Eric S

THE
ROUND DOZEN

A COLLECTION OF HIS STORIES
SELECTED BY
W. SOMERSET MAUGHAM

THE
ROUND DOZEN

A COLLECTION OF HIS STORIES

SELECTED BY

W. SOMERSET MAUGHAM

THE REPRINT SOCIETY
LONDON

PRINTED IN GREAT BRITAIN AT THE WINDMILL PRESS
KINGSWOOD, SURREY

CONTENTS

RAIN

IT was nearly bed-time and when they awoke next morning land would be in sight. Dr. Macphail lit his pipe and, leaning over the rail, searched the heavens for the Southern Cross. After two years at the front and a wound that had taken longer to heal than it should, he was glad to settle down quietly at Apia for twelve months at least, and he felt already better for the journey. Since some of the passengers were leaving the ship next day at Pago-Pago they had had a little dance that evening and in his ears hammered still the harsh notes of the mechanical piano. But the deck was quiet at last. A little way off he saw his wife in a long chair talking with the Davidsons, and he strolled over to her. When he sat down under the light and took off his hat you saw that he had very red hair, with a bald patch on the crown, and the red, freckled skin which accompanies red hair; he was a man of forty, thin, with a pinched face, precise and rather pedantic; and he spoke with a Scots accent in a very low, quiet voice.

Between the Macphails and the Davidsons, who were missionaries, there had arisen the intimacy of shipboard, which is due to propinquity rather than to any community of taste. Their chief tie was the disapproval they shared of the men who spent their days and nights in the smoking-room playing poker or bridge and drinking. Mrs. Macphail was not a little flattered to think that she and her husband were the only people on board with whom the Davidsons were willing to associate, and even the doctor, shy but no fool, half unconsciously acknowledged the compliment. It was only because he was of an argumentative mind that in their cabin at night he permitted himself to carp.

"Mrs. Davidson was saying she didn't know how they'd have got through the journey if it hadn't been for us," said Mrs. Macphail, as she neatly brushed out her transformation. "She said we were really the only people on the ship they cared to know."

"I shouldn't have thought a missionary was such a big bug that he could afford to put on frills."

"It's not frills. I quite understand what she means. It wouldn't have been very nice for the Davidsons to have to mix with all that rough lot in the smoking-room."

"The founder of their religion wasn't so exclusive," said Dr. Macphail with a chuckle.

"I've asked you over and over again not to joke about religion," answered his wife. "I shouldn't like to have a nature like yours, Alec. You never look for the best in people."

He gave her a sidelong glance with his pale, blue eyes, but did not reply. After many years of married life he had learned that it was more conducive to peace to leave his wife with the last word. He was undressed before she was, and climbing into the upper bunk he settled down to read himself to sleep.

When he came on deck next morning they were close to land. He looked at it with greedy eyes. There was a thin strip of silver beach rising quickly to hills covered to the top with luxuriant vegetation. The coconut trees, thick and green, came nearly to the water's edge, and among them you saw the grass houses of the Samoans; and here and there, gleaming white, a little church. Mrs. Davidson came and stood beside him. She was dressed in black and wore round her neck a gold chain, from which dangled a small cross. She was a little woman, with brown, dull hair very elaborately arranged, and she had prominent blue eyes behind invisible pince-nez. Her face was long, like a sheep's, but she gave no impression of foolishness, rather of extreme alertness; she had the quick movements of a bird. The most remarkable thing about her was her voice, high, metallic, and without inflection; it fell on the ear with a hard monotony, irritating to the nerves like the pitiless clamour of the pneumatic drill.

"This must seem like home to you," said Dr. Macphail, with his thin, difficult smile.

"Ours are low islands, you know, not like these. Coral. These are volcanic. We've got another ten days' journey to reach them."

"In these parts that's almost like being in the next street at home," said Dr. Macphail facetiously.

"Well, that's rather an exaggerated way of putting

A*

it, but one does look at distances differently in the South Seas. So far you're right."

Dr. Macphail sighed faintly.

"I'm glad we're not stationed here," she went on. "They say this is a terribly difficult place to work in. The steamers' touching makes the people unsettled; and then there's the naval station; that's bad for the natives. In our district we don't have difficulties like that to contend with. There are one or two traders, of course, but we take care to make them behave, and if they don't we make the place so hot for them they're glad to go."

Fixing the glasses on her nose, she looked at the green island with a ruthless stare.

"It's almost a hopeless task for the missionaries here. I can never be sufficiently thankful to God that we are at least spared that."

Davidson's district consisted of a group of islands to the north of Samoa; they were widely separated and he had frequently to go long distances by canoe. At these times his wife remained at their headquarters and managed the mission. Dr. Macphail felt his heart sink when he considered the efficiency with which she certainly managed it. She spoke of the depravity of the natives in a voice which nothing could hush, but with a vehemently unctuous horror. Her sense of delicacy was singular. Early in their acquaintance she had said to him:

"You know, their marriage customs when we first

settled in the islands were so shocking that I couldn't possibly describe them to you. But I'll tell Mrs. Macphail and she'll tell you."

Then he had seen his wife and Mrs. Davidson, their deck-chairs close together, in earnest conversation for about two hours. As he walked past them backwards and forwards for the sake of exercise, he had heard Mrs. Davidson's agitated whisper, like the distant flow of a mountain torrent, and he saw by his wife's open mouth and pale face that she was enjoying an alarming experience. At night in their cabin she repeated to him with bated breath all she had heard.

"Well, what did I say to you?" cried Mrs. Davidson, exultant, next morning. "Did you ever hear anything more dreadful? You don't wonder that I couldn't tell you myself, do you? Even though you are a doctor."

Mrs. Davidson scanned his face. She had a dramatic eagerness to see that she had achieved the desired effect.

"Can you wonder that when we first went there our hearts sank? You'll hardly believe me when I tell you it was impossible to find a single good girl in any of the villages."

She used the word *good* in a severely technical manner.

"Mr. Davidson and I talked it over, and we made up our minds the first thing to do was to put down the dancing. The natives were crazy about dancing."

"I was not averse to it myself when I was a young man." said Dr. Macphail.

"I guessed as much when I heard you ask Mrs. Macphail to have a turn with you last night. I don't think there's any real harm if a man dances with his wife, but I was relieved that she wouldn't. Under the circumstances I thought it better that we should keep ourselves to ourselves."

"Under what circumstances?"

Mrs. Davidson gave him a quick look through her pince-nez, but did not answer his question.

"But among white people it's not quite the same," she went on, "though I must say I agree with Mr. Davidson, who says he can't understand how a husband can stand by and see his wife in another man's arms, and as far as I'm concerned I've never danced a step since I married. But the native dancing is quite another matter. It's not only immoral in itself, but it distinctly leads to immorality. However, I'm thankful to God that we stamped it out, and I don't think I'm wrong in saying that no one has danced in our district for eight years."

But now they came to the mouth of the harbour and Mrs. Macphail joined them. The ship turned sharply and steamed slowly in. It was a great land-locked harbour big enough to hold a fleet of battleships; and all around it rose, high and steep, the green hills. Near the entrance, getting such breeze as blew from the sea, stood the governor's house in a garden. The Stars and Stripes dangled languidly from a flagstaff. They passed two or three trim bungalows, and a tennis court, and then they came to the quay with its warehouses. Mrs. Davidson pointed out the schooner, moored two or three hundred yards from the side, which was to take them to Apia. There was a crowd of eager, noisy, and good-humoured natives come from all parts of the island, some from curiosity, others to barter with the travellers on their way to Sydney; and they brought pineapples and huge bunches of bananas, *tapa* cloths, necklaces of shells or sharks' teeth, *kava*-bowls, and models of war canoes. American sailors, neat and trim, clean-shaven and frank of face, sauntered among them, and there was a little group of officials. While their luggage was being landed the Macphails and Mrs. Davidson watched the crowd. Dr. Macphail looked at the yaws from which most of the children and the young boys seemed to suffer, disfiguring sores like torpid ulcers, and his professional eyes glistened when he saw for the first time in his experience cases of elephantiasis, men going about with a huge, heavy arm or dragging along a grossly disfigured leg. Men and women wore the *lava-lava*.

"It's a very indecent costume," said Mrs. Davidson. "Mr. Davidson thinks it should be prohibited by law. How can you expect people to be moral when they wear nothing but a strip of red cotton round their loins?"

"It's suitable enough to the climate," said the doctor, wiping the sweat off his head.

Now that they were on land the heat, though it was

so early in the morning, was already oppressive. Closed in by its hills, not a breath of air came into Pago-Pago.

"In our islands," Mrs. Davidson went on in her high-pitched tones, "we've practically eradicated the *lava-lava*. A few old men still continue to wear it, but that's all. The women have all taken to the Mother Hubbard, and the men wear trousers and singlets. At the very beginning of our stay Mr. Davidson said in one of his reports: 'The inhabitants of these islands will never be thoroughly Christianised till every boy of more than ten years is made to wear a pair of trousers.'"

But Mrs. Davidson had given two or three of her birdlike glances at heavy grey clouds that came floating over the mouth of the harbour. A few drops began to fall.

"We'd better take shelter," said said.

They made their way with all the crowd to a great shed of corrugated iron, and the rain began to fall in torrents. They stood there for some time and then were joined by Mr. Davidson. He had been polite enough to the Macphails during the journey, but he had not his wife's sociability, and had spent much of his time reading. He was a silent, rather sullen man, and you felt that his affability was a duty that he imposed upon himself Christianly; he was by nature reserved and even morose. His appearance was singular. He was very tall and thin, with long limbs loosely jointed; hollow cheeks and curiously high cheek-bones; he had so cadaverous an air that it surprised you to notice how full and sensual

were his lips. He wore his hair very long. His dark
eyes, set deep in their sockets, were large and tragic;
and his hands, with their big, long fingers, were finely
shaped; they gave him a look of great strength. But
the most striking thing about him was the feeling he
gave you of suppressed fire. It was impressive and
vaguely troubling. He was not a man with whom any
intimacy was possible.

He brought now unwelcome news. There was an
epidemic of measles, a serious and often fatal disease
among the Kanakas, on the island, and a case had
developed among the crew of the schooner which was
to take them on their journey. The sick man had been
brought ashore and put in hospital on the quarantine
station, but telegraphic instructions had been sent from
Apia to say that the schooner would not be allowed to
enter the harbour till it was certain no other member
of the crew was affected.

"It means we shall have to stay here for ten days at
least."

"But I'm urgently needed at Apia," said Dr.
Macphail.

"That can't be helped. If no more cases develop on
board, the schooner will be allowed to sail with white
passengers, but all native traffic is prohibited for three
months."

"Is there a hotel here?" asked Mrs. Macphail.

Davidson gave a low chuckle.

"There's not."

"What shall we do then?"

"I've been talking to the governor. There's a trader along the front who has rooms that he rents, and my proposition is that as soon as the rain lets up we should go along there and see what we can do. Don't expect comfort. You've just got to be thankful if we get a bed to sleep on and a roof over our heads."

But the rain showed no sign of stopping, and at length with umbrellas and waterproofs they set out. There was no town, but merely a group of official buildings, a store or two, and at the back, among the coconut trees and plantains, a few native dwellings. The house they sought was about five minutes' walk from the wharf. It was a frame house of two storeys, with broad verandahs on both floors and a roof of corrugated iron. The owner was a half-caste named Horn, with a native wife surrounded by little brown children, and on the ground-floor he had a store where he sold canned goods and cottons. The rooms he showed them were almost bare of furniture. In the Macphails' there was nothing but a poor, worn bed with a ragged mosquito net, a rickety chair, and a washstand. They looked round with dismay. The rain poured down without ceasing.

"I'm not going to unpack more than we actually need," said Mrs. Macphail.

Mrs. Davidson came into the room as she was unlocking a portmanteau. She was very brisk and alert. The cheerless surroundings had no effect on her.

"If you'll take my advice you'll get a needle and cotton and start right in to mend the mosquito net," she said, "or you'll not be able to get a wink of sleep to-night."

"Will they be very bad?" asked Dr. Macphail.

"This is the season for them. When you're asked to a party at Government House at Apia you'll notice that all the ladies are given a pillow-slip to put their—their lower extremities in."

"I wish the rain would stop for a moment," said Mrs. Macphail. "I could try to make the place comfortable with more heart if the sun were shining."

"Oh, if you wait for that, you'll wait a long time. Pago-Pago is about the rainiest place in the Pacific. You see, the hills, and that bay, they attract the water, and one expects rain at this time of year anyway."

She looked from Macphail to his wife, standing helplessly in different parts of the room, like lost souls, and she pursed her lips. She saw that she must take them in hand. Feckless people like that made her impatient, but her hands itched to put everything in the order which came so naturally to her.

"Here, you give me a needle and cotton and I'll mend that net of yours, while you go on with your unpacking. Dinner's at one. Dr. Macphail, you'd better go down to the wharf and see that your heavy luggage has been put in a dry place. You know what these natives are, they're quite capable of storing it where the rain will beat in on it all the time."

The doctor put on his waterproof again and went downstairs. At the door Mr. Horn was standing in conversation with the quartermaster of the ship they had just arrived in and a second-class passenger whom Dr. Macphail had seen several times on board. The quartermaster, a little, shrivelled man, extremely dirty, nodded to him as he passed.

"This is a bad job about the measles, doc," he said. "I see you've fixed yourself up already."

Dr. Macphail thought he was rather familiar, but he was a timid man and he did not take offence easily.

"Yes, we've got a room upstairs."

"Miss Thompson was sailing with you to Apia, so I've brought her along here."

The quartermaster pointed with his thumb to the woman standing by his side. She was twenty-seven perhaps, plump, and in a coarse fashion pretty. She wore a white dress and a large white hat. Her fat calves in white cotton stockings bulged over the tops of long white boots in glacé kid. She gave Macphail an ingratiating smile.

"The feller's tryin' to soak me a dollar and a half a day for the meanest-sized room," she said in a hoarse voice.

"I tell you she's a friend of mine, Jo," said the quartermaster. "She can't pay more than a dollar, and you've sure got to take her for that."

The trader was fat and smooth and quietly smiling.

"Well, if you put it like that, Mr. Swan, I'll see what

I can do about it. I'll talk to Mrs. Horn and if we think we can make a reduction we will."

"Don't try to pull that stuff with me," said Miss Thompson. "We'll settle this right now. You get a dollar a day for the room and not one bean more."

Dr. Macphail smiled. He admired the effrontery with which she bargained. He was the sort of man who always paid what he was asked. He preferred to be overcharged than to haggle. The trader sighed.

"Well, to oblige Mr. Swan I'll take it."

"That's the goods," said Miss Thompson. "Come right in and have a shot of hooch. I've got some real good rye in that grip if you'll bring it along, Mr. Swan. You come along too, doctor."

"Oh, I don't think I will, thank you," he answered. "I'm just going down to see that our luggage is all right."

He stepped out into the rain. It swept in from the opening of the harbour in sheets and the opposite shore was all blurred. He passed two or three natives clad in nothing but the *lava-lava*, with huge umbrellas over them. They walked finely, with leisurely movements, very upright; and they smiled and greeted him in a strange tongue as they went by.

It was nearly dinner-time when he got back, and their meal was laid in the trader's parlour. It was a room designed not to live in but for purposes of prestige, and it had a musty, melancholy air. A suite of stamped plush was arranged neatly round the walls, and from the middle of the ceiling, protected from the flies by yellow tissue paper, hung a gilt chandelier. Davidson did not come.

"I know he went to call on the governor," said Mrs. Davidson, "and I guess he's kept him to dinner."

A little native girl brought them a dish of Hamburger steak, and after a while the trader came up to see that they had everything they wanted.

"I see we have a fellow lodger, Mr. Horn," said Dr. Macphail.

"She's taken a room, that's all," answered the trader. "She's getting her own board."

He looked at the two ladies with an obsequious air.

"I put her downstairs so she shouldn't be in the way. She won't be any trouble to you."

"Is it someone who was on the boat?" asked Mrs. Macphail.

"Yes, ma'am, she was in the second cabin. She was going to Apia. She has a position as cashier waiting for her."

"Oh!"

When the trader was gone Macphail said:

"I shouldn't think she'd find it exactly cheerful having her meals in her room."

"If she was in the second cabin I guess she'd rather," answered Mrs. Davidson. "I don't exactly know who it can be."

"I happened to be there when the quartermaster brought her along. Her name's Thompson."

"It's not the woman who was dancing with the quartermaster last night?" asked Mrs. Davidson.

"That's who it must be," said Mrs. Macphail. "I wondered at the time what she was. She looked rather fast to me."

"Not good style at all," said Mrs. Davidson.

They began to talk of other things, and after dinner, tired with their early rise, they separated and slept. When they awoke, though the sky was still grey and the clouds hung low, it was not raining and they went for a walk on the high road which the Americans had built along the bay.

On their return they found that Davidson had just come in.

"We may be here for a fortnight," he said irritably. "I've argued it out with the governor, but he says there is nothing to be done."

"Mr. Davidson's just longing to get back to his work," said his wife, with an anxious glance at him.

"We've been away for a year," he said, walking up and down the verandah. "The mission has been in charge of native missionaries and I'm terribly nervous that they've let things slide. They're good men, I'm not saying a word against them, God-fearing, devout, and truly Christian men—their Christianity would put many so-called Christians at home to the blush—but they're pitifully lacking in energy. They can make a stand once, they can make a stand twice, but they can't make a stand all the time. If you leave a mission in charge of a native missionary, no matter how trust-worthy he seems, in course of time you'll find he's let abuses creep in."

Mr. Davidson stood still. With his tall, spare form, and his great eyes flashing out of his pale face, he was an impressive figure. His sincerity was obvious in the fire of his gestures and in his deep, ringing voice.

"I expect to have my work cut out for me. I shall act and I shall act promptly. If the tree is rotten it shall be cut down and cast into the flames."

And in the evening after the high tea which was their last meal, while they sat in the stiff parlour, the ladies working and Dr. Macphail smoking his pipe, the missionary told them of his work in the islands.

"When we went there they had no sense of sin at all," he said. "They broke the commandments one after the other and never knew they were doing wrong. And I think that was the most difficult part of my work, to instil into the natives the sense of sin."

The Macphails knew already that Davidson had worked in the Solomons for five years before he met his wife. She had been a missionary in China, and they had become acquainted in Boston, where they were both spending part of their leave to attend a missionary congress. On their marriage they had been appointed to the islands, in which they had laboured ever since.

In the course of all the conversations they had had with Mr. Davidson one thing had shone out clearly and that was the man's unflinching courage. He was a medical missionary, and he was liable to be called at any time to one or other of the islands in the group. Even the whaleboat is not so very safe a conveyance in the stormy Pacific of the wet season, but often he would be sent for in a canoe, and then the danger was great. In cases of illness or accident he never hesitated. A dozen times he had spent the whole night baling for his life, and more than once Mrs. Davidson had given him up for lost.

"I'd beg him not to go sometimes," she said, "or at least to wait till the weather was more settled, but he'd never listen. He's obstinate, and when he's once made up his mind, nothing can move him."

"How can I ask the natives to put their trust in the Lord if I am afraid to do so myself?" cried Davidson. "And I'm not, I'm not. They know that if they send for me in their trouble I'll come if it's humanly possible. And do you think the Lord is going to abandon me when I am on His business? The wind blows at His bidding and the waves toss and rage at His word."

Dr. Macphail was a timid man. He had never been able to get used to the hurtling of the shells over the trenches, and when he was operating in an advanced dressing-station the sweat poured from his brow and dimmed his spectacles in the effort he made to control his unsteady hand. He shuddered a little as he looked at the missionary.

"I wish I could say that I've never been afraid," he said.

"I wish you could say that you believed in God," retorted the other.

But for some reason, that evening the missionary's thoughts travelled back to the early days he and his wife had spent on the islands.

"Sometimes Mrs. Davidson and I would look at one another and the tears would stream down our cheeks. We worked without ceasing, day and night, and we seemed to make no progress. I don't know what I should have done without her then. When I felt my heart sink, when I was very near despair, she gave me courage and hope."

Mrs. Davidson looked down at her work, and a slight colour rose to her thin cheeks. Her hands trembled a little. She did not trust herself to speak.

"We had no one to help us. We were alone, thousands of miles from any of our own people, surrounded by darkness. When I was broken and weary she would put her work aside and take the Bible and read to me till peace came and settled upon me like sleep upon the eyelids of a child, and when at last she closed the book she'd say: 'We'll save them in spite of themselves.' And I felt strong again in the Lord, and I answered: 'Yes, with God's help I'll save them. I must save them.'"

He came over to the table and stood in front of it as though it were a lectern.

"You see, they were so naturally depraved that they couldn't be brought to see their wickedness. We had to make sins out of what they thought were natural actions. We had to make it a sin, not only to commit adultery and to lie and thieve, but to expose their bodies, and to dance and not to come to church. I made it a sin for a girl to show her bosom and a sin for a man not to wear trousers."

"How?" asked Dr. Macphail, not without surprise.

"I instituted fines. Obviously the only way to make people realise that an action is sinful is to punish them if they commit it. I fined them if they didn't come to church, and I fined them if they danced. I fined them if they were improperly dressed. I had a tariff, and every sin had to be paid for either in money or work. And at last I made them understand."

"But did they never refuse to pay?"

"How could they?" asked the missionary.

"It would be a brave man who tried to stand up against Mr. Davidson," said his wife, tightening her lips.

Dr. Macphail looked at Davidson with troubled eyes. What he heard shocked him, but he hesitated to express his disapproval.

"You must remember that in the last resort I could expel them from their church membership."

"Did they mind that?"

Davidson smiled a little and gently rubbed his hands.

"They couldn't sell their copra. When the men fished they got no share of the catch. It meant something very like starvation. Yes, they minded quite a lot."

"Tell him about Fred Ohlson," said Mrs. Davidson.

The missionary fixed his fiery eyes on Dr. Macphail.

"Fred Ohlson was a Danish trader who had been in the islands a good many years. He was a pretty rich man as traders go and he wasn't very pleased when we came. You see, he'd had things very much his own way. He paid the natives what he liked for their copra, and he paid in goods and whisky. He had a native wife, but he was flagrantly unfaithful to her. He was a drunkard. I gave him a chance to mend his ways, but he wouldn't take it. He laughed at me."

Davidson's voice fell to a deep bass as he said the last words, and he was silent for a minute or two. The silence was heavy with menace.

"In two years he was a ruined man. He'd lost everything he'd saved in a quarter of a century. I broke him, and at last he was forced to come to me like a beggar and beseech me to give him a passage back to Sydney."

"I wish you could have seen him when he came to see Mr. Davidson," said the missionary's wife. "He had been a fine, powerful man, with a lot of fat on him, and he had a great big voice, but now he was half the size, and he was shaking all over. He'd suddenly become an old man."

With abstracted gaze Davidson looked out into the night. The rain was falling again.

Suddenly from below came a sound, and Davidson turned and looked questioningly at his wife. It was the sound of a gramophone, harsh and loud, wheezing out a syncopated tune.

"What's that?" he asked.

Mrs. Davidson fixed her pince-nez more firmly on her nose.

"One of the second-class passengers has a room in the house. I guess it comes from there."

They listened in silence, and presently they heard the sound of dancing. Then the music stopped, and they heard the popping of corks and voices raised in animated conversation.

"I daresay she's giving a farewell party to her friends on board," said Dr. Macphail. "The ship sails at twelve, doesn't it?"

Davidson made no remark, but he looked at his watch.

"Are you ready?" he asked his wife.

She got up and folded her work.

"Yes, I guess I am," she answered.

"It's early to go to bed yet, isn't it?" said the doctor.

"We have a good deal of reading to do," explained Mrs. Davidson. "Wherever we are, we read a chapter of the Bible before retiring for the night and we study it with the commentaries, you know, and discuss it thoroughly. It's a wonderful training for the mind."

The two couples bade one another good night. Dr. and Mrs. Macphail were left alone. For two or three minutes they did not speak.

"I think I'll go and fetch the cards," the doctor said at last.

Mrs. Macphail looked at him doubtfully. Her

conversation with the Davidsons had left her a little uneasy, but she did not like to say that she thought they had better not play cards when the Davidsons might come in at any moment. Dr. Macphail brought them and she watched him, though with a vague sense of guilt, while he laid out his patience. Below the sound of revelry continued.

It was fine enough next day, and the Macphails, condemned to spend a fortnight of idleness at Pago-Pago, set about making the best of things. They went down to the quay and got out of their boxes a number of books. The doctor called on the chief surgeon of the naval hospital and went round the beds with him. They left cards on the governor. They passed Miss Thompson on the road. The doctor took off his hat, and she gave him a "Good morning, doc.,' in a loud, cheerful voice. She was dressed as on the day before, in a white frock, and her shiny white boots with their high heels, her fat legs bulging over the tops of them, were strange things on that exotic scene.

"I don't think she's very suitably dressed, I must say," said Mrs. Macphail. "She looks extremely common to me."

When they got back to their house, she was on the verandah playing with one of the trader's dark children.

"Say a word to her," Dr. Macphail whispered to his wife. "She's all alone here, and it seems rather unkind to ignore her."

Mrs. Macphail was shy, but she was in the habit of doing what her husband bade her.

"I think we're fellow lodgers here," she said, rather foolishly.

"Terrible, ain't it, bein' cooped up in a one-horse burg like this?" answered Miss Thompson. "And they tell me I'm lucky to have gotten a room. I don't see myself livin' in a native house, and that's what some have to do. I don't know why they don't have a hotel."

They exchanged a few more words. Miss Thompson, loud-voiced and garrulous, was evidently quite willing to gossip, but Mrs. Macphail had a poor stock of small talk and presently she said:

"Well, I think we must go upstairs."

In the evening when they sat down to their high tea Davidson, on coming in, said:

"I see that woman downstairs has a couple of sailors sitting there. I wonder how she's gotten acquainted with them."

"She can't be very particular," said Mrs. Davidson.

They were all rather tired after the idle, aimless day.

"If there's going to be a fortnight of this I don't know what we shall feel like at the end of it," said Dr. Macphail.

"The only thing to do is to portion out the day to different activities," answered the missionary. "I shall set aside a certain number of hours to study and a certain number to exercise, rain or fine—in the wet season you can't afford to pay any attention to the rain—and a certain number to recreation."

Dr. Macphail looked at his companion with misgiving. Davidson's programme oppressed him. They were eating Hamburger steak again. It seemed the only dish the cook knew how to make. Then below the gramophone began. Davidson started nervously when he heard it, but said nothing. Men's voices floated up. Miss Thompson's guests were joining in a well-known song and presently they heard her voice too, hoarse and loud. There was a good deal of shouting and laughing. The four people upstairs, trying to make conversation, listened despite themselves to the clink of glasses and the scrape of chairs. More people had evidently come. Miss Thompson was giving a party.

"I wonder how she gets them all in," said Mrs. Macphail, suddenly breaking into a medical conversation between the missionary and her husband.

It showed whither her thoughts were wandering. The twitch of Davidson's face proved that, though he spoke of scientific things, his mind was busy in the same direction. Suddenly, while the doctor was giving some experience of practice on the Flanders front, rather prosily, he sprang to his feet with a cry.

"What's the matter, Alfred?" asked Mrs. Davidson.

"Of course! It never occurred to me. She's out of Iwelei."

"She can't be."

"She came on board at Honolulu. It's obvious. And she's carrying on her trade here. Here!"

He uttered the last word with a passion of indignation.

"What's Iwelei?" asked Mrs. Macphail.

He turned his gloomy eyes on her and his voice trembled with horror.

"The plague spot of Honolulu. The Red Light district. It was a blot on our civilisation."

Iwelei was on the edge of the city. You went down side streets by the harbour, in the darkness, across a rickety bridge, till you came to a deserted road, all ruts and holes, and then suddenly you came out into the light. There was parking room for motors on each side of the road, and there were saloons, tawdry and bright, each one noisy with its mechanical piano, and there were barbers' shops and tobacconists'. There was a stir in the air and a sense of expectant gaiety. You turned down a narrow alley, either to the right or to the left, for the road divided Iwelei into two parts, and you found yourself in the district. There were rows of little bungalows, trim and neatly painted in green, and the pathway between them was broad and straight. It was laid out like a garden city. In its respectable regularity, its order and spruceness, it gave an impression of sardonic horror; for never can the search for love have been so systematised and ordered. The pathways were lit by a rare lamp, but they would have been dark except for the lights that came from the open windows of the bungalows. Men wandered about, looking at the women who sat at their windows, reading or sewing, for the most part taking no notice of the passers-by; and like the women they were of all nationalities. There were Americans, sailors from the ships in port, enlisted men off the gunboats, sombrely drunk, and soldiers from the regiments, white and black, quartered on the island; there were Japanese, walking in twos and threes; Hawaiians, Chinese in long robes, and Filipinos in preposterous hats. They were silent and as it were oppressed. Desire is sad.

"It was the most crying scandal of the Pacific," exclaimed Davidson vehemently. "The missionaries had been agitating against it for years, and at last the local press took it up. The police refused to stir. You know their argument. They say that vice is inevitable and consequently the best thing is to localise and control it. The truth is, they were paid. Paid! They were paid by the saloon-keepers, paid by the bullies, paid by the women themselves. At last they were forced to move."

"I read about it in the papers that came on board in Honolulu," said Dr. Macphail.

"Iwelei, with its sin and shame, ceased to exist on the very day we arrived. The whole population was brought before the justices. I don't know why I didn't understand at once what that woman was."

"Now you come to speak of it," said Mrs. Macphail, "I remember seeing her come on board only a few minutes before the boat sailed. I remember thinking at the time she was cutting it rather fine."

"How dare she come here!" cried Davidson indignantly. "I'm not going to allow it."

He strode towards the door.

"What are you going to do?" asked Macphail.

"What do you expect me to do? I'm going to stop it. I'm not going to have this house turned into—into . . ."

He sought for a word that should not offend the ladies' ears. His eyes were flashing and his pale face was paler still in his emotion.

"It sounds as though there were three or four men down there," said the doctor. "Don't you think it's rather rash to go in just now?"

The missionary gave him a contemptuous look and without a word flung out of the room.

"You know Mr. Davidson very little if you think the fear of personal danger can stop him in the performance of his duty," said his wife.

She sat with her hands nervously clasped, a spot of colour on her high cheek-bones, listening to what was about to happen below. They all listened. They heard him clatter down the wooden stairs and throw open the door. The singing stopped suddenly, but the gramophone continued to bray out its vulgar tune. They heard Davidson's voice and then the noise of something heavy falling. The music stopped. He had hurled the gramophone on the floor. Then again they heard Davidson's voice, they could not make out the words, then Miss Thompson's, loud and shrill, then a confused clamour as though several people were shouting together at the top of their lungs. Mrs. Davidson gave a little gasp, and she clenched her hands

B

more tightly. Dr. Macphail looked uncertainly from her to his wife. He did not want to go down, but he wondered if they expected him to. Then there was something that sounded like a scuffle. The noise now was more distinct. It might be that Davidson was being thrown out of the room. The door was slammed. There was a moment's silence and they heard Davidson come up the stairs again. He went to his room.

"I think I'll go to him," said Mrs. Davidson.

She got up and went out.

"If you want me, just call," said Mrs. Macphail, and then when the other was gone: "I hope he isn't hurt."

"Why couldn't he mind his own business?" said Dr. Macphail.

They sat in silence for a minute or two and then they both started, for the gramophone began to play once more, defiantly, and mocking voices shouted hoarsely the words of an obscene song.

Next day Mrs. Davidson was pale and tired. She complained of headache, and she looked old and wizened. She told Mrs. Macphail that the missionary had not slept at all; he had passed the night in a state of frightful agitation and at five had got up and gone out. A glass of beer had been thrown over him and his clothes were stained and stinking. But a sombre fire glowed in Mrs. Davidson's eyes when she spoke of Miss Thompson.

"She'll bitterly rue the day when she flouted Mr. Davidson," she said. "Mr. Davidson has a wonderful heart and no one who is in trouble has ever gone to him without being comforted, but he has no mercy for sin, and when his righteous wrath is excited he's terrible."

"Why, what will he do?" asked Mrs. Macphail.

"I don't know, but I wouldn't stand in that creature's shoes for anything in the world."

Mrs. Macphail shuddered. There was something positively alarming in the triumphant assurance of the little woman's manner. They were going out together that morning, and they went down the stairs side by side. Miss Thompson's door was open, and they saw her in a bedraggled dressing-gown, cooking something in a chafing-dish.

"Good morning," she called. "Is Mr. Davidson better this morning?"

They passed her in silence, with their noses in the air, as if she did not exist. They flushed, however, when she burst into a shout of derisive laughter. Mrs. Davidson turned on her suddenly.

"Don't you dare to speak to me," she screamed. "If you insult me I shall have you turned out of here."

"Say, did I ask Mr. Davidson to visit with me?"

"Don't answer her," whispered Mrs. Macphail hurriedly.

They walked on till they were out of earshot.

"She's brazen, brazen," burst from Mrs. Davidson. Her anger almost suffocated her.

And on their way home they met her strolling toward the quay. She had all her finery on. Her great white hat with its vulgar, showy flowers was an affront. She called out cheerily to them as she went by, and a couple of American sailors who were standing there grinned as the ladies set their faces to an icy stare. They got in just before the rain began to fall again.

"I guess she'll get her fine clothes spoilt," said Mrs. Davidson with a bitter sneer.

Davidson did not come in till they were half way through dinner. He was wet through, but he would not change. He sat, morose and silent, refusing to eat more than a mouthful, and he stared at the slanting rain. When Mrs. Davidson told him of their two encounters with Miss Thompson he did not answer. His deepening frown alone showed that he had heard.

"Don't you think we ought to make Mr. Horn turn her out of here?" asked Mrs. Davidson. "We can't allow her to insult us."

"There doesn't seem to be any other place for her to go," said Macphail.

"She can live with one of the natives."

"In weather like this a native hut must be a rather uncomfortable place to live in."

"I lived in one for years," said the missionary.

When the little native girl brought in the fried bananas which formed the sweet they had every day, Davidson turned to her.

"Ask Miss Thompson when it would be convenient for me to see her," he said.

The girl nodded shyly and went out.

"What do you want to see her for, Alfred?" asked his wife.

"It's my duty to see her. I won't act till I've given her every chance."

"You don't know what she is. She'll insult you."

"Let her insult me. Let her spit on me. She has an immortal soul, and I must do all that is in my power to save it."

Mrs. Davidson's ears rang still with the harlot's mocking laughter.

"She's gone too far."

"Too far for the mercy of God?" His eyes lit up suddenly and his voice grew mellow and soft. "Never. The sinner may be deeper in sin than the depth of hell itself, but the love of the Lord Jesus can reach him still."

The girl came back with the message.

"Miss Thompson's compliments and as long as Rev. Davidson don't come in business hours she'll be glad to see him any time."

The party received it in stony silence, and Dr. Macphail quickly effaced from his lips the smile which had come upon them. He knew his wife would be vexed with him if he found Miss Thompson's effrontery amusing.

They finished the meal in silence. When it was over the two ladies got up and took their work, Mrs. Macphail was making another of the innumerable comforters which she had turned out since the beginning of the war, and the doctor lit his pipe. But Davidson remained in his chair and with abstracted eyes stared at the table. At last he got up and without a word went out of the room. They heard him go down and they heard Miss Thompson's defiant "Come in" when he knocked at the door. He remained with her for an hour. And Dr. Macphail watched the rain. It was beginning to get on his nerves. It was not like our soft English rain that drops gently on the earth; it was unmerciful and somehow terrible; you felt in it the malignancy of the primitive powers of nature. It did not pour, it flowed. It was like a deluge from heaven, and it rattled on the roof of corrugated iron with a steady persistence that was maddening. It seemed to have a fury of its own. And sometimes you felt that you must scream if it did not stop, and then suddenly you felt powerless, as though your bones had suddenly become soft; and you were miserable and hopeless.

Macphail turned his head when the missionary came back. The two women looked up.

"I've given her every chance. I have exhorted her to repent. She is an evil woman."

He paused, and Dr. Macphail saw his eyes darken and his pale face grow hard and stern.

"Now I shall take the whips with which the Lord Jesus drove the usurers and the money-changers out of the Temple of the Most High."

He walked up and down the room. His mouth was close-set, and his black brows were frowning.

"If she fled to the uttermost parts of the earth I should pursue her."

With a sudden movement he turned round and strode

out of the room. They heard him go downstairs again.

"What is he going to do?" asked Mrs. Macphail.

"I don't know." Mrs. Davidson took off her pince-nez and wiped them. "When he is on the Lord's work I never ask him questions."

She sighed a little.

"What is the matter?"

"He'll wear himself out. He doesn't know what it is to spare himself."

Dr. Macphail learnt the first results of the missionary's activity from the half-caste trader in whose house they lodged. He stopped the doctor when he passed the store and came out to speak to him on the stoop. His fat face was worried.

"The Rev. Davidson has been at me for letting Miss Thompson have a room here," he said, "but I didn't know what she was when I rented it to her. When people come and ask if I can rent them a room all I want to know is if they've the money to pay for it. And she paid me for hers a week in advance."

Dr. Macphail did not want to commit himself.

"When all's said and done it's your house. We're very much obliged to you for taking us in at all."

Horn looked at him doubtfully. He was not certain yet how definitely Macphail stood on the missionary's side.

"The missionaries are in with one another," he said, hesitatingly. "If they get it in for a trader he may just as well shut up his store and quit."

"Did he want you to turn her out?"

"No, he said so long as she behaved herself he couldn't ask me to do that. He said he wanted to be just to me. I promised she shouldn't have no more visitors. I've just been and told her."

"How did she take it?"

"She gave me hell."

The trader squirmed in his old ducks. He had found Miss Thompson a rough customer.

"Oh, well, I daresay she'll get out. I don't suppose she wants to stay here if she can't have anyone in."

"There's nowhere she can go, only a native house, and no native'll take her now, not now that the missionaries have got their knife in her."

Dr. Macphail looked at the falling rain.

"Well, I don't suppose it's any good waiting for it to clear up."

In the evening when they sat in the parlour Davidson talked to them of his early days at college. He had had no means and had worked his way through by doing odd jobs during the vacations. There was silence downstairs. Miss Thompson was sitting in her little room alone. But suddenly the gramophone began to play. She had set it on in defiance, to cheat her loneliness, but there was no one to sing, and it had a melancholy note. It was like a cry for help. Davidson took no notice. He was in the middle of a long anecdote and without change of expression went on. The gramophone continued. Miss Thompson put on one reel after another. It looked as though the silence of the night were getting on her nerves. It was breathless and sultry. When the Macphails went to bed they could not sleep. They lay side by side with their eyes wide open, listening to the cruel singing of the mosquitoes outside their curtain.

"What's that?" whispered Mrs. Macphail at last.

They heard a voice, Davidson's voice, through the wooden partition. It went on with a monotonous, earnest insistence. He was praying aloud. He was praying for the soul of Miss Thompson.

Two or three days went by. Now when they passed Miss Thompson on the road she did not greet them with ironic cordiality or smile; she passed with her nose in the air, a sulky look on her painted face, frowning, as though she did not see them. The trader told Macphail that she had tried to get lodging elsewhere, but had failed. In the evening she played through the various reels of her gramophone, but the pretence of mirth was obvious now. The ragtime had a cracked, heart-broken rhythm as though it were a one-step of despair. When she began to play on Sunday Davidson sent Horn to beg her to stop at once since it was the Lord's day. The reel was taken off and the house was silent except for the steady pattering of the rain on the iron roof.

"I think she's getting a bit worked up," said the trader next day to Macphail. "She don't know what Mr. Davidson's up to and it makes her scared."

Macphail had caught a glimpse of her that morning and it struck him that her arrogant expression had

B*

changed. There was in her face a hunted look. The half-caste gave him a sidelong glance.

"I suppose you don't know what Mr. Davidson is doing about it?" he hazarded.

"No, I don't."

It was singular that Horn should ask him that question, for he also had the idea that the missionary was mysteriously at work. He had an impression that he was weaving a net around the woman, carefully, systematically, and suddenly, when everything was ready, would pull the strings tight.

"He told me to tell her," said the trader, "that if at any time she wanted him she only had to send and he'd come."

"What did she say when you told her that?"

"She didn't say nothing. I didn't stop. I just said what he said I was to and then I beat it. I thought she might be going to start weepin'."

"I have no doubt the loneliness is getting on her nerves," said the doctor. "And the rain—that's enough to make anyone jumpy," he continued irritably. "Doesn't it ever stop in this confounded place?"

"It goes on pretty steady in the rainy season. We have three hundred inches in the year. You see, it's the shape of the bay. It seems to attract the rain from all over the Pacific."

"Damn the shape of the bay," said the doctor.

He scratched his mosquito bites. He felt very short-tempered. When the rain stopped and the sun shone, it was like a hothouse, seething, humid, sultry, breathless, and you had a strange feeling that everything was growing with a savage violence. The natives, blithe and childlike by reputation, seemed then, with their tattooing and their dyed hair, to have something sinister in their appearance; and when they pattered along at your heels with their naked feet you looked back instinctively. You felt they might at any moment come behind you swiftly and thrust a long knife between your shoulderblades. You could not tell what dark thoughts lurked behind their wide-set eyes. They had a little the look of ancient Egyptians painted on a temple wall, and there was about them the terror of what is immeasurably old.

The missionary came and went. He was busy, but the Macphails did not know what he was doing. Horn told the doctor that he saw the governor every day, and once Davidson mentioned him.

"He looks as if he had plenty of determination," he said, "but when you come down to brass tacks he has no backbone."

"I suppose that means he won't do exactly what you want," suggested the doctor facetiously.

The missionary did not smile.

"I want him to do what's right. It shouldn't be necessary to persuade a man to do that."

"But there may be differences of opinion about what is right."

"If a man had a gangrenous foot would you have patience with anyone who hesitated to amputate it?"

"Gangrene is a matter of fact."

"And Evil?"

What Davidson had done soon appeared. The four of them had just finished their midday meal, and they had not yet separated for the siesta which the heat imposed on the ladies and on the doctor. Davidson had little patience with the slothful habit. The door was suddenly flung open and Miss Thompson came in. She looked round the room and then went up to Davidson.

"You low-down skunk, what have you been saying about me to the governor?"

She was spluttering with rage. There was a moment's pause. Then the missionary drew forward a chair.

"Won't you be seated, Miss Thompson? I've been hoping to have another talk with you."

"You poor low-life bastard."

She burst into a torrent of insult, foul and insolent. Davidson kept his grave eyes on her.

"I'm indifferent to the abuse you think fit to heap on me, Miss Thompson," he said, "but I must beg you to remember that ladies are present."

Tears by now were struggling with her anger. Her face was red and swollen as though she were choking.

"What has happened?" asked Dr. Macphail.

"A feller's just been in here and he says I gotter beat it on the next boat."

Was there a gleam in the missionary's eyes? His face remained impassive.

"You could hardly expect the governor to let you

stay here under the circumstances."

"You done it," she shrieked. "You can't kid me. You done it."

"I don't want to deceive you. I urged the governor to take the only possible step consistent with his obligations."

"Why couldn't you leave me be? I wasn't doin' you no harm."

"You may be sure that if you had I should be the last man to resent it."

"Do you think I want to stay on in this poor imitation of a burg? I don't look no busher, do I?"

"In that case I don't see what cause of complaint you have," he answered.

She gave an inarticulate cry of rage and flung out of the room. There was a short silence.

"It's a relief to know that the governor has acted at last," said Davidson finally. "He's a weak man and he shilly-shallied. He said she was only here for a fortnight anyway, and if she went on to Apia that was under British jurisdiction and had nothing to do with him."

The missionary sprang to his feet and strode across the room.

"It's terrible the way the men who are in authority seek to evade their responsibility. They speak as though evil that was out of sight ceased to be evil. The very existence of that woman is a scandal and it does not help matters to shift it to another of the islands. In the end I had to speak straight from the shoulder."

Davidson's brow lowered, and he protruded his firm chin. He looked fierce and determined.

"What do you mean by that?"

"Our mission is not entirely without influence at Washington. I pointed out to the governor that it wouldn't do him any good if there was a complaint about the way he managed things here."

"When has she got to go?" asked the doctor, after a pause.

"The San Francisco boat is due here from Sydney next Tuesday. She's to sail on that."

That was in five days' time. It was next day, when he was coming back from the hospital where for want of something better to do Macphail spent most of his mornings, that the half-caste stopped him as he was going upstairs.

"Excuse me, Dr. Macphail, Miss Thompson's sick. Will you have a look at her?"

"Certainly."

Horn led him to her room. She was sitting in a chair idly, neither reading nor sewing, staring in front of her. She wore her white dress and the large hat with the flowers on it. Macphail noticed that her skin was yellow and muddy under her powder, and her eyes were heavy.

"I'm sorry to hear you're not well," he said.

"Oh, I ain't sick really. I just said that, because I just had to see you. I've got to clear on a boat that's going to 'Frisco."

She looked at him and he saw that her eyes were

suddenly startled. She opened and clenched her hands spasmodically. The trader stood at the door, listening.

"So I understand," said the doctor.

She gave a little gulp.

"I guess it ain't very convenient for me to go to 'Frisco just now. I went to see the governor yesterday afternoon, but I couldn't get to him. I saw the secretary, and he told me I'd got to take that boat and that was all there was to it. I just had to see the governor, so I waited outside his house this morning, and when he come out I spoke to him. He didn't want to speak to me, I'll say, but I wouldn't let him shake me off, and at last he said he hadn't no objection to my staying here till the next boat to Sydney if the Rev. Davidson will stand for it."

She stopped and looked at Dr. Macphail anxiously.

"I don't know exactly what I can do," he said.

"Well, I thought maybe you wouldn't mind asking him. I swear to God I won't start anything here if he'll just only let me stay. I won't go out of the house if that'll suit him. It's no more'n a fortnight."

"I'll ask him."

"He won't stand for it," said Horn. "He'll have you out on Tuesday, so you may as well make up your mind to it."

"Tell him I can get work in Sydney, straight stuff, I mean. 'Tain't asking very much."

"I'll do what I can."

"And come and tell me right away, will you? I can't set down to a thing till I get the dope one way or the other."

It was not an errand that much pleased the doctor, and, characteristically perhaps, he went about it indirectly. He told his wife what Miss Thompson had said to him and asked her to speak to Mrs. Davidson. The missionary's attitude seemed rather arbitrary and it could do no harm if the girl were allowed to stay in Pago-Pago another fortnight. But he was not prepared for the result of his diplomacy. The missionary came to him straightway.

"Mrs. Davidson tells me that Thompson has been speaking to you."

Dr. Macphail, thus directly tackled, had the shy man's resentment at being forced out into the open. He felt his temper rising, and he flushed.

"I don't see that it can make any difference if she goes to Sydney rather than to San Francisco, and so long as she promises to behave while she's here it's dashed hard to persecute her."

The missionary fixed him with his stern eyes.

"Why is she unwilling to go back to San Francisco?"

"I didn't enquire," answered the doctor with some asperity. "And I think one does better to mind one's own business."

Perhaps it was not a very tactful answer.

"The governor has ordered her to be deported by the first boat that leaves the island. He's only done his duty and I will not interfere. Her presence is a peril here."

"I think you're very harsh and tyrannical."

The two ladies looked up at the doctor with some

alarm, but they need not have feared a quarrel, for the missionary smiled gently.

"I'm terribly sorry you should think that of me, Dr. Macphail. Believe me, my heart bleeds for that unfortunate woman, but I'm only trying to do my duty."

The doctor made no answer. He looked out of the window sullenly. For once it was not raining and across the bay you saw nestling among the trees the huts of a native village.

"I think I'll take advantage of the rain stopping to go out," he said.

"Please don't bear me malice because I can't accede to your wish," said Davidson, with a melancholy smile. "I respect you very much, doctor, and I should be sorry if you thought ill of me."

"I have no doubt you have a sufficiently good opinion of yourself to bear mine with equanimity," he retorted.

"That's one on me," chuckled Davidson.

When Dr. Macphail, vexed with himself because he had been uncivil to no purpose, went downstairs, Miss Thompson was waiting for him with her door ajar.

"Well," she said, "have you spoken to him?"

"Yes, I'm sorry, he won't do anything," he answered, not looking at her in his embarrassment.

But then he gave her a quick glance, for a sob broke from her. He saw that her face was white with fear. It gave him a shock of dismay. And suddenly he had an idea.

"But don't give up hope yet. I think it's a shame the

way they're treating you and I'm going to see the
governor myself."

"Now?"

He nodded. Her face brightened.

"Say, that's real good of you. I'm sure he'll let me
stay if you speak for me. I just won't do a thing I didn't
ought all the time I'm here."

Dr. Macphail hardly knew why he had made up his
mind to appeal to the governor. He was perfectly
indifferent to Miss Thompson's affairs, but the missionary had irritated him, and with him temper was a
smouldering thing. He found the governor at home.
He was a large, handsome man, a sailor, with a grey
toothbrush moustache; and he wore a spotless uniform
of white drill.

"I've come to see you about a woman who's lodging
in the same house as we are," he said. "Her name's
Thompson."

"I guess I've heard nearly enough about her, Dr.
Macphail," said the governor, smiling. "I've given her
the order to get out next Tuesday and that's all I can do."

"I wanted to ask you if you couldn't stretch a point
and let her stay here till the boat comes in from San
Francisco so that she can go to Sydney. I will guarantee
her good behaviour."

The governor continued to smile, but his eyes grew
small and serious.

"I'd be very glad to oblige you, Dr. Macphail, but
I've given the order and it must stand."

The doctor put the case as reasonably as he could, but now the governor ceased to smile at all. He listened sullenly, with averted gaze. Macphail saw that he was making no impression.

"I'm sorry to cause any lady inconvenience, but she'll have to sail on Tuesday and that's all there is to it."

"But what difference can it make?"

"Pardon me, doctor, but I don't feel called upon to explain my official actions except to the proper authorities."

Macphail looked at him shrewdly. He remembered Davidson's hint that he had used threats, and in the governor's attitude he read a singular embarrassment.

"Davidson's a damned busybody," he said hotly.

"Between ourselves, Dr. Macphail, I don't say that I have formed a very favourable opinion of Mr. Davidson, but I am bound to confess that he was within his rights in pointing out to me the danger that the presence of a woman of Miss Thompson's character was to a place like this, where a number of enlisted men are stationed among a native population."

He got up and Dr. Macphail was obliged to do so too.

"I must ask you to excuse me. I have an engagement. Please give my respects to Mrs. Macphail."

The doctor left him crest-fallen. He knew that Miss Thompson would be waiting for him, and unwilling to tell her himself that he had failed, he went into the house by the back door and sneaked up the stairs as though he had something to hide.

At supper he was silent and ill-at-ease, but the missionary was jovial and animated. Dr. Macphail thought his eyes rested on him now and then with triumphant good-humour. It struck him suddenly that Davidson knew of his visit to the governor and of its ill success. But how on earth could he have heard of it? There was something sinister about the power of that man. After supper he saw Horn on the verandah and, as though to have a casual word with him, went out.

"She wants to know if you've seen the governor," the trader whispered.

"Yes. He wouldn't do anything. I'm awfully sorry, I can't do anything more."

"I knew he wouldn't. They daren't go against the missionaries."

"What are you talking about?" said Davidson affably, coming out to join them.

"I was just saying there was no chance of your getting over to Apia for at least another week," said the trader glibly.

He left them, and the two men returned into the parlour. Mr. Davidson devoted one hour after each meal to recreation. Presently a timid knock was heard at the door.

"Come in," said Mrs. Davidson, in her sharp voice.

The door was not opened. She got up and opened it. They saw Miss Thompson standing at the threshold. But the change in her appearance was extraordinary. This was no longer the flaunting hussy who had jeered at them in the road, but a broken, frightened woman.

Her hair, as a rule so elaborately arranged, was tumbling
untidily over her neck. She wore bedroom slippers and
a skirt and blouse. They were unfresh and bedraggled.
She stood at the door with the tears streaming down her
face and did not dare to enter.

"What do you want?" said Mrs. Davidson harshly.

"May I speak to Mr. Davidson?" she said in a choking
voice.

The missionary rose and went towards her.

"Come right in, Miss Thompson," he said in cordial
tones. "What can I do for you?"

She entered the room.

"Say, I'm sorry for what I said to you the other day
an' for—for everythin' else. I guess I was a bit lit up. I
beg pardon."

"Oh, it was nothing. I guess my back's broad
enough to bear a few hard words."

She stepped towards him with a movement that was
horribly cringing.

"You've got me beat. I'm all in. You won't make me
go back to 'Frisco?"

His genial manner vanished and his voice grew on a
sudden hard and stern.

"Why don't you want to go back there?"

She cowered before him.

"I guess my people live there. I don't want them to
see me like this. I'll go anywhere else you say."

"Why don't you want to go back to San Francisco?"

"I've told you."

He leaned forward, staring at her, and his great, shining eyes seemed to try to bore into her soul. He gave a sudden gasp.

"The penitentiary."

She screamed, and then she fell at his feet, clasping his legs.

"Don't send me back there. I swear to you before God I'll be a good woman. I'll give all this up."

She burst into a torrent of confused supplication and the tears coursed down her painted cheeks. He leaned over her and, lifting her face, forced her to look at him.

"Is that it, the penitentiary?"

"I beat it before they could get me," she gasped. "If the bulls grab me it's three years for mine."

He let go his hold of her and she fell in a heap on the floor, sobbing bitterly. Dr. Macphail stood up.

"This alters the whole thing," he said. "You can't make her go back when you know this. Give her another chance. She wants to turn over a new leaf."

"I'm going to give her the finest chance she's ever had. If she repents let her accept her punishment."

She misunderstood the words and looked up. There was a gleam of hope in her heavy eyes.

"You'll let me go?"

"No. You shall sail for San Francisco on Tuesday."

She gave a groan of horror and then burst into low, hoarse shrieks which sounded hardly human, and she beat her head passionately on the ground. Dr. Macphail sprang to her and lifted her up.

"Come on, you mustn't do that. You'd better go to your room and lie down. I'll get you something."

He raised her to her feet and partly dragging her, partly carrying her, got her downstairs. He was furious with Mrs. Davidson and with his wife because they made no effort to help. The half-caste was standing on the landing and with his assistance he managed to get her on the bed. She was moaning and crying. She was almost insensible. He gave her a hypodermic injection. He was hot and exhausted when he went upstairs again.

"I've got her to lie down."

The two women and Davidson were in the same positions as when he had left them. They could not have moved or spoken since he went.

"I was waiting for you," said Davidson, in a strange, distant voice. "I want you all to pray with me for the soul of our erring sister."

He took the Bible off a shelf, and sat down at the table at which they had supped. It had not been cleared, and he pushed the tea-pot out of the way. In a powerful voice, resonant and deep, he read to them the chapter in which is narrated the meeting of Jesus Christ with the woman taken in adultery.

"Now kneel with me and let us pray for the soul of our dear sister, Sadie Thompson."

He burst into a long, passionate prayer in which he implored God to have mercy on the sinful woman. Mrs. Macphail and Mrs. Davidson knelt with covered eyes.

The doctor, taken by surprise, awkward and sheepish, knelt too. The missionary's prayer had a savage eloquence. He was extraordinarily moved, and as he spoke the tears ran down his cheeks. Outside, the pitiless rain fell, fell steadily, with a fierce malignity that was all too human.

At last he stopped. He paused for a moment and said:

"We will now repeat the Lord's prayer."

They said it and then, following him, they rose from their knees. Mrs. Davidson's face was pale and restful. She was comforted and at peace, but the Macphails felt suddenly bashful. They did not know which way to look.

"I'll just go down and see how she is now," said Dr. Macphail.

When he knocked at her door it was opened for him by Horn. Miss Thompson was in a rocking-chair, sobbing quietly.

"What are you doing there?" exclaimed Macphail. "I told you to lie down."

"I can't lie down. I want to see Mr. Davidson."

"My poor child, what do you think is the good of it? You'll never move him."

"He said he'd come if I sent for him."

Macphail motioned to the trader.

"Go and fetch him."

He waited with her in silence while the trader went upstairs. Davidson came in.

"Excuse me for asking you to come here," she said, looking at him sombrely.

"I was expecting you to send for me. I knew the Lord would answer my prayer."

They stared at one another for a moment and then she looked away. She kept her eyes averted when she spoke.

"I've been a bad woman. I want to repent."

"Thank God! thank God! He has heard our prayers."

He turned to the two men.

"Leave me alone with her. Tell Mrs. Davidson that our prayers have been answered."

They went out and closed the door behind them.

"Gee whizz," said the trader.

That night Dr. Macphail could not get to sleep till late, and when he heard the missionary come upstairs he looked at his watch. It was two o'clock. But even then he did not go to bed at once, for through the wooden partition that separated their rooms he heard him praying aloud, till he himself, exhausted, fell asleep.

When he saw him next morning he was surprised at his appearance. He was paler than ever, tired, but his eyes shone with an inhuman fire. It looked as though he were filled with an overwhelming joy.

"I want you to go down presently and see Sadie," he said. "I can't hope that her body is better, but her soul—her soul is transformed."

The doctor was feeling wan and nervous.

"You were with her very late last night," he said.

"Yes, she couldn't bear to have me leave her."

"You look as pleased as Punch," the doctor said irritably.

Davidson's eyes shone with ecstasy.

"A great mercy has been vouchsafed me. Last night I was privileged to bring a lost soul to the loving arms of Jesus."

Miss Thompson was again in the rocking-chair. The bed had not been made. The room was in disorder. She had not troubled to dress herself, but wore a dirty dressing-gown, and her hair was tied in a sluttish knot. She had given her face a dab with a wet towel, but it was all swollen and creased with crying. She looked a drab.

She raised her eyes dully when the doctor came in. She was cowed and broken.

"Where's Mr. Davidson?" she asked.

"He'll come presently if you want him," answered Macphail acidly. "I came here to see how you were."

"Oh, I guess I'm O.K. You needn't worry about that."

"Have you had anything to eat?"

"Horn brought me some coffee."

She looked anxiously at the door.

"D'you think he'll come down soon? I feel as if it wasn't so terrible when he's with me."

"Are you still going on Tuesday?"

"Yes, he says I've got to go. Please tell him to come right along. You can't do me any good. He's the only one as can help me now."

"Very well," said Dr. Macphail.

During the next three days the missionary spent almost all his time with Sadie Thompson. He joined the others only to have his meals. Dr. Macphail noticed that he hardly ate.

"He's wearing himself out," said Mrs. Davidson pitifully. "He'll have a breakdown if he doesn't take care, but he won't spare himself."

She herself was white and pale. She told Mrs. Macphail that she had no sleep. When the missionary came upstairs from Miss Thompson he prayed till he was exhausted, but even then he did not sleep for long. After an hour or two he got up and dressed himself, and went for a tramp along the bay. He had strange dreams.

"This morning he told me that he'd been dreaming about the mountains of Nebraska," said Mrs. Davidson.

"That's curious," said Dr. Macphail.

He remembered seeing them from the windows of the train when he crossed America. They were like huge mole-hills, rounded and smooth, and they rose from the plain abruptly. Dr. Macphail remembered how it struck him that they were like a woman's breasts.

Davidson's restlessness was intolerable even to himself. But he was buoyed up by a wonderful exhilaration. He was tearing out by the roots the last vestiges of sin that lurked in the hidden corners of that poor woman's heart. He read with her and prayed with her.

"It's wonderful," he said to them one day at supper. "It's a true rebirth. Her soul, which was black as night, is now pure and white like the new-fallen snow. I am humble and afraid. Her remorse for all her sins is beautiful. I am not worthy to touch the hem of her garment."

"Have you the heart to send her back to San Francisco?" said the doctor. "Three years in an American prison. I should have thought you might have saved her from that."

"Ah, but don't you see? It's necessary. Do you think my heart doesn't bleed for her? I love her as I love my wife and my sister. All the time that she is in prison I shall suffer all the pain that she suffers."

"Bunkum," cried the doctor impatiently.

"You don't understand because you're blind. She's sinned, and she must suffer. I know what she'll endure. She'll be starved and tortured and humiliated. I want her to accept the punishment of man as a sacrifice to God. I want her to accept it joyfully. She has an opportunity which is offered to very few of us. God is very good and very merciful."

Davidson's voice trembled with excitement. He could hardly articulate the words that tumbled passionately from his lips.

"All day I pray with her and when I leave her I pray again, I pray with all my might and main, so that Jesus may grant her this great mercy. I want to put in her heart the passionate desire to be punished so that at the end, even if I offered to let her go, she would refuse. I want her to feel that the bitter punishment of prison is the thank-offering that she places at the feet of our Blessed Lord, who gave His life for her."

The days passed slowly. The whole household, intent on the wretched, tortured woman downstairs, lived in a state of unnatural excitement. She was like a victim that was being prepared for the savage rites of a bloody idolatry. Her terror numbed her. She could not bear to let Davidson out of her sight; it was only when he was with her that she had courage, and she hung upon him with a slavish dependence. She cried a great deal, and she read the Bible, and prayed. Sometimes she was exhausted and apathetic. Then she did indeed look forward to her ordeal, for it seemed to offer an escape, direct and concrete, from the anguish she was enduring. She could not bear much longer the vague terrors which now assailed her. With her sins she had put aside all personal vanity, and she slopped about her room, unkempt and dishevelled, in her tawdry dressing-gown. She had not taken off her night-dress for four days, nor put on stockings. Her room was littered and untidy. Meanwhile the rain fell with a cruel persistence. You felt that the heavens must at last be empty of water, but still it poured down, straight and heavy, with a maddening iteration, on the iron roof. Everything was damp and clammy. There was mildew on the walls and on the boots that stood on the floor. Through the sleepless nights the mosquitoes droned their angry chant.

"If it would only stop raining for a single day it wouldn't be so bad," said Dr. Macphail.

They all looked forward to the Tuesday when the boat for San Francisco was to arrive from Sydney. The strain was intolerable. So far as Dr. Macphail was concerned, his pity and his resentment were alike extinguished by his desire to be rid of the unfortunate woman. The inevitable must be accepted. He felt he would breathe more freely when the ship had sailed. Sadie Thompson was to be escorted on board by a clerk in the governor's office. This person called on the Monday evening and told Miss Thompson to be prepared at eleven in the morning. Davidson was with her.

"I'll see that everything is ready. I mean to come on board with her myself."

Miss Thompson did not speak.

When Dr. Macphail blew out his candle, and crawled cautiously under his mosquito curtains, he gave a sigh of relief.

"Well, thank God that's over. By this time tomorrow she'll be gone."

"Mrs. Davidson will be glad too. She says he's wearing himself to a shadow," said Mrs. Macphail. "She's a different woman."

"Who?"

"Sadie. I should never have thought it possible. It makes one humble."

Dr. Macphail did not answer, and presently he fell asleep. He was tired out, and he slept more soundly than usual.

He was awakened in the morning by a hand placed on his arm, and, starting up, saw Horn by the side of his bed. The trader put his finger on his mouth to prevent any exclamation from Dr. Macphail and beckoned to him to come. As a rule he wore shabby ducks, but now he was barefoot and wore only the *lava-lava* of the natives. He looked suddenly savage, and Dr. Macphail, getting out of bed, saw that he was heavily tattooed. Horn made him a sign to come on to the verandah. Dr. Macphail got out of bed and followed the trader out.

"Don't make a noise," he whispered. "You're wanted. Put on a coat and some shoes. Quick."

Dr. Macphail's first thought was that something had happened to Miss Thompson.

"What is it? Shall I bring my instruments?"

"Hurry, please, hurry."

Dr. Macphail crept back into the bedroom, put on a waterproof over his pyjamas, and a pair of rubber-soled shoes. He rejoined the trader, and together they tiptoed down the stairs. The door leading out to the road was open and at it were standing half a dozen natives.

"What is it?" repeated the doctor.

"Come along with me," said Horn.

He walked out and the doctor followed him. The natives came after them in a little bunch. They crossed the road and came on to the beach. The doctor saw a group of natives standing round some object at the water's edge. They hurried along, a couple of dozen yards perhaps, and the natives opened out as the doctor came up. The trader pushed him forwards. Then he saw, lying half in the water and half out, a dreadful object, the body of Davidson. Dr. Macphail bent down —he was not a man to lose his head in an emergency—

and turned the body over. The throat was cut from ear to ear, and in the right hand was still the razor with which the deed was done.

"He's quite cold," said the doctor. "He must have been dead some time."

"One of the boys saw him lying there on his way to work just now and came and told me. Do you think he did it himself?"

"Yes. Someone ought to go for the police."

Horn said something in the native tongue, and two youths started off.

"We must leave him here till they come," said the doctor.

"They mustn't take him into my house. I won't have him in my house."

"You'll do what the authorities say," replied the doctor sharply. "In point of fact I expect they'll take him to the mortuary."

They stood waiting where they were. The trader took a cigarette from a fold in his *lava-lava* and gave one to Dr. Macphail. They smoked while they stared at the corpse. Dr. Macphail could not understand.

"Why do you think he did it?" asked Horn.

The doctor shrugged his shoulders. In a little while native police came along, under the charge of a marine, with a stretcher, and immediately afterwards a couple of naval officers and a naval doctor. They managed everything in a businesslike manner.

"What about the wife?" said one of the officers.

"Now that you've come I'll go back to the house and get some things on. I'll see that it's broken to her. She'd better not see him till he's been fixed up a little."

"I guess that's right," said the naval doctor.

When Dr. Macphail went back he found his wife nearly dressed.

"Mrs. Davidson's in a dreadful state about her husband," she said to him as soon as he appeared. "He hasn't been to bed all night. She heard him leave Miss Thompson's room at two, but he went out. If he's been walking about since then he'll be absolutely dead."

Dr. Macphail told her what had happened and asked her to break the news to Mrs. Davidson.

"But why did he do it?" she asked, horror-stricken.

"I don't know."

"But I can't. I can't."

"You must."

She gave him a frightened look and went out. He heard her go into Mrs. Davidson's room. He waited a minute to gather himself together and then began to shave and wash. When he was dressed he sat down on the bed and waited for his wife. At last she came.

"She wants to see him," she said.

"They've taken him to the mortuary. We'd better go down with her. How did she take it?"

"I think she's stunned. She didn't cry. But she's trembling like a leaf."

"We'd better go at once."

When they knocked at her door, Mrs. Davidson

came out. She was very pale, but dry-eyed. To the doctor she seemed unnaturally composed. No word was exchanged, and they set out in silence down the road. When they arrived at the mortuary Mrs. Davidson spoke.

"Let me go in and see him alone."

They stood aside. A native opened a door for her and closed it behind her. They sat down and waited. One or two white men came and talked to them in undertones. Dr. Macphail told them again what he knew of the tragedy. At last the door was quietly opened and Mrs. Davidson came out. Silence fell upon them.

"I'm ready to go back now," she said.

Her voice was hard and steady. Dr. Macphail could not understand the look in her eyes. Her pale face was very stern. They walked back slowly, never saying a word, and at last they came round the bend on the other side of which stood their house. Mrs. Davidson gave a gasp, and for a moment they stopped still. An incredible sound assaulted their ears. The gramophone which had been silent for so long was playing, playing ragtime loud and harsh.

"What's that?" cried Mrs. Macphail with horror.

"Let's go on," said Mrs. Davidson.

They walked up the steps and entered the hall. Miss Thompson was standing at her door, chatting with a sailor. A sudden change had taken place in her. She was no longer the cowed drudge of the last days.

She was dressed in all her finery, in her white dress, with the high shiny boots over which her fat legs bulged in their cotton stockings; her hair was elaborately arranged; and she wore that enormous hat covered with gaudy flowers. Her face was painted, her eyebrows were boldly black, and her lips were scarlet. She held herself erect. She was the flaunting quean that they had known at first. As they came in she broke into a loud, jeering laugh; and then, when Mrs. Davidson involuntarily stopped, she collected the spittle in her mouth and spat. Mrs. Davidson cowered back, and two red spots rose suddenly to her cheeks. Then, covering her face with her hands, she broke away and ran quickly up the stairs. Dr. Macphail was outraged. He pushed past the woman into her room.

"What the devil are you doing?" he cried. "Stop that damned machine."

He went up to it and tore the record off. She turned on him.

"Say, doc., you can that stuff with me. What the hell are you doin' in my room?"

"What do you mean?" he cried. "What d'you mean?"

She gathered herself together. No one could describe the scorn of her expression or the contemptuous hatred she put into her answer.

"You men! You filthy, dirty pigs! You're all the same, all of you. Pigs! Pigs!"

Dr. Macphail gasped. He understood.

JANE

I REMEMBER very well the occasion on which I first saw Jane Fowler. It is indeed only because the details of the glimpse I had of her then are so clear that I trust my recollection at all, for, looking back, I must confess that I find it hard to believe that it has not played me a fantastic trick. I had lately returned to London from China and was drinking a dish of tea with Mrs. Tower. Mrs. Tower had been seized with the prevailing passion for decoration; and with the ruthlessness of her sex had sacrificed chairs in which she had comfortably sat for years, tables, cabinets, ornaments on which her eyes had dwelt in peace since she was married, pictures that had been familiar to her for a generation; and delivered herself into the hands of an expert. Nothing remained in her drawing-room with which she had any association, or to which any sentiment was attached; and she had invited me that day to see the fashionable glory in which she now lived. Everything that could be pickled was pickled and what couldn't be pickled was painted. Nothing matched, but everything harmonised.

"Do you remember that ridiculous drawing-room suite that I used to have?" asked Mrs. Tower.

The curtains were sumptuous yet severe; the sofa

was covered with Italian brocade; the chair on which I sat was in *petit point*. The room was beautiful, opulent without garishness and original without affectation; yet to me it lacked something; and while I praised with my lips I asked myself why I so much preferred the rather shabby chintz of the despised suite, the Victorian water-colours that I had known so long, and the ridiculous Dresden china that had adorned the chimney-piece. I wondered what it was that I missed in all these rooms that the decorators were turning out with a profitable industry. Was it heart? But Mrs. Tower looked about her happily.

"Don't you like my alabaster lamps?" she said. "They give such a soft light."

"Personally I have a weakness for a light that you can see by," I smiled.

"It's so difficult to combine that with a light that you can't be too much seen by," laughed Mrs. Tower.

I had no notion what her age was. When I was quite a young man she was a married woman a good deal older than I, but now she treated me as her contemporary. She constantly said that she made no secret of her age, which was forty, and then added with a smile that all women took five years off. She never sought to conceal the fact that she dyed her hair (it was a very pretty brown with reddish tints), and she said she did this because hair was hideous while it was going grey; as soon as hers was white she would cease to dye it.

"Then they'll say what a young face I have."

Meanwhile it was painted, though with discretion, and her eyes owed not a little of their vivacity to art. She was a handsome woman, exquisitely gowned, and in the sombre glow of the alabaster lamps did not look a day more than the forty she gave herself.

"It is only at my dressing-table that I can suffer the naked brightness of a thirty-two-candle electric bulb," she added with smiling cynicism. "There I need it to tell me first the hideous truth and then to enable me to take the necessary steps to correct it."

We gossiped pleasantly about our common friends and Mrs. Tower brought me up to date in the scandal of the day. After roughing it here and there it was very agreeable to sit in a comfortable chair, the fire burning brightly on the hearth, charming tea-things set out on a charming table, and talk with this amusing, attractive woman. She treated me as a prodigal returned from his husks and was disposed to make much of me. She prided herself on her dinner-parties; she took no less trouble to have her guests suitably assorted than to give them excellent food; and there were few persons who did not look upon it as a treat to be bidden to one of them. Now she fixed a date and asked me whom I would like to meet.

"There's only one thing I must tell you. If Jane Fowler is still here I shall have to put it off."

"Who is Jane Fowler?" I asked.

Mrs. Tower gave a rueful smile.

"Jane Fowler is my cross."

"Oh!"

"Do you remember a photograph that I used to have on the piano before I had my room done, of a woman in a tight dress with tight sleeves and a gold locket, with her hair drawn back from a broad forehead and her ears showing and spectacles on a rather blunt nose? Well, that was Jane Fowler."

"You had so many photographs about the room in your unregenerate days," I said, vaguely.

"It makes me shudder to think of them. I've made them into a huge brown-paper parcel and hidden them in an attic."

"Well, who is Jane Fowler?" I asked again, smiling.

"She's my sister-in-law. She was my husband's sister and she married a manufacturer in the North. She's been a widow for many years, and she's very well-to-do."

"And why is she your cross?"

"She's worthy, she's dowdy, she's provincial. She looks twenty years older than I do and she's quite capable of telling anyone she meets that we were at school together. She has an overwhelming sense of family affection and because I am her only living connection she's devoted to me. When she comes to London it never occurs to her that she should stay anywhere but here—she thinks it would hurt my feelings—and she'll pay me visits of three or four weeks. We sit here and she knits and reads. And sometimes she insists on taking me to dine at Claridge's and she looks like a funny old charwoman and everyone I particularly don't want to be seen by is sitting at the next table. When we are driving home she says she loves giving me a little treat. With her own hands she makes me tea-cosies that I am forced to use when she is here and doilies and centrepieces for the dining-room table."

Mrs. Tower paused to take breath.

"I should have thought a woman of your tact would find a way to deal with a situation like that."

"Ah, but don't you see, I haven't a chance. She's so immeasurably kind. She has a heart of gold. She bores me to death, but I wouldn't for anything let her suspect it."

"And when does she arrive?"

"To-morrow."

But the answer was hardly out of Mrs. Tower's mouth when the bell rang. There were sounds in the hall of a slight commotion and in a minute or two the butler ushered in an elderly lady.

"Mrs. Fowler," he announced.

"Jane," cried Mrs. Tower, springing to her feet. "I wasn't expecting you to-day."

"So your butler has just told me. I certainly said to-day in my letter."

Mrs. Tower recovered her wits.

"Well, it doesn't matter. I'm very glad to see you whenever you come. Fortunately I'm doing nothing this evening."

"You mustn't let me give you any trouble. If I can

have a boiled egg for my dinner that's all I shall want."

A faint grimace for a moment distorted Mrs. Tower's handsome features. A boiled egg!

"Oh, I think we can do a little better than that."

I chuckled inwardly when I recollected that the two ladies were contemporaries. Mrs. Fowler looked a good fifty-five. She was a rather big woman; she wore a black straw hat with a wide brim and from it a black lace veil hung over her shoulders, a cloak that oddly combined severity with fussiness, a long black dress, voluminous as though she wore several petticoats under it, and stout boots. She was evidently short-sighted, for she looked at you through large gold-rimmed spectacles.

"Won't you have a cup of tea?" asked Mrs. Tower.

"If it wouldn't be too much trouble. I'll take off my mantle."

She began by stripping her hands of the black gloves she wore, and then took off her cloak. Round her neck was a solid gold chain from which hung a large gold locket in which I felt certain was a photograph of her deceased husband. Then she took off her hat and placed it neatly with her gloves and cloak on the sofa corner. Mrs. Tower pursed her lips. Certainly those garments did not go very well with the austere but sumptuous beauty of Mrs. Tower's redecorated drawing-room. I wondered where on earth Mrs. Fowler had found the extraordinary clothes she wore. They were not old and the materials were expensive. It was astounding to think that dressmakers still made things that had

c*

not been worn for a quarter of a century. Mrs. Fowler's grey hair was very plainly done, showing all her forehead and her ears, with a parting in the middle. It had evidently never known the tongs of Monsieur Marcel. Now her eyes fell on the tea-table with its teapot of Georgian silver and its cups in old Worcester.

"What have you done with the tea-cosy I gave you last time I came up, Marion?" she asked. "Don't you use it?"

"Yes, I used it every day, Jane," answered Mrs. Tower glibly. "Unfortunately we had an accident with it a little while ago. It got burnt."

"But the last one I gave you got burnt."

"I'm afraid you'll think us very careless."

"It doesn't really matter," smiled Mrs. Fowler. "I shall enjoy making you another. I'll go to Liberty's to-morrow and buy some silks."

Mrs. Tower kept her face bravely.

"I don't deserve it, you know. Doesn't your vicar's wife need one?"

"Oh, I've just made her one," said Mrs. Fowler brightly.

I noticed that when she smiled she showed white, small and regular teeth. They were a real beauty. Her smile was certainly very sweet.

But I felt it high time for me to leave the two ladies to themselves, so I took my leave.

Early next morning Mrs. Tower rang me up and I heard at once from her voice that she was in high spirits.

"I've got the most wonderful news for you," she said. "Jane is going to be married."

"Nonsense."

"Her fiancé is coming to dine here to-night to be introduced to me and I want you to come too."

"Oh, but I shall be in the way."

"No, you won't. Jane suggested herself that I should ask you. Do come."

She was bubbling over with laughter.

"Who is he?"

"I don't know. She tells me he's an architect. Can you imagine the sort of man Jane would marry?"

I had nothing to do and I could trust Mrs. Tower to give me a good dinner.

When I arrived Mrs. Tower, very splendid in a tea-gown a little too young for her, was alone.

"Jane is putting the finishing touches to her appearance. I'm longing for you to see her. She's all in a flutter. She says he adores her. His name is Gilbert and when she speaks of him her voice gets all funny and tremulous. It makes me want to laugh."

"I wonder what he's like."

"Oh, I'm sure I know. Very big and massive, with a bald head and an immense gold chain across an immense tummy. A large, fat, clean-shaven, red face and a booming voice."

Mrs. Fowler came in. She wore a very stiff black silk dress with a wide skirt and a train. At the neck it was cut into a timid V and the sleeves came down to the elbows.

She wore a necklace of diamonds set in silver. She carried in her hands a long pair of black gloves and a fan of black ostrich feathers. She managed (as so few people do) to look exactly what she was. You could never have thought her anything in the world but the respectable relict of a North-country manufacturer of ample means.

"You've really got quite a pretty neck, Jane," said Mrs. Tower with a kindly smile.

It was indeed astonishingly young when you compared it with her weather-beaten face. It was smooth and unlined and the skin was white. And I noticed then that her head was very well placed on her shoulders.

"Has Marion told you my news?" she said, turning to me with that really charming smile of hers as if we were already old friends.

"I must congratulate you," I said.

"Wait to do that till you've seen my young man."

"I think it's too sweet to hear you talk of your young man," smiled Mrs. Tower.

Mrs. Fowler's eyes certainly twinkled behind her preposterous spectacles.

"Don't expect anyone too old. You wouldn't like me to marry a decrepit old gentleman with one foot in the grave, would you?"

This was the only warning she gave us. Indeed there was no time for any further discussion, for the butler flung open the door and in a loud voice announced:

"Mr. Gilbert Napier."

There entered a youth in a very well-cut dinner

jacket. He was slight, not very tall, with fair hair in which there was a hint of a natural wave, clean-shaven and blue-eyed. He was not particularly good-looking, but he had a pleasant, amiable face. In ten years he would probably be wizened and sallow; but now, in extreme youth, he was fresh and clean and blooming. For he was certainly not more than twenty-four. My first thought was that this was the son of Jane Fowler's fiancé (I had not known he was a widower) come to say that his father was prevented from dining by a sudden attack of gout. But his eyes fell immediately on Mrs. Fowler, his face lit up, and he went towards her with both hands outstretched. Mrs. Fowler gave him hers, a demure smile on her lips, and turned to her sister-in-law.

"This is my young man, Marion," she said.

He held out his hand.

"I hope you'll like me, Mrs. Tower," he said. "Jane tells me you're the only relation she has in the world."

Mrs. Tower's face was wonderful to behold. I saw then to admiration how bravely good breeding and social usage could combat the instincts of the natural woman. For the astonishment and then the dismay that for an instant she could not conceal were quickly driven away, and her face assumed an expression of affable welcome. But she was evidently at a loss for words. It was not unnatural if Gilbert felt a certain embarrassment and I was too busy preventing myself from laughing to think of anything to say. Mrs. Fowler alone kept perfectly calm.

"I know you'll like him, Marion. There's no one enjoys good food more than he does." She turned to the young man. "Marion's dinners are famous."

"I know," he beamed.

Mrs. Tower made some quick rejoinder and we went downstairs. I shall not soon forget the exquisite comedy of that meal. Mrs. Tower could not make up her mind whether the pair of them were playing a practical joke on her or whether Jane by wilfully concealing her fiancé's age had hoped to make her look foolish. But then Jane never jested and she was incapable of doing a malicious thing. Mrs. Tower was amazed, exasperated and perplexed. But she had recovered her self-control, and for nothing would she have forgotten that she was a perfect hostess whose duty it was to make her party go. She talked vivaciously; but I wondered if Gilbert Napier saw how hard and vindictive was the expression of her eyes behind the mask of friendliness that she turned to him. She was measuring him. She was seeking to delve into the secret of his soul. I could see that she was in a passion, for under her rouge her cheeks glowed with an angry red.

"You've got a very high colour, Marion," said Jane, looking at her amiably through her great round spectacles.

"I dressed in a hurry. I daresay I put on too much rouge."

"Oh, is it rouge? I thought it was natural. Otherwise I shouldn't have mentioned it." She gave Gilbert a shy little smile. "You know, Marion and I were at school together. You would never think it to look at us now, would you? But of course I've lived a very quiet life."

I do not know what she meant by these remarks; it was almost incredible that she made them in complete simplicity; but anyhow they goaded Mrs. Tower to such a fury that she flung her own vanity to the winds. She smiled brightly.

"We shall neither of us see fifty again, Jane," she said.

If the observation was meant to discomfit the widow it failed.

"Gilbert says I mustn't acknowledge to more than forty-nine for his sake," she answered blandly.

Mrs. Tower's hands trembled slightly, but she found a retort.

"There is of course a certain disparity of age between you," she smiled.

"Twenty-seven years," said Jane. "Do you think it's too much? Gilbert says I'm very young for my age. I told you I shouldn't like to marry a man with one foot in the grave."

I was really obliged to laugh and Gilbert laughed too. His laughter was frank and boyish. It looked as though he were amused at everything Jane said. But Mrs. Tower was almost at the end of her tether and I was afraid that unless relief came she would for once forget that she was a woman of the world. I came to the rescue as best I could.

"I suppose you're very busy buying your trousseau," I said.

"No. I wanted to get my things from the dress-maker in Liverpool I've been to ever since I was first married. But Gilbert won't let me. He's very masterful, and of course he has wonderful taste."

She looked at him with a little affectionate smile, demurely, as though she were a girl of seventeen.

Mrs. Tower went quite pale under her make-up.

"We're going to Italy for our honeymoon. Gilbert has never had a chance of studying Renaissance archi-tecture and of course it's important for an architect to see things for himself. And we shall stop in Paris on the way and get my clothes there."

"Do you expect to be away long?"

"Gilbert has arranged with his office to stay away for six months. It will be such a treat for him, won't it? You see, he's never had more than a fortnight's holiday before."

"Why not?" asked Mrs. Tower in a tone that no effort of will could prevent from being icy.

"He's never been able to afford it, poor dear."

"Ah!" said Mrs. Tower, and into the exclamation put volumes.

Coffee was served and the ladies went upstairs. Gilbert and I began to talk in the desultory way in which men talk who have nothing whatever to say to one another; but in two minutes a note was brought in to me by the butler. It was from Mrs. Tower and ran as follows:

*"Come upstairs quickly and then go as soon as you can.
Take him with you. Unless I have it out with Jane at once I
shall have a fit."*

I told a facile lie.

"Mrs. Tower has a headache and wants to go to bed.
I think if you don't mind we'd better clear out."

"Certainly," he answered.

We went upstairs and five minutes later were on the
doorstep. I called a taxi and offered the young man a lift.

"No, thanks," he answered. "I'll just walk to the
corner and jump on a bus."

Mrs. Tower sprang to the fray as soon as she heard
the front-door close behind us.

"Are you crazy, Jane?" she cried.

"Not more than most people who don't habitually
live in a lunatic asylum, I trust," Jane answered blandly.

"May I ask why you're going to marry this young
man?" asked Mrs. Tower with formidable politeness.

"Partly because he won't take no for an answer.
He's asked me five times. I grew positively tired of
refusing him."

"And why do you think he's so anxious to marry you?"

"I amuse him."

Mrs. Tower gave an exclamation of annoyance.

"He's an unscrupulous rascal. I very nearly told him
so to his face."

"You would have been wrong, and it wouldn't have
been very polite."

"He's penniless and you're rich. You can't be such a besotted fool as not to see that he's marrying you for your money."

Jane remained perfectly composed. She observed her sister-in-law's agitation with detachment.

"I don't think he is, you know," she replied. "I think he's very fond of me."

"You're an old woman, Jane."

"I'm the same age as you are, Marion," she smiled.

"I've never let myself go. I'm very young for my age. No one would think I was more than forty. But even I wouldn't dream of marrying a boy twenty years younger than myself."

"Twenty-seven," corrected Jane.

"Do you mean to tell me that you can bring yourself to believe that it's possible for a young man to care for a woman old enough to be his mother?"

"I've lived very much in the country for many years. I daresay there's a great deal about human nature that I don't know. They tell me there's a man called Freud, an Austrian, I believe . . ."

But Mrs. Tower interrupted her without any politeness at all.

"Don't be ridiculous, Jane. It's so undignified. It's so ungraceful. I always thought you were a sensible woman. Really you're the last person I should ever have thought likely to fall in love with a boy."

"But I'm not in love with him. I've told him that. Of course I like him very much or I wouldn't think of marrying him. I thought it only fair to tell him quite plainly what my feelings were towards him."

Mrs. Tower gasped. The blood rushed to her head and her breathing oppressed her. She had no fan, but she seized the evening paper and vigorously fanned herself with it.

"If you're not in love with him why do you want to marry him?"

"I've been a widow a very long time and I've led a very quiet life. I thought I'd like a change."

"If you want to marry just to be married why don't you marry a man of your own age?"

"No man of my own age has asked me five times. In fact no man of my own age has asked me at all."

Jane chuckled as she answered. It drove Mrs. Tower to the final pitch of frenzy.

"Don't laugh, Jane. I won't have it. I don't think you can be right in your mind. It's dreadful."

It was altogether too much for her and she burst into tears. She knew that at her age it was fatal to cry, her eyes would be swollen for twenty-four hours and she would look a sight. But there was no help for it. She wept. Jane remained perfectly calm. She looked at Marion through her large spectacles and reflectively smoothed the lap of her black silk dress.

"You're going to be so dreadfully unhappy," Mrs. Tower sobbed, dabbing her eyes cautiously in the hope that the black on her lashes would not smudge.

"I don't think so, you know," Jane answered in

those equable, mild tones of hers, as if there were a little smile behind the words. "We've talked it over very thoroughly. I always think I'm a very easy person to live with. I think I shall make Gilbert very happy and comfortable. He's never had anyone to look after him properly. We're only marrying after mature consideration. And we've decided that if either of us wants his liberty the other will place no obstacles in the way of his getting it."

Mrs. Tower had by now recovered herself sufficiently to make a cutting remark.

"How much has he persuaded you to settle on him?"

"I wanted to settle a thousand a year on him, but he wouldn't hear of it. He was quite upset when I made the suggestion. He says he can earn quite enough for his own needs."

"He's more cunning than I thought," said Mrs. Tower acidly.

Jane paused a little and looked at her sister-in-law with kindly but resolute eyes.

"You see, my dear, it's different for you," she said. "You've never been so very much a widow, have you?"

Mrs. Tower looked at her. She blushed a little. She even felt slightly uncomfortable. But of course Jane was much too simple to intend an innuendo. Mrs. Tower gathered herself together with dignity.

"I'm so upset that I really must go to bed," she said. "We'll resume the conversation to-morrow morning."

"I'm afraid that won't be very convenient, dear. Gilbert and I are going to get the licence to-morrow morning."

Mrs. Tower threw up her hands in a gesture of dismay, but she found nothing more to say.

The marriage took place at a registrar's office. Mrs. Tower and I were the witnesses. Gilbert in a smart blue suit looked absurdly young and he was obviously nervous. It is a trying moment for any man. But Jane kept her admirable composure. She might have been in the habit of marrying as frequently as a woman of fashion. Only a slight colour on her cheeks suggested that beneath her calm was some faint excitement. It is a thrilling moment for any woman. She wore a very full dress of silver grey velvet in the cut of which I recognised the hand of the dressmaker in Liverpool (evidently a widow of unimpeachable character), who had made her gowns for so many years; but she had so far succumbed to the frivolity of the occasion as to wear a large picture hat covered with blue ostrich feathers. Her gold-rimmed spectacles made it extraordinarily grotesque. When the ceremony was over the registrar (somewhat taken aback, I thought, by the difference of age between the pair he was marrying) shook hands with her, tendering his strictly official congratulations; and the bridegroom, blushing slightly, kissed her. Mrs. Tower, resigned but implacable, kissed her; and then the bride looked at me expectantly. It was evidently fitting that I should kiss her too. I did. I confess that I felt a little shy as we walked out of the registrar's office past loungers who waited cynically to see the bridal pairs, and it was with relief that I stepped into Mrs. Tower's car. We drove to Victoria Station, for the happy couple were to go over to Paris by the two o'clock train, and Jane had insisted that the wedding-breakfast should be eaten at the station restaurant. She said it always made her nervous not to be on the platform in good time. Mrs. Tower, present only from a strong sense of family duty, was able to do little to make the party go off well; she ate nothing (for which I could not blame her, since the food was execrable, and anyway I hate champagne at luncheon) and talked in a strained voice. But Jane went through the menu conscientiously.

"I always think one should make a hearty meal before starting out on a journey," she said.

We saw them off, and I drove Mrs. Tower back to her house.

"How long do you give it?" she said. "Six months?"

"Let's hope for the best," I smiled.

'Don't be so absurd. There can be no 'best.' You don't think he's marrying her for anything but her money, do you? Of course it can't last. My only hope is that she won't have to go through as much suffering as she deserves."

I laughed. The charitable words were spoken in such a tone as to leave me in small doubt of Mrs. Tower's meaning.

"Well, if it doesn't last you'll have the consolation of saying: 'I told you so,'" I said.

"I promise you I'll never do that."

"Then you'll have the satisfaction of congratulating yourself on your self-control in not saying: 'I told you so.'"

"She's old and dowdy and dull."

"Are you sure she's dull?" I said. "It's true she doesn't say very much, but when she says anything it's very much to the point."

"I've never heard her make a joke in my life."

I was once more in the Far East when Gilbert and Jane returned from their honeymoon and this time I remained away for nearly two years. Mrs. Tower was a bad correspondent and though I sent her an occasional picture-postcard I received no news from her. But I met her within a week of my return to London; I was dining out and found that I was seated next to her. It was an immense party, I think we were four-and-twenty, like the blackbirds in the pie, and, arriving somewhat late, I was too confused by the crowd in which I found myself to notice who was there. But when we sat down, looking round the long table I saw that a good many of my fellow-guests were well known to the public from their photographs in the illustrated papers. Our hostess had a weakness for the persons technically known as celebrities and this was an unusually brilliant gathering. When Mrs. Tower and I had exchanged the conventional remarks that two people make when they have not seen one another for a couple of years I asked about Jane.

"She's very well," said Mrs. Tower with a certain dryness.

"How has the marriage turned out?"

Mrs. Tower paused a little and took a salted almond from the dish in front of her.

"It appears to be quite a success."

"You were wrong then?"

"I said it wouldn't last and I still say it won't last. It's contrary to human nature."

"Is she happy?"

"They're both happy."

"I suppose you don't see very much of them."

"At first I saw quite a lot of them. But now . . ." Mrs. Tower pursed her lips a little. "Jane is becoming very grand."

"What *do* you mean?" I laughed.

"I think I should tell you that she's here to-night."

"Here?"

I was startled. I looked round the table again. Our hostess was a delightful and an entertaining woman, but I could not imagine that she would be likely to invite to a dinner such as this the elderly and dowdy wife of an obscure architect. Mrs. Tower saw my perplexity and was shrewd enough to see what was in my mind. She smiled thinly.

"Look on the left of our host."

I looked. Oddly enough the woman who sat there had by her fantastic appearance attracted my attention the moment I was ushered into the crowded drawing-

room. I thought I noticed a gleam of recognition in her
eye, but to the best of my belief I had never seen her
before. She was not a young woman, for her hair was
iron-grey; it was cut very short and clustered thickly
round her well-shaped head in tight curls. She made no
attempt at youth, for she was conspicuous in that
gathering by using neither lipstick, rouge nor powder.
Her face, not a particularly handsome one, was red and
weather-beaten; but because it owed nothing to artifice
had a naturalness that was very pleasing. It contrasted
oddly with the whiteness of her shoulders. They were
really magnificent. A woman of thirty might have been
proud of them. But her dress was extraordinary. I had
not seen often anything more audacious. It was cut very
low, with short skirts, which were then the fashion, in
black and yellow; it had almost the effect of fancy-dress
and yet so became her that though on anyone else
it would have been outrageous, on her it had the
inevitable simplicity of nature. And to complete the
impression of an eccentricity in which there was no
pose and of an extravagance in which there was no
ostentation she wore, attached by a broad black ribbon,
a single eye-glass.

"You're not going to tell me *that* is your sister-in-
law," I gasped.

"That is Jane Napier," said Mrs. Tower icily.

At that moment she was speaking. Her host was
turned towards her with an anticipatory smile. A
baldish white-haired man, with a sharp, intelligent face,

who sat on her left, was leaning forward eagerly, and the couple who sat opposite, ceasing to talk with one another, listened intently. She said her say and they all, with a sudden movement, threw themselves back in their chairs and burst into vociferous laughter. From the other side of the table a man addressed Mrs. Tower: I recognised a famous statesman.

"Your sister-in-law has made another joke, Mrs. Tower," he said.

Mrs. Tower smiled.

"She's priceless, isn't she?"

"Let me have a long drink of champagne and then for heaven's sake tell me about all it," I said.

Well, this is how I gathered it had all happened. At the beginning of their honeymoon Gilbert took Jane to various dressmakers in Paris and he made no objection to her choosing a number of 'gowns' after her own heart; but he persuaded her to have a 'frock' or two made according to his own design. It appeared that he had a knack for that kind of work. He engaged a smart French maid. Jane had never had such a thing before. She did her own mending and when she wanted 'doing up' was in the habit of ringing for the housemaid. The dresses Gilbert had devised were very different from anything she had worn before; but he had been careful not to go too far too quickly, and because it pleased him she persuaded herself, though not without misgivings, to wear them in preference to those she had chosen herself. Of course she could not wear them with the voluminous petticoats she had been in the habit of using, and these, though it cost her an anxious moment, she discarded.

"Now if you please," said Mrs. Tower, with something very like a sniff of disapproval, "she wears nothing but thin silk tights. It's a wonder to me she doesn't catch her death of cold at her age."

Gilbert and the French maid taught her how to wear her clothes, and, unexpectedly enough, she was very quick at learning. The French maid was in raptures over Madame's arms and shoulders. It was a scandal not to show anything so fine.

"Wait a little, Alphonsine," said Gilbert. "The next lot of clothes I design for Madame we'll make the most of her."

The spectacles of course were dreadful. No one could look really well in gold-rimmed spectacles. Gilbert tried some with tortoise-shell rims. He shook his head.

"They'd look all right on a girl," he said. "You're too old to wear spectacles, Jane." Suddenly he had an inspiration. "By George, I've got it. You must wear an eyeglass."

"Oh, Gilbert, I couldn't."

She looked at him and his excitement, the excitement of the artist, made her smile. He was so sweet to her she wanted to do what she could to please him.

"I'll try," she said.

When they went to an optician and, suited with the right size, she placed an eyeglass jauntily in her eye

Gilbert clapped his hands. There and then, before the astonished shopman, he kissed her on both cheeks.

"You look wonderful," he cried.

So they went down to Italy and spent happy months studying Renaissance and Baroque architecture. Jane not only grew accustomed to her changed appearance, but found she liked it. At first she was a little shy when she went into the dining-room of an hotel and people turned round to stare at her, no one had ever raised an eyelid to look at her before, but presently she found that the sensation was not disagreeable. Ladies came up to her and asked her where she got her dress.

"Do you like it?" she answered demurely. "My husband designed it for me."

"I should like to copy it if you don't mind."

Jane had certainly for many years lived a very quiet life, but she was by no means lacking in the normal instincts of her sex. She had her answer ready.

"I'm so sorry, but my husband's very particular and he won't hear of anyone copying my frocks. He wants me to be unique."

She had an idea that people would laugh when she said this, but they didn't; they merely answered:

"Oh, of course I quite understand. You *are* unique."

But she saw them making mental notes of what she wore, and for some reason this quite "put her about." For once in her life that she wasn't wearing what everybody else did, she reflected, she didn't see why everybody else should want to wear what she did.

"Gilbert," she said, quite sharply for her, "next time you're designing dresses for me I wish you'd design things that people *can't* copy."

"The only way to do that is to design things that only you can wear."

"Can't you do that?"

"Yes, if you'll do something for me."

"What is it?"

"Cut off your hair."

I think this was the first time that Jane jibbed. Her hair was long and thick and as a girl she had been quite vain of it; to cut it off was a very drastic proceeding. This really was burning her boats behind her. In her case it was not the first step that cost so much, it was the last; but she took it ("I know Marion will think me a perfect fool, and I shall *never* be able to go to Liverpool again," she said), and when they passed through Paris on their way home Gilbert led her (she felt quite sick, her heart was beating so fast) to the best hairdresser in the world. She came out of his shop with a jaunty, saucy, impudent head of crisp grey curls. Pygmalion had finished his fantastic masterpiece: Galatea was come to life.

"Yes," I said, "but that isn't enough to explain why Jane is here to-night amid this crowd of duchesses, cabinet ministers and such-like; nor why she is sitting on one side of her host with an Admiral of the Fleet on the other."

"Jane is a humorist," said Mrs. Tower. "Didn't you see them all laughing at what she said?"

There was no doubt now of the bitterness in Mrs. Tower's heart.

"When Jane wrote and told me they were back from their honeymoon I thought I must ask them both to dinner. I didn't much like the idea, but I felt it had to be done. I knew the party would be deadly and I wasn't going to sacrifice any of the people who really mattered. On the other hand I didn't want Jane to think I hadn't any nice friends. You know I never have more than eight, but on this occasion I thought it would make things go better if I had twelve. I'd been too busy to see Jane until the evening of the party. She kept us all waiting a little—that was Gilbert's cleverness—and at last she sailed in. You could have knocked me down with a feather. She made the rest of the women look dowdy and provincial. She made me feel like a painted old trollop."

Mrs. Tower drank a little champagne.

"I wish I could describe the frock to you. It would have been quite impossible on anyone else; on her it was perfect. And the eyeglass! I'd known her for thirty-five years and I'd never seen her without spectacles."

"But you knew she had a good figure."

"How should I? I'd never seen her except in the clothes you first saw her in. Did *you* think she had a good figure? She seemed not to be unconscious of the sensation she made but to take it as a matter of course. I thought of my dinner and I heaved a sigh of relief. Even if she was a little heavy in hand, with that appearance it didn't so very much matter. She was sitting at the other end of the table and I heard a good deal of laughter, I was glad to think that the other people were playing up well; but after dinner I was a good deal taken aback when no less than three men came up to me and told me that my sister-in-law was priceless, and did I think she would allow them to call on her? I didn't quite know whether I was standing on my head or my heels. Twenty-four hours later our hostess of to-night rang me up and said she had heard my sister-in-law was in London and she was priceless and would I ask her to luncheon to meet her? She has an infallible instinct, that woman: in a month everyone was talking about Jane. I am here to-night, not because I've known our hostess for twenty years and have asked her to dinner a hundred times, but because I'm Jane's sister-in-law."

Poor Mrs. Tower. The position was galling, and though I could not help being amused, for the tables were turned on her with a vengeance, I felt that she deserved my sympathy.

"People never can resist those who make them laugh," I said, trying to console her.

"She never makes *me* laugh."

Once more from the top of the table I heard a guffaw and guessed that Jane had said another amusing thing.

"Do you mean to say that you are the only person who doesn't think her funny?" I asked, smiling.

"Had it struck *you* that she was a humorist?"

"I'm bound to say it hadn't."

"She says just the same things as she's said for the last thirty-five years. I laugh when I see everyone else does because I don't want to seem a perfect fool, but I am not amused."

"Like Queen Victoria," I said.

It was a foolish jest and Mrs. Tower was quite right sharply to tell me so. I tried another tack.

"Is Gilbert here?" I asked, looking down the table.

"Gilbert was asked because she won't go out without him, but to-night he's at a dinner of the Architects' Institute or whatever it's called."

"I'm dying to renew my acquaintance with her."

"Go and talk to her after dinner. She'll ask you to her Tuesdays."

"Her Tuesdays?"

"She's at home every Tuesday evening. You'll meet there everyone you ever heard of. They're the best parties in London. She's done in one year what I've failed to do in twenty."

"But what you tell me is really miraculous. How has it been done?"

Mrs. Tower shrugged her handsome but adipose shoulders.

"I shall be glad if you'll tell me," she replied.

After dinner I tried to make my way to the sofa on which Jane was sitting, but I was intercepted and it was not till a little later that my hostess came up to me and said:

"I must introduce you to the star of my party. Do

you know Jane Napier? She's priceless. She's much more amusing than your comedies."

I was taken up to the sofa. The admiral who had been sitting beside her at dinner was with her still. He showed no sign of moving and Jane, shaking hands with me, introduced me to him.

"Do you know Sir Reginald Frobisher?"

We began to chat. It was the same Jane as I had known before, perfectly simple, homely and unaffected, but her fantastic appearance certainly gave a peculiar savour to what she said. Suddenly I found myself shaking with laughter. She had made a remark, sensible and to the point, but not in the least witty, which her manner of saying and the bland look she gave me through her eyeglass made perfectly irresistible. I felt light-hearted and buoyant. When I left her she said to me:

"If you've got nothing better to do, come and see us on Tuesday evening. Gilbert will be so glad to see you."

"When he's been a month in London he'll know that he *can* have nothing better to do," said the admiral.

So, on Tuesday but rather late, I went to Jane's. I confess I was a little surprised at the company. It was quite a remarkable collection of writers, painters and politicians, actors, great ladies and great beauties: Mrs. Tower was right, it was a grand party; I had seen nothing like it in London since Stafford House was sold. No particular entertainment was provided. The refreshments were adequate without being luxurious. Jane in her quiet way seemed to be enjoying herself; I

D

could not see that she took a great deal of trouble with her guests, but they seemed to like being there, and the gay, pleasant party did not break up till two in the morning. After that I saw much of her. I not only went often to her house, but seldom went out to luncheon or to dinner without meeting her. I am an amateur of humour and I sought to discover in what lay her peculiar gift. It was impossible to repeat anything she said, for the fun, like certain wines, would not travel. She had no gift for epigram. She never made a brilliant repartee. There was no malice in her remarks nor sting in her rejoinders. There are those who think that impropriety, rather than brevity, is the soul of wit; but she never said a thing that could have brought a blush to a Victorian cheek. I think her humour was unconscious and I am sure it was unpremeditated. It flew like a butterfly from flower to flower, obedient only to its own caprice and pursuivant of neither method nor intention. It depended on the way she spoke and on the way she looked. Its subtlety gained by the flaunting and extravagant appearance that Gilbert had achieved for her; but her appearance was only an element in it. Now of course she was the fashion and people laughed if she but opened her mouth. They no longer wondered that Gilbert had married a wife so much older than himself. They saw that Jane was a woman with whom age did not count. They thought him a devilish lucky young fellow. The admiral quoted Shakespeare to me: "Age cannot wither her, nor custom stale her infinite variety."

Gilbert was delighted with her success. As I came to know him better I grew to like him. It was quite evident that he was neither a rascal nor a fortune-hunter. He was not only immensely proud of Jane but genuinely devoted to her. His kindness to her was touching. He was a very unselfish and sweet-tempered young man.

"Well, what do you think of Jane now?" he said to me once, with boyish triumph.

"I don't know which of you is more wonderful," I said. "You or she."

"Oh, I'm nothing."

"Nonsense. You don't think I'm such a fool as not to see that it's you, and you only, who've made Jane what she is."

"My only merit is that I saw what was there when it wasn't obvious to the naked eye," he answered.

"I can understand your seeing that she had in her the possibility of that remarkable appearance, but how in the world have you made her into a humorist?"

"But I always thought the things she said a perfect scream. She was always a humorist."

"You're the only person who ever thought so."

Mrs. Tower, not without magnanimity, acknowledged that she had been mistaken in Gilbert. She grew quite attached to him. But notwithstanding appearances she never faltered in her opinion that the marriage could not last. I was obliged to laugh at her.

"Why, I've never seen such a devoted couple," I said.

"Gilbert is twenty-seven now. It's just the time for a

pretty girl to come along. Did you notice the other evening at Jane's that pretty little niece of Sir Reginald's? I thought Jane was looking at them both with a good deal of attention, and I wondered to myself."

"I don't believe Jane fears the rivalry of any girl under the sun."

"Wait and see," said Mrs. Tower.

"You gave it six months."

"Well, now I give it three years."

When anyone is very positive in an opinion it is only human nature to wish him proved wrong. Mrs. Tower was really too cocksure. But such a satisfaction was not mine, for the end that she had always and confidently predicted to the ill-assorted match did in point of fact come. Still, the fates seldom give us what we want in the way we want it, and though Mrs. Tower could flatter herself that she had been right, I think after all she would sooner have been wrong. For things did not happen at all in the way she expected.

One day I received an urgent message from her and fortunately went to see her at once. When I was shown into the room Mrs. Tower rose from her chair and came towards me with the stealthy swiftness of a leopard stalking his prey. I saw that she was excited.

"Jane and Gilbert have separated," she said.

"Not really? Well, you were right after all."

Mrs. Tower looked at me with an expression I could not understand.

"Poor Jane," I muttered.

"Poor Jane!" she repeated, but in tones of such derision that I was dumbfounded.

She found some difficulty in telling me exactly what had occurred.

Gilbert had left her a moment before she leaped to the telephone to summon me. When he entered the room, pale and distraught, she saw at once that something terrible had happened. She knew what he was going to say before he said it.

"Marion, Jane has left me."

She gave him a little smile and took his hand.

"I knew you'd behave like a gentleman. It would have been dreadful for her for people to think that *you* had left her."

"I've come to you because I knew I could count on your sympathy."

"Oh, I don't blame you, Gilbert," said Mrs. Tower, very kindly. "It was bound to happen."

He sighed.

"I suppose so. I couldn't hope to keep her always. She was too wonderful and I'm a perfectly common-place fellow."

Mrs. Tower patted his hand. He was really behaving beautifully.

"And what is going to happen now?"

"Well, she's going to divorce me."

"Jane always said she'd put no obstacle in your way if ever you wanted to marry a girl."

"You don't think it's likely I should ever be willing to marry anyone else after being Jane's husband," he answered.

Mrs. Tower was puzzled.

"Of course you mean that *you've* left Jane."

"I? That's the last thing I should ever do."

"Then why is she divorcing you?"

"She's going to marry Sir Reginald Frobisher as soon as the decree is made absolute."

Mrs. Tower positively screamed. Then she felt so faint that she had to get her smelling salts.

"After all you've done for her?"

"I've done nothing for her."

"Do you mean to say you're going to allow yourself to be made use of like that?"

"We arranged before we married that if either of us wanted his liberty the other should put no hindrance in the way."

"But that was done on your account. Because you were twenty-seven years younger than she was."

"Well, it's come in very useful for her," he answered bitterly.

Mrs. Tower expostulated, argued and reasoned; but Gilbert insisted that no rules applied to Jane, and he must do exactly what she wanted. He left Mrs. Tower prostrate. It relieved her a good deal to give me a full account of this interview. It pleased her to see that I was as surprised as herself and if I was not so indignant with Jane as she was she ascribed that to the criminal lack of morality incident to my sex. She was still in a state of extreme agitation when the door was opened and the butler showed in—Jane herself. She was dressed in black and white as no doubt befitted her slightly ambiguous position, but in a dress so original and fantastic, in a hat so striking, that I positively gasped at the sight of her. But she was as ever bland and collected. She came forward to kiss Mrs. Tower, but Mrs. Tower withdrew herself with icy dignity.

"Gilbert has been here," she said.

"Yes, I know," smiled Jane. "I told him to come and see you. I'm going to Paris to-night and I want you to be very kind to him while I am away. I'm afraid just at first he'll be rather lonely and I shall feel more comfortable if I can count on your keeping an eye on him."

Mrs. Tower clasped her hands.

"Gilbert has just told me something that I can hardly bring myself to believe. He tells me that you're going to divorce him to marry Reginald Frobisher."

"Don't you remember, before I married Gilbert you advised me to marry a man of my own age. The admiral is fifty-three."

"But, Jane, you owe everything to Gilbert," said Mrs. Tower indignantly. "You wouldn't exist without him. Without him to design your clothes, you'll be nothing."

"Oh, he's promised to go on designing my clothes," Jane answered blandly.

"No woman could want a better husband. He's always been kindness itself to you."

"Oh, I know he's been sweet."

"How *can* you be so heartless?"

"But I was never in love with Gilbert," said Jane. "I always told him that. I'm beginning to feel the need of the companionship of a man of my own age. I think I've probably been married to Gilbert long enough. The young have no conversation." She paused a little and gave us both a charming smile. "Of course I shan't lose sight of Gilbert. I've arranged that with Reginald. The admiral has a niece that would just suit him. As soon as we're married we'll ask them to stay with us at Malta—you know that the admiral is to have the Mediterranean Command—and I shouldn't be at all surprised if they fell in love with one another."

Mrs. Tower gave a little sniff.

"And have you arranged with the admiral that if you want your liberty neither should put any hindrance in the way of the other?"

"I suggested it," Jane answered with composure. "But the admiral says he knows a good thing when he sees it and he won't want to marry anyone else, and if anyone wants to marry me—he has eight twelve-inch guns on his flagship and he'll discuss the matter at short range." She gave us a look through her eyeglass which even the fear of Mrs. Tower's wrath could not prevent me from laughing at. "I think the admiral's a very passionate man."

Mrs. Tower indeed gave me an angry frown.

"I never thought you funny, Jane," she said. "I

never understood why people laughed at the things you said."

"I never thought I was funny myself, Marion," smiled Jane, showing her bright, regular teeth. "I am glad to leave London before too many people come round to our opinion."

"I wish you'd tell me the secret of your astonishing success," I said.

She turned to me with that bland, homely look I knew so well.

"You know, when I married Gilbert and settled in London and people began to laugh at what I said no one was more surprised than I was. I'd said the same things for thirty years and no one ever saw anything to laugh at. I thought it must be my clothes or my bobbed hair or my eyeglass. Then I discovered it was because I spoke the truth. It was so unusual that people thought it humorous. One of these days someone else will discover the secret and when people habitually tell the truth of course there'll be nothing funny in it."

"And why am I the only person not to think it funny?" asked Mrs. Tower.

Jane hesitated a little as though she were honestly searching for a satisfactory explanation.

"Perhaps you don't know the truth when you see it, Marion dear," she answered in her mild good-natured way.

It certainly gave her the last word. I felt that Jane would always have the last word. She *was* priceless.

D*

THE OUTSTATION

THE new assistant arrived in the afternoon. When
the Resident, Mr. Warburton, was told that the
prahu was in sight he put on his solar topee and went
down to the landing-stage. The guard, eight little
Dyak soldiers, stood to attention as he passed. He
noted with satisfaction that their bearing was martial,
their uniforms neat and clean, and their guns shining.
They were a credit to him. From the landing-stage he
watched the bend of the river round which in a moment
the boat would sweep. He looked very smart in his
spotless ducks and white shoes. He held under his arm a
gold-headed Malacca cane which had been given him by
the Sultan of Perak. He awaited the newcomer with
mingled feelings. There was more work in the district
than one man could properly do, and during his
periodical tours of the country under his charge it had
been inconvenient to leave the station in the hands of a
native clerk, but he had been so long the only white man
there that he could not face the arrival of another
without misgiving. He was accustomed to loneliness.
During the war he had not seen an English face for
three years; and once when he was instructed to put up
an afforestation officer he was seized with panic, so that
when the stranger was due to arrive, having arranged

everything for his reception, he wrote a note telling him he was obliged to go up-river, and fled; he remained away till he was informed by a messenger that his guest had left.

Now the prahu appeared in the broad reach. It was manned by prisoners, Dyaks under various sentences, and a couple of warders were waiting on the landing-stage to take them back to gaol. They were sturdy fellows, used to the river, and they rowed with a powerful stroke. As the boat reached the side a man got out from under the attap awning and stepped on shore. The guard presented arms.

"Here we are at last. By God! I'm as cramped as the devil. I've brought you your mail."

He spoke with exuberant joviality. Mr. Warburton politely held out his hand.

"Mr. Cooper, I presume?"

"That's right. Were you expecting anyone else?"

The question had a facetious intent, but the Resident did not smile.

"My name is Warburton. I'll show you your quarters. They'll bring your kit along."

He preceded Cooper along the narrow pathway and they entered a compound in which stood a small bungalow.

"I've had it made as habitable as I could, but of course no one has lived in it for a good many years."

It was built on piles. It consisted of a long living-room which opened on to a broad verandah, and behind, on each side of a passage, were two bedrooms.

"This'll do me all right," said Cooper.

"I daresay you want to have a bath and a change. I shall be very much pleased if you'll dine with me to-night. Will eight o'clock suit you?"

"Any old time will do for me."

The Resident gave a polite, but slightly disconcerted smile, and withdrew. He returned to the Fort where his own residence was. The impression which Allen Cooper had given him was not very favourable, but he was a fair man, and he knew that it was unjust to form an opinion on so brief a glimpse. Cooper seemed to be about thirty. He was a tall, thin fellow, with a sallow face in which there was not a spot of colour. It was a face all in one tone. He had a large, hooked nose and blue eyes. When, entering the bungalow, he had taken off his topee and flung it to a waiting boy, Mr. Warburton noticed that his large skull, covered with short, brown hair, contrasted somewhat oddly with a weak, small chin. He was dressed in khaki shorts and a khaki shirt, but they were shabby and soiled; and his battered topee had not been cleaned for days. Mr. Warburton reflected that the young man had spent a week on a coasting steamer and had passed the last forty-eight hours lying in the bottom of a prahu.

"We'll see what he looks like when he comes in to dinner."

He went into his room, where his things were as neatly laid out as if he had an English valet, undressed, and, walking down the stairs to the bathhouse, sluiced himself with cool water. The only concession he made to the climate was to wear a white dinner-jacket; but otherwise, in a boiled shirt and a high collar, silk socks and patent-leather shoes, he dressed as formally as though he were dining at his club in Pall Mall. A careful host, he went into the dining-room to see that the table was properly laid. It was gay with orchids, and the silver shone brightly. The napkins were folded into elaborate shapes. Shaded candles in silver candlesticks shed a soft light. Mr. Warburton smiled his approval and returned to the sitting-room to await his guest. Presently he appeared. Cooper was wearing the khaki shorts, the khaki shirt, and the ragged jacket in which he had landed. Mr. Warburton's smile of greeting froze on his face.

"Hulloa, you're all dressed up," said Cooper. "I didn't know you were going to do that. I very nearly put on a sarong."

"It doesn't matter at all. I daresay your boys were busy."

"You needn't have bothered to dress on my account, you know."

"I didn't. I always dress for dinner."

"Even when you're alone?"

"Especially when I'm alone," replied Mr. Warburton, with a frigid stare.

He saw a twinkle of amusement in Cooper's eyes, and he flushed an angry red. Mr. Warburton was a hot-tempered man; you might have guessed that from his red face with its pugnacious features and from his red hair now growing white; his blue eyes, cold as a rule and observing, could flash with sudden wrath; but he was a man of the world and, he hoped, a just one. He must do his best to get on with this fellow.

"When I lived in London I moved in circles in which it would have been just as eccentric not to dress for dinner every night as not to have a bath every morning. When I came to Borneo I saw no reason to discontinue so good a habit. For three years during the war I never saw a white man. I never omitted to dress on a single occasion on which I was well enough to come in to dinner. You have not been very long in this country; believe me, there is no better way to maintain the proper pride which you should have in yourself. When a white man surrenders in the slightest degree to the influences that surround him he very soon loses his self-respect, and when he loses his self-respect you may be quite sure that the natives will soon cease to respect him."

"Well, if you expect me to put on a boiled shirt and a stiff collar in this heat I'm afraid you'll be disappointed."

"When you are dining in your own bungalow you will, of course, dress as you think fit, but when you do me the pleasure of dining with me, perhaps you will come to the conclusion that it is only polite to wear the costume usual in civilised society."

Two Malay boys, in sarongs and songkoks, with

smart white coats and brass buttons, came in, one
bearing gin pahits, and the other a tray on which were
olives and anchovies. Then they went in to dinner.
Mr. Warburton flattered himself that he had the best
cook, a Chinese, in Borneo, and he took great trouble to
have as good food as in the difficult circumstances was
possible. He exercised much ingenuity in making the
best of his materials.

"Would you care to look at the menu?" he said,
handing it to Cooper.

It was written in French and the dishes had resounding names. They were waited on by the two boys.
In opposite corners of the room two more waved
immense fans, and so gave movement to the sultry air.
The fare was sumptuous and the champagne excellent.

"Do you do yourself like this every day?" said
Cooper.

Mr. Warburton gave the menu a careless glance.

"I have not noticed that the dinner is any different
from usual," he said. "I eat very little myself, but I
make a point of having a proper dinner served to me
every night. It keeps the cook in practice and it's good
discipline for the boys."

The conversation proceeded with effort. Mr.
Warburton was elaborately courteous, and it may be
that he found a slightly malicious amusement in the
embarrassment which he thereby occasioned in his
companion. Cooper had not been more than a few
months in Sembulu, and Mr. Warburton's enquiries

about friends of his in Kuala Solor were soon exhausted.

"By the way," he said presently, "did you meet a lad called Hennerley? He's come out recently, I believe."

"Oh, yes, he's in the police. A rotten bounder."

"I should hardly have expected him to be that. His uncle is my friend Lord Barraclough. I had a letter from Lady Barraclough only the other day asking me to look out for him."

"I heard he was related to somebody or other. I suppose that's how he got the job. He's been to Eton and Oxford and he doesn't forget to let you know it."

"You surprise me," said Mr. Warburton. "All his family have been at Eton and Oxford for a couple of hundred years. I should have expected him to take it as a matter of course."

"I thought him a damned prig."

"To what school did you go?"

"I was born in Barbados. I was educated there."

"Oh, I see."

Mr. Warburton managed to put so much offensiveness into his brief reply that Cooper flushed. For a moment he was silent.

"I've had two or three letters from Kuala Solor," continued Mr. Warburton, "and my impression was that young Hennerley was a great success. They say he's a first-rate sportsman."

"Oh, yes, he's very popular. He's just the sort of fellow they would like in K.S. I haven't got much use for the first-rate sportsman myself. What does it amount to in the long run that a man can play golf and tennis better than other people? And who cares if he can make a break of seventy-five at billiards? They attach a damned sight too much importance to that sort of thing in England."

"Do you think so? I was under the impression that the first-rate sportsman had come out of the war certainly no worse than anyone else."

"Oh, if you're going to talk of the war, then I do know what I'm talking about. I was in the same regiment as Hennerley and I can tell you that the men couldn't stick him at any price."

"How do you know?"

"Because I was one of the men."

"Oh, you hadn't got a commission."

"A fat chance I had of getting a commission. I was what was called a Colonial. I hadn't been to a public school and I had no influence. I was in the ranks the whole damned time."

Cooper frowned. He seemed to have difficulty in preventing himself from breaking out into violent invective. Mr. Warburton watched him, his little blue eyes narrowed, watched him and formed his opinion. Changing the conversation, he began to speak to Cooper about the work that would be required of him, and as the clock struck ten he rose.

"Well, I won't keep you any more. I daresay you're tired by your journey."

They shook hands.

"Oh, I say, look here," said Cooper, "I wonder if you can find me a boy. The boy I had before never turned up when I was starting from K.S. He took my kit on board and all that, and then disappeared. I didn't know he wasn't there till we were out of the river."

"I'll ask my head-boy. I have no doubt he can find you someone."

"All right. Just tell him to send the boy along and if I like the look of him I'll take him."

There was a moon, so that no lantern was needed. Cooper walked across from the Fort to his bungalow.

"I wonder why on earth they've sent me a fellow like that?" reflected Mr. Warburton. "If that's the kind of man they're going to get out now I don't think much of it."

He strolled down his garden. The Fort was built on the top of a little hill and the garden ran down to the river's edge; on the bank was an arbour, and hither it was his habit to come after dinner to smoke a cheroot. And often from the river that flowed below him a voice was heard, the voice of some Malay too timorous to venture into the light of day, and a complaint or an accusation was softly wafted to his ears, a piece of information was whispered to him or a useful hint, which otherwise would never have come into his official ken. He threw himself heavily into a long rattan chair. Cooper! An envious, ill-bred fellow, bumptious, self-assertive and vain. But Mr. Warburton's irritation could not withstand the silent beauty of the night. The air was scented with the sweet-smelling flowers of a tree that grew at the entrance to the arbour, and the fire-flies, sparkling dimly, flew with their slow and silvery flight. The moon made a pathway on the broad river for the light feet of Siva's bride, and on the further bank a row of palm trees was delicately silhouetted against the sky. Peace stole into the soul of Mr. Warburton.

He was a queer creature and he had had a singular career. At the age of twenty-one he had inherited a considerable fortune, a hundred thousand pounds, and when he left Oxford he threw himself into the gay life, which in those days (now Mr. Warburton was a man of four-and-fifty) offered itself to the young man of good family. He had his flat in Mount Street, his private hansom, and his hunting-box in Warwickshire. He went to all the places where the fashionable congregate. He was handsome, amusing, and generous. He was a figure in the society of London in the early 'nineties, and society then had not lost its exclusiveness nor its brilliance. The Boer War which shook it was unthought of; the Great War which destroyed it was prophesied only by the pessimists. It was no unpleasant thing to be a rich young man in those days, and Mr. Warburton's chimney-piece during the season was packed with cards for one great function after another. Mr. Warburton displayed them with complacency. For Mr. Warburton was a snob. He was not a timid snob, a little ashamed of being impressed by his betters, nor a snob who sought the intimacy of persons who had acquired celebrity in politics or notoriety in the arts, nor the snob who was dazzled by riches; he was the naked, unadulterated common snob who dearly loved a lord. He was touchy and quick-tempered, but he would much rather have been snubbed by a person of quality than flattered by a commoner. His name figured insignificantly in *Burke's Peerage* and it was marvellous to watch the ingenuity he used to mention his distant relationship to the noble family he belonged to; but never a word did he say of the honest Liverpool manufacturer from whom, through his mother, a Miss Gubbins, he had come by his fortune. It was the terror of his fashionable life that at Cowes, maybe, or at Ascot, when he was with a duchess or even with a prince of the blood, one of these relatives would claim acquaintance with him.

His failing was too obvious not soon to become notorious, but its extravagance saved it from being merely despicable. The great whom he adored laughed at him, but in their hearts felt his adoration not unnatural. Poor Warburton was a dreadful snob, of course, but after all he was a good fellow. He was always ready to back a bill for an impecunious nobleman, and if you were in a tight corner you could safely count on him for a hundred pounds. He gave good dinners. He played whist badly, but never minded how much he lost if the company was select. He happened to be a gambler, an unlucky one, but he was a good loser, and it was impossible not to admire the coolness with which he lost five hundred pounds at a sitting. His passion for cards, almost as strong as his passion for titles, was the cause of his undoing. The life he led was expensive and his gambling losses were formidable. He began to plunge more heavily, first on horses, and then on the Stock Exchange. He had a certain simplicity of character, and the unscrupulous found him an ingenuous prey. I do not know if he ever realised that his smart friends laughed at him behind his back, but I think he had an obscure instinct that he could not afford to appear other than careless of his money. He got into the hands of money-lenders. At the age of thirty-four he was ruined.

He was too much imbued with the spirit of his class to hesitate in the choice of his next step. When a man in his set had run through his money, he went out to the colonies. No one heard Mr. Warburton repine. He made no complaint because a noble friend had advised a disastrous speculation, he pressed nobody to whom he had lent money to repay it, he paid his debts (if he had only known it, the despised blood of the Liverpool manufacturer came out in him there), sought help from no one, and, never having done a stroke of work in his life, looked for a means of livelihood. He remained cheerful, unconcerned and full of humour. He had no wish to make anyone with whom he happened to be uncomfortable by the recital of his misfortune. Mr. Warburton was a snob, but he was also a gentleman.

The only favour he asked of any of the great friends in whose daily company he had lived for years was a recommendation. The able man who was at that time Sultan of Sembulu took him into his service. The night before he sailed he dined for the last time at his club.

"I hear you're going away, Warburton," the old Duke of Hereford said to him.

"Yes, I'm going to Borneo."

"Good God, what are you going there for?"

"Oh, I'm broke."

"Are you? I'm sorry. Well, let us know when you come back. I hope you have a good time."

"Oh yes. Lots of shooting, you know."

The Duke nodded and passed on. A few hours later Mr. Warburton watched the coast of England recede into the mist, and he left behind everything which to him made life worth living.

Twenty years had passed since then. He kept up a busy correspondence with various great ladies and his letters were amusing and chatty. He never lost his love for titled persons and paid careful attention to the announcements in *The Times* (which reached him six weeks after publication) of their comings and goings. He perused the column which records births, marriages, and deaths, and he was always ready with his letter of congratulation or condolence. The illustrated papers told him how people looked and on his periodical visits to England, able to take up the threads as though they had never been broken, he knew all about any new person who might have appeared on the social surface. His interest in the world of fashion was as vivid as when himself had been a figure in it. It still seemed to him the only thing that mattered.

But insensibly another interest had entered into his life. The position he found himself in flattered his vanity; he was no longer the sycophant craving the smiles of the great, he was the master whose word was law. He was gratified by the guard of Dyak soldiers who presented arms as he passed. He liked to sit in judgment on his fellow men. It pleased him to compose quarrels between rival chiefs. When the head-hunters were troublesome in the old days he set out to chastise them with a thrill of pride in his own behaviour. He was too vain not to be of dauntless courage, and a pretty story was told of his coolness in adventuring single-handed into a stockaded village and demanding the surrender of a bloodthirsty pirate. He became a skilful administrator. He was strict, just and honest.

And little by little he conceived a deep love for the Malays. He interested himself in their habits and customs. He was never tired of listening to their talk. He admired their virtues, and with a smile and a shrug of the shoulders condoned their vices.

"In my day," he would say, "I have been on intimate terms with some of the greatest gentlemen in England, but I have never known finer gentlemen than some well-born Malays whom I am proud to call my friends."

He liked their courtesy and their distinguished

manners, their gentleness and their sudden passions. He knew by instinct exactly how to treat them. He had a genuine tenderness for them. But he never forgot that he was an English gentleman, and he had no patience with the white men who yielded to native customs. He made no surrenders. And he did not imitate so many of the white men in taking a native woman to wife, for an intrigue of this nature, however sanctified by custom, seemed to him not only shocking but undignified. A man who had been called George by Albert Edward, Prince of Wales could hardly be expected to have any connection with a native. And when he returned to Borneo from his visits to England it was now with something like relief. His friends, like himself, were no longer young, and there was a new generation which looked upon him as a tiresome old man. It seemed to him that the England of to-day had lost a good deal of what he had loved in the England of his youth. But Borneo remained the same. It was home to him now, He meant to remain in the service as long as was possible. and the hope in his heart was that he would die before at last he was forced to retire. He had stated in his will that wherever he died he wished his body to be brought back to Sembulu, and buried among the people he loved within the sound of the softly flowing river.

But these emotions he kept hidden from the eyes of men; and no one, seeing this spruce, stout, well-set-up man, with his clean-shaven strong face and his whitening hair, would have dreamed that he cherished so profound a sentiment.

He knew how the work of the station should be done, and during the next few days he kept a suspicious eye on his assistant. He saw very soon that he was painstaking and competent. The only fault he had to find with him was that he was brusque with the natives.

"The Malays are shy and very sensitive," he said to him. "I think you will find that you will get much better results if you take care always to be polite, patient and kindly."

Cooper gave a short, grating laugh.

"I was born in Barbadoes and I was in Africa in the war. I don't think there's much about niggers that I don't know."

"I know nothing," said Mr. Warburton acidly. "But we were not talking of them. We were talking of Malays."

"Aren't they niggers?"

"You are very ignorant," replied Mr. Warburton.

He said no more.

On the first Sunday after Cooper's arrival he asked him to dinner. He did everything ceremoniously, and though they had met on the previous day in the office and later, on the Fort verandah, where they drank a gin and bitters together at six o'clock, he sent a polite note across to the bungalow by a boy. Cooper, however unwillingly, came in evening dress and Mr. Warburton, though gratified that his wish was respected, noticed with disdain that the young man's clothes were badly cut and his shirt ill-fitting. But Mr. Warburton was in a good temper that evening.

"By the way," he said to him, as he shook hands, "I've talked to my head-boy about finding you someone and he recommends his nephew. I've seen him and he seems a bright and willing lad. Would you like to see him?"

"I don't mind."

"He's waiting now."

Mr. Warburton called his boy and told him to send for his nephew. In a moment a tall, slender youth of twenty appeared. He had large dark eyes and a good profile. He was very neat in his sarong, a little white coat, and a fez, without a tassel, of plum-coloured velvet. He answered to the name of Abas. Mr. Warburton looked on him with approval, and his manner insensibly softened as he spoke to him in fluent and idiomatic Malay. He was inclined to be sarcastic with white people, but with the Malays he had a happy mixture of condescension and kindliness. He stood in the place of the Sultan. He knew perfectly how to preserve his own dignity, and at the same time put a native at his ease.

"Will he do?" said Mr. Warburton, turning to Cooper.

"Yes, I daresay he's no more of a scoundrel than any of the rest of them."

Mr. Warburton informed the boy that he was engaged, and dismissed him.

"You're very lucky to get a boy like that," he told Cooper. "He belongs to a very good family. They came over from Malacca nearly a hundred years ago."

"I don't much mind if the boy who cleans my shoes and brings me a drink when I want it has blue blood in his veins or not. All I ask is that he should do what I tell him and look sharp about it."

Mr. Warburton pursed his lips, but made no reply.

They went in to dinner. It was excellent, and the wine was good. Its influence presently had its effect on them, and they talked not only without acrimony, but even with friendliness. Mr. Warburton liked to do himself well, and on Sunday night he made it a habit to do himself even a little better than usual. He began to think he was unfair to Cooper. Of course he was not a gentleman, but that was not his fault, and when you got to know him it might be that he would turn out a very good fellow. His faults, perhaps, were faults of manner. And he was certainly good at his work, quick, conscientious and thorough. When they reached the dessert Mr. Warburton was feeling kindly disposed towards all mankind.

"This is your first Sunday, and I'm going to give you a very special glass of port. I've only got about two dozen of it left and I keep it for special occasions."

He gave his boy instructions and presently the bottle was brought. Mr. Warburton watched the boy open it.

"I got this port from my old friend Charles Hollington. He'd had it for forty years, and I've had it for a good many. He was well known to have the best cellar in England."

"Is he a wine merchant?"

"Not exactly," smiled Mr. Warburton; "I was speaking of Lord Hollington of Castle Reagh. He's one of the richest peers in England. A very old friend of mine. I was at Eton with his brother."

This was an opportunity that Mr. Warburton could never resist, and he told a little anecdote of which the only point seemed to be that he knew an Earl. The port was certainly very good; he drank a glass and then a second. He lost all caution. He had not talked to a white man for months. He began to tell stories. He showed himself in the company of the great. Hearing him, you would have thought that at one time ministries were formed and policies decided on his suggestion whispered into the ear of a duchess or thrown over the dinner-table to be gratefully acted on by the confidential adviser of the sovereign. The old days at Ascot, Goodwood and Cowes lived again for him. Another glass of port. There were the great house-parties in Yorkshire and in Scotland to which he went every year.

"I had a man called Foreman then, the best valet I ever had, and why do you think he gave me notice? You know in the Housekeeper's Room the ladies' maids and the gentlemen's gentlemen sit according to the precedence of their masters. He told me he was sick of going to party after party at which I was the only commoner. It meant that he always had to sit at the bottom of the table, and all the best bits were taken before a dish reached him. I told the story to the old

Duke of Hereford, and he roared. 'By God, sir,' he said, 'if I were King of England, I'd make you a Viscount just to give your man a chance.' 'Take him yourself, Duke,' I said. 'He's the best valet I've ever had.' 'Well, Warburton,' he said, 'if he's good enough for you he's good enough for me. Send him along.' "

Then there was Monte Carlo where Mr. Warburton and the Grand Duke Fyodor, playing in partnership, had broken the bank one evening; and there was Marienbad. At Marienbad Mr. Warburton had played baccarat with Edward VII.

"He was only Prince of Wales then, of course. I remember him saying to me, 'George, if you draw on a five you'll lose your shirt.' He was right; I don't think he ever said a truer word in his life. He was a wonderful man. I always said he was the greatest diplomatist in Europe. But I was a young fool in those days, I hadn't the sense to take his advice. If I had, if I'd never drawn on a five, I daresay I shouldn't be here to-day."

Cooper was watching him. His brown eyes, deep in their sockets, were hard and supercilious, and on his lips was a mocking smile. He had heard a good deal about Mr. Warburton in Kuala Solor, not a bad sort, and he ran his district like clockwork, they said, but by heaven, what a snob! They laughed at him good-naturedly, for it was impossible to dislike a man who was so generous and so kindly, and Cooper had already heard the story of the Prince of Wales and the game of baccarat. But Cooper listened without indulgence. From the beginning he had resented the Resident's manner. He was very sensitive, and he writhed under Mr. Warburton's polite sarcasms. Mr. Warburton had a knack of receiving a remark of which he disapproved with a devastating silence. Cooper had lived little in England and he had a peculiar dislike of the English. He resented especially the public-school boy, since he always feared that he was going to patronise him. He was so much afraid of others putting on airs with him that, in order as it were to get in first, he put on such airs as to make everyone think him insufferably conceited.

"Well, at all events the war has done one good thing for us," he said at last. "It's smashed up the power of the aristocracy. The Boer War started it, and 1914 put the lid on."

"The great families of England are doomed," said Mr. Warburton with the complacent melancholy of an *émigré* who remembered the court of Louis XV. "They cannot afford any longer to live in their splendid palaces and their princely hospitality will soon be nothing but a memory."

"And a damned good job too, in my opinion."

"My poor Cooper, what can you know of the glory that was Greece and the grandeur that was Rome?"

Mr. Warburton made an ample gesture. His eyes for an instant grew dreamy with a vision of the past.

"Well, believe me, we're fed up with all that rot. What we want is a business government by business men. I was born in a Crown Colony, and I've lived practically all my life in the colonies. I don't give a row of pins for a lord. What's wrong with England is snobbishness. And if there's anything that gets my goat it's a snob."

A snob! Mr. Warburton's face grew purple and his eyes blazed with anger. That was a word that had pursued him all his life. The great ladies whose society he had enjoyed in his youth were not inclined to look upon his appreciation of themselves as unworthy, but even great ladies are sometimes out of temper and more than once Mr. Warburton had had the dreadful word flung in his teeth. He knew, he could not help knowing, that there were odious people who called him a snob. How unfair it was! Why, there was no vice he found so detestable as snobbishness. After all, he liked to mix with people of his own class, he was only at home in their company, and how in heaven's name could anyone say that was snobbish? Birds of a feather.

"I quite agree with you," he answered. "A snob is a man who admires or despises another because he is of a higher social rank than his own. It is the most vulgar failing of our English middle-class."

He saw a flicker of amusement in Cooper's eyes. Cooper put up his hand to hide the broad smile that rose to his lips, and so made it more noticeable. Mr. Warburton's hands trembled a little.

Probably Cooper never knew how greatly he had offended his chief. A sensitive man himself, he was strangely insensitive to the feelings of others.

Their work forced them to see one another for a few minutes now and then during the day, and they met at six to have a drink on Mr. Warburton's verandah. This was an old-established custom of the country which Mr. Warburton would not for the world have broken. But they ate their meals separately, Cooper in his bungalow and Mr. Warburton at the Fort. After the office work was over they walked till dusk fell, but they walked apart. There were but few paths in this country where the jungle pressed close upon the plantations of the village, and when Mr. Warburton caught sight of his assistant passing along with his loose stride, he would make a circuit in order to avoid him. Cooper, with his bad manners, his conceit in his own judgment and his intolerance, had already got on his nerves; but it was not till Cooper had been on the station for a couple of months that an incident happened which turned the Resident's dislike into bitter hatred.

Mr. Warburton was obliged to go up-country on a tour of inspection, and he left the station in Cooper's charge with more confidence, since he had definitely come to the conclusion that he was a capable fellow. The only thing he did not like was that he had no indulgence. He was honest, just and painstaking, but he had no sympathy for the natives. It bitterly amused Mr. Warburton to observe that this man, who looked upon himself as every man's equal, should look upon so many men as his own inferiors. He was hard, he had no patience with the native mind, and he was a bully. Mr.

Warburton very quickly realised that the Malays disliked and feared him. He was not altogether displeased.
He would not have liked it very much if his assistant
had enjoyed a popularity which might rival his own.
Mr. Warburton made his elaborate preparations, set out
on his expedition, and in three weeks returned. Meanwhile the mail had arrived. The first thing that struck
his eyes when he entered his sitting-room was a great
pile of open newspapers. Cooper had met him, and they
went into the room together. Mr. Warburton turned to
one of the servants who had been left behind, and
sternly asked him what was the meaning of those open
papers. Cooper hastened to explain.

"I wanted to read all about the Wolverhampton
murder, and so I borrowed your *Times*. I brought them
back again. I knew you wouldn't mind."

Mr. Warburton turned on him, white with anger.

"But I do mind. I mind very much."

"I'm sorry," said Cooper, with composure. "The
fact is, I simply couldn't wait till you came back."

"I wonder you didn't open my letters as well."

Cooper, unmoved, smiled at his chief's exasperation.

"Oh, that's not quite the same thing. After all, I
couldn't imagine you'd mind my looking at your
newspapers. There's nothing private in them."

"I very much object to anyone reading my paper
before me." He went up to the pile. There were nearly
thirty numbers there. "I think it extremely impertinent
of you. They're all mixed up."

E

"We can easily put them in order," said Cooper, joining him at the table.

"Don't touch them," cried Mr. Warburton.

"I say, it's childish to make a scene about a little thing like that."

"How dare you speak to me like that?"

"Oh, go to hell," said Cooper, and he flung out of the room.

Mr. Warburton, trembling with passion, was left contemplating his papers. His greatest pleasure in life had been destroyed by those callous, brutal hands. Most people living in out-of-the-way places when the mail comes tear open impatiently their papers and taking the last ones first glance at the latest news from home. Not so Mr. Warburton. His newsagent had instructions to write on the outside of the wrapper the date of each paper he despatched, and when the great bundle arrived Mr. Warburton looked at these dates and with his blue pencil numbered them. His head-boy's orders were to place one on the table every morning in the verandah with the early cup of tea, and it was Mr. Warburton's especial delight to break the wrapper as he sipped his tea, and read the morning paper. It gave him the illusion of living at home. Every Monday morning he read the Monday *Times* of six weeks back, and so went through the week. On Sunday he read *The Observer*. Like his habit of dressing for dinner it was a tie to civilisation. And it was his pride that, no matter how exciting the news was, he had never yielded to the temptation of opening a paper before its allotted time. During the war the suspense sometimes had been intolerable, and when he read one day that a push was begun he had undergone agonies of suspense which he might have saved himself by the simple expedient of opening a later paper which lay waiting for him on a shelf. It had been the severest trial to which he had ever exposed himself, but he victoriously surmounted it. And that clumsy fool had broken open those neat tight packages because he wanted to know whether some horrid woman had murdered her odious husband.

Mr. Warburton sent for his boy and told him to bring wrappers. He folded up the papers as neatly as he could, placed a wrapper round each and numbered it. But it was a melancholy task.

"I shall never forgive him," he said. "Never."

Of course his boy had been with him on his expedition; he never travelled without him, for his boy knew exactly how he liked things, and Mr. Warburton was not the kind of jungle traveller who was prepared to dispense with his comforts; but in the interval since their arrival he had been gossiping in the servants' quarters. He had learnt that Cooper had had trouble with his boys. All but the youth Abas had left him. Abas had desired to go too, but his uncle had placed him there on the instructions of the Resident, and he was afraid to leave without his uncle's permission.

"I told him he had done well, Tuan," said the boy. "But he is unhappy. He says it is not a good house, and he wishes to know if he may go as the others have gone."

"No, he must stay. The Tuan must have servants. Have those who went been replaced?"

"No, Tuan, no one will go."

Mr. Warburton frowned. Cooper was an insolent fool, but he had an official position and must be suitably provided with servants. It was not seemly that his house should be improperly conducted.

"Where are the boys who ran away?"

"They are in the kampong, Tuan."

"Go and see them to-night, and tell them that I expect them to be back in Tuan Cooper's house at dawn to-morrow."

"They say they will not go, Tuan."

"On my order?"

The boy had been with Mr. Warburton for fifteen years, and he knew every intonation of his master's voice. He was not afraid of him, they had gone through too much together; once in the jungle the Resident had saved his life, and once, upset in some rapids, but for him the Resident would have been drowned; but he knew when the Resident must be obeyed without question.

"I will go to the kampong," he said.

Mr. Warburton expected that his subordinate would take the first opportunity to apologise for his rudeness, but Cooper had the ill-bred man's inability to express regret; and when they met next morning in the office he ignored the incident. Since Mr. Warburton had been away for three weeks it was necessary for them to have a somewhat prolonged interview. At the end of it, Mr. Warburton dismissed him.

"I don't think there's anything else, thank you." Cooper turned to go, but Mr. Warburton stopped him. "I understand you've been having some trouble with your boys."

Cooper gave a harsh laugh.

"They tried to blackmail me. They had the damned cheek to run away, all except that incompetent fellow Abas—he knew when he was well off—but I just sat tight. They've all come to heel again."

"What do you mean by that?"

"This morning they were all back on their jobs, the Chinese cook and all. There they were, as cool as cucumbers; you would have thought they owned the place. I suppose they'd come to the conclusion that I wasn't such a fool as I looked."

"By no means. They came back on my express order."

Cooper flushed slightly.

"I should be obliged if you wouldn't interfere with my private concerns."

"They're not your private concerns. When your servants run away it makes you ridiculous. You are perfectly free to make a fool of yourself, but I cannot allow you to be made a fool of. It is unseemly that your house should not be properly staffed. As soon as I heard that your boys had left you, I had them told to be back in their places at dawn. That'll do."

Mr. Warburton nodded to signify that the interview was at an end. Cooper took no notice.

"Shall I tell you what I did? I called them and gave the whole bally lot the sack. I gave them ten minutes to get out of the compound."

Mr. Warburton shrugged his shoulders.

"What makes you think you can get others?"

"I've told my own clerk to see about it."

Mr. Warburton reflected for a moment.

"I think you behaved very foolishly. You will do well to remember in future that good masters make good servants."

"Is there anything else you want to teach me?"

"I should like to teach you manners, but it would be an arduous task, and I have not the time to waste. I will see that you get boys."

"Please don't put yourself to any trouble on my account. I'm quite capable of getting them for myself."

Mr. Warburton smiled acidly. He had an inkling that Cooper disliked him as much as he disliked Cooper, and he knew that nothing is more galling than to be forced to accept the favours of a man you detest.

"Allow me to tell you that you have no more chance of getting Malay or Chinese servants here now than you have of getting an English butler or a French chef. No one will come to you except on an order from me. Would you like me to give it?"

"No."

"As you please. Good morning."

Mr. Warburton watched the development of the situation with acrid humour. Cooper's clerk was unable to persuade Malay, Dyak or Chinese to enter the house of such a master. Abas, the boy who remained faithful to him, knew how to cook only native food, and Cooper, a coarse feeder, found his gorge rise against the ever-lasting rice. There was no water-carrier, and in that great heat he needed several baths a day. He cursed Abas, but Abas opposed him with sullen resistance and would not do more than he chose. It was galling to know that the lad stayed with him only because the Resident insisted. This went on for a fortnight and then, one morning, he found in his house the very servants whom he had previously dismissed. He fell into a violent rage, but he had learnt a little sense, and this time, without a word, he let them stay. He swallowed his humiliation, but the impatient contempt he had felt for Mr. Warburton's idiosyncrasies changed into a sullen hatred: the Resident with this malicious stroke had made him the laughing-stock of all the natives.

The two men now held no communication with one another. They broke the time-honoured custom of sharing, notwithstanding personal dislike, a drink at six o'clock with any white man who happened to be at the station. Each lived in his own house as though the other did not exist. Now that Cooper had fallen into the work, it was necessary for them to have little to do with one another in the office. Mr. Warburton used his orderly to send any message he had to give his assistant, and his instructions he sent by formal letter. They saw one another constantly, that was inevitable, but did not exchange half a dozen words in a week. The fact that they could not avoid catching sight of one another got on their nerves. They brooded over their antagonism, and Mr. Warburton, taking his daily walk, could think of nothing but how much he detested his assistant.

And the dreadful thing was that in all probability they would remain thus, facing each other in deadly enmity, till Mr. Warburton went on leave. It might be three years. He had no reason to send in a complaint to headquarters: Cooper did his work very well, and at that time men were hard to get. True, vague complaints reached him and hints that the natives found Cooper harsh. There was certainly a feeling of dissatisfaction among them. But when Mr. Warburton looked into specific cases, all he could say was that Cooper had shown severity where mildness would not have been misplaced, and had been unfeeling when himself would have been sympathetic. He had done nothing for which he could be taken to task. But Mr. Warburton watched him. Hatred will often make a man clear-sighted, and he had a suspicion that Cooper was using the natives without consideration, yet keeping within the law, because he felt that thus he could exasperate his chief. One day perhaps he would go too far. None knew better than Mr. Warburton how irritable the incessant heat could make a man and how difficult it was to keep

one's self-control after a sleepless night. He smiled
softly to himself. Sooner or later Cooper would deliver
himself into his hand.

When at last the opportunity came, Mr. Warburton
laughed aloud. Cooper had charge of the prisoners;
they made roads, built sheds, rowed when it was
necessary to send the prahu up- or down-stream, kept the
town clean and otherwise usefully employed themselves.
If well behaved they even on occasion served as house-
boys. Cooper kept them hard at it. He liked to see them
work. He took pleasure in devising tasks for them;
and seeing quickly enough that they were being made
to do useless things the prisoners worked badly. He
punished them by lengthening their hours. This was
contrary to the regulations, and as soon as it was
brought to the attention of Mr. Warburton, without
referring the matter back to his subordinate, he gave
instructions that the old hours should be kept; Cooper,
going out for his walk, was astounded to see the
prisoners strolling back to the gaol; he had given
instructions that they were not to knock off till dusk.
When he asked the warder in charge why they had left
off work he was told that it was the Resident's bidding.

White with rage he strode to the Fort. Mr. Warburton, in his spotless white ducks and his neat topee,
with a walking-stick in his hand, followed by his dogs,
was on the point of starting out on his afternoon stroll.
He had watched Cooper go, and knew that he had taken
the road by the river. Cooper jumped up the steps and

E*

went straight up to the Resident.

"I want to know what the hell you mean by countermanding my order that the prisoners were to work till six," he burst out, beside himself with fury.

Mr. Warburton opened his cold blue eyes very wide and assumed an expression of great surprise.

"Are you out of your mind? Are you so ignorant that you do not know that that is not the way to speak to your official superior?"

"Oh, go to hell. The prisoners are my pidgin, and you've got no right to interfere. You mind your business and I'll mind mine. I want to know what the devil you mean by making a damned fool of me. Everyone in the place will know that you've countermanded my order."

Mr. Warburton kept very cool.

"You had no power to give the order you did. I countermanded it because it was harsh and tyrannical. Believe me, I have not made half such a damned fool of you as you have made of yourself."

"You disliked me from the first moment I came here. You've done everything you could to make the place impossible for me because I wouldn't lick your boots for you. You got your knife into me because I wouldn't flatter you."

Cooper, spluttering with rage, was nearing dangerous ground, and Mr. Warburton's eyes grew on a sudden colder and more piercing.

"You are wrong. I thought you were a cad, but I

was perfectly satisfied with the way you did your work."

"You snob. You damned snob. You thought me a cad because I hadn't been to Eton. Oh, they told me in K.S. what to expect. Why, don't you know that you're the laughing-stock of the whole country? I could hardly help bursting into a roar of laughter when you told your celebrated story about the Prince of Wales. My God, how they shouted at the club when they told it. By God, I'd rather be the cad I am than the snob you are."

He got Mr. Warburton on the raw.

"If you don't get out of my house this minute I shall knock you down," he cried.

The other came a little closer to him and put his face in his.

"Touch me, touch me," he said. "By God, I'd like to see you hit me. Do you want me to say it again? Snob. Snob."

Cooper was three inches taller than Mr. Warburton, a strong, muscular young man. Mr. Warburton was fat and fifty-four. His clenched fist shot out. Cooper caught him by the arm and pushed him back.

"Don't be a damned fool. Remember I'm not a gentleman. I know how to use my hands."

He gave a sort of hoot, and grinning all over his pale, sharp face jumped down the verandah steps. Mr. Warburton, his heart in his anger pounding against his ribs, sank exhausted into a chair. His body tingled as though he had prickly heat. For one horrible moment he thought he was going to cry. But suddenly he was conscious that his head-boy was on the verandah and instinctively regained control of himself. The boy came forward and filled him a glass of whisky and soda. Without a word Mr. Warburton took it and drank it to the dregs.

"What do you want to say to me?" asked Mr. Warburton, trying to force a smile on to his strained lips.

"Tuan, the assistant tuan is a bad man. Abas wishes again to leave him."

"Let him wait a little. I shall write to Kuala Solor and ask that Tuan Cooper should go elsewhere."

"Tuan Cooper is not good with the Malays."

"Leave me."

The boy silently withdrew. Mr. Warburton was left alone with his thoughts. He saw the club at Kuala Solor, the men sitting round the table in the window in their flannels, when the night had driven them in from golf and tennis, drinking whiskies and gin pahits, and laughing when they told the celebrated story of the Prince of Wales and himself at Marienbad. He was hot with shame and misery. A snob! They all thought him a snob. And he had always thought them very good fellows, he had always been gentleman enough to let it make no difference to him that they were of very second-rate position. He hated them now. But his hatred for them was nothing compared with his hatred for Cooper. And if it had come to blows

Cooper could have thrashed him. Tears of mortification ran down his red, fat face. He sat there for a couple of hours smoking cigarette after cigarette, and he wished he were dead.

At last the boy came back and asked him if he would dress for dinner. Of course! He always dressed for dinner. He rose wearily from his chair and put on his stiff shirt and the high collar. He sat down at the prettily decorated table, and was waited on as usual by the two boys while two others waved their great fans. Over there in the bungalow, two hundred yards away, Cooper was eating a filthy meal clad only in a sarong and a baju. His feet were bare and while he ate he probably read a detective story. After dinner Mr. Warburton sat down to write a letter. The Sultan was away, but he wrote, privately and confidentially, to his representative. Cooper did his work very well, he said, but the fact was that he couldn't get on with him. They were getting dreadfully on each other's nerves and he would look upon it as a very great favour if Cooper could be transferred to another post.

He despatched the letter next morning by special messenger. The answer came a fortnight later with the month's mail. It was a private note, and ran as follows:

"*My dear Warburton,*

I do not want to answer your letter officially, and so I am writing you a few lines myself. Of course if you insist I will put the matter up to the Sultan, but I think you would be much wiser to drop it. I know Cooper is a rough diamond, but he is capable, and he had a pretty thin time in the war, and I think he should be given every chance. I think you are a little too much inclined to attach importance to a man's social position. You must remember that times have changed. Of course it's a very good thing for a man to be a gentleman, but it's better that he should be competent and hard-working. I think if you'll exercise a little tolerance you'll get on very well with Cooper.

Yours very sincerely,
Richard Temple."

The letter dropped from Mr. Warburton's hand. It was easy to read between the lines. Dick Temple, whom he had known for twenty years, Dick Temple who came from quite a good county family, thought him a snob, and for that reason had no patience with his request. Mr. Warburton felt on a sudden discouraged with life. The world of which he was a part had passed away and the future belonged to a meaner generation. Cooper represented it and Cooper he hated with all his heart. He stretched out his hand to fill his glass, and at the gesture his head-boy stepped forward.

"I didn't know you were there."

The boy picked up the official letter. Ah, that was why he was waiting.

"Does Tuan Cooper go, Tuan?"

"No."

"There will be a misfortune."

For a moment the words conveyed nothing to his lassitude. But only for a moment. He sat up in his chair and looked at the boy. He was all attention.

"What do you mean by that?"

"Tuan Cooper is not behaving rightly with Abas."

Mr. Warburton shrugged his shoulders. How should a man like Cooper know how to treat servants? Mr. Warburton knew the type: he would be grossly familiar with them at one moment and rude and inconsiderate the next.

"Let Abas go back to his family."

"Tuan Cooper holds back his wages so that he may not run away. He has paid him nothing for three months. I tell him to be patient. But he is angry, he will not listen to reason. If the Tuan continues to use him ill there will be a misfortune."

"You were right to tell me."

The fool! Did he know so little of the Malays as to think he could safely injure them? It would serve him damned well right if he got a kriss in his back. A kriss. Mr. Warburton's heart seemed on a sudden to miss a beat. He had only to let things take their course and one fine day he would be rid of Cooper. He smiled faintly as the phrase, a masterly inactivity, crossed his mind. And now his heart beat a little quicker, for he saw the man he hated lying on his face in a pathway of the jungle with a knife in his back. A fit end for the cad and the bully. Mr. Warburton sighed. It was his duty to warn him, and of course he must do it. He wrote a brief and formal note to Cooper asking him to come to the Fort at once.

In ten minutes Cooper stood before him. They had not spoken to one another since the day when Mr. Warburton had nearly struck him. He did not now ask him to sit down.

"Did you wish to see me?" asked Cooper.

He was untidy and none too clean. His face and hands were covered with little red blotches where mosquitoes had bitten him and he had scratched himself till the blood came. His long, thin face bore a sullen look.

"I understand that you are again having trouble with your servants. Abas, my head-boy's nephew, complains that you have held back his wages for three months. I consider it a most arbitrary proceeding. The lad wishes to leave you, and I certainly do not blame him. I must insist on your paying what is due to him."

"I don't choose that he should leave me. I am holding back his wages as a pledge of his good behaviour."

"You do not know the Malay character. The Malays are very sensitive to injury and ridicule. They are passionate and revengeful. It is my duty to warn you that if you drive this boy beyond a certain point you run a great risk."

Cooper gave a contemptuous chuckle

"What do you think he'll do?"

"I think he'll kill you."

"Why should you mind?"

"Oh, I wouldn't," replied Mr. Warburton, with a faint laugh. "I should bear it with the utmost fortitude. But I feel the official obligation to give you a proper warning."

"Do you think I'm afraid of a damned nigger?"

"It's a matter of entire indifference to me."

"Well, let me tell you this, I know how to take care of myself; that boy Abas is a dirty, thieving rascal, and if he tries any monkey tricks on me, by God, I'll wring his bloody neck."

"That was all I wished to say to you," said Mr. Warburton. "Good-evening."

Mr. Warburton gave him a little nod of dismissal. Cooper flushed, did not for a moment know what to say or do, turned on his heel and stumbled out of the room. Mr. Warburton watched him go with an icy smile on his lips. He had done his duty. But what would he have thought had he known that when Cooper got back to his bungalow, so silent and cheerless, he threw himself down on his bed and in his bitter loneliness on a sudden lost all control of himself? Painful sobs tore his chest and heavy tears rolled down his thin cheeks.

After this Mr. Warburton seldom saw Cooper, and never spoke to him. He read his *Times* every morning, did his work at the office, took his exercise, dressed for dinner, dined and sat by the river smoking his cheroot. If by chance he ran across Cooper he cut him dead. Each, though never for a moment unconscious of the

propinquity, acted as though the other did not exist.
Time did nothing to assuage their animosity. They
watched one another's actions and each knew what the
other did. Though Mr. Warburton had been a keen
shot in his youth, with age he had acquired a distaste
for killing the wild things of the jungle, but on Sundays
and holidays Cooper went out with his gun: if he got
something it was a triumph over Mr. Warburton; if not,
Mr. Warburton shrugged his shoulders and chuckled.
These counter-jumpers trying to be sportsmen! Christmas was a bad time for both of them: they ate their
dinners alone, each in his own quarters, and they got
deliberately drunk. They were the only white men
within two hundred miles and they lived within
shouting distance of each other. At the beginning of the
year Cooper went down with fever, and when Mr.
Warburton caught sight of him again he was surprised
to see how thin he had grown. He looked ill and worn.
The solitude, so much more unnatural because it was due
to no necessity, was getting on his nerves. It was getting
on Mr. Warburton's too, and often he could not sleep
at night. He lay awake brooding. Cooper was drinking
heavily and surely the breaking-point was near; but in
his dealings with the natives he took care to do nothing
that might expose him to his chief's rebuke. They
fought a grim and silent battle with one another. It
was a test of endurance. The months passed, and
neither gave sign of weakening. They were like men
dwelling in regions of eternal night, and their souls

were oppressed with the knowledge that never would the day dawn for them. It looked as though their lives would continue for ever in this dull and hideous monotony of hatred.

And when at last the inevitable happened it came upon Mr. Warburton with all the shock of the unexpected. Cooper accused the boy Abas of stealing some of his clothes, and when the boy denied the theft took him by the scruff of the neck and kicked him down the steps of the bungalow. The boy demanded his wages and Cooper flung at his head every word of abuse he knew. If he saw him in the compound in an hour he would hand him over to the police. Next morning the boy waylaid him outside the Fort when he was walking over to his office, and again demanded his wages. Cooper struck him in the face with his clenched fist. The boy fell to the ground and got up with blood streaming from his nose.

Cooper walked on and set about his work. But he could not attend to it. The blow had calmed his irritation, and he knew that he had gone too far. He was worried. He felt ill, miserable and discouraged. In the adjoining office sat Mr. Warburton, and his impulse was to go and tell him what he had done; he made a movement in his chair, but he knew with what icy scorn he would listen to the story. He could see his patronising smile. For a moment he had an uneasy fear of what Abas might do. Warburton had warned him all right. He sighed. What a fool he had been! But he shrugged nis shoulders impatiently. He did not care; a fat lot he had to live for. It was all Warburton's fault; if he hadn't put his back up nothing like this would have happened. Warburton had made life a hell for him from the start. The snob. But they were all like that: it was because he was a Colonial. It was a damned shame that he had never got his commission in the war; he was as good as anyone else. They were a lot of dirty snobs. He was damned if he was going to knuckle under now. Of course Warburton would hear of what had happened; the old devil knew everything. He wasn't afraid. He wasn't afraid of any Malay in Borneo, and Warburton could go to blazes.

He was right in thinking that Mr. Warburton would know what had happened. His head-boy told him when he went in to tiffin.

"Where is your nephew now?"

"I do not know, Tuan. He has gone."

Mr. Warburton remained silent. After luncheon as a rule he slept a little, but to-day he found himself very wide awake. His eyes involuntarily sought the bungalow where Cooper was now resting.

The idiot! Hesitation for a little was in Mr. Warburton's mind. Did the man know in what peril he was? He supposed he ought to send for him. But each time he had tried to reason with Cooper, Cooper had insulted him. Anger, furious anger welled up suddenly in Mr. Warburton's heart, so that the veins on his temples stood out and he clenched his fists. The cad had had his warning. Now let him take what was coming to him. It was no business of his, and if anything happened it was not his fault. But perhaps they would wish in Kuala Solor that they had taken his advice and transferred Cooper to another station.

He was strangely restless that night. After dinner he walked up and down the verandah. When the boy went away to his own quarters, Mr. Warburton asked him whether anything had been seen of Abas.

"No, Tuan, I think maybe he has gone to the village of his mother's brother."

Mr. Warburton gave him a sharp glance, but the boy was looking down, and their eyes did not meet. Mr. Warburton went down to the river and sat in his arbour. But peace was denied him. The river flowed ominously silent. It was like a great serpent gliding with sluggish movement towards the sea. And the trees of the jungle over the water were heavy with a breathless menace. No bird sang. No breeze ruffled the leaves of the cassias. All around him it seemed as though something waited.

He walked across the garden to the road. He had Cooper's bungalow in full view from there. There was a light in his sitting-room, and across the road floated the sound of rag-time. Cooper was playing his gramophone. Mr. Warburton shuddered; he had never got over his instinctive dislike of that instrument. But for that he would have gone over and spoken to Cooper. He turned and went back to his own house. He read late into the night, and at last he slept. But he did not sleep very long, he had terrible dreams, and he seemed to be awakened by a cry. Of course that was a dream too, for no cry—from the bungalow, for instance—could be heard in his room. He lay awake till dawn. Then he heard hurried steps and the sound of voices, his head-boy burst suddenly into the room without his fez, and Mr. Warburton's heart stood still.

"Tuan! Tuan!"

Mr. Warburton jumped out of bed.

"I'll come at once."

He put on his slippers, and in his sarong and pyjama-jacket walked across his compound and into Cooper's. Cooper was lying in bed, with his mouth open, and a kriss sticking in his heart. He had been killed in his sleep. Mr. Warburton started, but not because he had not expected to see just such a sight, he started because he felt in himself a sudden glow of exultation. A great burden had been lifted from his shoulders.

Cooper was quite cold. Mr. Warburton took the kriss out of the wound, it had been thrust in with such force that he had to use an effort to get it out, and looked at it. He recognised it. It was a kriss that a dealer had offered him some weeks before, and which he knew Cooper had bought.

"Where is Abas?" he asked sternly.

"Abas is at the village of his mother's brother."

The sergeant of the native police was standing at the foot of the bed.

"Take two men and go to the village and arrest him."

Mr. Warburton did what was immediately necessary. With set face he gave orders. His words were short and peremptory. Then he went back to the Fort. He shaved and had his bath, dressed and went into the dining-room. By the side of his plate *The Times* in its wrapper lay waiting for him. He helped himself to some fruit. The head-boy poured out his tea while the second handed him a dish of eggs. Mr. Warburton ate with a good appetite. The head-boy waited.

"What is it?" asked Mr. Warburton.

"Tuan, Abas, my nephew, was in the house of his mother's brother all night. It can be proved. His uncle will swear that he did not leave the kampong."

Mr. Warburton turned upon him with a frown.

"Tuan Cooper was killed by Abas. You know it as well as I know it. Justice must be done."

"Tuan, you would not hang him?"

Mr. Warburton hesitated an instant, and though his voice remained set and stern a change came into his eyes. It was a flicker which the Malay was quick to notice and across his own eyes flashed an answering look of understanding.

"The provocation was very great. Abas will be sentenced to a term of imprisonment." There was a pause while Mr. Warburton helped himself to marmalade. "When he has served a part of his sentence in prison I will take him into this house as a boy. You can train him in his duties. I have no doubt that in the house of Tuan Cooper he got into bad habits."

"Shall Abas give himself up, Tuan?"

"It would be wise of him."

The boy withdrew. Mr. Warburton took his *Times* and neatly slit the wrapper. He loved to unfold the heavy, rustling pages. The morning, so fresh and cool, was delicious and for a moment his eyes wandered out over the garden with a friendly glance. A great weight had been lifted from his mind. He turned to the columns in which were announced the births, marriages, and deaths. That was what he always looked at first. A name he knew caught his attention. Lady Ormskirk had had a son at last. By George, how pleased the old gowager must be! He would write her a note of conpratulation by the next mail.

Abas would make a very good house-boy.

That fool Cooper!

THE ROUND DOZEN

I LIKE Elsom. It is a seaside resort in the South of England, not very far from Brighton, and it has something of the late Georgian charm of that agreeable town. But it is neither bustling nor garish. Ten years ago, when I used to go there not infrequently, you might still see here and there an old house, solid and pretentious in no unpleasing fashion (like a decayed gentlewoman of good family whose discreet pride in her ancestry amuses rather than offends you), which was built in the reign of the First Gentleman in Europe and where a courtier of fallen fortunes may well have passed his declining years. The main street had a lackadaisical air and the doctor's motor seemed a trifle out of place. The housewives did their housekeeping in a leisurely manner. They gossiped with the butcher as they watched him cut from his great joint of South Down a piece of the best-end of the neck, and they asked amiably after the grocer's wife as he put half a pound of tea and a packet of salt into their string bag. I do not know whether Elsom was ever fashionable: it certainly was not so then; but it was respectable and cheap. Elderly ladies, maiden and widowed, lived there, Indian civilians and retired soldiers: they looked forward with little shudders of dismay to August and September which would bring holiday-makers; but did not disdain to let them their houses and on the proceeds spend a few worldly weeks in a Swiss pension. I never knew Elsom at that hectic time when the lodging-houses were full and young men in blazers sauntered along the front, when Pierrots performed on the beach and in the billiard-room at the Dolphin you heard the click of balls till eleven at night. I only knew it in winter. Then in every house on the sea-front, stucco houses with bow-windows built a hundred years ago, there was a sign to inform you that apartments were to let; and the guests of the Dolphin were waited on by a single waiter and the boots. At ten o'clock the porter came into the smoking-room and looked at you in so marked a manner that you got up and went to bed. Then Elsom was a restful place and the 'Dolphin' a very comfortable inn. It was pleasing to think that the Prince Regent drove over with Mrs. Fitzherbert more than once to drink a dish of tea in its coffee-room. In the hall was a framed letter from Mr. Thackeray ordering a sitting-room and two bedrooms overlooking the sea and giving instructions that a fly should be sent to the station to meet him.

One November, two or three years after the war, having had a bad attack of influenza, I went down to Elsom to regain my strength. I arrived in the afternoon and when I had unpacked my things went for a stroll on the front. The sky was overcast and the calm sea grey and cold. A few seagulls flew close to the shore. Sailing boats, their masts taken down for the winter, were drawn up high on the shingly beach and the bathing huts stood side by side in a long, grey and tattered row. No one was sitting on the benches that the town council had put here and there, but a few people were trudging up and down for exercise. I passed an old colonel with a red nose who stamped along in plus-fours followed by a terrier, two elderly women in short skirts and stout shoes and a plain girl in a Tam o' Shanter. I had never seen the front so deserted. The lodging-houses looked like bedraggled old maids waiting for lovers who would never return, and even the friendly 'Dolphin' seemed wan and desolate. My heart sank. Life on a sudden seemed very drab. I returned to the hotel, drew the curtains of my sitting-room, poked the fire and with a book sought to dispel my melancholy. But I was glad enough when it was time to dress for dinner. I went into the coffee-room and found the guests of the hotel already seated. I gave them a casual glance. There was one lady of middle age by herself and there were two elderly gentlemen, golfers probably, with red faces and baldish heads, who ate their food in moody silence. The only other persons in the room were a group of three who sat in the bow-window, and they immediately attracted my surprised attention. The party consisted of an old gentleman and two ladies, one of whom was old and probably his wife, while the other was younger and possibly his daughter. It was the old lady who first excited my interest. She wore a voluminous dress of black silk and a black lace cap; on her wrists were heavy gold bangles and round her neck a substantial gold chain from which hung a large gold locket; at her neck was a large gold brooch. I did not know that anyone still wore jewellery of that sort. Often, passing second-hand jewellers and pawnbrokers, I had lingered for a moment to look at these strangely old-fashioned articles, so solid, costly and hideous, and thought, with a smile in which there was a tinge of sadness, of the women long since dead who had worn them. They suggested the period when the bustle and the flounce were taking the place of the crinoline and the porkpie hat was ousting the poke-bonnet. The British people liked things solid and good in those days. They went to church on Sunday morning and after church walked in the Park. They gave dinner parties of twelve courses where the master of the house carved the beef and the chickens, and after dinner the ladies who could play favoured the company with Mendelssohn's *Songs without Words* and the gentleman with the fine baritone voice sang an old English ballad.

The younger woman had her back turned to me and at first I could see only that she had a slim and youthful figure. She had a great deal of brown hair which seemed to be elaborately arranged. She wore a grey dress. The three of them were chatting in low tones and presently she turned her head so that I saw her profile. It was astonishingly beautiful. The nose was straight and delicate, the line of the cheek exquisitely modelled; I saw then that she wore her hair after the manner of Queen Alexandra. The dinner proceeded to its close and the party got up. The old lady sailed out of the room, looking neither to the right nor to the left, and the young one followed her. Then I saw with a shock that she was old. Her frock was simple enough, the skirt was longer than was at that time worn, and there was something slightly old-fashioned in the cut, I daresay the waist was more clearly indicated than was then usual, but it was a girl's frock. She was tall, like a heroine of Tennyson's, slight, with long legs and a graceful carriage. I had seen the nose before, it was the nose of a Greek goddess, her mouth was beautiful, and her eyes were large and blue. Her skin was of course a little tight on the bones and there were wrinkles on her forehead and about her eyes, but in youth it must have been lovely. She reminded you of those Roman ladies with features of an exquisite regularity whom Alma Tadema used to paint, but who, notwithstanding their antique dress, were so stubbornly English. It was a type of cold perfection that one had not seen for five-and-twenty years. Now it is as dead as the epigram. I was like an archæologist who finds some long-buried statue and I was thrilled in so unexpected a manner to hit upon this survival of a past era. For no day is so dead as the day before yesterday.

The gentleman rose to his feet when the two ladies left, and then resumed his chair. A waiter brought him a glass of heavy port. He smelt it, sipped it, and rolled it round his tongue. I observed him. He was a little man, much shorter than his imposing wife, well-covered without being stout, with a fine head of curling grey hair. His face was much wrinkled and it bore a faintly humorous expression. His lips were tight and his chin was square. He was, according to our present notions, somewhat extravagantly dressed. He wore a black velvet jacket, a frilled shirt with a low collar and a large black tie, and very wide evening trousers. It gave you vaguely the effect of costume. Having drunk his port with deliberation, he got up and sauntered out of the room.

When I passed through the hall, curious to know who these singular people were, I glanced at the visitors' book. I saw written in an angular feminine hand, the writing that was taught to young ladies in modish schools forty years or so ago, the names: Mr. and Mrs. Edwin St. Clair and Miss Porchester. Their address was given as 68, Leinster Square, Bayswater, London. These must be the names and this the address of the persons who had so much interested me. I asked the manageress who Mr. St. Clair was and she told me that she believed he was something in the City. I went into the billiard-room and knocked the balls about for a little while and then on my way upstairs passed through the lounge. The two red-faced gentlemen were reading the evening paper and the elderly lady was dozing over a novel. The party of three sat in a corner. Mrs. St. Clair was knitting, Miss Porchester was busy with embroidery, and Mr. St. Clair was reading aloud in a discreet but resonant tone. As I passed I discovered that he was reading *Bleak House*.

I read and wrote most of the next day, but in the afternoon I went for a walk and on my way home I sat down for a little on one of those convenient benches on the sea-front. It was not quite so cold as the day before and the air was pleasant. For want of anything better to do I watched a figure advancing towards me from a distance. It was a man and as he came nearer I saw that it was rather a shabby little man. He wore a thin black greatcoat and a somewhat battered bowler. He walked with his hands in his pockets and looked cold. He gave me a glance as he passed by, went on a few steps, hesitated, stopped and turned back. When he came up once more to the bench on which I sat he took a hand out of his pocket and touched his hat. I noticed that he wore shabby black gloves, and surmised that he was a widower in straitened circumstances. Or he might have been a mute recovering, like myself, from influenza.

"Excuse me, sir," he said, "but could you oblige me with a match?"

"Certainly."

He sat down beside me and while I put my hand in my pocket for matches he hunted in his for cigarettes. He took out a small packet of Goldflake and his face fell.

"Dear, dear, how very annoying! I haven't got a cigarette left."

"Let me offer you one," I replied, smiling.

I took out my case and he helped himself.

"Gold?" he asked, giving the case a tap as I closed it. "Gold? That's a thing I never could keep. I've had three. All stolen."

His eyes rested in a melancholy way on his boots which were sadly in need of repair. He was a wizened little man with a long thin nose and pale blue eyes. His skin was sallow and he was much lined. I could not tell what his age was; he might have been five-and-thirty or he might have been sixty. There was nothing remarkable about him except his insignificance. But though evidently poor he was neat and clean. He was respectable and he clung to respectability. No, I did not think he was a mute, I thought he was a solicitor's clerk who had lately buried his wife and been sent to Elsom by an indulgent employer to get over the first shock of his grief.

"Are you making a long stay, sir?" he asked me.

"Ten days or a fortnight."

"Is this your first visit to Elsom, sir?"

"I have been here before."

"I know it well, sir. I flatter myself there are very few seaside resorts that I have not been to at one time or another. Elsom is hard to beat, sir. You get a very nice class of people here. There's nothing noisy or vulgar about Elsom, if you understand what I mean. Elsom has very pleasant recollections for me, sir. I knew Elsom well in bygone days. I was married in St. Martin's Church, sir."

"Really," I said feebly.

"It was a very happy marriage, sir."

"I'm very glad to hear it," I returned.

"Nine months that one lasted," he said reflectively.

Surely the remark was a trifle singular. I had not looked forward with any enthusiasm to the probability which I so clearly foresaw that he would favour me with an account of his matrimonial experiences, but now I waited if not with eagerness at least with curiosity for a further observation. He made none. He sighed a little. At last I broke the silence.

"There don't seem to be very many people about," I remarked.

"I like it so. I'm not one for crowds. As I was saying just now I reckon I've spent a good many years at one seaside resort after the other, but I never came in the season. It's the winter I like."

"Don't you find it a little melancholy?"

He turned towards me and placed his black-gloved hand for an instant on my arm.

"It is melancholy. And because it's melancholy a little ray of sunshine is very welcome."

The remark seemed to me perfectly idiotic and I did not answer. He withdrew his hand from my arm and got up.

"Well, I mustn't keep you, sir. Pleased to have made your acquaintance."

He took off his dingy hat very politely and strolled away. It was beginning now to grow chilly and I thought I would return to the 'Dolphin.' As I reached its broad steps a landau drove up, drawn by two scraggy horses, and from it stepped Mr. St. Clair. He wore a hat that looked like the unhappy result of a union between a bowler and a top-hat. He gave his hand to his wife and then to his niece. The porter carried in after them rugs and cushions. As Mr. St. Clair paid the driver I heard him tell him to come at the usual time next day and I understood that the St. Clairs took a drive every afternoon in a landau. It would not have surprised me to learn that none of them had ever been in a motorcar.

The manageress told me that they kept very much to themselves and sought no acquaintance among the other persons staying at the hotel. I rode my imagination on a loose rein. I watched them eat three meals a day. I watched Mr. and Mrs. St. Clair sit at the top of the hotel steps in the morning. He read *The Times* and she knitted. I suppose Mrs. St. Clair had never read a paper in her life, for they never took anything but *The Times* and Mr. St. Clair of course took it with him every day to the City. At about twelve Miss Porchester joined them.

"Have you enjoyed your walk, Eleanor?" asked Mrs. St. Clair.

"It was very nice, Aunt Gertrude," answered Miss Porchester.

And I understood that just as Mrs. St. Clair took 'her drive' every afternoon Miss Porchester took 'her walk' every morning.

"When you have come·to the end of your row, my dear," said Mr. St. Clair, with a glance at his wife's knitting, "we might go for a constitutional before luncheon."

"That will be very nice," answered Mrs. St. Clair. She folded up her work and gave it to Miss Porchester. "If you're going upstairs, Eleanor, will you take my work?"

"Certainly, Aunt Gertrude."

"I daresay you're a little tired after your walk, my dear."

"I shall have a little rest before luncheon."

Miss Porchester went into the hotel and Mr. and Mrs. St. Clair walked slowly along the sea-front, side by side, to a certain point, and then walked slowly back.

When I met one of them on the stairs I bowed and received an unsmiling, polite bow in return, and in the morning I ventured upon a good-day, but there the matter ended. It looked as though I should never have a chance to speak to any of them. But presently I thought that Mr. St. Clair gave me now and then a glance, and thinking he had heard my name I imagined, perhaps vainly, that he looked at me with curiosity. And a day or two after that I was sitting in my room when the porter came in with a message.

"Mr. St. Clair presents his compliments and could you oblige him with the loan of *Whitaker's Almanack*."

I was astonished.

"Why on earth should he think that I have a

Whitaker's Almanack?"

"Well, sir, the manageress told him you wrote."

I could not see the connection.

"Tell Mr. St. Clair that I'm very sorry that I haven't got a *Whitaker's Almanack*, but if I had I would very gladly lend it to him."

Here was my opportunity. I was by now filled with eagerness to know these fantastic persons more closely. Now and then in the heart of Asia I have come upon a lonely tribe living in a little village among an alien population. No one knows how they came there or why they settled in that spot. They live their own lives, speak their own language, and have no communication with their neighbours. No one knows whether they are the descendants of a band that was left behind when their nation swept in a vast horde across the continent or whether they are the dying remnant of some great people that in that country once held empire. They are a mystery. They have no future and no history. This odd little family seemed to me to have something of the same character. They were of an era that is dead and gone. They reminded me of persons in one of those leisurely, old-fashioned novels that one's father read. They belonged to the 'eighties and they had not moved since then. How extraordinary it was that they could have lived through the last forty years as though the world stood still! They took me back to my childhood and I recollected people who are long since dead. I wonder if it is only distance that gives me the impression that they were more peculiar than any one is now. When a person was described then as 'quite a character,' by heaven, it meant something.

So that evening after dinner I went into the lounge and boldly addressed Mr. St. Clair.

"I'm so sorry I haven't got a *Whitaker's Almanack*," I said, "but if I have any other book that can be of service to you I shall be delighted to lend it to you."

Mr. St. Clair was obviously startled. The two ladies kept their eyes on their work. There was an embarrassed hush.

"It does not matter at all, but I was given to understand by the manageress that you were a novelist."

I racked my brain. There was evidently some connection between my profession and *Whitaker's Almanack* that escaped me.

"In days gone by Mr. Trollope used often to dine with us in Leinster Square and I remember him saying that the two most useful books to a novelist were the Bible and *Whitaker's Almanack*."

"I see that Thackeray once stayed in this hotel," I remarked, anxious not to let the conversation drop.

"I never very much cared for Mr. Thackeray, though he dined more than once with my wife's father, the late Mr. Sargeant Saunders. He was too cynical for me. My niece has not read *Vanity Fair* to this day."

Miss Porchester blushed slightly at this reference to herself. A waiter brought in the coffee and Mrs. St. Clair turned to her husband.

"Perhaps, my dear, this gentleman would do us the pleasure to have his coffee with us."

Although not directly addressed I answered promptly:

"Thank you very much."

I sat down.

"Mr. Trollope was always my favourite novelist," said Mr. St. Clair. "He was so essentially a gentleman. I admire Charles Dickens. But Charles Dickens could never draw a gentleman. I am given to understand that young people nowadays find Mr. Trollope a little slow. My niece, Miss Porchester, prefers the novels of Mr. William Black."

"I'm afraid I've never read any," I said.

"Ah, I see that you are like me; you are not up to date. My niece once persuaded me to read a novel by a Miss Rhoda Broughton, but I could not manage more than a hundred pages of it."

"I did not say I liked it, Uncle Edwin," said Miss Porchester, defending herself, with another blush, "I told you it was rather fast, but everybody was talking about it."

"I'm quite sure it is not the sort of book your Aunt Gertrude would have wished you to read, Eleanor."

"I remember Miss Broughton telling me once that when she was young people said her books were fast and when she was old they said they were slow, and it was very hard since she had written exactly the same sort of book for forty years."

"Oh, did you know Miss Broughton?" asked Miss

Porchester, addressing me for the first time. "How very interesting! And did you know Ouida?"

"My dear Eleanor, what will you say next! I'm quite sure you've never read anything by Ouida."

"Indeed, I have, Uncle Edwin. I've read *Under Two Flags* and I liked it very much."

"You amaze and shock me. I don't know what girls are coming to nowadays."

"You always said that when I was thirty you gave me complete liberty to read anything I liked."

"There is a difference, my dear Eleanor, between liberty and licence," said Mr. St. Clair, smiling a little in order not to make his reproof offensive, but with a certain gravity.

I do not know if in recounting this conversation I have managed to convey the impression it gave me of a charming and old-fashioned air. I could have listened all night to them discussing the depravity of an age that was young in the eighteen-eighties. I would have given a good deal for a glimpse of their large and roomy house in Leinster Square. I should have recognised the suite covered in red brocade that stood stiffly about the drawing-room, each piece in its appointed place; and the cabinets filled with Dresden china would have brought me back my childhood. In the dining-room, where they habitually sat, for the drawing-room was used only for parties, was a Turkey carpet and a vast mahogany sideboard 'groaning' with silver. On the walls were the pictures that had excited the admiration of Mrs.

Humphrey Ward and her uncle Matthew in the Academy of eighteen-eighty.

Next morning, strolling through a pretty lane at the back of Elsom, I met Miss Porchester, who was taking 'her walk.' I should have liked to go a little way with her, but felt certain that it would embarrass this maiden of fifty to saunter alone with a man even of my respectable years. She bowed as I passed her and blushed. Oddly enough, a few yards behind her I came upon the funny shabby little man in black gloves with whom I had spoken for a few minutes on the front. He touched his old bowler hat.

"Excuse me, sir, but could you oblige me with a match?" he said.

"Certainly," I retorted, "but I'm afraid I have no cigarettes on me."

"Allow me to offer you one of mine," he said, taking out the paper case. It was empty. "Dear, dear, I haven't got one either. What a curious coincidence!"

He went on and I had a notion that he a little hastened his steps. I was beginning to have my doubts about him. I hoped he was not going to bother Miss Porchester. For a moment I thought of walking back, but I did not. He was a civil little man and I did not believe he would make a nuisance of himself to a single lady.

I saw him again that very afternoon. I was sitting on the front. He walked towards me with little, halting steps. There was something of a wind and he looked like a dried leaf being driven before it. This time he did not hesitate, but sat down beside me.

"We meet again, sir. The world is a small place. If it will not inconvenience you perhaps you will allow me to rest a few minutes. I am a wee bit tired."

"This is a public bench, and you have just as much right to sit on it as I."

I did not wait for him to ask me for a match, but at once offered him a cigarette.

"How very kind of you, sir! I have to limit myself to so many cigarettes a day, but I enjoy those I smoke. As one grows older the pleasures of life diminish, but my experience is that one enjoys more those that remain."

"That is a very consoling thought."

"Excuse me, sir, but am I right in thinking that you are the well-known author?"

"I am an author," I replied. "But what made you think it?"

"I have seen your portrait in the illustrated papers. I suppose you don't recognise me?"

I looked at him again, a weedy little man in neat, but shabby black clothes, with a long nose and watery blue eyes.

"I'm afraid I don't."

"I daresay I've changed," he sighed. "There was a time when my photograph was in every paper in the United Kingdom. Of course, those press photographs never do you justice. I give you my word, sir, that if I hadn't seen my name underneath I should never have guessed that some of them were meant for me."

F*

He was silent for a while. The tide was out and beyond the shingle of the beach was a strip of yellow mud. The breakwaters were half buried in it like the backbones of prehistoric beasts.

"It must be a wonderfully interesting thing to be an author, sir. I've often thought I had quite a turn for writing myself. At one time and another I've done a rare lot of reading. I haven't kept up with it much lately. For one thing my eyes are not so good as they used to be. I believe I could write a book if I tried."

"They say anybody can write one," I answered.

"Not a novel, you know. I'm not much of a one for novels; I prefer histories and that like. But memoirs. If anybody was to make it worth my while I wouldn't mind writing my memoirs."

"It's very fashionable just now."

"There are not many people who've had the experiences I've had in one way and another. I did write to one of the Sunday papers about it some little while back, but they never answered my letter."

He gave me a long, appraising look. He had too respectable an air to be about to ask me for half a crown.

"Of course you don't know who I am, sir, do you?"

"I honestly don't."

He seemed to ponder for a moment, then he smoothed down his black gloves on his fingers, looked for a moment at a hole in one of them, and then turned to me not without self-consciousness.

"I am the celebrated Mortimer Ellis," he said.

"Oh?"

I did not know what other ejaculation to make, for to the best of my belief I had never heard the name before. I saw a look of disappointment come over his face, and I was a trifle embarrassed.

"Mortimer Ellis," he repeated. "You're not going to tell me you don't know."

"I'm afraid I must. I'm very often out of England."

I wondered to what he owed his celebrity. I passed over in my mind various possibilities. He could never have been an athlete, which alone in England gives a man real fame, but he might have been a faith-healer or a champion billiard-player. There is of course no one so obscure as a cabinet minister out of office and he might have been the President of the Board of Trade in a defunct administration. But he had none of the look of a politician.

"That's fame for you," he said bitterly. "Why, for weeks I was the most talked-about man in England. Look at me. You must have seen my photograph in the papers. Mortimer Ellis."

"I'm sorry," I said, shaking my head.

He paused a moment to give his disclosure effectiveness.

"I am the well-known bigamist."

Now what are you to reply when a person who is practically a stranger to you informs you that he is a well-known bigamist? I will confess that I have sometimes had the vanity to think that I am not as a rule at a loss for a retort, but here I found myself speechless.

"I've had eleven wives, sir," he went on.

"Most people find one about as much as they can manage."

"Ah, that's want of practice. When you've had eleven there's very little you don't know about women."

"But why did you stop at eleven?"

"There now, I knew you'd say that. The moment I set eyes on you I said to myself, he's got a clever face. You know, sir, that's the thing that always grizzles me. Eleven does seem a funny number, doesn't it? There's something unfinished about it. Now three anyone might have, and seven's all right, they say nine's lucky, and there's nothing wrong with ten. But eleven! That's the one thing I regret. I shouldn't have minded anything if I could have brought it up to the Round Dozen."

He unbuttoned his coat and from an inside pocket produced a bulging and very greasy pocket book. From this he took a large bundle of newspaper cuttings; they were worn and creased and dirty. But he spread out two or three.

"Now just you look at those photographs. I ask you, are they like me? It's an outrage. Why, you'd think I was a criminal to look at them."

The cuttings were of imposing length. In the opinion of sub-editors Mortimer Ellis had obviously been a news item of value. One was headed, A Much Married Man; another, Heartless Ruffian Brought to

Book; a third, Contemptible Scoundrel Meets his Waterloo.

"Not what you would call a good press," I murmured.

"I never pay any attention to what the newspapers say," he answered, with a shrug of his thin shoulders. "I've known too many journalists myself for that. No, it's the judge I blame. He treated me shocking and it did him no good, mind you; he died within the year."

I ran my eyes down the report I held.

"I see he gave you five years."

"Disgraceful, I call it, and see what it says." He pointed to a place with his forefinger. " 'Three of his victims pleaded for mercy to be shown to him.' That shows what they thought of me. And after that he gave me five years. And just look what he called me, a heartless scoundrel—me, the best-hearted man that ever lived—a pest of society and a danger to the public. Said he wished he had the power to give me the cat. I don't so much mind his giving me five years, though you'll never get me to say it wasn't excessive, but I ask you, had he the right to talk to me like that? No, he hadn't, and I'll never forgive him, not if I live to be a hundred."

The bigamist's cheeks flushed and his watery eyes were filled for a moment with fire. It was a sore subject with him.

"May I read them?" I asked him.

"That's what I gave them you for. I want you to read them, sir. And if you can read them without saying that I'm a much wronged man, well, you're not the man I took you for."

As I glanced through one cutting after another I saw why Mortimer Ellis had so wide an acquaintance with the seaside resorts of England. They were his hunting-ground. His method was to go to some place when the season was over and take apartments in one of the empty lodging-houses. Apparently it did not take him long to make acquaintance with some woman or other, widow or spinster, and I noticed that their ages at the time were between thirty-five and fifty. They stated in the witness-box that they had met him first on the sea-front. He generally proposed marriage to them within a fortnight of this and they were married shortly after. He induced them in one way or another to entrust him with their savings and in a few months, on the pretext that he had to go to London on business, he left them never to return. Only one had ever seen him again till, obliged to give evidence, they saw him in the dock. They were women of a certain respectability; one was the daughter of a doctor and another of a clergyman; there was a lodging-house keeper, there was the widow of a commercial traveller, and there was a retired dress-maker. For the most part, their fortunes ranged from five hundred to a thousand pounds, but whatever the sum the misguided women were stripped of every penny. Some of them told really pitiful stories of the destitution to which they had been reduced. But they all acknowledged that he had been a good husband to them. Not only had three actually pleaded for mercy to be shown him, but one said in the witness box that, if he was willing to come, she was ready to take him back. He noticed that I was reading this.

"And she'd have worked for me," he said, "there's no doubt about that. But I said, better let bygones be bygones. No one likes a cut off the best end of the neck better than I do, but I'm not much of a one for cold roast mutton, I will confess."

It was only by an accident that Mortimer Ellis did not marry his twelfth wife and so achieve the Round Dozen which I understand appealed to his love of symmetry. For he was engaged to be married to a Miss Hubbard—"two thousand pounds she had, if she had a penny, in war-loan," he confided to me, and the banns had been read, when one of his former wives saw him, made enquiries, and communicated with the police. He was arrested on the very day before his twelfth wedding.

"She was a bad one, she was," he told me. "She deceived me something cruel."

"How did she do that?"

"Well, I met her at Eastbourne, one December it was, on the pier, and she told me in course of conversation that she'd been in the millinery business and had retired. She said she'd made a tidy bit of money. She wouldn't say exactly how much it was, but she gave me to understand it was something like fifteen hundred pounds. And when I married her, would you believe it, she hadn't got three hundred. And that's the one who gave me away. And mind you, I'd never blamed her. Many a man would have cut up rough when he found out he'd been made a fool of. I never showed her that I was disappointed even, I just went away without a word."

"But not without the three hundred pounds, I take it."

"Oh come, sir, you must be reasonable," he returned in an injured tone. "You can't expect three hundred pounds to last for ever and I'd been married to her four months before she confessed the truth."

"Forgive my asking," I said, "and pray don't think my question suggests a disparaging view of your personal attractions, but—why did they marry you?"

"Because I asked them," he answered, evidently very much surprised at my enquiry.

"But did you never have any refusals?"

"Very seldom. Not more than four or five in the whole course of my career. Of course I didn't propose till I was pretty sure of my ground and I don't say I didn't draw a blank sometimes. You can't expect to click every time, if you know what I mean, and I've often wasted several weeks making up to a woman before I saw there was nothing doing."

I surrendered myself for a time to my reflections. But I noticed presently that a broad smile spread over the mobile features of my friend.

"I understand what you mean," he said. "It's my

appearance that puzzles you. You don't know what it is they see in me. That's what comes of reading novels and going to the pictures. You think what women want is the cowboy type, or the romance of old Spain touch, flashing eyes, an olive skin, and a beautiful dancer. You make me laugh."

"I'm glad," I said.

"Are you a married man, sir?"

"I am. But I only have one wife.'

"You can't judge by that. You can't generalise from a single instance, if you know what I mean. Now, I ask you, what would you know about dogs if you'd never had anything but one bull-terrier?"

The question was rhetorical and I felt sure did not require an answer. He paused for an effective moment and went on.

"You're wrong, sir. You're quite wrong. They may take a fancy to a good-looking young fellow, but they don't want to marry him. They don't really care about looks."

"Douglas Jerrold, who was as ugly as he was witty, used to say that if he was given ten minutes' start with a woman he could cut out the handsomest man in the room."

"They don't want wit. They don't want a man to be funny; they think he's not serious. They don't want a man who's too handsome; they think he's not serious either. That's what they want, they want a man who's serious. Safety first. And then—attention. I may not be handsome and I may not be amusing, but believe me, I've got what every woman wants. Poise. And the proof is, I've made every one of my wives happy."

"It certainly is much to your credit that three of them pleaded for mercy to be shown to you and that one was willing to take you back."

"You don't know what an anxiety that was to me all the time I was in prison. I thought she'd be waiting for me at the gate when I was released and I said to the Governor, for God's sake, sir, smuggle me out so as no one can see me."

He smoothed his gloves again over his hands and his eye once more fell upon the hole in the first finger.

"That's what comes of living in lodgings, sir. How's a man to keep himself neat and tidy without a woman to look after him? I've been married too often to be able to get along without a wife. There are men who don't like being married. I can't understand them. The fact is, you can't do a thing really well unless you've got your heart in it, and I like being a married man. It's no difficulty to me to do the little things that women like and that some men can't be bothered with. As I was saying just now, it's attention a woman wants. I never went out of the house without giving my wife a kiss and I never came in without giving her another. And it was very seldom I came in without bringing her some chocolates or a few flowers. I never grudged the expense."

"After all, it was her money you were spending," I interposed.

"And what if it was? It's not the money that you've paid for a present that signifies, it's the spirit you give it in. That's what counts with women. No, I'm not one to boast, but I will say this for myself, I am a good husband."

I looked desultorily at the reports of the trial which I still held.

"I'll tell you what surprises me," I said. "All these women were very respectable, of a certain age, quiet, decent persons. And yet they married you without any enquiry after the shortest possible acquaintance."

He put his hand impressively on my arm.

"Ah, that's what you don't understand, sir. Women have got a craving to be married. It doesn't matter how young they are or how old they are, if they're short or tall, dark or fair, they've all got one thing in common: they want to be married. And mind you, I married them in church. No woman feels really safe unless she's married in church. You say I'm no beauty, well, I never thought I was, but if I had one leg and a hump on my back I could find any number of women who'd jump at the chance of marrying me. It's not the man they care about, it's marriage. It's a mania with them. It's a disease. Why, there's hardly one of them who wouldn't have accepted me the second time I saw her only I like to make sure of my ground before I commit myself. When it all came out there was a rare to-do because I'd married eleven times. Eleven times? Why, it's nothing, it's not even a Round Dozen. I could have married thirty times if I'd wanted to. I give you my word, sir, when I consider my opportunities, I'm astounded at my moderation."

"You told me you were very fond of reading history."

"Yes, Warren Hastings said that, didn't he? It struck me at the time I read it. It seemed to fit me like a glove."

"And you never found these constant courtships a trifle monotonous?"

"Well, sir, I think I've got a logical mind, and it always gave me a rare lot of pleasure to see how the same effects followed on the same causes, if you know what I mean. Now, for instance, with a woman who'd never been married before I always passed myself off as a widower. It worked like a charm. You see, a spinster likes a man who knows a thing or two. But with a widow I always said I was a bachelor: a widow's afraid a man who's been married before knows too much."

I gave him back his cuttings; he folded them up neatly and replaced them in his greasy pocket book.

"You know, sir, I always think I've been misjudged. Just see what they say about me: a pest of society, unscrupulous villain, contemptible scoundrel. Now just look at me. I ask you, do I look that sort of man? You know me, you're a judge of character, I've told you all about myself; do you think me a bad man?"

"My acquaintance with you is very slight," I answered with what I thought considerable tact.

"I wonder if the judge, I wonder if the jury, I wonder if the public ever thought about my side of the question.

The public booed me when I was taken into court and the police had to protect me from their violence. Did any of them think what I'd done for these women?"

"You took their money."

"Of course I took their money. I had to live the same as anybody has to live. But what did I give them in exchange for their money?"

This was another rhetorical question and though he looked at me as though he expected an answer I held my tongue. Indeed I did not know the answer. His voice was raised and he spoke with emphasis. I could see that he was serious.

"I'll tell you what I gave them in exchange for their money. Romance. Look at this place." He made a wide, circular gesture that embraced the sea and the horizon. "There are a hundred places in England like this. Look at that sea and that sky; look at these lodging houses; look at that pier and the front. Doesn't it make your heart sink? It's dead as mutton. It's all very well for you who come down here for a week or two because you're run down. But think of all those women who live here from one year's end to another. They haven't a chance. They hardly know anyone. They've just got enough money to live on and that's all. I wonder if you know how terrible their lives are. Their lives are just like the front, a long, straight, cemented walk that goes on and on from one seaside resort to another. Even in the season there's nothing for them. They're out of it. They might as well be dead. And then I come along.

Mind you, I never made advances to a woman who wouldn't have gladly acknowledged to thirty-five. And I give them love. Why, many of them had never known what it was to have a man do them up behind. Many of them had never known what it was to sit on a bench in the dark with a man's arm round their waist. I bring them change and excitement. I give them a new pride in themselves. They were on the shelf and I come along quite quietly and I deliberately take them down. A little ray of sunshine in those drab lives, that's what I was. No wonder they jumped at me, no wonder they wanted me to go back to them. The only one who gave me away was the milliner, she said she was a widow, my private opinion is that she'd never been married at all. You say I did the dirty on them; why, I brought happiness and glamour into eleven lives that never thought they had even a dog's chance of it again. You say I'm a villain and a scoundrel, you're wrong. I'm a philanthropist. Five years, they gave me; they should have given me the medal of the Royal Humane Society."

He took out his empty packet of Goldflake and looked at it with a melancholy shake of the head. When I handed him my cigarette case he helped himself without a word. I watched the spectacle of a good man struggling with his emotion.

"And what did I get out of it, I ask you?" he continued presently. "Board and lodging and enough to buy cigarettes. But I never was able to save, and the proof is that now, when I'm not so young as I was, I haven't got half a crown in my pocket." He gave me a sidelong glance. "It's a great come-down for me to find myself in this position. I've always paid my way and I've never asked a friend for a loan in all my life. I was wondering, sir, if you could oblige me with a trifle. It's humiliating to me to have to suggest it, but the fact is, if you could oblige me with a pound it would mean a great deal to me."

Well, I had certainly had a pound's worth of entertainment out of the bigamist and I dived for my pocket-book.

"I shall be very glad," I said.

He looked at the notes I took out.

"I suppose you couldn't make it two, sir?"

"I think I could."

I handed him a couple of pound notes and he gave a little sigh as he took them.

"You don't know what it means to a man who's used to the comforts of home life not to know where to turn for a night's lodging."

"But there is one thing I should like you to tell me," I said. "I shouldn't like you to think me cynical, but I had a notion that women on the whole take the maxim, 'It is more blessed to give than to receive,' as applicable exclusively to our sex. How did you persuade these respectable, and no doubt thrifty, women to entrust you so confidently with all their savings?"

An amused smile spread over his undistinguished features.

"Well, sir, you know what Shakespeare said about ambition o'erleaping itself. That's the explanation. Tell a woman you'll double her capital in six months if she'll give it you to handle and she won't be able to give you the money quick enough. Greed, that's what it is. Just greed."

It was a sharp sensation, stimulating to the appetite (like hot sauce with ice cream), to go from this diverting ruffian to the respectability, all lavender bags and crinolines, of the St. Clairs and Miss Porchester. I spent every evening with them now. No sooner had the ladies left him than Mr. St. Clair sent his compliments to my table and asked me to drink a glass of port with him. When we had finished it we went into the lounge and drank coffee. Mr. St. Clair enjoyed his glass of old brandy. The hour I thus spent with them was so exquisitely boring that it had for me a singular fascination. They were told by the manageress that I had written plays.

"We used often to go to the theatre when Sir Henry Irving was at the Lyceum," said Mr. St. Clair. "I once had the pleasure of meeting him. I was taken to supper at the Garrick Club by Sir Everard Millais and I was introduced to Mr. Irving, as he then was."

"Tell him what he said to you, Edwin," said Mrs. St. Clair.

Mr. St. Clair struck a dramatic attitude and gave not at all a bad imitation of Henry Irving.

" 'You have the actor's face, Mr. St. Clair,' he said to me. 'If you ever think of going on the stage, come to me and I will give you a part.' " Mr. St. Clair resumed his natural manner. "It was enough to turn a young man's head."

"But it didn't turn yours," I said.

"I will not deny that if I had been otherwise situated I might have allowed myself to be tempted. But I had my family to think of. It would have broken my father's heart if I had not gone into the business."

"What is that?" I asked.

"I am a tea merchant, sir. My firm is the oldest in the City of London. I have spent forty years of my life in combating to the best of my ability the desire of my fellow-countrymen to drink Ceylon tea instead of the China tea which was universally drunk in my youth."

I thought it charmingly characteristic of him to spend a lifetime in persuading the public to buy something they didn't want rather than something they did.

"But in his younger days my husband did a lot of amateur acting and he was thought very clever," said Mrs. St. Clair.

"Shakespeare, you know, and sometimes *The School for Scandal*. I would never consent to act trash. But that is a thing of the past. I had a gift, perhaps it was a pity to waste it, but it's too late now. When we have a dinner-party I sometimes let the ladies persuade me to recite the great soliloquies of Hamlet. But that is all I do."

Oh! Oh! Oh! I thought with shuddering fascination of those dinner-parties and wondered whether I should ever be asked to one of them. Mrs. St. Clair gave me a little smile, half shocked, half prim.

"My husband was very bohemian as a young man," she said.

"I sowed my wild oats. I knew quite a lot of painters and writers, Wilkie Collins, for instance, and even men who wrote for the papers. Watts painted a portrait of my wife, and I bought a picture of Millais. I knew a number of the pre-Raphaelites."

"Have you a Rossetti?" I asked.

"No. I admired Rossetti's talent, but I could not approve of his private life. I would never buy a picture by an artist whom I should not care to ask to dinner at my house."

My brain was reeling when Miss Porchester, looking at her watch, said: "Are you not going to read to us to-night, Uncle Edwin?"

I withdrew.

It was while I was drinking a glass of port with Mr. St. Clair one evening that he told me the sad story of Miss Porchester. She was engaged to be married to a nephew of Mrs. St. Clair, a barrister, when it was discovered that he had had an intrigue with the daughter of his laundress.

"It was a terrible thing," said Mr. St. Clair. "A terrible thing. But of course my niece took the only possible course. She returned him his ring, his letters and his photograph, and said that she could never marry him. She implored him to marry the young person he had wronged and said she would be a sister to her. It broke her heart. She has never cared for any one since."

"And did he marry the young person?"

Mr. St. Clair shook his head and sighed.

"No, we were greatly mistaken in him. It has been a sore grief to my dear wife to think that a nephew of hers should behave in such a dishonourable manner. Some time later we heard that he was engaged to a young lady in a very good position with ten thousand pounds of her own. I considered it my duty to write to her father and put the facts before him. He answered my letter in a most insolent fashion. He said he would much rather his son-in-law had a mistress before marriage than after."

"What happened then?"

"They were married and now my wife's nephew is one of His Majesty's Judges of the High Court, and his wife is My Lady. But we've never consented to receive them. When my wife's nephew was knighted Eleanor suggested that we should ask them to dinner, but my wife said that he should never darken our doors and I upheld her."

"And the laundress's daughter?"

"She married in her own class of life and has a public-house at Canterbury. My niece, who has a little money of her own, did everything for her and is godmother to her eldest child."

Poor Miss Porchester. She had sacrificed herself on the altar of Victorian morality and I am afraid the consciousness that she had behaved beautifully was the only benefit she had got from it.

"Miss Porchester is a woman of striking appearance," I said. "When she was younger she must have been perfectly lovely. I wonder she never married somebody else."

"Miss Porchester was considered a great beauty. Alma Tadema admired her so much that he asked her to sit as a model for one of his pictures, but of course we couldn't very well allow that." Mr. St. Clair's tone conveyed that the suggestion had deeply outraged his sense of decency. "No, Miss Porchester never cared for anyone but her cousin. She never speaks of him and it is now thirty years since they parted, but I am convinced that she loves him still. She is a true woman, my dear sir, one life, one love, and though perhaps I regret that she has been deprived of the joys of marriage and motherhood I am bound to admire her fidelity."

But the heart of woman is incalculable and rash is the man who thinks she will remain in one stay. Rash, Uncle Edwin. You have known Eleanor for many years, for when, her mother having fallen into a decline and died, you brought the orphan to your comfortable and even luxurious house in Leinster Square, she was but a child; but what, when it comes down to brass tacks, Uncle Edwin, do you really know of Eleanor?

It was but two days after Mr. St. Clair had confided to me the touching story which explained why Miss Porchester had remained a spinster that, coming back to the hotel in the afternoon after a round of golf, the manageress came up to me in an agitated manner.

"Mr. St. Clair's compliments and will you go up to number twenty-seven the moment you come in."

"Certainly. But why?"

"Oh, there's a rare upset. They'll tell you."

I knocked at the door. I heard a 'come in, come in,' which reminded me that Mr. St. Clair had played Shakespearean parts in probably the most refined amateur dramatic company in London. I entered and found Mrs. St. Clair lying on the sofa with a handkerchief soaked in eau-de-Cologne on her brow and a bottle of smelling salts in her hand. Mr. St. Clair was standing in front of the fire in such a manner as to prevent anyone else in the room from obtaining any benefit from it.

"I must apologise for asking you to come up in this unceremonious fashion, but we are in great distress, and we thought you might be able to throw some light on what has happened."

His perturbation was obvious.

"What *has* happened?"

"Our niece, Miss Porchester, has eloped. This morning she sent in a message to my wife that she had one of her sick headaches. When she has one of her sick headaches she likes to be left absolutely alone and it wasn't till this afternoon that my wife went to see if there was anything she could do for her. The room was empty. Her trunk was packed. Her dressing-case with silver fittings was gone. And on the pillow was a letter telling us of her rash act."

"I'm very sorry," I said. "I don't know exactly what I can do."

"We were under the impression that you were the only gentleman at Elsom with whom she had any acquaintance."

His meaning flashed across me.

"I haven't eloped with her," I said. "I happen to be a married man."

"I see you haven't eloped with her. At the first moment we thought perhaps . . . but if it isn't you, who is it?"

"I'm sure I don't know."

"Show him the letter, Edwin," said Mrs. St. Clair from the sofa.

"Don't move, Gertrude. It will bring on your lumbago."

Miss Porchester had 'her' sick headaches and Mrs. St. Clair had 'her' lumbago. What had Mr. St. Clair? I was willing to bet a fiver that Mr. St. Clair had 'his' gout. He gave me the letter and I read it with an air of decent commiseration.

Dearest Uncle Edwin and Aunt Gertrude,

When you receive this I shall be far away. I am going to be married this morning to a gentleman who is very dear to me. I know I am doing wrong in running away like this, but I was afraid you would endeavour to set obstacles in the way of my marriage and since nothing would induce me to change my mind I thought it would save us all much unhappiness if I did it without telling you anything about it. My fiancé is a very retiring man, owing to his long residence in tropical countries not in the best of health, and he thought it much better that we should be married quite privately. When you know how radiantly happy I am I hope you will forgive me. Please send my box to the luggage office at Victoria Station.

Your loving niece,

Eleanor.

"I will never forgive her," said Mr. St. Clair as I returned him the letter. "She shall never darken my doors again. Gertrude, I forbid you ever to mention Eleanor's name in my hearing."

Mrs. St. Clair began to sob quietly.

"Aren't you rather hard?" I said. "Is there any reason why Miss Porchester shouldn't marry?"

"At her age," he answered angrily. "It's ridiculous. We shall be the laughing-stock of everyone in Leinster Square. Do you know how old she is? She's fifty-one."

"Fifty-four," said Mrs. St. Clair through her sobs.

"She's been the apple of my eye. She's been like a daughter to us. She's been an old maid for years.

I think it's positively improper for her to think of marriage."

"She was always a girl to us, Edwin," pleaded Mrs. St. Clair.

"And who is this man she's married? It's the deception that rankles. She must have been carrying on with him under our very noses. She does not even tell us his name. I fear the very worst."

Suddenly I had an inspiration. That morning after breakfast I had gone out to buy myself some cigarettes and at the tobacconist's I ran across Mortimer Ellis. I had not seen him for some days.

"You're looking very spruce," I said.

His boots had been repaired and were neatly blacked, his hat was brushed, he was wearing a clean collar and new gloves. I thought he had laid out my two pounds to advantage.

"I have to go to London this morning on business," he said.

I nodded and left the shop.

I remembered that a fortnight before, walking in the country, I had met Miss Porchester and, a few yards behind, Mortimer Ellis. Was it possible that they had been walking together and he had fallen back as they caught sight of me? By heaven, I saw it all.

"I think you said that Miss Porchester had money of her own," I said.

"A trifle. She has three thousand pounds."

Now I was certain. I looked at them blankly.

Suddenly Mrs. St. Clair, with a cry, sprang to her feet.

"Edwin, Edwin, supposing he doesn't marry her?"

Mr. St. Clair at this put his hand to his head and in a state of collapse sank into a chair.

"The disgrace would kill me," he groaned.

"Don't be alarmed," I said. "He'll marry her all right. He always does. He'll marry her in church."

They paid no attention to what I said. I suppose they thought I'd suddenly taken leave of my senses. I was quite sure now. Mortimer Ellis had achieved his ambition after all. Miss Porchester completed the Round Dozen.

THE LETTER

OUTSIDE on the quay the sun beat fiercely. A stream of motors, lorries and buses, private cars and hirelings, sped up and down the crowded thoroughfare, and every chauffeur blew his horn; rickshaws threaded their nimble path amid the throng, and the panting coolies found breath to yell at one another; coolies, carrying heavy bales, sidled along with their quick jog-trot and shouted to the passer-by to make way; itinerant vendors proclaimed their wares. Singapore is the meeting-place of a hundred peoples; and men of all colours, black Tamils, yellow Chinks, brown Malays, Armenians, Jews and Bengalis, called to one another in raucous tones. But inside the office of Messrs. Ripley, Joyce and Naylor it was pleasantly cool; it was dark after the dusty glitter of the street and agreeably quiet after its unceasing din. Mr. Joyce sat in his private room, at the table, with an electric fan turned full on him. He was leaning back, his elbows on the arms of the chair, with the tips of the outstretched fingers of one hand resting neatly against the tips of the outstretched fingers of the other. His gaze rested on the battered volumes of the Law Reports which stood on a long shelf in front of him. On the top of a cupboard were square boxes of japanned tin, on which were painted the names of various clients.

There was a knock at the door.

"Come in."

A Chinese clerk, very neat in his white ducks, opened it.

"Mr. Crosbie is here, sir."

He spoke beautiful English, accenting each word with precision, and Mr. Joyce had often wondered at the extent of his vocabulary. Ong Chi Seng was a Cantonese and he had studied law at Gray's Inn. He was spending a year or two with Messrs. Ripley, Joyce and Naylor in order to prepare himself for practice on his own account. He was industrious, obliging, and of exemplary character.

"Show him in," said Mr. Joyce.

He rose to shake hands with his visitor and asked him to sit down. The light fell on him as he did so. The face of Mr. Joyce remained in shadow. He was by nature a silent man, and now he looked at Robert Crosbie for quite a minute without speaking. Crosbie was a big fellow, well over six feet high, with broad shoulders, and muscular. He was a rubber-planter, hard with the constant exercise of walking over the estate, and with the tennis which was his relaxation when the day's work was over. He was deeply sunburned. His hairy hands, his feet in clumsy boots, were enormous, and Mr. Joyce found himself thinking that a blow of that great fist would easily kill the fragile Tamil. But there was no fierceness in his blue eyes; they were confiding and gentle; and his face, with its big, undistinguished features, was open, frank and honest. But at this moment it bore a look of deep distress. It was drawn and haggard.

"You look as though you hadn't had much sleep the last night or two," said Mr. Joyce.

"I haven't."

Mr. Joyce noticed now the old felt hat, with its broad double brim, which Crosbie had placed on the table; and then his eyes travelled to the khaki shorts he wore, showing his red hairy thighs, the tennis shirt open at the neck, without a tie, and the dirty khaki jacket with the ends of the sleeves turned up. He looked as though he had just come in from a long tramp among the rubber trees. Mr. Joyce gave a slight frown.

"You must pull yourself together, you know. You must keep your head."

"Oh, I'm all right."

"Have you seen your wife to-day?"

"No, I'm to see her this afternoon. You know, it is a damned shame that they should have arrested her."

"I think they had to do that," Mr. Joyce answered in his level, soft tone.

"I should have thought they'd have let her out on bail."

"It's a very serious charge."

"It is damnable. She did what any decent woman would do in her place. Only, nine women out of ten wouldn't have the pluck. Leslie's the best woman in the world. She wouldn't hurt a fly. Why, hang it all, man, I've been married to her for twelve years, do you think I don't know her? God, if I'd got hold of the man I'd have wrung his neck, I'd have killed him without a moment's hesitation. So would you."

"My dear fellow, everybody's on your side. No one has a good word to say for Hammond. We're going to get her off. I don't suppose either the assessors or the judge will go into court without having already made up their minds to bring in a verdict of not guilty."

"The whole thing's a farce," said Crosbie violently. "She ought never to have been arrested in the first place, and then it's terrible, after all the poor girl's gone through, to subject her to the ordeal of a trial. There's not a soul I've met since I've been in Singapore, man or woman, who hasn't told me that Leslie was absolutely justified. I think it's awful to keep her in prison all these weeks."

"The law is the law. After all, she confesses that she killed the man. It is terrible, and I'm dreadfully sorry for both you and for her."

"I don't matter a hang," interrupted Crosbie.

"But the fact remains that murder has been committed, and in a civilised community a trial is inevitable."

"Is it murder to exterminate noxious vermin? She shot him as she would have shot a mad dog."

Mr. Joyce leaned back again in his chair and once more placed the tips of his ten fingers together. The

little construction he formed looked like the skeleton of
a roof. He was silent for a moment.

"I should be wanting in my duty as your legal
adviser," he said at last, in an even voice, looking at his
client with his cool, brown eyes, "if I did not tell you
that there is one point which causes me just a little
anxiety. If your wife had only shot Hammond once, the
whole thing would be absolutely plain sailing. Unfortunately she fired six times."

"Her explanation is perfectly simple. In the circumstances anyone would have done the same."

"I daresay," said Mr. Joyce, "and of course I think
the explanation is very reasonable. But it's no good
closing our eyes to the facts. It's always a good plan to
put yourself in another man's place, and I can't deny
that if I were prosecuting for the Crown that is the point
on which I should centre my enquiry."

"My dear fellow, that's perfectly idiotic."

Mr. Joyce shot a sharp glance at Robert Crosbie.
The shadow of a smile hovered over his shapely lips.
Crosbie was a good fellow, but he could hardly be
described as intelligent.

"I daresay it's of no importance," answered the
lawyer, "I just thought it was a point worth mentioning.
You haven't got very long to wait now, and when it's all
over I recommend you to go off somewhere with your
wife on a trip, and forget all about it. Even though we
are almost dead certain to get an acquittal, a trial of that
sort is anxious work, and you'll both want a rest."

For the first time Crosbie smiled, and his smile strangely changed his face. You forgot the uncouthness and saw only the goodness of his soul.

"I think I shall want it more than Leslie. She's borne up wonderfully. By God, there's a plucky little woman for you."

"Yes, I've been very much struck by her self-control," said the lawyer. "I should never have guessed that she was capable of such determination."

His duties as her counsel had made it necessary for him to have a good many interviews with Mrs. Crosbie since her arrest. Though things had been made as easy as could be for her, the fact remained that she was in gaol, awaiting her trial for murder, and it would not have been surprising if her nerves had failed her. She appeared to bear her ordeal with composure. She read a great deal, took such exercise as was possible, and by favour of the authorities worked at the pillow lace which had always formed the entertainment of her long hours of leisure. When Mr. Joyce saw her, she was neatly dressed in cool, fresh, simple frocks, her hair was carefully arranged, and her nails were manicured. Her manner was collected. She was able even to jest upon the little inconveniences of her position. There was something casual about the way in which she spoke of the tragedy, which suggested to Mr. Joyce that only her good breeding prevented her from finding something a trifle ludicrous in a situation which was eminently serious. It surprised him, for he had never thought that she had a sense of humour.

He had known her off and on for a good many years. When she paid visits to Singapore she generally came to dine with his wife and himself, and once or twice she had passed a week-end with them at their bungalow by the sea. His wife had spent a fortnight with her on the estate, and had met Geoffrey Hammond several times. The two couples had been on friendly, if not on intimate, terms, and it was on this account that Robert Crosbie had rushed over to Singapore immediately after the catastrophe and begged Mr. Joyce to take charge personally of his unhappy wife's defence.

The story she told him the first time he saw her, she had never varied in the smallest detail. She told it as coolly then, a few hours after the tragedy, as she told it now. She told it connectedly, in a level, even voice, and her only sign of confusion was when a slight colour came into her cheeks as she described one or two of its incidents. She was the last woman to whom one would have expected such a thing to happen. She was in the early thirties, a fragile creature, neither short nor tall, and graceful rather than pretty. Her wrists and ankles were very delicate, but she was extremely thin, and you could see the bones of her hands through the white skin, and the veins were large and blue. Her face was colourless, slightly sallow, and her lips were pale. You did not notice the colour of her eyes. She had a great deal of light brown hair, and it had a slight natural wave; it was the sort of hair that with a little touching-up would have been very pretty, but you could not imagine that Mrs. Crosbie would think of resorting to any such device. She was a quiet, pleasant, unassuming woman. Her manner was engaging, and if she was not very popular it was because she suffered from a certain shyness. This was comprehensible enough, for the planter's life is lonely, and in her own house, with people she knew, she was in her quiet way charming. Mrs. Joyce, after her fortnight's stay, had told her husband that Leslie was a very agreeable hostess. There was more in her, she said, than people thought; and when you came to know her you were surprised how much she had read and how entertaining she could be.

She was the last woman in the world to commit murder.

Mr. Joyce dismissed Robert Crosbie with such reassuring words as he could find and, once more alone in his office, turned over the pages of the brief. But it was a mechanical action, for all its details were familiar to him. The case was the sensation of the day, and it was discussed in all the clubs, at all the dinner tables, up and down the Peninsula, from Singapore to Penang. The facts that Mrs. Crosbie gave were simple. Her husband had gone to Singapore on business, and she was alone for the night. She dined by herself, late, at a quarter to nine, and after dinner sat in the sitting-room working at her lace. It opened on the verandah. There was no one in the bungalow, for the servants had retired to their own quarters at the back of the compound. She was surprised to hear a step on the gravel path in the garden, a booted step, which suggested a white man rather than a native, for she had not heard a motor drive up, and she could not imagine who could be coming to see her at that time of night. Someone ascended the few stairs that led up to the bungalow, walked across the verandah, and appeared at the door of the room in which she sat. At the first moment she did not recognise the visitor. She sat with a shaded lamp, and he stood with his back to the darkness.

"May I come in?" he said.

She did not even recognise the voice.

"Who is it?" she asked.

She worked with spectacles, and she took them off as she spoke.

"Geoff. Hammond."

"Of course. Come in and have a drink."

She rose and shook hands with him cordially. She was a little surprised to see him, for though he was a neighbour neither she nor Robert had been lately on very intimate terms with him, and she had not seen him for some weeks. He was the manager of a rubber estate nearly eight miles from theirs, and she wondered why he had chosen this late hour to come and see them.

"Robert's away," she said. "He had to go to Singapore for the night."

Perhaps he thought his visit called for some explanation, for he said:

"I'm sorry. I felt rather lonely to-night, so I thought

I'd just come along and see how you were getting on."

"How on earth did you come? I never heard a car."

"I left it down the road. I thought you might both be in bed and asleep."

This was natural enough. The planter gets up at dawn in order to take the roll-call of the workers, and soon after dinner he is glad to go to bed. Hammond's car was, in point of fact, found next day a quarter of a mile from the bungalow.

Since Robert was away there was no whisky and soda in the room. Leslie did not call the boy, who was probably asleep, but fetched it herself. Her guest mixed himself a drink and filled his pipe.

Geoff. Hammond had a host of friends in the colony. He was at this time in the late thirties, but he had come out as a lad. He had been one of the first to volunteer on the outbreak of war, and had done very well. A wound in the knee caused him to be invalided out of the army after two years, but he returned to the Federated Malay States with a D.S.O. and an M.C. He was one of the best billiard-players in the colony. He had been a beautiful dancer and a fine tennis player, but though able no longer to dance, and his tennis, with a stiff knee, was not so good as it had been, he had the gift of popularity and was universally liked. He was a tall, good-looking fellow, with attractive blue eyes and a fine head of black, curling hair. Old stagers said his only fault was that he was too fond of the girls, and after the catastrophe they shook their heads and vowed that they had always known this would get him into trouble.

He began now to talk to Leslie about the local affairs, the forthcoming races in Singapore, the price of rubber, and his chances of killing a tiger which had been lately seen in the neighbourhood. She was anxious to finish by a certain date the piece of lace on which she was working, for she wanted to send it home for her mother's birthday, and so put on her spectacles again, and drew towards her chair the little table on which stood the pillow.

"I wish you wouldn't wear those great horn-spectacles," he said. "I don't know why a pretty woman should do her best to look plain."

She was a trifle taken aback at this remark. He had never used that tone with her before. She thought the best thing was to make light of it.

"I have no pretensions to being a raving beauty, you know, and if you ask me point-blank, I'm bound to tell you that I don't care two pins if you think me plain or not."

"I don't think you're plain. I think you're awfully pretty."

"Sweet of you," she answered, ironically. "But in that case I can only think you half-witted."

He chuckled. But he rose from his chair and sat down in another by her side.

"You're not going to have the face to deny that you have the prettiest hands in the world," he said.

He made a gesture as though to take one of them. She gave him a little tap.

"Don't be an idiot. Sit down where you were before and talk sensibly, or else I shall send you home."

He did not move.

"Don't you know that I'm awfully in love with you?" he said.

She remained quite cool.

"I don't. I don't believe it for a minute, and even if it were true I don't want you to say it."

She was the more surprised at what he was saying, since during the seven years she had known him he had never paid her any particular attention. When he came back from the war they had seen a good deal of one another, and once when he was ill Robert had gone over and brought him back to their bungalow in his car. He had stayed with them then for a fortnight. But their interests were dissimilar, and the acquaintance had never ripened into friendship. For the last two or three years they had seen little of him. Now and then he came over to play tennis, now and then they met him at some planter's who was giving a party, but it often happened that they did not set eyes on him for a month at a time.

Now he took another whisky and soda. Leslie wondered if he had been drinking before. There was something odd about him, and it made her a trifle uneasy. She watched him help himself with disapproval.

"I wouldn't drink any more if I were you," she said, good-humouredly still.

He emptied his glass and put it down.

"Do you think I'm talking to you like this because I'm drunk?" he asked abruptly.

"That is the most obvious explanation, isn't it?"

"Well, it's a lie. I've loved you ever since I first knew you. I've held my tongue as long as I could, and now it's got to come out. I love you, I love you, I love you."

She rose and carefully put aside the pillow.

"Good-night," she said.

"I'm not going now."

At last she began to lose her temper.

"But, you poor fool, don't you know that I've never loved anyone but Robert, and even if I didn't love Robert you're the last man I should care for."

"What do I care? Robert's away."

"If you don't go away this minute I shall call the boys, and have you thrown out."

"They're out of earshot."

She was very angry now. She made a movement as though to go on to the verandah from which the house-boy would certainly hear her, but he seized her arm.

"Let me go," she cried furiously.

"Not much. I've got you now."

She opened her mouth and called "Boy! boy!" but with a quick gesture he put his hand over it. Then before she knew what he was about he had taken her in his arms and was kissing her passionately. She struggled, turning her lips away from his burning mouth.

"No, no, no," she cried. "Leave me alone. I won't."

She grew confused about what happened then. All that had been said before she remembered accurately, but now his words assailed her ears through a mist of horror and fear. He seemed to plead for her love. He broke into violent protestations of passion. And all the time he held her in his tempestuous embrace. She was helpless, for he was a strong, powerful man, and her arms were pinioned to her sides; her struggles were unavailing, and she felt herself grow weaker; she was afraid she would faint, and his hot breath on her face made her feel desperately sick. He kissed her mouth, her eyes, her cheeks, her hair. The pressure of his arms was killing her. He lifted her off her feet. She tried to kick him, but he only held her more closely. He was carrying her now. He wasn't speaking any more, but she knew that his face was pale and his eyes hot with desire. He was taking her into the bedroom. He was no longer a civilised man, but a savage. And as he ran he stumbled against a table which was in the way. His stiff knee made him a little awkward on his feet, and with the burden of the woman in his arms he fell. In a moment she had snatched herself away from him. She ran round the sofa. He was up in a flash, and flung himself towards her. There was a revolver on the desk. She was not a nervous woman, but Robert was to be away for the night, and she had meant to take it into her room when she went to bed. That was why it happened to be there. She was frantic with terror now. She did not know what she was doing. She heard a report. She saw

Hammond stagger. He gave a cry. He said something, she didn't know what. He lurched out of the room on to the verandah. She was in a frenzy now, she was beside herself, she followed him out, yes, that was it, she must have followed him out, though she remembered nothing of it, she followed firing automatically, shot after shot, till the six chambers were empty. Hammond fell down on the floor of the verandah. He crumpled up into a bloody heap.

When the boys, startled by the reports, rushed up, they found her standing over Hammond with the revolver still in her hand, and Hammond lifeless. She looked at them for a moment without speaking. They stood in a frightened, huddled bunch. She let the revolver fall from her hand, and without a word turned and went into the sitting-room. They watched her go into her bedroom and turn the key in the lock. They dared not touch the dead body, but looked at it with terrified eyes, talking excitedly to one another in undertones. Then the head-boy collected himself; he had been with them for many years, he was Chinese and a level-headed fellow. Robert had gone into Singapore on his motor-cycle, and the car stood in the garage. He told the seis to get it out; they must go at once to the Assistant District Officer and tell him what had happened. He picked up the revolver and put it in his pocket. The A.D.O., a man called Withers, lived on the outskirts of the nearest town, which was about thirty-five miles away. It took them an hour and a half to reach him. Everyone was asleep, and they had to rouse the boys. Presently Withers came out and they told him their errand. The head-boy showed him the revolver in proof of what he said. The A.D.O. went into his room to dress, sent for his car, and in a little while was following them back along the deserted road. The dawn was just breaking as he reached the Crosbies' bungalow. He ran up the steps of the verandah, and stopped short as he saw Hammond's body lying where he fell. He touched the face. It was quite cold.

"Where's mem?" he asked the house-boy.

The Chinese pointed to the bedroom. Withers went to the door and knocked. There was no answer. He knocked again.

"Mrs. Crosbie," he called.

"Who is it?"

"Withers."

There was another pause. Then the door was unlocked and slowly opened. Leslie stood before him. She had not been to bed, and wore the tea-gown in which she had dined. She stood and looked silently at the A.D.O.

"Your house-boy fetched me," he said. "Hammond. What have you done?"

"He tried to rape me, and I shot him."

"My God. I say, you'd better come out here. You must tell me exactly what happened."

"Not now. I can't. You must give me time. Send for my husband."

Withers was a young man, and he did not know exactly what to do in an emergency which was so out of the run of his duties. Leslie refused to say anything till at last Robert arrived. Then she told the two men the story, from which since then, though she had repeated it over and over again, she had never in the slightest degree diverged.

The point to which Mr. Joyce recurred was the shooting. As a lawyer he was bothered that Leslie had fired not once, but six times, and the examination of the dead man showed that four of the shots had been fired close to the body. One might almost have thought that when the man fell she stood over him and emptied the contents of the revolver into him. She confessed that her memory, so accurate for all that had preceded, failed her here. Her mind was blank. It pointed to an uncontrollable fury; but uncontrollable fury was the last thing you would have expected from this quiet and demure woman. Mr. Joyce had known her a good many years, and had always thought her an unemotional person; during the weeks that had passed since the tragedy her composure had been amazing.

Mr. Joyce shrugged his shoulders.

"The fact is, I suppose," he reflected, "that you can never tell what hidden possibilities of savagery there are in the most respectable of women."

There was a knock at the door.

"Come in."

The Chinese clerk entered and closed the door

behind him. He closed it gently, with deliberation, but decidedly, and advanced to the table at which Mr. Joyce was sitting.

"May I trouble you, sir, for a few words private conversation?" he said.

The elaborate accuracy with which the clerk expressed himself always faintly amused Mr. Joyce, and now he smiled.

"It's no trouble, Chi Seng," he replied.

"The matter on which I desire to speak to you, sir, is delicate and confidential."

"Fire away."

Mr. Joyce met his clerk's shrewd eyes. As usual Ong Chi Seng was dressed in the height of local fashion. He wore very shiny patent-leather shoes and gay silk socks. In his black tie was a pearl and ruby pin, and on the fourth finger of his left hand a diamond ring. From the pocket of his neat white coat protruded a gold fountain pen and a gold pencil. He wore a gold wrist-watch, and on the bridge of his nose invisible pince-nez. He gave a little cough.

"The matter has to do with the case R. *v.* Crosbie, sir."

"Yes?"

"A circumstance has come to my knowledge, sir, which seems to me to put a different complexion on it."

"What circumstance?"

"It has come to my knowledge, sir, that there is a letter in existence from the defendant to the unfortunate victim of the tragedy."

"I shouldn't be at all surprised. In the course of the last seven years I have no doubt that Mrs. Crosbie often had occasion to write to Mr. Hammond."

Mr. Joyce had a high opinion of his clerk's intelligence and his words were designed to conceal his thoughts.

"That is very probable, sir. Mrs. Crosbie must have communicated with the deceased frequently, to invite him to dine with her for example, or to propose a tennis game. That was my first thought when the matter was brought to my notice. This letter, however, was written on the day of the late Mr. Hammond's death."

Mr. Joyce did not flicker an eyelash. He continued to look at Ong Chi Seng with the smile of faint amusement with which he generally talked to him.

"Who has told you this?"

"The circumstances were brought to my knowledge, sir, by a friend of mine."

Mr. Joyce knew better than to insist.

"You will no doubt recall, sir, that Mrs. Crosbie has stated that until the fatal night she had had no communication with the deceased for several weeks."

"Have you got the letter?"

"No, sir."

"What are its contents?"

"My friend gave me a copy. Would you like to peruse it, sir?"

"I should."

Ong Chi Seng took from an inside pocket a bulky wallet. It was filled with papers, Singapore dollar notes and cigarette cards. From the confusion he presently extracted a half-sheet of thin note-paper and placed it before Mr. Joyce. The letter read as follows:

R. *will be away for the night. I absolutely must see you. I shall expect you at eleven. I am desperate, and if you don't come I won't answer for the consequences. Don't drive up.*—L.

It was written in the flowing hand which the Chinese were taught at the foreign schools. The writing, so lacking in character, was oddly incongruous with the ominous words.

"What makes you think that this note was written by Mrs. Crosbie?"

"I have every confidence in the veracity of my informant, sir," replied Ong Chi Seng. "And the matter can very easily be put to the proof. Mrs. Crosbie will, no doubt, be able to tell you at once whether she wrote such a letter or not."

Since the beginning of the conversation Mr. Joyce had not taken his eyes off the respectable countenance of his clerk. He wondered now if he discerned in it a faint expression of mockery.

"It is inconceivable that Mrs. Crosbie should have written such a letter," said Mr. Joyce.

"If that is your opinion, sir, the matter is of course ended. My friend spoke to me on the subject only because he thought, as I was in your office, you might like to know of the existence of this letter before a communication was made to the Deputy Public Prosecutor."

"Who has the original?" asked Mr. Joyce sharply.

Ong Chi Seng made no sign that he perceived in this question and its manner a change of attitude.

"You will remember, sir, no doubt, that after the death of Mr. Hammond it was discovered that he had had relations with a Chinese woman. The letter is at present in her possession."

That was one of the things which had turned public opinion most vehemently against Hammond. It came to be known that for several months he had had a Chinese woman living in his house.

For a moment neither of them spoke. Indeed everything had been said and each understood the other perfectly.

"I'm obliged to you, Chi Seng. I will give the matter my consideration."

"Very good, sir. Do you wish me to make a communication to that effect to my friend?"

"I daresay it would be as well if you kept in touch with him," Mr. Joyce answered with gravity.

"Yes, sir."

The clerk noiselessly left the room, shutting the door again with deliberation, and left Mr. Joyce to his reflections. He stared at the copy, in its neat, impersonal writing, of Leslie's letter. Vague suspicions troubled him. They were so disconcerting that he made an effort to put them out of his mind. There must be a simple explanation of the letter, and Leslie without doubt could give it at once, but, by heaven, an explanation was needed. He rose from his chair, put the letter in his pocket, and took his topee. When he went out Ong Chi Seng was busily writing at his desk.

"I'm going out for a few minutes, Chi Seng," he said.

"Mr. George Reed is coming by appointment at twelve o'clock, sir. Where shall I say you've gone?"

Mr. Joyce gave him a thin smile.

"You can say that you haven't the least idea."

But he knew perfectly well that Ong Chi Seng was aware that he was going to the gaol. Though the crime had been committed in Belanda and the trial was to take place at Belanda Bharu, since there was in the gaol no convenience for the detention of a white woman Mrs. Crosbie had been brought to Singapore.

When she was led into the room in which he waited she held out her thin, distinguished hand, and gave him a pleasant smile. She was, as ever, neatly and simply dressed, and her abundant, pale hair was arranged with care.

"I wasn't expecting to see you this morning," she said, graciously.

She might have been in her own house, and Mr. Joyce almost expected to hear her call the boy and tell him to bring the visitor a gin pahit.

"How are you?" he asked.

"I'm in the best of health, thank you." A flicker of

amusement flashed across her eyes. "This is a wonderful place for a rest cure."

The attendant withdrew and they were left alone.

"Do sit down," said Leslie.

He took a chair. He did not quite know how to begin. She was so cool that it seemed almost impossible to say to her the thing he had come to say. Though she was not pretty there was something agreeable in her appearance. She had elegance, but it was the elegance of good breeding in which there was nothing of the artifice of society. You had only to look at her to know what sort of people she had and what kind of surroundings she had lived in. Her fragility gave her a singular refinement. It was impossible to associate her with the vaguest idea of grossness.

"I'm looking forward to seeing Robert this afternoon," she said, in her good-humoured, easy voice. (It was a pleasure to hear her speak, her voice and her accent were so distinctive of her class.) "Poor dear, it's been a great trial to his nerves. I'm thankful it'll all be over in a few days."

"It's only five days now."

"I know. Each morning when I awake I say to myself, 'one less.'" She smiled then. "Just as I used to do at school and the holidays were coming."

"By the way, am I right in thinking that you had no communication whatever with Hammond for several weeks before the catastrophe?"

"I'm quite positive of that. The last time we met was

at a tennis-party at the MacFarrens. I don't think I said more than two words to him. They have two courts, you know, and we didn't happen to be in the same sets."

"And you haven't written to him?"

"Oh, no."

"Are you quite sure of that?"

"Oh, quite," she answered, with a little smile. "There was nothing I should write to him for except to ask him to dine or to play tennis, and I hadn't done either for months."

"At one time you'd been on fairly intimate terms with him. How did it happen that you had stopped asking him to anything?"

Mrs. Crosbie shrugged her thin shoulders.

"One gets tired of people. We hadn't anything very much in common. Of course, when he was ill Robert and I did everything we could for him, but the last year or two he'd been quite well, and he was very popular. He had a good many calls on his time, and there didn't seem to be any need to shower invitations upon him."

"Are you quite certain that was all?"

Mrs. Crosbie hesitated for a moment.

"Well, I may just as well tell you. It had come to our ears that he was living with a Chinese woman, and Robert said he wouldn't have him in the house. I had seen her myself."

Mr. Joyce was sitting in a straight-backed armchair, resting his chin on his hand, and his eyes were fixed on Leslie. Was it his fancy that, as she made this remark, her black pupils were filled on a sudden, for the fraction of a second, with a dull red light? The effect was startling. Mr. Joyce shifted in his chair. He placed the tips of his ten fingers together. He spoke very slowly, choosing his words.

"I think I should tell you that there is in existence a letter in your handwriting to Geoff. Hammond."

He watched her closely. She made no movement, nor did her face change colour, but she took a noticeable time to reply.

"In the past I've often sent him little notes to ask him to something or other, or to get me something when I knew he was going to Singapore."

"This letter asks him to come and see you because Robert was going to Singapore."

"That's impossible. I never did anything of the kind."

"You'd better read it for yourself."

He took it out of his pocket and handed it to her. She gave it a glance and with a smile of scorn handed it back to him.

"That's not my handwriting."

"I know, it's said to be an exact copy of the original."

She read the words now, and as she read a horrible change came over her. Her colourless face grew dreadful to look at. It turned green. The flesh seemed on a sudden to fall away and her skin was tightly stretched over the bones. Her lips receded, showing her teeth, so that she had the appearance of making a grimace. She stared at Mr. Joyce with eyes that started from their sockets. He was looking now at a gibbering death's head.

"What does it mean?" she whispered.

Her mouth was so dry that she could utter no more than a hoarse sound. It was no longer a human voice.

"That is for you to say," he answered.

"I didn't write it. I swear I didn't write it."

"Be very careful what you say. If the original is in your handwriting it would be useless to deny it."

"It would be a forgery."

"It would be difficult to prove that. It would be easy to prove that it was genuine."

A shiver passed through her lean body. But great beads of sweat stood on her forehead. She took a handkerchief from her bag and wiped the palms of her hands. She glanced at the letter again and gave Mr. Joyce a sidelong look.

"It's not dated. If I had written it and forgotten all about it, it might have been written years ago. If you'll give me time, I'll try and remember the circumstances."

"I noticed there was no date. If this letter were in the hands of the prosecution they would cross-examine the boys. They would soon find out whether someone took a letter to Hammond on the day of his death."

Mrs. Crosbie clasped her hands violently and swayed in her chair so that he thought she would faint.

"I swear to you that I didn't write that letter."

Mr. Joyce was silent for a little while. He took his eyes from her distraught face, and looked down on the floor. He was reflecting.

"In these circumstances we need not go into the matter further," he said slowly, at last breaking the silence. "If the possessor of this letter sees fit to place it in the hands of the prosecution you will be prepared."

His words suggested that he had nothing more to say to her, but he made no movement of departure. He waited. To himself he seemed to wait a very long time. He did not look at Leslie, but he was conscious that she sat very still. She made no sound. At last it was he who spoke.

"If you have nothing more to say to me I think I'll be getting back to my office."

"What would anyone who read the letter be inclined to think that it meant?" she asked then.

"He'd know that you had told a deliberate lie," answered Mr. Joyce sharply.

"When?"

"You have stated definitely that you had had no communication with Hammond for at least three months."

"The whole thing has been a terrible shock to me. The events of that dreadful night have been a nightmare. It's not very strange if one detail has escaped my memory."

"It would be unfortunate when your memory has reproduced so exactly every particular of your interview with Hammond, that you should have forgotten so important a point as that he came to see you in the bungalow on the night of his death at your express desire."

"I hadn't forgotten. After what happened I was afraid to mention it. I thought you'd none of you believe my story if I admitted that he'd come at my invitation. I daresay it was stupid of me; but I lost my head, and after I'd said once that I'd had no communication with Hammond I was obliged to stick to it."

By now Leslie had recovered her admirable composure, and she met Mr. Joyce's appraising glance with candour. Her gentleness was very disarming.

"You will be required to explain, then, *why* you asked Hammond to come and see you when Robert was away for the night."

She turned her eyes full on the lawyer. He had been mistaken in thinking them insignificant, they were rather fine eyes, and unless he was mistaken they were bright now with tears. Her voice had a little break in it.

"It was a surprise I was preparing for Robert. His birthday is next month. I knew he wanted a new gun and you know I'm dreadfully stupid about sporting things. I wanted to talk to Geoff. about it. I thought I'd get him to order it for me."

"Perhaps the terms of the letter are not very clear to your recollection. Will you have another look at it?"

"No, I don't want to," she said quickly.

"Does it seem to you the sort of letter a woman would write to a somewhat distant acquaintance because she wanted to consult him about buying a gun?"

"I daresay it's rather extravagant and emotional. I do express myself like that, you know. I'm quite prepared to admit it's very silly." She smiled. "And after all, Geoff. Hammond wasn't quite a distant acquaintance. When he was ill I'd nursed him like a mother. I asked him to come when Robert was away, because Robert wouldn't have him in the house."

Mr. Joyce was tired of sitting so long in the same position. He rose and walked once or twice up and down the room, choosing the words he proposed to say; then he leaned over the back of the chair in which he had been sitting. He spoke slowly in a tone of deep gravity.

"Mrs. Crosbie, I want to talk to you very, very seriously. This case was comparatively plain sailing. There was only one point which seemed to me to require explanation: as far as I could judge, you had fired no less than four shots into Hammond when he was lying on the ground. It was hard to accept the possibility that a delicate, frightened, and habitually self-controlled woman, of gentle nature and refined instincts, should have surrendered to an absolutely uncontrolled frenzy. But of course it was admissible. Although Geoffrey Hammond was much liked and on the whole thought highly of, I was prepared to prove that he was the sort of man who might be guilty of the crime which in justification of your act you accused him of. The fact, which was discovered after his death, that he had been living with a Chinese woman gave us something very definite to go upon. That robbed him of any sympathy which might have been felt for him. We made up our minds to make use of the odium which such a connection cast upon him in the minds of all respectable people. I told your husband this morning that I was certain of an acquittal, and I wasn't just telling him that to give him heart. I do not believe the assessors would have left the court."

They looked into one another's eyes. Mrs. Crosbie was strangely still. She was like a little bird paralysed by the fascination of a snake. He went on in the same quiet tones.

"But this letter has thrown an entirely different complexion on the case. I am your legal adviser, I shall represent you in court. I take your story as you tell it me, and I shall conduct your defence according to its terms. It may be that I believe your statements, and it may be that I doubt them. The duty of counsel is to persuade the Court that the evidence placed before it is not such as to justify it in bringing in a verdict of guilty, and any private opinion he may have of the guilt or innocence of his client is entirely beside the point."

He was astonished to see in Leslie's eyes the flicker of a smile. Piqued, he went on somewhat dryly.

"You're not going to deny that Hammond came to your house at your urgent, and I may even say, hysterical invitation?"

Mrs. Crosbie, hesitating for an instant, seemed to consider.

"They can prove that the letter was taken to his bungalow by one of the house-boys. He rode over on his bicycle."

"You mustn't expect other people to be stupider than you. The letter will put them on the track of suspicions which have entered nobody's head. I will not tell you what I personally thought when I saw the copy. I do not wish you to tell me anything but what is needed to save your neck."

Mrs. Crosbie gave a shrill cry. She sprang to her feet, white with terror.

"You don't think they'd hang me?"

"If they came to the conclusion that you hadn't killed Hammond in self-defence, it would be the duty of the assessors to bring in a verdict of guilty. The charge is murder. It would be the duty of the judge to sentence you to death."

"But what can they prove?" she gasped.

"I don't know what they can prove. You know. I don't want to know. But if their suspicions are aroused, if they begin to make inquiries, if the natives are questioned—what is it that can be discovered?"

She crumpled up suddenly. She fell on the floor before he could catch her. She had fainted. He looked round the room for water, but there was none there, and he did not want to be disturbed. He stretched her out on the floor, and kneeling beside her waited for her to recover. When she opened her eyes he was disconcerted by the ghastly fear that he saw in them.

"Keep quite still," he said. "You'll be better in a moment."

"You won't let them hang me," she whispered.

She began to cry, hysterically, while in undertones he sought to quieten her.

"For goodness sake pull yourself together," he said.

"Give me a minute."

Her courage was amazing. He could see the effort she made to regain her self-control, and soon she was once more calm.

"Let me get up now."

He gave her his hand and helped her to her feet. Taking her arm, he led her to the chair. She sat down wearily.

"Don't talk to me for a minute or two," she said.

"Very well."

When at last she spoke it was to say something which he did not expect. She gave a little sigh.

"I'm afraid I've made rather a mess of things," she said.

He did not answer, and once more there was a silence.

"Isn't it possible to get hold of the letter?" she said at last.

"I do not think anything would have been said to me about it if the person in whose possession it is was not prepared to sell it."

"Who's got it?"

"The Chinese woman who was living in Hammond's house."

H

A spot of colour flickered for an instant on Leslie's cheek-bones.

"Does she want an awful lot for it?"

"I imagine that she has a very shrewd idea of its value. I doubt if it would be possible to get hold of it except for a very large sum."

"Are you going to let me be hanged?"

"Do you think it's so simple as all that to secure possession of an unwelcome piece of evidence? It's no different from suborning a witness. You have no right to make any such suggestion to me."

"Then what is going to happen to me?"

"Justice must take its course."

She grew very pale. A little shudder passed through her body.

"I put myself in your hands. Of course I have no right to ask you to do anything that isn't proper."

Mr. Joyce had not bargained for the little break in her voice which her habitual self-restraint made quite intolerably moving. She looked at him with humble eyes, and he thought that if he rejected their appeal they would haunt him for the rest of his life. After all, nothing could bring poor Hammond back to life again. He wondered what really was the explanation of that letter. It was not fair to conclude from it that she had killed Hammond without provocation. He had lived in the East a long time and his sense of professional honour was not perhaps so acute as it had been twenty years before. He stared at the floor. He made up his mind to do something which he knew was unjustifiable, but it stuck in his throat and he felt dully resentful towards Leslie. It embarrassed him a little to speak.

"I don't know exactly what your husband's circumstances are?"

Flushing a rosy red, she shot a swift glance at him.

"He has a good many tin shares and a small share in two or three rubber estates. I suppose he could raise money."

"He would have to be told what it was for."

She was silent for a moment. She seemed to think.

"He's in love with me still. He would make any sacrifice to save me. Is there any need for him to see the letter?"

Mr. Joyce frowned a little, and, quick to notice, she went on:

"Robert is an old friend of yours. I'm not asking you to do anything for me, I'm asking you to save a rather simple, kind man who never did you any harm from all the pain that's possible."

Mr. Joyce did not reply. He rose to go and Mrs. Crosbie, with the grace that was natural to her, held out her hand. She was shaken by the scene, and her look was haggard, but she made a brave attempt to speed him with courtesy.

"It's so good of you to take all this trouble for me. I can't begin to tell you how grateful I am."

Mr. Joyce returned to his office. He sat in his own room, quite still, attempting to do no work, and pondered. His imagination brought him many strange ideas. He shuddered a little. At last there was the discreet knock on the door which he was expecting. Ong Chi Seng came in.

"I was just going out to have my tiffin, sir," he said.

"All right."

"I didn't know if there was anything you wanted before I went, sir."

"I don't think so. Did you make another appointment for Mr. Reed?"

"Yes, sir. He will come at three o'clock."

"Good."

Ong Chi Seng turned away, walked to the door, and put his long slim fingers on the handle. Then, as though on an afterthought, he turned back.

"Is there anything you wish me to say to my friend, sir?"

Although Ong Chi Seng spoke English so admirably he had still a difficulty with the letter R, and he pronounced it 'fliend.'

"What friend?"

"About the letter Mrs. Crosbie wrote to Hammond deceased, sir."

"Oh! I'd forgotten about that. I mentioned it to Mrs. Crosbie and she denies having written anything of the sort. It's evidently a forgery."

Mr. Joyce took the copy from his pocket and handed it to Ong Chi Seng. Ong Chi Seng ignored the gesture.

"In that case, sir, I suppose there would be no

objection if my fliend delivered the letter to the Deputy Public Prosecutor."

"None. But I don't quite see what good that would do your friend."

"My fliend, sir, thought it was his duty in the interests of justice."

"I am the last man in the world to interfere with anyone who wishes to do his duty, Chi Seng."

The eyes of the lawyer and of the Chinese clerk met. Not the shadow of a smile hovered on the lips of either, but they understood each other perfectly.

"I quite understand, sir," said Ong Chi Seng, "but from my study of the case R. *v.* Crosbie I am of opinion that the production of such a letter would be damaging to our client."

"I have always had a very high opinion of your legal acumen, Chi Seng."

"It has occurred to me, sir, that if I could persuade my fliend to induce the Chinese woman who has the letter to deliver it into our hands it would save a great deal of trouble."

Mr. Joyce idly drew faces on his blotting-paper.

"I suppose your friend is a business man. In what circumstances do you think he would be induced to part with the letter?"

"He has not got the letter. The Chinese woman has the letter. He is only a relation of the Chinese woman. She is an ignorant woman; she did not know the value of that letter till my fliend told her."

"What value did he put on it?"

"Ten thousand dollars, sir."

"Good God! Where on earth do you suppose Mrs. Crosbie can get ten thousand dollars! I tell you the letter's a forgery."

He looked up at Ong Chi Seng as he spoke. The clerk was unmoved by the outburst. He stood at the side of the desk, civil, cool and observant.

"Mr. Crosbie owns an eighth share of the Betong Rubber Estate and a sixth share of the Selantan River Rubber Estate. I have a fliend who will lend him the money on the security of his property."

"You have a large circle of acquaintances, Chi Seng."

"Yes, sir."

"Well, you can tell them all to go to hell. I would never advise Mr. Crosbie to give a penny more than five thousand for a letter that can be very easily explained."

"The Chinese woman does not want to sell the letter, sir. My fliend took a long time to persuade her. It is useless to offer her less than the sum mentioned."

Mr. Joyce looked at Ong Chi Seng for at least three minutes. The clerk bore the searching scrutiny without embarrassment. He stood in a respectful attitude with downcast eyes. Mr. Joyce knew his man. Clever fellow, Chi Seng, he thought, I wonder how much he's going to get out of it.

"Ten thousand dollars is a very large sum."

"Mr. Crosbie will certainly pay it rather than see his wife hanged, sir."

Again Mr. Joyce paused. What more did Chi Seng know than he had said? He must be pretty sure of his ground if he was obviously so unwilling to bargain. That sum had been fixed because whoever it was that was managing the affair knew it was the largest amount that Robert Crosbie could raise.

"Where is the Chinese woman now?" asked Mr. Joyce.

"She is staying at the house of my fliend, sir."

"Will she come here?"

"I think it more better if you go to her, sir. I can take you to the house to-night and she will give you the letter. She is a very ignorant woman, sir, and she does not understand cheques."

"I wasn't thinking of giving her a cheque. I will bring banknotes with me."

"It would only be waste of valuable time to bring less than ten thousand dollars, sir."

"I quite understand."

"I will go and tell my fliend after I have had my tiffin, sir."

"Very good. You'd better meet me outside the club at ten o'clock to-night."

"With pleasure, sir," said Ong Chi Seng.

He gave Mr. Joyce a little bow and left the room. Mr. Joyce went out to have luncheon, too. He went to the club and here, as he had expected, he saw Robert Crosbie. He was sitting at a crowded table, and as he passed him, looking for a place, Mr. Joyce touched him on the shoulder.

"I'd like a word or two with you before you go," he said.

"Right you are. Let me know when you're ready."

Mr. Joyce had made up his mind how to tackle him. He played a rubber of bridge after luncheon in order to allow time for the club to empty itself. He did not want on this particular matter to see Crosbie in his office. Presently Crosbie came into the card-room and looked on till the game was finished. The other players went on their various affairs, and the two were left alone.

"A rather unfortunate thing has happened, old man," said Mr. Joyce, in a tone which he sought to render as casual as possible. "It appears that your wife sent a letter to Hammond asking him to come to the bungalow on the night he was killed."

"But that's impossible," cried Crosbie. "She's always stated that she had had no communication with Hammond. I know from my own knowledge that she hadn't set eyes on him for a couple of months."

"The fact remains that the letter exists. It's in the possession of the Chinese woman Hammond was living with. Your wife meant to give you a present on your birthday, and she wanted Hammond to help her to get it. In the emotional excitement that she suffered from after the tragedy, she forgot all about it, and having once denied having any communication with Hammond she was afraid to say that she had made a mistake. It was, of course, very unfortunate, but I daresay it was not unnatural."

Crosbie did not speak. His large, red face bore an expression of complete bewilderment, and Mr. Joyce was at once relieved and exasperated by his lack of comprehension. He was a stupid man, and Mr. Joyce had no patience with stupidity. But his distress since the catastrophe had touched a soft spot in the lawyer's heart; and Mrs. Crosbie had struck the right note when she asked him to help her, not for her sake, but for her husband's.

"I need not tell you that it would be very awkward if this letter found its way into the hands of the prosecution. Your wife has lied, and she would be asked to explain the lie. It alters things a little if Hammond did not intrude, an unwanted guest, but came to your house by invitation. It would be easy to arouse in the assessors a certain indecision of mind."

Mr. Joyce hesitated. He was face to face now with his decision. If it had been a time for humour, he could have smiled at the reflection that he was taking so grave a step, and that the man for whom he was taking it had not the smallest conception of its gravity. If he gave the matter a thought, he probably imagined that what Mr. Joyce was doing was what any lawyer did in the ordinary run of business.

"My dear Robert, you are not only my client, but my friend. I think we must get hold of that letter. It'll cost a good deal of money. Except for that I should have preferred to say nothing to you about it."

"How much?"

H*

"Ten thousand dollars."

"That's a devil of a lot. With the slump and one thing and another it'll take just about all I've got."

"Can you get it at once?"

"I suppose so. Old Charlie Meadows will let me have it on my tin shares and on those two estates I'm interested in."

"Then will you?"

"Is it absolutely necessary?"

"If you want your wife to be acquitted."

Crosbie grew very red. His mouth sagged strangely.

"But . . ." he could not find words, his face now was purple. "But I don't understand. She can explain. You don't mean to say they'd find her guilty? They couldn't hang her for putting a noxious vermin out of the way."

"Of course they wouldn't hang her. They might only find her guilty of manslaughter. She'd probably get off with two or three years."

Crosbie started to his feet and his face was distraught with horror.

"Three years!"

Then something seemed to dawn in that slow intelligence of his. His mind was darkness across which shot suddenly a flash of lightning, and though the succeeding darkness was as profound, there remained the memory of something not seen but perhaps just descried. Mr. Joyce saw that Crosbie's big red hands, coarse and hard with all the odd jobs he had set them to, trembled.

"What was the present she wanted to make me?"

"She says she wanted to give you a new gun."

Once more that great red face flushed a deeper red.

"When have you got to have the money ready?"

There was something odd in his voice now. It sounded as though he spoke with invisible hands clutching at his throat.

"At ten o'clock to-night. I thought you could bring it to my office at about six."

"Is the woman coming to you?"

"No, I'm going to her."

"I'll bring the money. I'll come with you."

Mr. Joyce looked at him sharply.

"Do you think there's any need for you to do that? I think it would be better if you left me to deal with this matter by myself."

"It's my money, isn't it? I'm going to come."

Mr. Joyce shrugged his shoulders. They rose and shook hands. Mr. Joyce looked at him curiously.

At ten o'clock they met in the empty club.

"Everything all right?" asked Mr. Joyce.

"Yes. I've got the money in my pocket."

"Let's go then."

They walked down the steps. Mr. Joyce's car was waiting for them in the square, silent at that hour, and as they came to it Ong Chi Seng stepped out of the shadow of a house. He took his seat beside the driver and gave him a direction. They drove past the Hôtel de l'Europe and turned up by the Sailors' Home to get into Victoria Street. Here the Chinese shops were still open, idlers lounged about, and in the roadway rickshaws and motor cars and gharries gave a busy air to the scene. Suddenly their car stopped and Chi Seng turned round.

"I think it more better if we walk here, sir," he said.

They got out and he went on. They followed a step or two behind. Then he asked them to stop.

"You wait here, sir. I go in and speak to my fliend."

He went into a shop, open to the street, where three or four Chinese were standing behind the counter. It was one of those strange shops where nothing was on view, and you wondered what it was they sold there. They saw him address a stout man in a duck suit with a large gold chain across his breast, and the man shot a quick glance out into the night. He gave Chi Seng a key and Chi Seng came out. He beckoned to the two men waiting and slid into a doorway at the side of the shop. They followed him and found themselves at the foot of a flight of stairs.

"If you wait a minute I will light a match," he said, always resourceful. "You come upstairs, please."

He held a Japanese match in front of them, but it scarcely dispelled the darkness and they groped their way up behind him. On the first floor he unlocked a door and going in lit a gas-jet.

"Come in, please," he said.

It was a small square room, with one window, and the only furniture consisted of two low Chinese beds covered with matting. In one corner was a large chest, with an elaborate lock, and on this stood a shabby tray with an opium pipe on it and a lamp. There was in the room the faint, acrid scent of the drug. They sat down and Ong Chi Seng offered them cigarettes. In a moment the door was opened by the fat Chinaman whom they had seen behind the counter. He bade them good-evening in very good English, and sat down by the side of his fellow-countryman.

"The Chinese woman is just coming," said Chi Seng.

A boy from the shop brought in a tray with a teapot and cups and the Chinaman offered them a cup of tea. Crosbie refused. The Chinese talked to one another in undertones, but Crosbie and Mr. Joyce were silent. At last there was the sound of a voice outside; someone was calling in a low tone; and the Chinaman went to the door. He opened it, spoke a few words, and ushered a woman in. Mr. Joyce looked at her. He had heard much about her since Hammond's death, but he had never seen her. She was a stoutish person, not very young, with a broad, phlegmatic face, she was powdered and rouged and her eyebrows were a thin black line, but she gave you the impression of a woman of character. She wore a pale blue jacket and a white skirt, her costume was not quite European nor quite Chinese, but on her feet were little Chinese silk slippers. She wore heavy gold chains round her neck, gold bangles on her wrists, gold ear-rings and elaborate gold pins in her black hair. She walked in slowly, with the air of a woman sure of herself, but with a certain heaviness of tread, and sat down on the bed beside Ong Chi Seng. He said something to her and nodding she gave an incurious glance at the two white men.

"Has she got the letter?" asked Mr. Joyce.

"Yes, sir."

Crosbie said nothing, but produced a roll of five hundred-dollar notes. He counted out twenty and handed them to Chi Seng.

"Will you see if that is correct?"

The clerk counted them and gave them to the fat Chinaman.

"Quite correct, sir."

The Chinaman counted them once more and put them in his pocket. He spoke again to the woman and she drew from her bosom a letter. She gave it to Chi Seng, who cast his eyes over it.

"This is the right document, sir," he said, and was about to give it to Mr. Joyce when Crosbie took it from him.

"Let me look at it," he said.

Mr. Joyce watched him read and then held out his hand for it.

"You'd better let me have it."

Crosbie folded it up deliberately and put it in his pocket.

"No, I'm going to keep it myself. It's cost me enough money."

Mr. Joyce made no rejoinder. The three Chinese

watched the little passage, but what they thought about it, or whether they thought, it was impossible to tell from their impassive countenances. Mr. Joyce rose to his feet.

"Do you want me any more to-night, sir?" said Ong Chi Seng.

"No." He knew that the clerk wished to stay behind in order to get his agreed share of the money, and he turned to Crosbie. "Are you ready?"

Crosbie did not answer, but stood up. The Chinaman went to the door and opened it for them. Chi Seng found a bit of candle and lit it in order to light them down, and the two Chinese accompanied them to the street. They left the woman sitting quietly on the bed smoking a cigarette. When they reached the street the Chinese left them and went once more upstairs.

"What are you going to do with that letter?" asked Mr. Joyce.

"Keep it."

They walked to where the car was waiting for them and here Mr. Joyce offered his friend a lift. Crosbie shook his head.

"I'm going to walk." He hesitated a little and shuffled his feet. "I went to Singapore on the night of Hammond's death partly to buy a new gun that a man I knew wanted to dispose of. Good-night."

He disappeared quickly into the darkness.

Mr. Joyce was quite right about the trial. The assessors went into court fully determined to acquit

Mrs. Crosbie. She gave evidence on her own behalf. She told her story simply and with straightforwardness. The D.P.P. was a kindly man and it was plain that he took no great pleasure in his task. He asked the necessary questions in a deprecating manner. His speech for the prosecution might really have been a speech for the defence, and the assessors took less than five minutes to consider their popular verdict. It was impossible to prevent the great outburst of applause with which it was received by the crowd that packed the court-house. The judge congratulated Mrs. Crosbie and she was a free woman.

No one had expressed a more violent disapprobation of Hammond's behaviour than Mrs. Joyce; she was a woman loyal to her friends and she had insisted on the Crosbies staying with her after the trial—for she in common with everyone else had no doubt of the result—till they could make arrangements to go away. It was out of the question for poor, dear, brave Leslie to return to the bungalow at which the horrible catastrophe had taken place. The trial was over by half-past twelve and when they reached the Joyces' house a grand luncheon was awaiting them. Cocktails were ready, Mrs. Joyce's million-dollar cocktail was celebrated through all the Malay States, and Mrs. Joyce drank Leslie's health. She was a talkative, vivacious woman, and now she was in the highest spirits. It was fortunate, for the rest of them were silent. She did not wonder, her husband never had much to say, and the other two were naturally exhausted from the long strain to which they had been subjected. During luncheon she carried on a bright and spirited monologue. Then coffee was served.

"Now, children," she said in her gay, bustling fashion, "you must have a rest and after tea I shall take you both for a drive to the sea."

Mr. Joyce, who lunched at home only by exception, had of course to go back to his office.

"I'm afraid I can't do that, Mrs. Joyce," said Crosbie. "I've got to get back to the estate at once."

"Not to-day?" she cried.

"Yes, now. I've neglected it for too long and I have urgent business. But I shall be very grateful if you will keep Leslie until we have decided what to do."

Mrs. Joyce was about to expostulate, but her husband prevented her.

"If he must go, he must, and there's an end of it."

There was something in the lawyer's tone which made her look at him quickly. She held her tongue and there was a moment's silence. Then Crosbie spoke again.

"If you'll forgive me, I'll start at once so that I can get there before dark." He rose from the table. "Will you come and see me off, Leslie?"

"Of course."

They went out of the dining-room together.

"I think that's rather inconsiderate of him," said Mrs. Joyce. "He must know that Leslie wants to be with him just now."

"I'm sure he wouldn't go if it wasn't absolutely necessary."

"Well, I'll just see that Leslie's room is ready for her. She wants a complete rest, of course, and then amusement."

Mrs. Joyce left the room and Joyce sat down again. In a short time he heard Crosbie start the engine of his motor-cycle and then noisily scrunch over the gravel of the garden path. He got up and went into the drawing-room. Mrs. Crosbie was standing in the middle of it, looking into space, and in her hand was an open letter. He recognised it. She gave him a glance as he came in and he saw that she was deathly pale.

"He knows," she whispered.

Mr. Joyce went up to her and took the letter from her hand. He lit a match and set the paper afire. She watched it burn. When he could hold it no longer he dropped it on the tiled floor and they both looked at the paper curl and blacken. Then he trod it into ashes with his foot.

"What does he know?"

She gave him a long, long stare and into her eyes came a strange look. Was it contempt or despair? Mr. Joyce could not tell.

"He knows that Geoff. was my lover."

Mr. Joyce made no movement and uttered no sound.

"He'd been my lover for years. He became my lover almost immediately after he came back from the war. We knew how careful we must be. When we became lovers I pretended I was tired of him, and he seldom came to the house when Robert was there. I used to drive out to a place we knew and he met me, two or three times a week, and when Robert went to Singapore he used to come to the bungalow late, when the boys had gone for the night. We saw one another constantly, all the time, and not a soul had the smallest suspicion of it. And then lately, a year ago, he began to change. I didn't know what was the matter. I couldn't believe that he didn't care for me any more. He always denied it. I was frantic. I made him scenes. Sometimes I thought he hated me. Oh, if you knew what agonies I endured. I passed through hell. I knew he didn't want me any more and I wouldn't let him go. Misery! Misery! I loved him. I'd given him everything. He was all my life. And then I heard he was living with a Chinese woman. I couldn't believe it. I wouldn't believe it. At last I saw her, I saw her with my own eyes, walking in the village, with her gold bracelets and her necklaces, an old, fat, Chinese woman. She was older than I was. Horrible! They all knew in the kampong that she was his mistress. And when I passed her, she looked at me and I knew that she knew I was his mistress too. I sent for him. I told him I must see him. You've read the letter. I was mad to write it. I didn't know what I was doing. I didn't care. I hadn't seen him for ten days. It was a lifetime. And when last we'd parted he took me in his arms and kissed me, and told me not to worry. And he went straight from my arms to hers."

She had been speaking in a low voice, vehemently, and now she stopped and wrung her hands.

"That damned letter. We'd always been so careful. He always tore up any word I wrote to him the moment he'd read it. How was I to know he'd leave that one? He came, and I told him I knew about the Chinawoman. He denied it. He said it was only scandal. I was beside myself. I don't know what I said to him. Oh, I hated him then. I tore him limb from limb. I said everything I could to wound him. I insulted him. I could have spat in his face. And at last he turned on me. He told me he was sick and tired of me and never wanted to see me again. He said I bored him to death. And then he acknowledged that it was true about the Chinawoman. He said he'd known her for years, before the war, and she was the only woman who really meant anything to him, and the rest just pastime. And he said he was glad I knew, and now at last I'd leave him alone. And then I don't know what happened, I was beside myself, I saw red. I seized the revolver and I fired. He gave a cry and I saw I'd hit him. He staggered and rushed for the verandah. I ran after him and fired again. He fell, and then I stood over him and I fired and fired till the revolver went click, click, and I knew there were no more cartridges."

At last she stopped, panting. Her face was no longer human, it was distorted with cruelty, and rage and pain. You would never have thought that this quiet, refined woman was capable of such fiendish passion. Mr. Joyce took a step backwards. He was absolutely aghast at the sight of her. It was not a face, it was a gibbering, hideous mask. Then they heard a voice calling from another room, a loud, friendly, cheerful voice. It was Mrs. Joyce.

"Come along, Leslie darling, your room's ready. You must be dropping with sleep."

Mrs. Crosbie's features gradually composed themselves. Those passions, so clearly delineated, were smoothed away as with your hand you would smooth a crumpled paper, and in a minute the face was cool and calm and unlined. She was a trifle pale, but her lips broke into a pleasant, affable smile. She was once more the well-bred and even distinguished woman.

"I'm coming, Dorothy dear. I'm sorry to give you so much trouble."

THE ALIEN CORN

I HAD known the Blands a long time before I discovered that they had any connection with Ferdy Rabenstein. Ferdy must have been nearly fifty when I first knew him and at the time of which I write he was well over seventy. He had altered little. His hair, coarse but abundant and curly, was white, but he had kept his figure and held himself as gallantly as ever. It was not hard to believe that in youth he had been as beautiful as people said. He had still his fine Semitic profile and the lustrous black eyes that had caused havoc in so many a Gentile breast. He was very tall, lean, with an oval face and a clear skin. He wore his clothes very well and in evening dress, even now, he was one of the handsomest men I had ever seen. He wore then large black pearls in his shirt-front and platinum and sapphire rings on his fingers. Perhaps he was rather flashy, but you felt it was so much in character that it would have ill become him to be anything else.

"After all, I am an Oriental," he said. "I can carry a certain barbaric magnificence."

I have often thought that Ferdy Rabenstein would make an admirable subject for a biography. He was not a great man, but within the limits he set himself he made of his life a work of art. It was a masterpiece in little, like a Persian miniature, and derived its interest from its perfection. Unfortunately the materials are scanty. They would consist of letters that may very well have been destroyed and the recollections of people who are old now and will soon be dead. His memory is extraordinary, but he would never write his memoirs, for he looks upon his past as a source of purely private entertainment; and he is a man of the most perfect discretion. Nor do I know anyone who could do justice to the subject but Max Beerbohm. There is no one else in this hard world of to-day who can look upon the trivial with such tender sympathy and wring such a delicate pathos from futility. I wonder that Max who must have known Ferdy much better than I, and long before, was never tempted to exercise his exquisite fancy on such a theme. He was born for Max to write about. And who should have illustrated the elegant book that I see in my mind's eye but Aubrey Beardsley? Thus would have been erected a monument of triple brass and the ephemera imprisoned to succeeding ages in the amber's exquisite translucency.

Ferdy's conquests were social and his venue was the great world. He was born in South Africa and did not come to England till he was twenty. For some time he was on the Stock Exchange, but on the death of his father he inherited a considerable fortune, and retiring from business devoted himself to the life of a man about town. At that period English society was still a closed body and it was not easy for a Jew to force its barriers, but to Ferdy they fell like the walls of Jericho. He was handsome, he was rich, he was a sportsman and he was good company. He had a house in Curzon Street, furnished with the most beautiful French furniture, and a French chef, and a brougham. It would be interesting to know the first steps in his wonderful career: they are lost in the dark abysm of time. When I first met him he had been long established as one of the smartest men in London: this was at a very grand house in Norfolk to which I had been asked as a promising young novelist by the hostess who took an interest in letters, but the company was very distinguished and I was overawed. We were sixteen, and I felt shy and alone among these cabinet ministers, great ladies and peers of the realm who talked of people and things of which I knew nothing. They were civil to me, but indifferent, and I was conscious that I was somewhat of a burden to my hostess. Ferdy saved me. He sat with me, walked with me and talked with me. He discovered that I was a writer and we discussed the drama and the novel; he learnt that I had lived much on the continent and he talked to me pleasantly of France, Germany and Spain. He seemed really to seek my society. He gave me the flattering impression that he and I stood apart from the other members of the company and by our conversation upon affairs of the spirit made that of the rest of them, the political situation, the scandal of somebody's divorce and the growing disinclination of pheasants to be killed, seem a little ridiculous. But if Ferdy had at the bottom of his heart a feeling of ever so faint a contempt for the hearty British gentry that surrounded us I am sure that it was only to me that he allowed an inkling of it to appear, and looking back I cannot but wonder whether it was not after all a suave and very delicate compliment that he paid me. I think of course that he liked to exercise his charm and I dare say the obvious pleasure his conversation gave me gratified him, but he could have had no motive for taking so much trouble over an obscure novelist other than his real interest in art and letters. I felt that he and I at bottom were equally alien in that company, I because I was a writer and he because he was a Jew, but I envied the ease with which he bore himself. He was completely at home. Everyone called him Ferdy. He seemed to be always in good spirits. He was never at a loss for a quip, a jest or a repartee. They liked him in that house because he made them laugh, but never made them uncomfortable by talking above their heads. He brought a faint savour of Oriental romance into their lives, but so cleverly that they only felt more English. You could never be dull when he was by and with him present you were safe from the fear of the devastating silences that sometimes overwhelm a British company. A pause looked inevitable and Ferdy Rabenstein had broken into a topic that interested everyone. An invaluable asset to any party. He had an inexhaustible fund of Jewish stories. He was a very good mimic and he assumed the Yiddish accent and reproduced the Jewish gestures to perfection;

his head sank into his body, his face grew cunning, his voice oily, and he was a rabbi or an old clothes merchant or a smart commercial traveller or a fat procuress in Frankfort. It was as good as a play. Because he was himself a Jew and insisted on it you laughed without reserve, but for my own part not without an under-current of discomfort. I was not quite sure of a sense of humour that made such cruel fun of his own race. I discovered afterwards that Jewish stories were his speciality and I seldom met him anywhere without hearing him tell sooner or later the last he had heard.

But the best story he told me on this occasion was not a Jewish one. It struck me so that I have never forgotten it, but for one reason or another I have never had occasion to tell it again. I give it here because it is a curious little incident concerning persons whose names at least will live in the social history of the Victorian Era and I think it would be a pity if it were lost. He told me then that once when quite a young man he was staying in the country in a house where Mrs. Langtry, at that time at the height of her beauty and astounding reputation, was also a guest. It happened to be within driving distance of that in which lived the Duchess of Somerset, who had been Queen of Beauty at the Eglinton Tournament, and knowing her slightly, it occurred to him that it would be interesting to bring the two women together. He suggested it to Mrs. Langtry, who was willing, and forthwith wrote to the Duchess asking if he might bring the celebrated beauty

to call on her. It was fitting, he said, that the loveliest
woman of this generation (this was in the 'eighties)
should pay her respects to the loveliest woman of the
last. 'Bring her by all means,' answered the Duchess,
'but I warn you that it will be a shock to her.' They
drove over in a carriage and pair, Mrs. Langtry in a
close-fitting blue bonnet with long satin strings,
which showed the exquisite shape of her head and made
her blue eyes even bluer, and were received by a little
ugly old hag who looked with irony out of her beady
eyes at the radiant beauty who had come to see her.
They had tea, they talked and they drove home again.
Mrs. Langtry was very silent and when Ferdy looked at
her he saw that she was quietly weeping. When they
got back to the house she went to her room and would
not come down to dinner that night. For the first time
she had realised that beauty dies.

Ferdy asked me for my address and a few days after I
got back to London invited me to dinner. There were
only six of us, an American woman married to an
English peer, a Swedish painter, an actress and a well-
known critic. We ate very good food and drank excellent wine. The conversation was easy and intelligent.
After dinner Ferdy was persuaded to play the piano.
He only played Viennese waltzes, I discovered later
that they were his speciality, and the light, tuneful and
sensual music seemed to accord well with his discreet
flamboyance. He played without affectation, with a

lilt, and he had a graceful touch. This was the first of a
good many dinners I had with him, he would ask me
two or three times a year, and as time passed I met him
more and more frequently at other people's houses.
I rose in the world and perhaps he came down a little.
Of late years I had sometimes found him at parties where
other Jews were and I fancied that I read in his shining
liquid eyes, resting for a moment on these members of
his race, a certain good-natured amusement at the
thought of what the world was coming to. There were
people who said he was a snob, but I do not think he
was; it just happened that in his early days he had never
met any but the great. He had a real passion for art and
in his commerce with those that produced it was at his
best. With them he had never that faint air of persiflage
which when he was with very grand persons made you
suspect that he was never quite the dupe of their
grandeur. His taste was exquisite and many of his
friends were glad to avail themselves of his knowledge.
He was one of the first to value old furniture and he
rescued many an exquisite piece from the attics of
ancestral mansions and gave it an honourable place
in the drawing-room. It amused him to saunter round
the auction rooms and he was always willing to give his
advice to great ladies who desired at once to acquire a
beautiful thing and make a profitable investment. He
was rich and good-natured. He liked to patronise the
arts and would take a great deal of trouble to get
commissions for some young painter whose talent he

admired or an engagement to play at a rich man's house
for a violinist who could in no other way get a hearing.
But he never let his rich man down. His taste was too
good to deceive and civil though he might be to the
mediocre he would not lift a finger to help them. His
own musical parties, very small and carefully chosen,
were a treat.

He never married.

"I am a man of the world," he said, "and I flatter
myself that I have no prejudices, *tous les goûts sont dans
la nature*, but I do not think I could bring myself to
marry a Gentile. There's no harm in going to the opera
in a dinner jacket, but it just would never occur to me
to do so."

"Then why didn't you marry a Jewess?"

(I did not hear this conversation, but the lively and
audacious creature who thus tackled him told me of it.)

"Oh, my dear, our women are so prolific. I could not
bear the thought of peopling the world with a little Ikey
and a little Jacob and a little Rebecca and a little Leah
and a little Rachel."

But he had had affairs of note and the glamour of
past romance still clung to him. He was in his youth of
an amorous complexion. I have met old ladies who told
me that he was irresistible, and when in reminiscent mood
they talked to me of this woman and that who had
completely lost her head over him, I divined that, such
was his beauty, they could not find it in their hearts to
blame them. It was interesting to hear of great ladies

that I had read of in the memoirs of the day or had met
as respectable dowagers garrulous over their grandsons
at Eton or making a mess of a hand at bridge and be-
think myself that they had been consumed with sinful
passion for the handsome Jew. Ferdy's most notorious
amour was with the Duchess of Hereford, the loveliest,
the most gallant and dashing of the beauties of the end of
Queen Victoria's reign. It lasted for twenty years.
He had doubtless flirtations meanwhile, but their
relations were stable and recognised. It was proof
of his marvellous tact that when at last they ended he
exchanged an ageing mistress for a loyal friend. I
remember meeting the pair not so very long ago at
luncheon. She was an old woman, tall and of a commanding presence, but with a mask of paint on a
ravaged face. We were lunching at the Carlton and
Ferdy, our host, came a few minutes late. He offered us
a cocktail and the Duchess told him we had already had
one.

"Ah, I wondered why your eyes were so doubly
bright," he said.

The old raddled woman flushed with pleasure.

My youth passed, I grew middle-aged, I wondered
how soon I must begin to describe myself as elderly; I
wrote books and plays, I travelled, I underwent experiences, I fell in love and out of it; and still I kept
meeting Ferdy at parties. War broke out and was
waged, millions of men were killed and the face of the
world was changed. Ferdy did not like the war. He was

too old to take part in it, and his German name was
awkward, but he was discreet and took care not to
expose himself to humiliation. His old friends were
faithful to him and he lived in a dignified but not too
strict seclusion. But then peace came and with courage
he set himself to making the best of changed conditions.
Society was mixed now, parties were rowdy, but Ferdy
fitted himself to the new life. He still told his funny
Jewish stories, he still played charmingly the waltzes of
Strauss, he still went round auction rooms and told the
new rich what they ought to buy. I went to live abroad,
but whenever I was in London I saw Ferdy and now
there was something a little uncanny in him. He did not
give in. He had never known a day's illness. He seemed
never to grow tired. He still dressed beautifully. He was
interested in everybody. His mind was alert and people
asked him to dinner, not for old times' sake, but
because he was worth his salt. He still gave charming
little concerts at his house in Curzon Street.

It was when he invited me to one of these that I
made the discovery that started the recollections of him
I have here set down. We were dining at a house in
Hill Street, a large party, and the women having gone
upstairs Ferdy and I found ourselves side by side. He
told me that Lea Makart was coming to play for him
on the following Friday evening and he would be glad
if I would come.

"I'm awfully sorry," I said, "but I'm going down to
the Blands."

"What Blands?"

"They live in Sussex at a place called Tilby."

"I didn't know you knew them."

He looked at me rather strangely. He smiled. I didn't know what amused him.

"Oh, yes, I've known them for years. It's a very nice house to stay at."

"Adolph is my nephew."

"Sir Adolphus?"

"It suggests one of the bucks of the Regency, doesn't it? But I will not conceal from you that he was named Adolph."

"Everyone I know calls him Freddy."

"I know, and I understand that Miriam, his wife, only answers to the name of Muriel."

"How does he happen to be your nephew?"

"Because Hannah Rabenstein, my sister, married Alphonse Bleikogel, who ended life as Sir Alfred Bland, first Baronet, and Adolph, their only son, in due course became Sir Adolphus Bland, second Baronet."

"Then Freddy Bland's mother, the Lady Bland who lives in Portland Place, is your sister?"

"Yes, my sister Hannah. She was the eldest of the family. She's eighty, but in full possession of her faculties and a remarkable woman."

"I've never met her."

"I think your friends the Blands would just as soon you didn't. She has never lost her German accent."

"Do you never see them?" I asked.

"I haven't spoken to them for twenty years. I am such a Jew and they are so English." He smiled. "I could never remember that their names were Freddy and Muriel. I used to come out with an Adolph or a Miriam at awkward moments. And they didn't like my stories. It was better that we should not meet. When the war broke out and I would not change my name it was the last straw. It was too late, I could never have accustomed my friends to think of me as anything but Ferdy Rabenstein; I was quite content. I was not ambitious to be a Smith, a Brown or a Robinson."

Though he spoke facetiously, there was in his tone the faintest possible derision and I felt, hardly felt even, the sensation was so shadowy, that, as it had often vaguely seemed to me before, there was in the depth of his impenetrable heart a cynical contempt for the Gentiles he had conquered.

"Then you don't know the two boys?" I said.

"No."

"The eldest is called George, you know. I don't think he's so clever as Harry, the other one, but he's an engaging youth. I think you'd like him."

"Where is he now?"

"Well, he's just been sent down from Oxford. I suppose he's at home. Harry's still at Eton."

"Why don't you bring George to lunch with me?"

"I'll ask him. I should think he'd love to come."

I

"It has reached my ears that he's been a little trouble-some."

"Oh, I don't know. He wouldn't go into the army, which is what they wanted. They rather fancied the Guards. And so he went to Oxford instead. He didn't work and he spent a great deal of money and he painted the town red. It was all quite normal."

"What was he sent down for?"

"I don't know. Nothing of any consequence."

At that moment our host rose and we went upstairs. When Ferdy bade me good-night he asked me not to forget about his great-nephew.

"Ring me up," he said. "Wednesday would suit me. Or Friday."

Next day I went down to Tilby. It was an Eliza-bethan mansion standing in a spacious park, in which roamed fallow deer, and from its windows you had wide views of rolling downs. It seemed to me that as far as the eye could reach the land belonged to the Blands. His tenants must have found Sir Adolphus a wonderful landlord, for I never saw farms kept in such order, the barns and cow-sheds were spick and span and the pigsties were a picture; the public-houses looked like old English water-colours and the cottages he had built on the estate combined admirably picturesqueness and convenience. It must have cost him a pot of money to run the place on these lines. Fortunately he had it. The park with its grand old trees (and its nine-hole golf course) was tended like a garden, and the wide-stretch-ing gardens were the pride of the neighbourhood. The magnificent house, with its steep roofs and mullioned windows, had been restored by the most celebrated architect in England and furnished by Lady Bland, with taste and knowledge, in a style that perfectly fitted it.

"Of course it's very simple," she said. "Just an English house in the country."

The dining-room was adorned with old English sporting pictures and the Chippendale chairs were of incredible value. In the drawing-room were portraits by Reynolds and Gainsborough and landscapes by Old Crome and Richard Wilson. Even in my bedroom with its four-post bed were water-colours by Birket Foster. It was very beautiful and a treat to stay there, but though it would have distressed Muriel Bland beyond anything to know it, it missed oddly enough entirely the effect she had sought. It did not give you for a moment the impression of an English house. You had the feeling that every object had been bought with a careful eye to the general scheme. You missed the dull Academy portraits that hung in the dining-room beside a Carlo Dolci that an ancestor had brought back from the grand tour, and the water-colours painted by a great aunt that cluttered up the drawing-room so engagingly. There was no ugly Victorian sofa that had always been there and that it never occurred to anybody to take away and no needlework chairs that an unmarried daughter had so painstakingly worked at about the time of the Great

Exhibition. There was beauty but no sentiment.

And yet how comfortable it was and how well looked after you were! And what a cordial greeting the Blands gave you! They seemed really to like people. They were generous and kindly. They were never happier than when they were entertaining the county, and though they had not owned the property for more than twenty years they had established themselves firmly in the favour of their neighbours. Except perhaps in their splendour and the competent way in which the estate was run there was nothing to suggest that they had not been settled there for centuries.

Freddy had been at Eton and Oxford. He was now in the early fifties. He was quiet in manner, courtly, very clever, I imagine, but a trifle reserved. He had great elegance, but it was not an English elegance; he had grey hair and a short pointed grey beard, fine dark eyes and an aquiline nose. He was just above middle-height; I don't think you would have taken him for a Jew, but rather for a foreign diplomat of some distinction. He was a man of character, but gave you, strangely enough, notwithstanding the success he had had in life, an impression of faint melancholy. His successes had been financial and political; in the world of sport, for all his perseverance, he had never shone. For many years he had followed hounds, but he was a bad rider and I think it must have been a relief to him when he could persuade himself that middle-age and pressure of business forced him to give up hunting. He had excellent shooting and gave grand parties for it, but he was a poor shot; and despite the course in his park he never succeeded in being more than an indifferent golfer. He knew only too well how much these things meant in England and his incapacity was a bitter disappointment to him. However George would make up for it.

George was scratch at golf, and though tennis was not his game he played much better than the average; the Blands had had him taught to shoot as soon as he was old enough to hold a gun and he was a fine shot; they had put him on a pony when he was two and Freddy, watching him mount his horse, knew that out hunting when the boy came to a fence he felt exhilaration and not that sickening feeling in the pit of his stomach, which, though he had chased the fox with such grim determination, had always made the sport a torture to him. George was so tall and slim, his curly hair, of a palish brown, was so fine, his eyes were so blue, he was the perfect type of the young Englishman. He had the engaging candour of the breed. His nose was straight, though perhaps a trifle fleshy, and his lips were perhaps a little full and sensual, but he had beautiful teeth, and his smooth skin was like ivory. George was the apple of his father's eye. He did not like Harry, his second son, so well. He was rather stocky, broad-shouldered and strong for his age, but his black eyes, shining with cleverness, his coarse dark hair and his big nose revealed his race. Freddy was severe with him, and often impatient, but with George he was all indulgence. Harry would go into the business, he had brains and push, but George was the heir. George would be an English gentleman.

George had offered to motor me down in the roadster his father had given him as a birthday present. He drove very fast and we arrived before the rest of the guests. The Blands were sitting on the lawn and tea was laid out under a magnificent cedar.

"By the way," I said presently, "I saw Ferdy Rabenstein the other day and he wants me to bring George to lunch with him."

I had not mentioned the invitation to George on the way because I thought that if there had been a family coldness I had better address his parents as well.

"Who in God's name is Ferdy Rabenstein?" said George.

How brief is human glory! A generation back such a question would have seemed grotesque.

"He's by way of being your great-uncle," I replied.

A glance had passed from father to mother when I first spoke.

"He's a horrid old man," said Muriel.

"I don't think it's in the least necessary for George to resume relationships that were definitely severed before he was born," said Freddy with decision.

"Anyhow I've delivered the message," said I, feeling somewhat snubbed.

"I don't want to see the old blighter," said George.

The conversation was broken off by the arrival of other guests and in a little while George went off to play golf with one of his Oxford friends.

It was not till next day that the matter was referred to again. I had played an indifferent round with Freddy Bland in the morning and several sets of what is known as country-house tennis in the afternoon and was sitting alone with Muriel on the terrace. In England we have so much bad weather that it is only fair that a beautiful day should be more beautiful than anywhere in the world and this June evening was perfect. The blue sky was cloudless and the air was balmy; before us stretched green rolling downs, and woods, and in the distance you saw the red roofs of a little village and the grey tower of the village church. It was a day when to be alive was sufficient happiness. Detached lines of poetry hovered vaguely in my memory. Muriel and I had been chatting desultorily.

"I hope you didn't think it rather horrid of us to refuse to let George lunch with Ferdy," she said suddenly. "He's such a fearful snob, isn't he?"

"D'you think so? He's always been very nice to me."

"We haven't been on speaking terms for twenty years. Freddy never forgave him for his behaviour during the war. So unpatriotic, I thought, and one really must draw the line somewhere. You know, he absolutely refused to drop his horrible German name. With Freddy in Parliament and running muni-

tions and all that sort of thing it was quite impossible.
I don't know why he should want to see George. He
can't mean anything to him."

"He's an old man. George and Harry are his great-
nephews. He must leave his money to some one."

"We'd rather not have his money," said Muriel
coldly.

Of course I didn't care a row of pins whether George
went to lunch with Ferdy Rabenstein, and I was quite
willing to let the matter drop, but evidently the Blands
had talked it over and Muriel felt that some explanation
was due to me.

"Of course you know that Freddy has Jewish blood
in him," she said.

She looked at me sharply. Muriel was rather a big
blonde woman and she spent a great deal of time trying
to keep down the corpulence to which she was pre-
disposed. She had been very pretty when young and
even now was a comely person; but her round blue eyes,
slightly prominent, her fleshy nose, the shape of her face
and the back of her neck, her exuberant manner,
betrayed her race. No Englishwoman, however fair-
haired, ever looked like that. And yet her observation
was designed to make me take it for granted that she was
a Gentile. I answered discreetly:

"So many people have nowadays."

"I know. But there's no reason to dwell on it, is
there? After all, we're absolutely English; no one
could be more English than George, in appearance

and manner and everything; I mean, he's such a fine sportsman and all that sort of thing, I can't see any object in his knowing Jews just because they happen to be distant connections of his."

"It's very difficult in England now not to know Jews, isn't it?"

"Oh, I know, in London one does meet a good many, and I think some of them are very nice. They're so artistic. I don't go so far as to say that Freddy and I deliberately avoid them, of course I wouldn't do that, but it just happens that we don't really know any of them very well. And down here, there simply aren't any to know."

I could not but admire the convincing manner in which she spoke. It would not have surprised me to be told that she really believed every word she said.

"You say that Ferdy might leave George his money. Well, I don't believe it's so very much anyway; it was quite a comfortable fortune before the war, but that's nothing nowadays. Besides, we're hoping that George will go in for politics when he's a little older, and I don't think it would do him any good in the constituency to inherit money from a Mr. Rabenstein."

"Is George interested in politics?" I asked, to change the conversation.

"Oh, I do hope so. After all, there's the family constituency waiting for him. It's a safe Conservative seat and one can't expect Freddy to go on with the grind of the House of Commons indefinitely."

I*

Muriel was grand. She talked already of the constituency as though twenty generations of Blands had sat for it. Her remark, however, was my first intimation that Freddy's ambition was not satisfied.

"I suppose Freddy would go to the House of Lords when George was old enough to stand."

"We've done a good deal for the party," said Muriel.

Muriel was a Catholic and she often told you that she had been educated in a convent—"Such sweet women, those nuns, I always said that if I had a daughter I should have sent her to a convent too"—but she liked her servants to be Church of England, and on Sunday evenings we had what was called supper because the fish was cold and there was ice-cream, so that they could go to church, and we were waited on by two footmen instead of four. It was still light when we finished and Freddy and I, smoking our cigars, walked up and down the terrace in the gloaming. I suppose Muriel had told him of her conversation with me, and it may be that his refusal to let George see his great-uncle still troubled him, but being subtler than she he attacked the question more indirectly. He told me that he had been very much worried about George. It had been a great disappointment that he had refused to go into the army.

"I should have thought he'd have loved the life," he said.

"And he would certainly have looked marvellous in his Guards uniform."

"He would, wouldn't he?" returned Freddy, ingenuously. "I wonder he could resist that."

He had been completely idle at Oxford; although his father had given him a very large allowance, he had got monstrously into debt; and now he had been sent down. But though he spoke so tartly I could see that he was not a little proud of his scapegrace son, he loved him with oh, such an unEnglish love, and in his heart it flattered him that George had cut such a dash.

"Why should you worry?" I said. "You don't really care if George has a degree or not."

Freddy chuckled.

"No, I don't suppose I do really. I always think the only important thing about Oxford is that people know you were there, and I daresay that George isn't any wilder than the other young men in his set. It's the future I'm thinking of. He's so damned idle. He doesn't seem to want to do anything but have a good time."

"He's young, you know."

"He's not interested in politics, and though he's so good at games he's not even very keen on sport. He seems to spend most of his time strumming the piano."

"That's a harmless amusement."

"Oh, yes, I don't mind that, but he can't go on loafing indefinitely. You see, all this will be his one day." Freddy gave a sweeping gesture that seemed to embrace the whole county, but I knew that he did not own it all yet. "I'm very anxious that he should be fit to assume his responsibilities. His mother is very ambitious for him, but I only want him to be an English gentleman."

Freddy gave me a sidelong glance as though he wanted to say something but hesitated in case I thought it ridiculous; but there is one advantage in being a writer that, since people look upon you as of no account, they will often say things to you that they would not to their equals. He thought he would risk it.

"You know, I've got an idea that nowhere in the world now is the Greek ideal of life so perfectly cultivated as by the English country gentleman living on his estates. I think his life has the beauty of a work of art."

I could not but smile when I reflected that it was impossible for the English country gentleman in these days to do anything of the sort without a packet of money safely invested in American Bonds, but I smiled with sympathy. I thought it rather touching that this Jewish financier should cherish so romantic a dream.

"I want him to be a good landlord. I want him to take his part in the affairs of the country. I want him to be a thorough sportsman."

"Poor mutt," I thought, but said: "Well, what are your plans for George now?"

"I think he has a fancy for the diplomatic service. He's suggested going to Germany to learn the language."

"A very good idea, I should have thought."

"For some reason he's got it into his head that he wants to go to Munich."

"A nice place."

Next day I went back to London and shortly after my arrival rang up Ferdy.

"I'm sorry, but George isn't able to come to lunch on Wednesday."

"What about Friday?"

"Friday's no good either." I thought it useless to beat about the bush. "The fact is, his people aren't keen on his lunching with you."

There was a moment's silence. Then:

"I see. Well, will you come on Wednesday anyway?"

"Yes, I'd like to," I answered.

So on Wednesday at half-past one I strolled round to Curzon Street. Ferdy received me with the somewhat elaborate graciousness that he cultivated. He made no reference to the Blands. We sat in the drawing-room and I could not help reflecting what an eye for beautiful objects that family had. The room was more crowded than the fashion of to-day approves and the gold snuff-boxes in vitrines, the French china, appealed to a taste that was not mine; but they were no doubt choice pieces; and the Louis XV suite, with its beautiful *petit point*, must have been worth an enormous lot of money. The pictures on the walls by Lancret, Pater and Watteau did not greatly interest me, but I recognised their

intrinsic excellence. It was a proper setting for this aged
man of the world. It fitted his period. Suddenly the
door opened and George was announced. Ferdy saw my
surprise and gave me a little smile of triumph.

"I'm very glad you were able to come after all," he
said as he shook George's hand.

I saw him in a glance take in his great-nephew whom
he saw to-day for the first time. George was very
elegantly dressed. He wore a short black coat, striped
trousers and the grey double-breasted waistcoat which
at that time was the mode. You could only wear it with
elegance if you were tall and thin and your belly was
slightly concave. I felt sure that Ferdy knew exactly
who George's tailor was and what haberdasher he went
to and approved of them. George, so smart and trim,
wearing his clothes so beautifully, certainly looked very
handsome. We went down to luncheon. Ferdy had
the social graces at his fingers' ends and he put the
boy at his ease, but I saw that he was carefully appraising
him; then, I do not know why, he began to tell some of
his Jewish stories. He told them with gusto and with
his wonderful mimicry. I saw George flush, and though
he laughed at them, I could see that it was with embarrassment. I wondered what on earth had induced
Ferdy to be so tactless. But he was watching George
and he told story after story. It looked as though he
would never stop. I wondered if for some reason I
could not grasp he was taking a malicious pleasure in
the boy's obvious discomfiture. At last we went up-

stairs and to make things easier I asked Ferdy to play the piano. He played us three or four little waltzes. He had lost none of his exquisite lightness nor his sense of their lilting rhythm. Then he turned to George.

"Do you play?" he asked him.

"A little."

"Won't you play something?"

"I'm afraid I only play classical music. I don't think it would interest you."

Ferdy smiled slightly, but did not insist. I said it was time for me to go and George accompanied me.

"What a filthy old Jew," he said as soon as we were in the street. "I hated those stories of his."

"They're his great stunt. He always tells them."

"Would you if you were a Jew?"

I shrugged my shoulders.

"How is it you came to lunch after all?" I asked George.

He chuckled. He was a light-hearted creature, with a sense of humour, and he shook off the slight irritation his great-uncle had caused him.

"He went to see Granny. You don't know Granny, do you?"

"No."

"She treats daddy like a kid in Etons. Granny said I was to go to lunch with great-uncle Ferdy and what Granny says goes."

"I see."

A week or two later George went to Munich to learn German. I happened then to go on a journey and it was not till the following spring that I was again in London. Soon after my arrival I found myself sitting next to Muriel Bland at dinner. I asked after George.

"He's still in Germany," she said.

"I see in the papers that you're going to have a great beano at Tilby for his coming of age."

"We're going to entertain the tenants and they're making George a presentation."

She was less exuberant than usual, but I did not pay much attention to the fact. She led a strenuous life and it might be that she was tired. I knew she liked to talk of her son, so I continued.

"I suppose George has been having a grand time in Germany," I said.

She did not answer for a moment and I gave her a glance. I was surprised to see that her eyes were filled with tears.

"I'm afraid George has gone mad," she said.

"What *do* you mean?"

"We've been so frightfully worried. Freddy's so angry, he won't even discuss it. I don't know what we're going to do."

Of course it immediately occurred to me that George, who, I supposed, like most young Englishmen sent to learn the language, had been put with a German family, had fallen in love with the daughter of the house and wanted to marry her. I had a pretty strong suspicion that the Blands were intent on his making a very grand marriage.

"Why, what's happened?" I asked.

"He wants to become a pianist."

"A what?"

"A professional pianist."

"What on earth put that idea in his head?"

"Heaven knows. We didn't know anything about it. We thought he was working for his exam. I went out to see him. I thought I'd like to know that he was getting on all right. Oh, my dear. He looks like nothing on earth. And he used to be so smart; I could have cried. He told me he wasn't going in for the exam. and had never had any intention of doing so; he'd only suggested the diplomatic service so that we'd let him go to Germany and he'd be able to study music."

"But has he any talent?"

"Oh, that's neither here nor there. Even if he had the genius of Paderewski we couldn't have George traipsing around the country playing at concerts. No one can deny that I'm very artistic, and so is Freddy, we love music and we've always known a lot of artists, but George will have a very great position, it's out of the question. We've set our hearts on his going into Parliament. He'll be very rich one day. There's nothing he can't aspire to."

"Did you point all that out to him?"

"Of course I did. He laughed at me. I told him he'd break his father's heart. He said his father could always fall back on Harry. Of course I'm devoted to Harry, and he's as clever as a monkey, but it was always understood that he was to go into the business; even though I am his mother I can see that he hasn't got the advantages that George has. Do you know what he said to me? He said that if his father would settle five pounds a week on him he would resign everything in Harry's favour and Harry could be his father's heir and succeed to the baronetcy and everything. It's too ridiculous. He said that if the Crown Prince of Roumania could abdicate a throne he didn't see why he couldn't abdicate a baronetcy. But you can't do that. Nothing can prevent him from being third baronet and if Freddy should be granted a peerage from succeeding to it at Freddy's death. Do you know, he even wants to drop the name of Bland and take some horrible German name."

I could not help asking what.

"Bleikogel or something like that," she answered.

That was a name I recognised. I remembered Ferdy telling me that Hannah Rabenstein had married Alphonse Bleikogel who became eventually Sir Alfred Bland, first Baronet. It was all very strange. I wondered what had happened to the charming and so typically English boy whom I had seen only a few months before.

"Of course when I came home and told Freddy he was furious. I've never seen him so angry. He foamed at the mouth. He wired to George to come back immediately and George wired back to say he couldn't on account of his work."

"Is he working?"

"From morning till night. That's the maddening part of it. He never did a stroke of work in his life. Freddy used to say he was born idle."

"H'm."

"Then Freddy wired to say that if he didn't come he'd stop his allowance and George wired back: 'Stop it.' That put the lid on. You don't know what Freddy can be when his back is up."

I knew that Freddy had inherited a large fortune, but I knew also that he had immensely increased it, and I could well imagine that behind the courteous and amiable Squire of Tilby there was a ruthless man of affairs. He had been used to having his own way and I could believe that when crossed he would be hard and cruel.

"We'd been making George a very handsome allowance, but you know how frightfully extravagant he was. We didn't think he'd be able to hold out long and in point of fact within a month he wrote to Ferdy and asked him to lend him a hundred pounds. Ferdy went to my mother-in-law, she's his sister, you know, and asked her what it meant. Though they hadn't spoken for twenty years Freddy went to see him and begged him not to send George a penny, and he promised he wouldn't. I don't know how George has been making both ends meet. I'm sure Freddy's right, but I can't help being rather worried. If I hadn't given Freddy my word of honour that I wouldn't send him anything I think I'd have slipped a few notes in a letter in case of accident. I mean, it's awful to think that perhaps he hasn't got enough to eat."

"It'll do him no harm to go short for a bit."

"We were in an awful hole, you know. We'd made all sorts of preparations for his coming of age, and I'd issued hundreds of invitations. Suddenly George said he wouldn't come. I was simply frantic. I wrote and wired. I would have gone over to Germany only Freddy wouldn't let me. I practically went down on my bended knees to George. I begged him not to put us in such a humiliating position. I mean, it's the sort of thing it's so difficult to explain. Then my mother-in-law stepped in. You don't know her, do you? She's an extraordinary old woman. You'd never think she was Freddy's mother. She was German originally, but of very good family."

"Oh?"

"To tell you the truth I'm rather frightened of her. She tackled Freddy and then she wrote to George herself. She said that if he'd come home for his twenty-first birthday she'd pay any debts he had in Munich and we'd all give a patient hearing to anything he had to say. He agreed to that and we're expecting him one day next week. But I'm not looking forward to it, I can tell you."

She gave a deep sigh. When we were walking up-stairs after dinner Freddy addressed me.

"I see Muriel has been telling you about George.

The damned fool! I have no patience with him. Fancy
wanting to be a pianist. It's so ungentlemanly."

"He's very young, you know," I said soothingly.

"He's had things too easy for him. I've been much
too indulgent. There's never been a thing he wanted
that I haven't given him. I'll learn him."

The Blands had a discreet apprehension of the uses of
advertisement and I gathered from the papers that the
celebrations at Tilby of George's twenty-first birthday
were conducted in accordance with the usage of English
county families. There was a dinner-party and a ball for
the gentry and a collation and a dance in marquees on
the lawn for the tenants. Expensive bands were brought
down from London. In the illustrated papers were
pictures of George surrounded by his family being
presented with a solid silver tea set by the tenantry.
They had subscribed to have his portrait painted, but
since his absence from the country had made it impossible for him to sit, the tea service had been sub-
stituted. I read in the columns of the gossip writers that
his father had given him a hunter, his mother a gramophone that changed its own records, his grandmother
the dowager Lady Bland an *Encyclopædia Britannica*
and his great-uncle Ferdinand Rabenstein a *Virgin and
Child* by Pellegrino da Modena. I could not help
observing that these gifts were bulky and not readily
convertible into cash. From Ferdy's presence at the
festivities I concluded that George's unaccountable

vagary had effected a reconciliation between uncle and nephew. I was right. Ferdy did not at all like the notion of his great-nephew becoming a professional pianist. At the first hint of danger to its prestige the family drew together and a united front was presented to oppose George's designs. Since I was not there I only know from hearsay what happened when the birthday celebrations were over. Ferdy told me something and so did Muriel, and later George gave me his version. The Blands had very much the impression that when George came home and found himself occupying the centre of the stage, when, surrounded by splendour, he saw for himself once more how much it meant to be the heir of a great estate, he would weaken. They surrounded him with love. They flattered him. They hung on his words. They counted on the goodness of his heart and thought that if they were very kind to him he would not have the courage to cause them pain. They seemed to take it for granted that he had no intention of going back to Germany and in conversation included him in all their plans. George did not say very much. He seemed to be enjoying himself. He did not open a piano. Things looked as though they were going very well. Peace descended on the troubled house. Then one day at luncheon when they were discussing a garden-party to which they had all been asked for one day of the following week, George said pleasantly:

"Don't count on me. I shan't be here."

"Oh, George, why not?" asked his mother.

"I must get back to my work. I'm leaving for Munich on Monday."

There was an awful pause. Everyone looked for something to say, but was afraid of saying the wrong thing, and at last it seemed impossible to break it. Luncheon was finished in silence. Then George went into the garden and the others, old Lady Bland and Ferdy, Muriel and Sir Adolphus, into the morning-room. There was a family council. Muriel wept. Freddy flew into a temper. Presently from the drawing-room they heard the sound of someone playing a nocturne of Chopin. It was George. It was as though now he had announced his decision he had gone for comfort, rest and strength to the instrument he loved. Freddy sprang to his feet.

"Stop that noise," he cried. "I won't have him play the piano in my house."

Muriel rang for a servant and gave him a message.

"Will you tell Mr. Bland that her ladyship has a bad headache and would he mind not playing the piano."

Ferdy, the man of the world, was deputed to have a talk with George. He was authorised to make him certain promises if he would give up the idea of becoming a pianist. If he did not wish to go into the diplomatic service his father would not insist, but if he would stand for Parliament he was prepared to pay his election expenses, give him a flat in London and make him an allowance of five thousand a year. I must say it was a handsome offer. I do not know what Ferdy said to the boy. I suppose he painted to him the life that a young man could lead in London on such an income. I am sure he made it very alluring. It availed nothing. All George asked was five pounds a week to be able to continue his studies and to be left alone. He was indifferent to the position that he might some day enjoy. He didn't want to hunt. He didn't want to shoot. He didn't want to be a Member of Parliament. He didn't want to be a millionaire. He didn't want to be a baronet. He didn't want to be a peer. Ferdy left him defeated and in a state of considerable exasperation.

After dinner that evening there was a battle royal. Freddy was a quick-tempered man, unused to opposition, and he gave George the rough side of his tongue. I gather that it was very rough indeed. The women who sought to restrain his violence were sternly silenced. Perhaps for the first time in his life Freddy would not listen to his mother. George was obstinate and sullen. He had made up his mind and if his father didn't like it he could lump it. Freddy was peremptory. He forbade George to go back to Germany. George answered that he was twenty-one and his own master. He would go where he chose. Freddy swore he would not give him a penny.

"All right, I'll earn money."

"You! You've never done a stroke of work in your life. What do you expect to do to earn money?"

"Sell old clothes," grinned George.

There was a gasp from all of them. Muriel was so taken aback that she said a stupid thing.

"Like a Jew?"

"Well, aren't I a Jew? And aren't you a Jewess and isn't daddy a Jew? We're all Jews, the whole gang of us, and everyone knows it and what the hell's the good of pretending we're not?"

Then a very dreadful thing happened. Freddy burst suddenly into tears. I'm afraid he didn't behave very much like Sir Adolphus Bland, Bart., M.P., and the good old English gentleman he so much wanted to be, but like an emotional Adolph Bleikogel who loved his son and wept with mortification because the great hopes he had set on him were brought to nothing and the ambition of his life was frustrated. He cried noisily with great loud sobs and pulled his beard and beat his breast and rocked to and fro. Then they all began to cry, old Lady Bland and Muriel, and Ferdy, who sniffed and blew his nose and wiped the tears streaming down his face, and even George cried. Of course it was very painful, but to our rough Anglo-Saxon temperament I am afraid it must seem also a trifle ridiculous. No one tried to console anybody else. They just sobbed and sobbed. It broke up the party.

But it had no result on the situation. George remained obdurate. His father would not speak to him. There were more scenes. Muriel sought to excite his pity; he was deaf to her piteous entreaties, he did not

seem to mind if he broke her heart, he did not care two
hoots if he killed his father. Ferdy appealed to him as a
sportsman and a man of the world. George was flippant
and indeed personally offensive. Old Lady Bland with
her guttural German accent and strong common sense
argued with him, but he would not listen to reason. It
was she, however, who at last found a way out. She
made George acknowledge that it was no use to throw
away all the beautiful things the world laid at his feet
unless he had talent. Of course he thought he had, but
he might be mistaken. It was not worth while to be a
second-rate pianist. His only excuse, his only justification, was genius. If he had genius his family had no
right to stand in his way.

"You can't expect me to show genius already,"
said George. "I shall have to work for years."

"Are you sure you are prepared for that?"

"It's my only wish in the world. I'll work like a dog.
I only want to be given my chance."

This was the proposition she made. His father was
determined to give him nothing and obviously they
could not let the boy starve. He had mentioned
five pounds a week. Well, she was willing to give
him that herself. He could go back to Germany and
study for two years. At the end of that time he must
come back and they would get some competent and
disinterested person to hear him play, and if then that
person said he showed promise of becoming a first-rate
pianist no further obstacles would be placed in his way.

He would be given every advantage, help and encouragement. If on the other hand that person decided that his natural gifts were not such as to ensure ultimate success he must promise faithfully to give up all thoughts of making music his profession and in every way accede to his father's wishes. George could hardly believe his ears.

"Do you mean that, Granny?"

"I do."

"But will daddy agree?"

"I vill see dat he does," she answered.

George seized her in his arms and impetuously kissed her on both cheeks.

"Darling," he cried.

"Ah, but de promise?"

He gave her his solemn word of honour that he would faithfully abide by the terms of the arrangement. Two days later he went back to Germany. Though his father consented unwillingly to his going, and indeed could not help doing so, he would not be reconciled to him and when he left refused to say good-bye to him. I imagine that in no manner could he have caused himself such pain. I permit myself a trite remark. It is strange that men, inhabitants for so short a while of an alien and inhuman world, should go out of their way to cause themselves so much unhappiness.

George had stipulated that during his two years of study his family should not visit him, so that when

Muriel heard some months before he was due to come home that I was passing through Munich on my way to Vienna, whither business called me, it was not unnatural that she should ask me to look him up. She was anxious to have first-hand information about him. She gave me George's address and I wrote ahead, telling him I was spending a day in Munich, and asked him to lunch with me. His answer awaited me at the hotel. He said he worked all day and could not spare the time to lunch with me, but if I would come to his studio about six he would like to show me that and if I had nothing better to do would love to spend the evening with me. So soon after six I went to the address he gave me. He lived on the second floor of a large block of flats and when I came to his door I heard the sound of piano-playing. It stopped when I rang and George opened the door for me. I hardly recognised him. He had grown very fat. His hair was extremely long, it curled all over his head in picturesque confusion; and he had certainly not shaved for three days. He wore a grimy pair of Oxford bags, a tennis shirt and slippers. He was not very clean and his finger-nails were rimmed with black. It was a startling change from the spruce, slim youth so elegantly dressed in such beautiful clothes that I had last seen. I could not but think it would be a shock to Ferdy to see him now. The studio was large and bare; on the walls were three or four unframed canvases of a highly cubist nature, there were several armchairs much the worse for wear, and a grand piano. Books were littered about and old newspapers and art magazines. It was dirty and untidy and there was a frowzy smell of stale beer and stale smoke.

"Do you live here alone?" I asked.

"Yes, I have a woman who comes in twice a week and cleans up. But I make my own breakfast and lunch."

"Can you cook?"

"Oh, I only have bread and cheese and a bottle of beer for lunch. I dine at a *Bierstube*."

It was pleasant to discover that he was very glad to see me. He seemed in great spirits and extremely happy. He asked after his relations and we talked of one thing and another. He had a lesson twice a week and for the rest of the time practised. He told me that he worked ten hours a day.

"That's a change," I said.

He laughed.

"Daddy said I was born tired. I wasn't really lazy. I didn't see the use of working at things that bored me."

I asked him how he was getting on with the piano. He seemed to be satisfied with his progress and I begged him to play to me.

"Oh, not now, I'm all in, I've been at it all day. Let's go out and dine and come back here later and then I'll play. I generally go to the same place, there are several students I know there, and it's rather fun."

Presently we set out. He put on socks and shoes and a very old golf coat, and we walked together through the wide quiet streets. It was a brisk cold day. His step was buoyant. He looked round him with a sigh of delight.

"I love Munich," he said. "It's the only city in the world where there's art in the very air you breathe. After all art is the only thing that matters, isn't it? I loathe the idea of going home."

"All the same I'm afraid you'll have to."

"I know. I'll go all right, but I'm not going to think about it till the time comes."

"When you do, you might do worse than get a haircut. If you don't mind my saying so you look almost too artistic to be convincing."

"You English, you're such Philistines," he said.

He took me to a rather large restaurant in a side street, crowded even at that early hour with people dining and furnished heavily in the German medieval style. A table covered with a red cloth, well away from the air, was reserved for George and his friends and when we went to it four or five youths were at it. There was a Pole studying Oriental languages, a student of philosophy, a painter (I suppose the author of George's cubist pictures), a Swede, and a young man who introduced himself to me, clicking his heels, as Hans Reiting, *Dichter*, namely Hans Reiting, poet. Not one of them was more than twenty-two and I felt a trifle out of it. They all addressed George as *du* and I noticed that his

German was extremely fluent. I had not spoken it for some time and mine was rusty, so that I could not take much part in the lively conversation. But nevertheless I thoroughly enjoyed myself. They ate sparingly, but drank a good deal of beer. They talked of art and literature and life and ethics and motor-cars and women. They were very revolutionary and though gay very much in earnest. They were contemptuous of everyone you had ever heard of, and the only point on which they all agreed was that in this topsy-turvy world only the vulgar could hope for success. They argued points of technique with animation, and contradicted one another, and shouted and were obscene. They had a grand time.

At about eleven George and I walked back to his studio. Munich is a city that frolics demurely and except about the Marienplatz the streets were still and empty. When we got in he took off his coat and said:

"Now I'll play to you."

I sat in one of the dilapidated armchairs and a broken spring stuck into my behind, but I made myself as comfortable as I could. George played Chopin. I know very little of music and that is one of the reasons for which I have found this story difficult to write. When I go to a concert at the Queen's Hall and in the intervals read the programme it is all Greek to me. I know nothing of harmony and counterpoint. I shall never forget how humiliated I felt once when, having come to Munich for a Wagner Festival, I went to a wonderful performance of *Tristan und Isolde* and never heard a note of it. The first few bars sent me off and I began to think of what I was writing, my characters leapt into life and I heard their long conversations, I suffered their pains and was a party to their joy; the years swept by and all sorts of things happened to me, the spring brought me its rapture and in the winter I was cold and hungry; and I loved and I hated and I died. I suppose there were intervals in which I walked round and round the garden and probably ate *Schinken-Brödchen* and drank beer, but I have no recollection of them. The only thing I know is that when the curtain for the last time fell I woke with a start. I had had a wonderful time, but I could not help thinking it was very stupid of me to come such a long way and spend so much money if I couldn't pay attention to what I heard and saw.

I knew most of the things George played. They were the familiar pieces of concert programmes. He played with a great deal of dash. Then he played Beethoven's *Appassionata*. I used to play it myself when I played the piano (very badly) in my far distant youth and I still knew every note of it. Of course it is a classic and a great work, it would be foolish to deny it, but I confess that at this time of day it leaves me cold. It is like *Paradise Lost*, splendid, but a trifle stolid. This too George played with vigour. He sweated profusely. At first I could not make out what was the matter with his playing, something did not seem to me quite right, and then it struck me that the two hands did not exactly synchronise, so that there was ever so slight an interval between the bass and the treble; but I repeat, I am ignorant of these things; what disconcerted me might have been merely the effect of his having drunk a good deal of beer that evening or indeed only my fancy. I said all I could think of to praise him.

"Of course I know I need a lot more work. I'm only a beginner, but I know I can do it. I feel it in my bones. It'll take me ten years, but then I shall be a pianist."

He was tired and came away from the piano. It was after midnight and I suggested going, but he would not hear of it. He opened a couple of bottles of beer and lit his pipe. He wanted to talk.

"Are you happy here?" I asked him.

"Very," he answered gravely. "I'd like to stay for ever. I've never had such fun in my life. This evening, for instance. Wasn't it grand?"

"It was very jolly. But one can't go on leading the student's life. Your friends here will grow older and go away."

"Others'll come. There are always students here and people like that."

"Yes, but you'll grow older too. Is there anything more lamentable than the middle-aged man who tries to go on living the undergraduate's life? The old fellow who wants to be a boy among boys, and tries to persuade himself that they'll accept him as one of themselves—how ridiculous he is. It can't be done."

"I feel so at home here. My poor father wants me to

K

be an English gentleman. It gives me gooseflesh. I'm
not a sportsman. I don't care a damn for hunting and
shooting and playing cricket. I was only acting."

"You gave a very natural performance."

"It wasn't till I came here that I knew it wasn't real.
I loved Eton, and Oxford was a riot, but all the same I
knew I didn't belong. I played the part all right,
because acting's in my blood, but there was always
something in me that wasn't satisfied. The house in
Grosvenor Square is a freehold and daddy paid a
hundred and eighty thousand pounds for Tilby; I don't
know if you understand what I mean, I felt they were
just furnished houses we'd taken for the season and one
of these days we'd pack up and the real owners would
come back."

I listened to him attentively, but I wondered how
much he was describing what he had obscurely felt and
how much he imagined now in his changed circumstances that he had felt.

"I used to hate hearing Great-Uncle Ferdy tell his
Jewish stories. I thought it so damned mean. I understand now; it was a safety valve. My God, the strain of
being a man about town. It's easier for daddy, he can
play the old English squire at Tilby, but in the City he
can be himself. He's all right. I've taken the make-up
off and my stage clothes and at last I can be my real self
too. What a relief! You know, I don't like English
people. I never really know where I am with you.
You're so dull and conventional. You never let your-

selves go. There's no freedom in you, freedom of the soul, and you're such funks. There's nothing in the world you're so frightened of as doing the wrong thing."

"Don't forget that you're English yourself, George," I murmured.

He laughed.

"I? I'm not English. I haven't got a drop of English blood in me. I'm a Jew and you know it, and a German Jew into the bargain. I don't want to be English. I want to be a Jew. My friends are Jews. You don't know how much more easy I feel with them. I can be myself. We did everything we could to avoid Jews at home; Mummy, because she was blonde, thought she could get away with it and pretended she was a Gentile. What rot! D'you know, I have a lot of fun wandering about the Jewish parts of Munich and looking at the people. I went to Frankfort once, there are a lot of them there, and I walked about and looked at the frowzy old men with their hooked noses and the fat women with their false hair. I felt such a sympathy for them, I felt I belonged to them, I could have kissed them. When they looked at me I wondered if they knew that I was one of them. I wish to God I knew Yiddish. I'd like to become friends with them, and go into their houses and eat Kosher food and all that sort of thing. I wanted to go to a synagogue, but I was afraid I'd do the wrong thing and be kicked out. I like the smell of the Ghetto and the sense of life, and the mystery and the dust and the squalor and the romance. I shall never get the longing for it out of my head now. That's the real thing. All the rest is only pretence."

"You'll break your father's heart," I said.

"It's his or mine. Why can't he let me go? There's Harry. Harry would love to be squire of Tilby. He'd be an English gentleman all right. You know, mummy's set her heart on my marrying a Christian. Harry would love to. He'll found the good old English family all right. After all, I ask so little. I only want five pounds a week, and they can keep the title and the park and the Gainsboroughs and the whole bag of tricks."

"Well, the fact remains that you gave your solemn word of honour to go back after two years."

"I'll go back all right," he said sullenly. "Lea Makart has promised to come and hear me play."

"What'll you do if she says you're no good?"

"Shoot myself," he said gaily.

"What nonsense," I answered in the same tone.

"Do *you* feel at home in England?"

"No," I said, "but then I don't feel at home anywhere else."

But he was quite naturally not interested in me.

"I loathe the idea of going back. Now that I know what life has to offer I wouldn't be an English country gentleman for anything in the world. My God, the boredom of it!"

"Money's a very nice thing and I've always understood it's very pleasant to be an English peer."

"Money means nothing to me. I want none of the things it can buy, and I don't happen to be a snob."

It was growing very late and I had to get up early next day. It seemed unnecessary for me to pay too much attention to what George said. It was the sort of nonsense a young man might very well indulge in when thrown suddenly among painters and poets. Art is strong wine and needs a strong head to carry it. The divine fire burns most efficiently in those who temper its fury with horse sense. After all, George was not twenty-three yet. Time teaches. And when all was said and done his future was no concern of mine. I bade him good-night and walked back to my hotel. The stars were shining in the indifferent sky. I left Munich in the morning.

I did not tell Muriel on my return to London what George had said to me, or what he looked like, but contented myself with assuring her that he was well and happy, working very hard, and seemed to be leading a virtuous and sober life. Six months later he came home. Muriel asked me to go down to Tilby for the week-end: Ferdy was bringing Lea Makart to hear George play and he particularly wished me to be there. I accepted. Muriel met me at the station.

"How did you find George?" I asked.

"He's very fat, but he seems in great spirits. I think he's pleased to be back again. He's been very sweet to his father."

"I'm glad of that."

"Oh, my dear, I do hope Lea Makart will say he's no good. It'll be such a relief to all of us."

"I'm afraid it'll be a terrible disappointment to him."

"Life is full of disappointments," said Muriel crisply. "But one learns to put up with them."

I gave her a smile of amusement. We were sitting in a Rolls, and there was a footman as well as a chauffeur on the box. She wore a string of pearls that had probably cost forty thousand pounds. I recollected that in the birthday honours Sir Adolphus Bland had not been one of the three gentlemen on whom the King had been pleased to confer a peerage.

Lea Makart was able to make only a flying visit. She was playing that evening at Brighton and would motor over to Tilby on the Sunday morning for luncheon. She was returning to London the same day because she had a concert in Manchester on the Monday. George was to play in the course of the afternoon.

"He's practising very hard," his mother told me. "That's why he didn't come with me to meet you."

We turned in at the park gates and drove up the imposing avenue of elms that led to the house. I found that there was no party.

I met the dowager Lady Bland for the first time. I had always been curious to see her. I had had in my mind's eye a somewhat sensational picture of an old, old Jewish woman who lived alone in her grand house in Portland Place and, with a finger in every pie, ruled her family with a despotic hand. She did not disappoint me. She was of a commanding presence, rather tall, and stout without being corpulent. Her countenance was markedly Hebraic. She wore a rather heavy moustache and a wig of a peculiarly metallic brown. Her dress was very grand, of black brocade, and she had a row of large diamond stars on her breast and round her neck a chain of diamonds. Diamond rings gleamed on her wrinkled hands. She spoke in a rather loud harsh voice and with a strong German accent. When I was introduced to her she fixed me with shining eyes. She summed me up with despatch and to my fancy at all events made no attempt to conceal from me that the judgment she formed was unfavourable.

"You have known my brother Ferdinand for many years, is it not so?" she said, rolling a guttural R. "My brother Ferdinand has always moved in very good society. Where is Sir Adolphus, Muriel? Does he know your guest is arrived? And will you not send for George? If he does not know his pieces by now he will not know them by to-morrow."

Muriel explained that Freddy was finishing a round of golf with his secretary and that she had had George told I was there. Lady Bland looked as though she thought Muriel's replies highly unsatisfactory and turned again to me.

"My daughter tells me you have been in Italy?"

"Yes, I've only just come back."

"It is a beautiful country. How is the King?"

I said I did not know.

"I used to know him when he was a little boy. He was not very strong then. His mother, Queen Margherita, was a great friend of mine. They thought he would never marry. The Duchess of Aosta was very angry when he fell in love with that Princess of Montenegro."

She seemed to belong to some long-past period of history, but she was very alert and I imagine that little escaped her beady eyes. Freddy, very spruce in plus-fours, presently came in. It was amusing and yet a little touching to see this grey-bearded man, as a rule somewhat domineering, so obviously on his best behaviour with the old lady. He called her Mamma. Then George came in. He was as fat as ever, but he had taken my advice and had his hair cut; he was losing his boyish looks, but he was a powerful and well set-up young man. It was good to see the pleasure he took in his tea. He ate quantities of sandwiches and great hunks of cake. He had still a boy's appetite. His father watched him with a tender smile and as I looked at him I could not be surprised at the attachment which they all so obviously felt for him. He had an ingenuousness, a charm and an enthusiasm which were certainly very pleasant. There was about him a generosity of demeanour, a frankness and a natural cordiality which could not but make people take to him. I do not know whether it was owing to a hint from his grandmother or merely of his own good nature, but it was plain that he was going out of his way to be nice to his father; and in his father's soft eyes, in the way he hung upon the boy's words, in his pleased, proud and happy look, you felt how bitterly the estrangement of the last two years had weighed on him. He adored George.

We played golf in the morning, a three-ball match, since Muriel, having to go to Mass, could not join us, and at one Ferdy arrived in Lea Makart's car. We sat down to luncheon. Of course Lea Makart's reputation was well known to me. She was acknowledged to be the greatest woman pianist in Europe. She was a very old friend of Ferdy's, who with his interest and patronage had greatly helped her at the beginning of her career, and it was he who had arranged for her to come and give her opinion of George's chances. At one time I went as often as I could to hear her play. She had no affectations; she played as a bird sings, without any appearance of effort, very naturally and the silvery notes dripped from her light fingers in a curiously spontaneous manner, so that it gave you the impression that she was improvising those complicated rhythms. They used to tell me that her technique was wonderful. I could never make up my mind how much the delight her playing gave me was due to her person. In those days she was the most ethereal thing you could imagine, and it was surprising that a creature so sylphlike should be capable of so much power. She was very slight, pale, with enormous eyes and magnificent black hair, and at the piano she had a child-like wistfulness that was most appealing. She was very beautiful in a hardly human way and when she played, a little smile on her closed lips, she seemed to be remembering things she had heard in another world. Now, however, a woman in the early forties, she was sylphlike no more; she was stout and her face had broadened; she had no longer that lovely remoteness, but the authority of her long succession of triumphs. She was brisk, business-like and somewhat over-whelming. Her vitality lit her with a natural spotlight as his sanctity surrounds the saint with a halo. She was not interested in anything very much but her own affairs, but since she had humour and knew the world she was able to invest them with gaiety. She held the conversation, but did not absorb it. George talked little. Every now and then she gave him a glance, but did not try to draw him in. I was the only Gentile at the table. All but old Lady Bland spoke perfect English, yet I could not help feeling that they did not speak like English people; I think they rounded their vowels more than we do, they certainly spoke louder, and the words seemed not to fall, but to gush from their lips. I think if I had been in another room where I could hear the tone but not the words of their speech I should have thought it was in a foreign language that they were conversing. The effect was slightly disconcerting.

Lea Makart wished to set out for London at about six, so it was arranged that George should play at four. Whatever the result of the audition, I felt that I, a stranger in the circle which her departure must render exclusively domestic, would be in the way and so, pretexting an early engagement in town next morning, I asked her if she would take me with her in her car.

At a little before four we all wandered into the drawing-room. Old Lady Bland sat on a sofa with Ferdy; Freddy, Muriel and I made ourselves comfortable in armchairs; and Lea Makart sat by herself. She chose instinctively a high-backed Jacobean chair that had somewhat the air of a throne, and in a yellow dress, with her olive skin, she looked very handsome. She had magnificent eyes. She was very much made up and her mouth was scarlet.

George gave no sign of nervousness. He was already seated at the piano when I went in with his father and mother, and he watched us quietly settling ourselves down. He gave me the shadow of a smile. When he saw that we were all at our ease he began to play. He played Chopin. He played two waltzes that were familiar to me, a polonaise and an *étude*. He played with a great deal of *brio*. I wish I knew music well enough to give an exact description of his playing. It had strength, and a youthful exuberance, but I felt that he missed what to me is the peculiar charm of Chopin, the tenderness, the nervous melancholy, the wistful gaiety and the slightly faded romance that reminds me always of an Early Victorian keepsake. And again I had the vague sensation, so slight that it almost escaped me, that the two hands did not quite synchronise. I looked at Ferdy and

saw him give his sister a look of faint surprise, Muriel's
eyes were fixed on the pianist, but presently she dropped
them and for the rest of the time stared at the floor. His
father looked at him too, and his eyes were steadfast, but
unless I was much mistaken he went pale and his face
betrayed something like dismay. Music was in the blood
of all of them, all their lives they had heard the greatest
pianists in the world, and they judged with instinctive
precision. The only person whose face betrayed no
emotion was Lea Makart. She listened very attentively.
She was as still as an image in a niche.

At last he stopped and turning round on his seat faced
her. He did not speak.

"What is it you want me to tell you?" she asked.

They looked into one another's eyes.

"I want you to tell me whether I have any chance of
becoming in time a pianist in the first rank."

"Not in a thousand years."

For a moment there was a dead silence. Freddy's head
sank and he looked down at the carpet at his feet. His
wife put out her hand and took his. But George
continued to look steadily at Lea Makart.

"Ferdy has told me the circumstances," she said at
last. "Don't think I'm influenced by them. Nothing of
this is very important." She made a great sweeping
gesture that took in the magnificent room with the
beautiful things it contained and all of us. "If I thought
you had in you the makings of an artist I shouldn't
hesitate to beseech you to give up everything for art's

sake. Art is the only thing that matters. In comparison with art, wealth and rank and power are not worth a row of pins." She gave us a look so sincere that it was void of insolence. "We are the only people who count. We give the world significance. You are only our raw material."

I was not too pleased to be included with the rest under that heading, but that is neither here nor there.

"Of course I can see that you've worked very hard. Don't think it's been wasted. It will always be a pleasure to you to be able to play the piano and it will enable you to appreciate great playing as no ordinary person can hope to do. Look at your hands. They're not a pianist's hands."

Involuntarily I glanced at George's hands. I had never noticed them before. I was astounded to see how podgy they were and how short and stumpy the fingers.

"Your ear is not quite perfect. I don't think you can ever hope to be more than a very competent amateur. In art the difference between the amateur and the professional is immeasurable."

George did not reply. Except for his pallor no one would have known that he was listening to the blasting of all his hopes. The silence that fell was quite awful. Lea Makart's eyes suddenly filled with tears.

"But don't take my opinion alone," she said. "After all, I'm not infallible. Ask somebody else. You know how good and generous Paderewski is. I'll write to him about you and you can go down and play to him. I'm sure he'll hear you."

George now gave a little smile. He had very good manners and whatever he was feeling did not want to make the situation too difficult for others.

"I don't think that's necessary, I am content to accept your verdict. To tell you the truth it's not so very different from my master's in Munich."

He got up from the piano and lit a cigarette. It eased the strain. The others moved a little in their chairs. Lea Makart smiled at George.

"Shall I play to you?" she said.

"Yes, do."

She got up and went to the piano. She took off the rings with which her fingers were laden. She played Bach. I do not know the names of the pieces, but I recognised the stiff ceremonial of the frenchified little German courts and the sober, thrifty comfort of the burghers, and the dancing on the village green, the green trees that looked like Christmas trees, and the sunlight on the wide German country, and a tender cosiness; and in my nostrils there was a warm scent of the soil and I was conscious of a sturdy strength that seemed to have its roots deep in mother earth, and of an elemental power that was timeless and had no home in space. She played exquisitely, with a soft brilliance that made you think of the full moon shining at dusk in the summer sky. With another part of me I watched the others and I saw how intensely they were conscious of the experience. They were rapt. I wished with all my heart that I could get from music the wonderful exaltation that possessed them. She stopped, a smile hovered on her lips, and she put on her rings. George gave a little chuckle.

"That clinches it, I fancy," he said.

The servants brought in tea and after tea Lea Makart and I bade the company farewell and got into the car. We drove up to London. She talked all the way, if not brilliantly at all events with immense gusto; she told me of her early years in Manchester and of the struggle of her beginnings. She was very interesting. She never even mentioned George; the episode was of no consequence, it was finished and she thought of it no more.

We little knew what was happening at Tilby. When we left George went out on the terrace and presently his father joined him. Freddy had won the day, but he was not happy. With his more than feminine sensitiveness he felt all that George was feeling, and George's anguish simply broke his heart. He had never loved his son more than then. When he appeared George greeted him with a little smile. Freddy's voice broke. In a sudden and overwhelming emotion he found it in him to surrender the fruits of his victory.

"Look here, old boy," he said, "I can't bear to think that you've had such a disappointment. Would you like to go back to Munich for another year and then see?"

George shook his head.

"No, it wouldn't be any good. I've had my chance. Let's call it a day."

"Try not to take it too hard."

"You see, the only thing in the world I want is to be a pianist. And there's nothing doing. It's a bit thick if you come to think of it."

George, trying so hard to be brave, smiled wanly.

"Would you like to go round the world? You can get one of your Oxford pals to go with you and I'll pay all the expenses. You've been working very hard for a long time."

"Thanks awfully, daddy, we'll talk about it. I'm just going for a stroll now."

"Shall I come with you?"

"I'd rather go alone."

Then George did a strange thing. He put his arm round his father's neck, and kissed him on the lips. He gave a funny little moved laugh and walked away. Freddy went back to the drawing-room. His mother, Ferdy and Muriel were sitting there.

"Freddy, why don't you marry the boy?" said the old lady. "He is twenty-three. It would take his mind off his troubles and when he is married and has a baby he will soon settle down like everybody else."

"Whom is he to marry, mamma?" asked Sir Adolphus, smiling.

"That's not so difficult. Lady Frielinghausen came to see me the other day with her daughter Violet. She is a very nice maiden and she will have money of her own. Lady Frielinghausen gave me to understand that her Sir Jacob would come down very handsome if Violet made a good match."

Muriel flushed.

"I hate Lady Frielinghausen. George is much too young to marry. He can afford to marry anyone he likes."

Old Lady Bland gave her daughter a strange look.

"You are a very foolish girl, Miriam," she said, using the name Muriel had long discarded. "As long as I am here I shall not allow you to commit a foolishness."

She knew as well as if Muriel had said it in so many words that she wanted George to marry a Gentile, but she knew also that so long as she was alive neither Freddy nor his wife would dare to suggest it.

But George did not go for a walk. Perhaps because the shooting season was about to open he took it into his head to go into the gun-room. He began to clean the gun that his mother had given him on his twentieth birthday. No one had used it since he went to Germany. Suddenly the servants were startled by a report. When they went into the gun-room they found George lying on the floor shot through the heart. Apparently the gun had been loaded and George while playing about with it had accidentally shot himself. One reads of such accidents in the paper often.

THE CREATIVE IMPULSE

I SUPPOSE that very few people know how Mrs. Albert Forrester came to write *The Achilles Statue;* and since it has been acclaimed as one of the great novels of our time I cannot but think that a brief account of the circumstances that gave it birth must be of interest to all serious students of literature; and indeed, if, as the critics say, this is a book that will live, the following narrative, serving a better purpose than to divert an idle hour, may be regarded by the historian of the future as a curious footnote to the literary annals of our day.

Everyone of course remembers the success that attended the publication of *The Achilles Statue*. Month after month printers were kept busy printing, binders were kept busy binding, edition after edition; and the publishers, both in England and America, were hard put to it to fulfil the pressing orders of the booksellers. It was promptly translated into every European tongue and it has been recently announced that it will soon be possible to read it in Japanese and in Urdu. But it had previously appeared serially in magazines on both sides of the Atlantic and from the editors of these Mrs. Albert Forrester's agent had wrung a sum that can only be described as thumping. A dramatisation of the work was made, which ran for a season in New York, and there is little doubt that when the play is produced in London it will have an equal success. The film rights have been sold at a great price. Though the amount that Mrs. Albert Forrester is reputed (in literary circles) to have made is probably exaggerated, there can be no doubt that she will have earned enough money from this one book to save her for the rest of her life from any financial anxiety.

It is not often that a book meets with equal favour from the public and the critics, and that she, of all persons, had (if I may so put it) squared the circle must have proved the more gratifying to Mrs. Albert Forrester, since, though she had received the commendation of the critics in no grudging terms (and indeed had come to look upon it as her due) the public had always remained strangely insensible to her merit. Each work she published, a slender volume beautifully printed and bound in white buckram, was hailed as a masterpiece, always to the length of a column, and in the weekly reviews which you see only in the dusty library of a very long-established club even to the extent of a page; and all well-read persons read and praised it. But well-read persons apparently do not buy books, and she did not sell. It was indeed a scandal that so distinguished an author, with an imagination so delicate and a style so exquisite, should remain neglected of the vulgar. In America she was almost completely unknown; and though Mr. Carl van Vechten had written an article berating the public for its obtuseness, the public remained callous. Her agent, a warm admirer of her genius, had blackmailed an American publisher into taking two of her books by refusing, unless he did so, to let him have others (trashy novels doubtless) that he badly wanted, and they had been duly published. The reception they received from the press was flattering and showed that in America the best minds were sensitive to her talent; but when it came to the third book the American publisher (in the coarse way publishers have) told the agent that any money he had to spare he preferred to spend on synthetic gin.

Since *The Achilles Statue* Mrs. Albert Forrester's previous books have been republished (and Mr. Carl van Vechten has written another article pointing out sadly, but firmly, that he had drawn the attention of the reading world to the merits of this exceptional writer fully fifteen years ago), and they have been so widely advertised that they can scarcely have escaped the cultured reader's attention. It is unnecessary, therefore, for me to give an account of them; and it would certainly be no more than cold potatoes after those two subtle articles by Mr. Carl van Vechten. Mrs. Albert Forrester began to write early. Her first work (a volume of elegies) appeared when she was a maiden of eighteen; and from then on she published, every two or three years, for she had too exalted a conception of her art to hurry her production, a volume either of verse or prose. When *The Achilles Statue* was written she had reached the respectable age of fifty-seven, so that it will be readily surmised that the number of her works was considerable. She had given the world half a dozen volumes of verse, published under Latin titles, such as *Felicitas*, *Pax Maris* and *Aes Triplex*, all of the graver kind, for her muse, disinclined to skip on a light, fantastic toe, trod a somewhat solemn measure. She remained faithful to the Elegy, and the Sonnet claimed much of her attention; but her chief distinction was to revive the Ode, a form of poetry that the poets of the present day somewhat neglect; and it may be asserted with confidence that her *Ode to President Fallières* will find a place in every anthology of English verse. It is admirable not only for the noble sonority of its rhythms, but also for its felicitous description of the pleasant land of France. Mrs. Albert Forrester wrote of the valley of the Loire with its memories of du Bellay, of Chartres and the jewelled windows of its cathedral, of the sun-swept cities of Provence, with a sympathy all the more remarkable since she had never penetrated further into France than Boulogne, which she visited shortly after her marriage on an excursion steamer from Margate. But the physical mortification of being extremely sea-sick and the intellectual humiliation of discovering that the inhabitants of that popular sea-side resort could not understand her fluent and idiomatic French made her determine not to expose herself a second time to experiences that were at once undignified and unpleasant; and she never again embarked on the treacherous element which she, however, sang (*Pax Maris*) in numbers both grave and sweet.

There are some fine passages too in the *Ode to Woodrow Wilson*, and I regret that, owing to a change in her sentiments towards that no doubt excellent man, the author decided not to reprint it. But I think it must be admitted that Mrs. Albert Forrester's most distinguished work was in prose. She wrote several volumes of brief, but perfectly constructed, essays on such subjects as Autumn in Sussex, Queen Victoria, Death, Spring in Norfolk, Georgian Architecture, Monsieur de Diaghileff and Dante; she also wrote works, both erudite and whimsical, on the Jesuit Architecture of the XVIIth Century and on the Literary Aspect of the Hundred Years' War. It was her prose that gained her that body of devoted admirers, fit though few, as with her rare gift of phrase she herself put it, that proclaimed her the greatest master of the English language that this century has seen. She admitted herself that it was her style, sonorous yet racy, polished yet eloquent, that was her strong point; and it was only in her prose that she had occasion to exhibit the delicious, but restrained, humour that her readers found so irresistible. It was not a humour of ideas, nor even a humour of words; it was much more subtle than that, it was a humour of punctuation: in a flash of inspiration she had discovered the comic possibilities of the semi-colon, and of this she had made abundant and exquisite use. She was able to place it in such a way that if you were a person of culture with a keen sense of humour, you did not exactly laugh through a horse-collar, but you giggled delightedly, and the greater your culture the more delightedly you giggled. Her friends said that it made every other form of humour coarse and exaggerated. Several writers had tried to imitate her; but in vain: whatever else you might say about Mrs. Albert Forrester you were bound to admit that she was able to get every ounce of humour out of the semi-colon and no one else could get within a mile of her.

Mrs. Albert Forrester lived in a flat not far from the Marble Arch, which combined the advantage of a good address and a moderate rent. It had a handsome drawing-room on the street and a large bedroom foi Mrs. Albert Forrester, a darkish dining-room at the back and a small poky bedroom, next door to the kitchen, for Mr. Albert Forrester who paid the rent. It was in the handsome drawing-room that Mrs. Albert Forrester every Tuesday afternoon received her friends. It was a severe and chaste apartment. On the walls was a paper designed by William Morris himself and on this, in plain black frames, mezzotints collected before mezzotints grew expensive; the furniture was of the Chippendale period, but for the roll-top desk, vaguely Louis XVI in character, at which Mrs. Albert Forrester wrote her works. This was pointed out to visitors the first time they came to see her, and there were few who looked at it without emotion. The carpet was thick and the lights discreet. Mrs. Albert Forrester sat in a straight-backed grandfather's chair covered with red damask. There was nothing ostentatious about it, but since it was the only comfortable chair in the room it set her apart as it were and above her guests. Tea was dispensed by a female of uncertain age, silent and colourless, who was never introduced to anyone but who was known to look upon it as a privilege to be allowed to save Mrs. Albert Forrester from the irksome duty of pouring out tea. She was thus able to devote herself entirely to conversation, and it must be admitted that her conversation was excellent. It was not sprightly; and since it is difficult to indicate punctuation in speech it may have seemed to some slightly lacking in humour, but it was of wide range, solid, instructive and interesting. Mrs. Albert Forrester was well acquainted with social science, jurisprudence and theology. She had read much and her memory was retentive. She had a pretty gift for quotation, which is a serviceable substitute for wit, and having for thirty years known more or less intimately a great many distinguished people, she had a great many interesting anecdotes to tell, which she placed with tact and which she did not repeat more than was pardonable. Mrs. Albert Forrester had the gift of attracting the most varied persons and you were liable at one and the same time to meet in her drawing-room an ex-Prime Minister, a newspaper proprietor and the ambassador of a First Class Power. I always imagined that these great people came because they thought that here they rubbed shoulders with Bohemia, but with a Bohemia sufficiently neat and clean for them to be in no danger that the dirt would come off on them. Mrs. Albert Forrester was deeply interested in politics and I myself heard a Cabinet Minister tell her frankly that she had a masculine intelligence. She had been opposed to Female Suffrage, but when it was at last granted to women she began to dally with the idea of going into Parliament. Her difficulty was that she did not know which party to choose.

"After all," she said, with a playful shrug of her somewhat massive shoulders, "I cannot form a party of one."

Like many serious patriots, in her inability to know for certain which way the cat would jump she held her political opinions in suspense; but of late she had been definitely turning towards Labour as the best hope of the country, and if a safe seat were offered her it was felt fairly certain that she would not hesitate to come out into the open as a champion of the oppressed proletariat.

Her drawing-room was always open to foreigners, to Cheko-Slovaks, Italians and Frenchmen if they were distinguished and to Americans even if they were obscure. But she was not a snob and you seldom met there a duke unless he was of a peculiarly serious turn and a peeress only if in addition to her rank she had the passport of some small social solecism such as having been divorced, written a novel or forged a cheque, which might give her claim on Mrs. Albert Forrester's Catholic sympathies. She did not much care for painters,

who were shy and silent; and musicians did not interest
her: even if they consented to play, and if they were
celebrated they were too often reluctant, their music was
a hindrance to conversation: if people wanted music
they could go to a concert; for her part she preferred the
more subtle music of the soul. But her hospitality to
writers, especially if they were promising and little
known, was warm and constant. She had an eye for
budding talent and there were few of the famous
writers who from time to time drank a dish of tea with
her whose first efforts she had not encouraged and whose
early steps she had not guided. Her own position was
too well assured for her to be capable of envy, and she
had heard the word genius attached to her name too
often to feel a trace of jealousy because the talents of
others brought them a material success that was denied
to her.

Mrs. Albert Forrester, confident in the judgment
of posterity, could afford to be disinterested. With
these elements then it is no wonder that she had
succeeded in creating something as near the French
Salon of the Eighteenth Century as our barbarous
nation has ever reached. To be invited to "eat a bun
and drink a cup of tea on Tuesday" was a privilege that
few failed to recognise; and when you sat on your
Chippendale chair in the discreetly lit, but austere room,
you could not but feel that you were living literary
history. The American ambassador once said to Mrs.
Albert Forrester:

"A cup of tea with you, Mrs. Forrester, is one of the richest intellectual treats which it has ever been my lot to enjoy."

It was indeed on occasion a trifle overwhelming. Mrs. Albert Forrester's taste was so perfect, she so inevitably admired the right thing and made the just observation about it, that sometimes you almost gasped for air. For my part I found it prudent to fortify myself with a cocktail or two before I exposed myself to the rarefied atmosphere of her society. Indeed, I very nearly found myself for ever excluded from it, for one afternoon, presenting myself at the door, instead of asking the maid who opened it: "Is Mrs. Forrester at home?" I asked: "Is there Divine Service to-day?"

Of course it was said in pure inadvertence, but it was unfortunate that the maid sniggered and one of Mrs. Albert Forrester's most devoted admirers, Ellen Hannaway, happened to be at the moment in the hall taking off her goloshes. She told my hostess what I had said before I got into the drawing-room, and as I entered Mrs. Albert Forrester fixed me with an eagle eye.

"Why did you ask if there was Divine Service to-day?" she inquired.

I explained that I was absent-minded, but Mrs. Albert Forrester held me with a gaze that I can only describe as compelling.

"Do you mean to suggest that my parties are . . ."

she searched for a word. "Sacramental?"

I did not know what she meant, but did not like to show my ignorance before so many clever people, and I decided that the only thing was to seize my trowel and the butter.

"Your parties are like you, dear lady, perfectly beautiful and perfectly divine."

A little tremor passed through Mrs. Albert Forrester's substantial frame. She was like a man who enters suddenly a room filled with hyacinths; the perfume is so intoxicating that he almost staggers. But she relented.

"If you were trying to be facetious," she said, "I should prefer you to exercise your facetiousness on my guests rather than on my maids. . . . Miss Warren will give you some tea."

Mrs. Albert Forrester dismissed me with a wave of the hand, but she did not dismiss the subject, since for the next two or three years whenever she introduced me to someone she never failed to add:

"You must make the most of him, he only comes here as a penance. When he comes to the door he always asks: Is there Divine Service to-day? So amusing, isn't he?"

But Mrs. Albert Forrester did not confine herself to weekly tea-parties: every Saturday she gave a luncheon of eight persons; this according to her opinion being the perfect number for general conversation and her dining-room conveniently holding no more. If Mrs. Albert Forrester flattered herself upon anything it was not that her knowledge of English prosody was unique, but that her luncheons were celebrated. She chose her guests with care and an invitation to one of them was more than a compliment, it was a consecration. Over the luncheon-table it was possible to keep the conversation on a higher level than in the mixed company of a tea-party and few can have left her dining-room without taking away with them an enhanced belief in Mrs. Albert Forrester's ability and a brighter faith in human nature. She only asked men, since, stout enthusiast for her sex as she was and glad to see women on other occasions, she could not but realise that they were inclined at table to talk exclusively to their next-door neighbours and thus hinder the general exchange of ideas that made her own parties an entertainment not only of the body but of the soul. For it must be said that Mrs. Albert Forrester gave you uncommonly good food, excellent wine and a first-rate cigar. Now to anyone who has partaken of literary hospitality this must appear very remarkable, since literary persons for the most part think highly and live plainly; their minds are occupied with the things of the spirit and they do not notice that the roast mutton is underdone and the potatoes cold: the beer is all right, but the wine has a sobering effect, and it is unwise to touch the coffee. Mrs. Albert Forrester was pleased enough to receive compliments on the fare she provided.

"If people do me the honour to break bread with me," she said, "it is only fair that I should give them as good food as they can get at home."

But if the flattery was excessive she deprecated it.

"You really embarrass me when you give me a meed of praise which is not my due. You must praise Mrs. Bulfinch."

"Who is Mrs. Bulfinch?"

"My cook."

"She's a treasure then, but you're not going to ask me to believe that she's responsible for the wine."

"Is it good? I'm terribly ignorant of such things; I put myself entirely in the hands of my wine merchant."

But if mention was made of the cigars Mrs. Albert Forrester beamed.

"Ah, for them you must compliment Albert. It is Albert who chooses the cigars and I am given to understand that no one knows more about a cigar than Albert."

She looked at her husband, who sat at the end of the table, with the proud bright eyes of a pedigree hen (a Buff Orpington for choice) looking at her only chick. Then there was a quick flutter of conversation as the guests, anxious to be civil to their host and relieved at length to find an occasion, expressed their appreciation of his peculiar merit.

"You're very kind," he said. "I'm glad you like them."

Then he would give a little discourse on cigars, explaining the excellencies he sought and regretting the deterioration in quality which had followed on the commercialisation of the industry. Mrs. Albert Forrester listened to him with a complacent smile, and it was plain that she enjoyed this little triumph of his. Of course you cannot go on talking of cigars indefinitely and as soon as she perceived that her guests were growing restive she broached a topic of more general, and it may be of more significant, interest. Albert subsided into silence. But he had had his moment.

It was Albert who made Mrs. Forrester's luncheons to some less attractive than her tea-parties, for Albert was a bore; but though without doubt perfectly conscious of the fact, she made a point that he should come to them and in fact had fixed upon Saturdays (for the rest of the week he was busy) in order that he should be able to. Mrs. Albert Forrester felt that her husband's presence on these festive occasions was an unavoidable debt that she paid to her own self-respect. She would never by a negligence admit to the world that she had married a man who was not spiritually her equal, and it may be that in the silent watches of the night she asked herself where indeed such could have been found. Mrs. Albert Forrester's friends were troubled by no such reticence and they said it was dreadful that such a woman should be burdened with such a man. They asked each other how she had ever come to marry him and (being most celibate) answered despairingly that no one ever knew why anybody married anybody else.

It was not that Albert was a verbose and aggressive

bore; he did not buttonhole you with interminable stories or pester you with pointless jokes; he did not crucify you on a platitude or hamstring you with a commonplace; he was just dull. A cipher. Clifford Boyleston, for whom the French Romantics had no secrets and who was himself a writer of merit, had said that when you looked into a room into which Albert had just gone there was nobody there. This was thought very clever by Mrs. Albert Forrester's friends and Rose Waterford, the well-known novelist and the most fearless of women, had ventured to repeat it to Mrs. Albert Forrester. Though she pretended to be annoyed, she had not been able to prevent the smile that rose to her lips. Her behaviour towards Albert could not but increase the respect in which her friends held her. She insisted that whatever in their secret hearts they thought of him, they should treat him with the decorum that was due to her husband. Her own demeanour was admirable. If he chanced to make an observation she listened to him with a pleasant expression and when he fetched her a book that she wanted or gave her his pencil to make a note of an idea that had occurred to her, she always thanked him. Nor would she allow her friends pointedly to neglect him, and though, being a woman of tact, she saw that it would be asking too much of the world if she took him about with her always, and she went out much alone, yet her friends knew that she expected them to ask him to dinner at least once a year. He always accompanied her to public banquets when she was going to make a speech, and if she delivered a lecture she took care that he should have a seat on the platform.

Albert was, I believe, of average height, but perhaps because you never thought of him except in connection with his wife (of imposing dimensions) you only thought of him as a little man. He was spare and frail and looked older than his age. This was the same as his wife's. His hair, which he kept very short, was white and meagre, and he wore a stubby white moustache; his was a face, thin and lined, without a noticeable feature; and his blue eyes, which once might have been attractive, were now pale and tired. He was always very neatly dressed in pepper-and-salt trousers, which he chose always of the same pattern, a black coat and a grey tie with a small pearl pin in it. He was perfectly unobtrusive, and when he stood in Mrs. Albert Forrester's drawing-room to receive the guests whom she had asked to luncheon you noticed him as little as you noticed the quiet and gentlemanly furniture. He was well-mannered and it was with a pleasant, courteous smile that he shook hands with them.

"How do you do? I'm very glad to see you," he said if they were friends of some standing. "Keeping well, I hope?"

But if they were strangers of distinction coming for the first time to the house, he went to the door as they entered the drawing-room, and said:

"I am Mrs. Albert Forrester's husband. I will

introduce you to my wife."

Then he led the visitor to where Mrs. Albert
Forrester stood, with her back to the light, and she with
a glad and eager gesture advanced to make the stranger
welcome.

It was agreeable to see the demure pride he took in his
wife's literary reputation and the self-effacement with
which he furthered her interests. He was always there
when he was wanted and never when he wasn't. His
tact, if not deliberate, was instinctive. Mrs. Albert
Forrester was the first to acknowledge his merits.

"I really don't know what I should do without him,"
she said. "He's invaluable to me. I read him everything
I write and his criticisms are often very useful."

"Molière and his cook," said Miss Waterford.

"Is that funny, dear Rose?" asked Mrs. Forrester,
somewhat acidly.

When Mrs. Albert Forrester did not approve of
a remark, she had a way that put many persons to
confusion of asking you whether it was a joke which
she was too dense to see. But it was impossible to
embarrass Miss Waterford. She was a lady who in
the course of a long life had had many affairs, but only
one passion, and this was for printer's ink. Mrs. Albert
Forrester tolerated rather than approved her.

"Come, come, my dear," she replied, "you know
very well that he wouldn't exist without you. He
wouldn't know us. It must be wonderful to him
to come in contact with all the best brains and the

most distinguished people of our day."

"It may be that the bee would perish without the hive which shelters it, but the bee nevertheless has a significance of its own."

And since Mrs. Albert Forrester's friends, though they knew all about art and literature, knew little about natural history, they had no reply to this observation. She went on.

"He doesn't interfere with me. He knows subconsciously when I don't want to be disturbed and, indeed, when I am following out a train of thought I find his presence in the room a comfort rather than a hindrance to me."

"Like a Persian cat," said Miss Waterford.

"But like a very well-trained, well-bred, and well-mannered Persian cat," answered Mrs. Forrester severely, thus putting Miss Waterford in her place.

But Mrs. Albert Forrester had not finished with her husband.

"We who belong to the intelligentsia," she said, "are apt to live in a world too exclusively our own. We are interested in the abstract rather than in the concrete, and sometimes I think that we survey the bustling world of human affairs in too detached a manner and from too serene a height. Do you not think that we stand in danger of becoming a little inhuman? I shall always be grateful to Albert because he keeps me in contact with the man in the street."

It was on account of this remark, to which none of her

friends could deny the rare insight and subtlety that characterised so many of her utterances, that for some time Albert was known in her immediate circle as The Man in the Street. But this was only for a while, and it was forgotten. He then became known as The Philatelist. It was Clifford Boyleston, with his wicked wit, who invented the name. One day, his poor brain exhausted by the effort to sustain a conversation with Albert, he had asked in desperation:

"Do you collect stamps?"

"No," answered Albert mildly. "I'm afraid I don't."

But Clifford Boyleston had no sooner asked the question than he saw its possibilities. He had written a book on Baudelaire's aunt by marriage, which had attracted the attention of all who were interested in French literature, and was well known in his exhaustive studies of the French spirit to have absorbed a goodly share of the Gallic quickness and the Gallic brilliancy. He paid no attention to Albert's disclaimer, but at the first opportunity informed Mrs. Albert Forrester's friends that he had at last discovered Albert's secret. He collected stamps. He never met him afterwards without asking him:

"Well, Mr. Forrester, how is the stamp collection?" Or: "Have you been buying any stamps since I saw you last?"

It mattered little that Albert continued to deny that he collected stamps, the invention was too apt not to be made the most of; Mrs. Albert Forrester's

friends insisted that he did, and they seldom spoke
to him without asking him how he was getting on.
Even Mrs. Albert Forrester, when she was in a specially
gay humour, would sometimes speak of her husband as
The Philatelist. The name really did seem to fit Albert
like a glove. Sometimes they spoke of him thus to his
face and they could not but appreciate the good nature
with which he took it; he smiled unresentfully and
presently did not even protest that they were mistaken.

Of course Mrs. Albert Forrester had too keen a social
sense to jeopardise the success of her luncheons by
allowing her more distinguished guests to sit on either
side of Albert. She took care that only her older and
more intimate friends should do this, and when the
appointed victims came in she would say to them:

"I know you won't mind sitting by Albert, will
you?"

They could only say that they would be delighted,
but if their faces too plainly expressed their dismay
she would pat their hands playfully and add:

"Next time you shall sit by me. Albert is so shy with
strangers and you know so well how to deal with him.'

They did: they simply ignored him. So far as they
were concerned the chair in which he sat might as well
have been empty. There was so sign that it annoyed
him to be taken no notice of by persons who after all
were eating food he paid for, since the earnings of Mrs.
Forrester could certainly not have provided her guests
with spring salmon and forced asparagus. He sat quiet

and silent, and if he opened his mouth it was only to give a direction to one of the maids. If a guest were new to him he would let his eyes rest on him in a stare that would have been embarrassing if it had not been so childlike. He seemed to be asking himself what this strange creature was; but what answer his mild scrutiny gave him he never revealed. When the conversation grew animated he would look from one speaker to the other, but again you could not tell from his thin, lined face what he thought of the fantastic notions that were bandied across the table.

Clifford Boyleston said that all the wit and wisdom he heard passed over his head like water over a duck's back. He had given up trying to understand and now only made a semblance of listening. But Harry Oakland, the versatile critic, said that Albert was taking it all in; he found it all too, too marvellous, and with his poor, muddled brain he was trying desperately to make head or tail of the wonderful things he heard. Of course in the City he must boast of the distinguished persons he knew, perhaps there he was a light of learning and letters, an authority on the ideal; it would be perfectly divine to hear what he made of it all. Harry Oakland was one of Mrs. Albert Forrester's staunchest admirers, and had written a brilliant and subtle essay on her style. With his refined and even beautiful features he looked like a San Sebastian who had had an accident with a hair-restorer; for he was uncommonly hirsute. He was a very young man, not thirty, but he had been in turn a

dramatic critic, and a critic of fiction, a musical critic
and a critic of painting. But he was getting a little tired
of art and threatened to devote his talents in future to
the criticism of sport.

Albert, I should explain, was in the City and it was a
misfortune that Mrs. Forrester's friends thought she
bore with meritorious fortitude that he was not even
rich. There would have been something romantic in it
if he had been a merchant prince who held the fate of
nations in his hand or sent argosies, laden with rare
spices, to those ports of the Levant the names of which
have provided many a poet with so rich and rare a
rhyme. But Albert was only a currant merchant and was
supposed to make no more than just enabled Mrs.
Albert Forrester to conduct her life with distinction and
even with liberality. Since his occupation kept him
in his office till six o'clock he never managed to get to
Mrs. Albert Forrester's Tuesdays till the most important
visitors were gone. By the time he arrived, there were
seldom more than three or four of her more intimate
friends in the drawing-room, discussing with freedom and
humour the guests who had departed, and when they
heard Albert's key in the front-door they realised with
one accord that it was late. In a moment he opened the
door in his hesitating way and looked mildly in. Mrs.
Albert Forrester greeted him with a bright smile.

"Come in, Albert, come in. I think you know everybody here."

Albert entered and shook hands with his wife's friends,

"Have you just come from the City?" she asked eagerly, though she knew there was nowhere else he could have come from. "Would you like a cup of tea?"

"No, thank you, my dear. I had tea in my office."

Mrs. Albert Forrester smiled still more brightly and the rest of the company thought she was perfectly wonderful with him.

"Ah, but I know you like a second cup. I will pour it out for you myself."

She went to the tea-table and forgetting that the tea had been stewing for an hour and a half and was stone cold, poured him out a cup and added milk and sugar. Albert took it with a word of thanks, and meekly stirred it, but when Mrs. Forrester resumed the conversation which his appearance had interrupted, without tasting it put it quietly down. His arrival was the signal for the party finally to break up and one by one the remaining guests took their departure. On one occasion, however, the conversation was so absorbing and the point at issue so important that Mrs. Albert Forrester would not hear of their going.

"It must be settled once for all. And after all," she remarked in a manner that for her was almost arch, "this is a matter on which Albert may have something to say. Let us have the benefit of his opinion."

It was when women were beginning to cut their hair and the subject of discussion was whether Mrs. Albert Forrester should or should not shingle. Mrs. Albert Forrester was a woman of authoritative presence.

She was large-boned and her bones were well covered; had she not been so tall and strong it might have suggested itself to you that she was corpulent. But she carried her weight gallantly. Her features were a little larger than life-size and it was this that gave her face doubtless the look of virile intellectuality that it certainly possessed. Her skin was dark and you might have thought that she had in her veins some trace of Levantine blood: she admitted that she could not but think there was in her a gypsy strain and that would account, she felt, for the wild and lawless passion that sometimes characterised her poetry. Her eyes were large and black and bright, her nose like the great Duke of Wellington's, but more fleshy, and her chin square and determined. She had a big mouth, with full red lips, which owed nothing to cosmetics, for of these Mrs. Albert Forrester had never deigned to make use; and her hair, thick, solid and grey, was piled on the top of her head in such a manner as to increase her already commanding height. She was in appearance an imposing, not to say an alarming, female.

She was always very suitably dressed in rich materials of sombre hue and she looked every inch a woman of letters; but in her discreet way (being after all human and susceptible to vanity) she followed the fashions and the cut of her gowns was modish. I think for some time she had hankered to shingle her hair, but she thought it more becoming to do it at the solicitation of her friends than on her own initiative.

L*

"Oh, you must, you must," said Harry Oakland, in his eager, boyish way. "You'd look too, too wonderful."

Clifford Boyleston, who was now writing a book on Madame de Maintenon, was doubtful. He thought it a dangerous experiment.

"I think," he said, wiping his eye-glasses with a cambric handkerchief, "I think when one has made a type one should stick to it. What would Louis XIV have been without his wig?"

"I'm hesitating," said Mrs. Forrester. "After all, we must move with the times. I am of my day and I do not wish to lag behind. America, as Wilhelm Meister said, is here and now." She turned brightly to Albert. "What does my lord and master say about it? What is your opinion, Albert? To shingle or not to shingle, that is the question."

"I'm afraid my opinion is not of great importance, my dear," he answered mildly.

"To me it is of the greatest importance," answered Mrs. Albert Forrester, flatteringly.

She could not but see how beautifully her friends thought she treated the philatelist.

"I insist," she proceeded, "I insist. No one knows me as you do, Albert. Will it suit me?"

"It might," he answered. "My only fear is that with your—statuesque appearance short hair would perhaps suggest,—well, shall we say, the Isle of Greece where burning Sappho loved and sung."

There was a moment's embarrassed pause. Rose

Waterford smothered a giggle, but the others preserved a stony silence. Mrs. Forrester's smile froze on her lips. Albert had dropped a brick.

"I always thought Byron a very mediocre poet," said Mrs. Albert Forrester at last.

The company broke up. Mrs. Albert Forrester did not shingle, nor indeed was the matter ever again referred to.

It was towards the end of another of Mrs. Albert Forrester's Tuesdays that the event occurred that had so great an influence on her literary career.

It had been one of her most successful parties. The leader of the Labour Party had been there and Mrs. Albert Forrester had gone as far as she could without definitely committing herself to intimate to him that she was prepared to throw in her lot with labour. The time was ripe and if she was ever to adopt a political career she must come to a decision. A member of the French Academy had been brought by Clifford Boyleston and, though she knew he was wholly unacquainted with English, it had gratified her to receive his affable compliment on her ornate and yet pellucid style. The American ambassador had been there and a young Russian prince whose authentic Romanoff blood alone prevented him from looking a gigolo. A duchess who had recently divorced her duke and married a jockey had been very gracious; and her strawberry leaves, albeit sere and yellow, undoubtedly added tone to the assembly. There had been quite a galaxy of literary lights. But now all, all were gone but Clifford Boyleston, Harry Oakland, Rose Waterford, Oscar Charles and Simmons. Oscar Charles was a little, gnome-like creature, young but with the wizened face of a cunning monkey, with gold spectacles, who earned his living in a government office but spent his leisure in the pursuit of literature. He wrote little articles for the sixpenny weeklies and had a spirited contempt for the world in general. Mrs. Albert Forrester liked him, thinking he had talent, but though he always expressed the keenest admiration for her style (it was indeed he who had named her the mistress of the semi-colon), his acerbity was so general that she also somewhat feared him. Simmons was her agent; a round-faced man who wore glasses so strong that his eyes behind them looked strange and misshapen. They reminded you of the eyes of some uncouth crustacean that you had seen in an aquarium. He came regularly to Mrs. Albert Forrester's parties, partly because he had the greatest admiration for her genius and partly because it was convenient for him to meet prospective clients in her drawing-room.

Mrs. Albert Forrester, for whom he had long laboured with but a trifling recompense, was not sorry to put him in the way of earning an honest penny, and she took care to introduce him, with warm expressions of gratitude, to anyone who might be supposed to have literary wares to sell. It was not without pride that she remembered that the notorious and vastly lucrative memoirs of Lady St. Swithin had been first mooted in her drawing-room.

They sat in a circle of which Mrs. Albert Forrester was the centre and discussed brightly, and, it must be confessed, somewhat maliciously the various persons who had been that day present. Miss Warren, the pallid female who had stood for two hours at the tea-table, was walking silently round the room collecting cups that had been left here and there. She had some vague employment, but was always able to get off in order to pour out tea for Mrs. Albert Forrester, and in the evening she typed Mrs. Albert Forrester's manuscripts. Mrs. Albert Forrester did not pay her for this, thinking quite rightly that as it was she did a great deal for the poor thing; but she gave her the seats for the cinema that were sent her for nothing and often presented her with articles of clothing for which she had no further use.

Mrs. Albert Forrester in her rather deep, full voice was talking in a steady flow and the rest were listening to her with attention. She was in good form and the words that poured from her lips could have gone straight down on paper without alteration. Suddenly there was a noise in the passage as though something heavy had fallen and then the sound of an altercation.

Mrs. Albert Forrester stopped and a slight frown darkened her really noble brow.

"I should have thought they knew by now that I

will not have this devastating racket in the flat. Would you mind ringing the bell, Miss Warren, and asking what is the reason of this tumult?"

Miss Warren rang the bell and in a moment the maid appeared. Miss Warren at the door, in order not to interrupt Mrs. Albert Forrester, spoke to her in undertones. But Mrs. Albert Forrester somewhat irritably interrupted herself.

"Well, Carter, what is it? Is the house falling down or has the Red Revolution at last broken out?"

"If you please, ma'am, it's the new cook's box," answered the maid. "The porter dropped it as he was bringing it in and the cook got all upset about it."

"What do you mean by 'the new cook'?"

"Mrs. Bulfinch went away this afternoon, ma'am," said the maid.

Mrs. Albert Forrester stared at her.

"This is the first I've heard of it. Had Mrs. Bulfinch given notice? The moment Mr. Forrester comes in tell him that I wish to speak to him."

"Very good, ma'am."

The maid went out and Miss Warren slowly returned to the tea-table. Mechanically, though nobody wanted them, she poured out several cups of tea.

"What a catastrophe!" cried Miss Waterford.

"You must get her back," said Clifford Boyleston. "She's a treasure, that woman, a remarkable cook, and she gets better and better every day."

But at that moment the maid came in again with a

letter on a small plated salver and handed it to her mistress.

"What is this?" said Mrs. Albert Forrester.

"Mr. Forrester said I was to give you this letter when you asked for him, ma'am," said the maid.

"Where is Mr. Forrester then?"

"Mr. Forrester's gone, ma'am," answered the maid as though the question surprised her.

"Gone? That'll do. You can go."

The maid left the room and Mrs. Albert Forrester, with a look of perplexity on her large face, opened the letter. Rose Waterford has told me that her first thought was that Albert, fearful of his wife's displeasure at the departure of Mrs. Bulfinch, had thrown himself in the Thames. Mrs. Albert Forrester read the letter and a look of consternation crossed her face.

"Oh, monstrous," she cried. "Monstrous! Monstrous!"

"What is it, Mrs. Forrester?"

Mrs. Albert Forrester pawed the carpet with her foot like a restive, high-spirited horse pawing the ground, and crossing her arms with a gesture that is indescribable (but that you sometimes see in a fishwife who is going to make the very devil of a scene) bent her looks upon her curious and excessively startled friends.

"Albert has eloped with the cook."

There was a gasp of dismay. Then something terrible happened. Miss Warren, who was standing behind the tea-table, suddenly choked. Miss Warren, who never opened her mouth and whom no one ever spoke to, Miss Warren, whom not one of them, though he had seen her every week for three years, would have recognised in the street, Miss Warren suddenly burst into uncontrollable laughter. With one accord, aghast, they turned and stared at her. They felt as Balaam must have felt when his ass broke into speech. She positively shrieked with laughter. There was a nameless horror about the sight, as though something had on a sudden gone wrong with a natural phenomenon, and you were just as startled as though the chairs and tables without warning began to skip about the floor in an antic dance. Miss Warren tried to contain herself, but the more she tried the more pitilessly the laughter shook her, and seizing a handkerchief she stuffed it in her mouth and hurried from the room. The door slammed behind her.

"Hysteria," said Clifford Boyleston.

"Pure hysteria, of course," said Harry Oakland.

But Mrs. Albert Forrester said nothing.

The letter had dropped at her feet and Simmons, the agent, picked it up and handed it to her. She would not take it.

"Read it," she said. "Read it aloud."

Mr. Simmons pushed his spectacles up on his forehead and holding the letter very close to his eyes read as follows:

My Dear,

Mrs. Bulfinch is in need of a change and has decided to leave, and as I do not feel inclined to stay on here without her I am going too. I have had all the literature I can stand and I am fed up with art.

Mrs. Bulfinch does not care about marriage, but if you care to divorce me she is willing to marry me. I hope you will find the new cook satisfactory. She has excellent references. It may save you trouble if I inform you that Mrs. Bulfinch and I are living at 411, Kennington Road, S.E.

Albert.

No one spoke. Mr. Simmons slipped his spectacles back on to the bridge of his nose. The fact was that none of them, brilliant as they were and accustomed to find topics of conversation to suit every occasion, could think of an appropriate remark. Mrs. Albert Forrester was not the kind of woman to whom you could offer condolences and each was too much afraid of the other's ridicule to venture upon the obvious. At last Clifford Boyleston came bravely to the rescue.

"One doesn't know what to say," he observed.

There was another silence and then Rose Waterford spoke.

"What does Mrs. Bulfinch look like?" she asked.

"How should I know?" answered Mrs. Albert Forrester, somewhat peevishly. "I have never looked at her, Albert always engaged the servants, she just came in for a moment so that I could see if her aura was satisfactory."

"But you must have seen her every morning when you did the housekeeping."

"Albert did the housekeeping. It was his own wish, so that I might be free to devote myself to my work. In this life one has to limit oneself."

"Did Albert order your luncheons?" asked Clifford Boyleston.

"Naturally. It was his province."

Clifford Boyleston slightly raised his eyebrows. What a fool he had been never to guess that it was Albert who was responsible for Mrs. Forrester's beautiful food! And of course it was owing to him that the excellent Chablis was always just sufficiently chilled to run coolly over the tongue, but never so cold as to lose its bouquet and its savour.

"He certainly knew good food and good wine."

"I always told you he had his points," answered Mrs. Albert Forrester, as though he were reproaching her. "You all laughed at him. You would not believe me when I told you that I owed a great deal to him."

There was no answer to this and once more silence, heavy and ominous, fell on the party. Suddenly Mr. Simmons flung a bombshell.

"You must get him back."

So great was her surprise that if Mrs. Albert Forrester had not been standing against the chimney-piece she would undoubtedly have staggered two paces to the rear.

"What on earth do you mean?" she cried. "I will never see him again as long as I live. Take him back? Never. Not even if he came and begged me on his bended knees."

"I didn't say take him back; I said, get him back."

But Mrs. Albert Forrester paid no attention to the misplaced interruption.

"I have done everything for him. What would he be without me? I ask you. I have given him a position which never in his remotest dreams could he have aspired to."

None could deny that there was something magnificent in the indignation of Mrs. Albert Forrester, but it appeared to have little effect on Mr. Simmons.

"What are you going to live on?"

Mrs. Albert Forrester flung him a glance totally devoid of amiability.

"God will provide," she answered in freezing tones.

"I think it very unlikely," he returned.

Mrs. Albert Forrester shrugged her shoulders. She wore an outraged expression. But Mr. Simmons made himself as comfortable as he could on his chair and lit a cigarette.

"You know you have no warmer admirer of your art than me," he said.

"Than I," corrected Clifford Boyleston.

"Or than you," went on Mr. Simmons blandly. "We all agree that there is no one writing now whom you need fear comparison with. Both in prose and verse you are absolutely first class. And your style—well, everyone knows your style."

"The opulence of Sir Thomas Browne with the limpidity of Cardinal Newman," said Clifford Boyleston. "The raciness of John Dryden with the precision of Jonathan Swift."

The only sign that Mrs. Albert Forrester heard was the smile that hesitated for a brief moment at the corners of her tragic mouth.

"And you have humour."

"Is there anyone in the world," cried Miss Waterford, "who can put such a wealth of wit and satire and comic observation into a semi-colon?"

"But the fact remains that you don't sell," pursued Mr. Simmons imperturbably. "I've handled your work for twenty years and I tell you frankly that I shouldn't have grown fat on my commission, but I've handled it because now and again I like to do what I can for good work. I've always believed in you and I've hoped that sooner or later we might get the public to swallow you. But if you think you can make your living by writing the sort of stuff you do I'm bound to tell you that you haven't a chance."

"I have come into the world too late," said Mrs. Albert Forrester. "I should have lived in the eighteenth century when the wealthy patron rewarded a dedication with a hundred guineas."

"What do you suppose the currant business brings in?"

Mrs. Albert Forrester gave a little sigh.

"A pittance. Albert always told me he made about twelve hundred a year."

"He must be a very good manager. But you couldn't expect him on that income to allow you very much. Take my word for it, there's only one thing for you to do and that's to get him back."

"I would rather live in a garret. Do you think I'm going to submit to the affront he has put upon me? Would you have me battle for his affections with my cook? Do not forget that there is one thing which is more valuable to a woman like me than her ease and that is her dignity."

"I was just coming to that," said Mr. Simmons coldly.

He glanced at the others and those strange, lopsided eyes of his looked more than ever monstrous and fish-like.

"There is no doubt in my mind," he went on, "that you have a very distinguished and almost unique position in the world of letters. You stand for something quite apart. You never prostituted your genius for filthy lucre and you have held high the banner of pure art. You're thinking of going into Parliament. I don't think much of politics myself, but there's no denying that it would be a good advertisement and if you get in I daresay we could get you a lecture tour in America on the strength of it. You have ideals and this I can say, that even the people who've never read a word you've written respect you. But in your position there's one thing you can't afford to be and that's a joke."

Mrs. Albert Forrester gave a distinct start.

"What on earth do you mean by that?"

"I know nothing about Mrs. Bulfinch and for all I know she's a very respectable woman, but the fact remains that a man doesn't run away with his cook without making his wife ridiculous. If it had been a dancer or a lady of title I daresay it wouldn't have done you any harm, but a cook would finish you. In a week you'd have all London laughing at you, and if there's one thing that kills an author or a politician it is ridicule. You must get your husband back and you must get him back pretty damned quick."

A dark flush settled on Mrs. Albert Forrester's face, but she did not immediately reply. In her ears there rang on a sudden the outrageous and unaccountable laughter that had sent Miss Warren flying from the room.

"We're all friends here and you can count on our discretion."

Mrs. Forrester looked at her friends and she thought that in Rose Waterford's eyes there was already a malicious gleam. On the wizened face of Oscar Charles was a whimsical look. She wished that in a moment of abandon she had not betrayed her secret. Mr. Simmons, however, knew the literary world and allowed his eyes to rest on the company.

"After all you are the centre and head of their set. Your husband has not only run away from you but also from them. It's not too good for them either. The fact is that Albert Forrester has made you all look a lot of damned fools."

"All," said Clifford Boyleston. "We're all in the same boat. He's quite right, Mrs. Forrester, the philatelist must come back."

"*Et tu, Brute.*"

Mr. Simmons did not understand Latin and if he had would probably not have been moved by Mrs. Albert Forrester's exclamation. He cleared his throat.

"My suggestion is that Mrs. Albert Forrester should go and see him to-morrow, fortunately we have his address, and beg him to reconsider his decision. I don't know what sort of things a woman says on these occasions, but Mrs. Forrester has tact and imagination and she must say them. If Mr. Forrester makes any conditions she must accept them. She must leave no stone unturned."

"If you play your cards well there is no reason why you shouldn't bring him back here with you to-morrow evening," said Rose Waterford lightly.

"Will you do it, Mrs. Forrester?"

For two minutes, at least, turned away from them, she stared at the empty fireplace; then, drawing herself to her full height, she faced them.

"For my art's sake, not for mine. I will not allow the ribald laughter of the Philistine to besmirch all that I hold good and true and beautiful."

"Capital," said Mr. Simmons, rising to his feet, "I'll look in on my way home to-morrow and I hope to find you and Mr. Forrester billing and cooing side by side like a pair of turtle doves."

He took his leave, and the others, anxious not to be left alone with Mrs. Albert Forrester and her agitation, in a body followed his example.

It was latish in the afternoon next day when Mrs. Albert Forrester, imposing in black silk and a velvet toque, set out from her flat in order to get a bus from the Marble Arch that would take her to Victoria Station. Mr. Simmons had explained to her by telephone how to reach the Kennington Road with expedition and economy. She neither felt nor looked like Delilah. At Victoria she took the tram that runs down the Vauxhall Bridge Road. When she crossed the river she found herself in a part of London more noisy, sordid and bustling than that to which she was accustomed, but she was too much occupied with her thoughts to notice the varied scene. She was relieved to find that the tram went along the Kennington Road and asked the conductor to put her down a few doors from the house she sought. When it did and rumbled on leaving her alone in the busy street, she felt strangely lost, like a traveller in an eastern tale set down by a djinn in an unknown city. She walked slowly, looking to right and left, and notwithstanding the emotions of indignation and embarrassment that fought for the possession of her somewhat opulent bosom, she could not but reflect that here was the material for a very pretty piece of prose. The little houses held about them the feeling of a bygone age when here it was still almost country, and Mrs. Albert Forrester registered in her retentive memory a note that she must look into the literary associations of the Kennington Road. Number four hundred and eleven was one of a row of shabby houses that stood some way back from the street; in front of it was a narrow strip of shabby grass, and a paved way led up to a latticed wooden porch that badly needed a coat of paint. This and the straggling, stunted creeper that grew over the front of the house gave it a falsely rural air which was strange and even sinister in that road down which thundered a tumultuous traffic. There was something equivocal about the house that suggested that here lived women to whom a life of pleasure had brought an inadequate reward.

The door was opened by a scraggy girl of fifteen with long legs and a tousled head.

"Does Mrs. Bulfinch live here, do you know?"

"You've rung the wrong bell. Second floor." The girl pointed to the stairs and at the same time screamed shrilly: "Mrs. Bulfinch, a party to see you. Mrs. Bulfinch."

Mrs. Albert Forrester walked up the dingy stairs. They were covered with torn carpet. She walked slowly, for she did not wish to get out of breath. A door opened as she reached the second floor and she recognised her cook.

"Good afternoon, Bulfinch," said Mrs. Albert Forrester, with dignity. "I wish to see your master."

Mrs. Bulfinch hesitated for the shadow of a second, then held the door wide open.

"Come in, ma'am." She turned her head. "Albert, here's Mrs. Forrester to see you."

Mrs. Forrester stepped by quickly and there was Albert sitting by the fire in a leather-covered, but rather shabby armchair, with his feet in slippers, and in shirt sleeves. He was reading the evening paper and smoking a cigar. He rose to his feet as Mrs. Albert Forrester came in. Mrs. Bulfinch followed her visitor into the room and closed the door.

"How are you, my dear?" said Albert cheerfully. "Keeping well, I hope."

"You'd better put on your coat, Albert," said Mrs. Bulfinch. "What *will* Mrs. Forrester think of you, finding you like that? I never."

She took the coat, which was hanging on a peg, and helped him into it; and like a woman familiar with the peculiarities of masculine dress pulled down his waistcoat so that it should not ride over his collar.

"I received your letter, Albert," said Mrs. Forrester.

"I supposed you had, or you wouldn't have known my address, would you?"

"Won't you sit down, ma'am?" said Mrs. Bulfinch, deftly dusting a chair, part of a suite covered in plum-coloured velvet, and pushing it forwards.

Mrs. Albert Forrester with a slight bow seated herself.

"I should have preferred to see you alone, Albert," she said.

His eyes twinkled.

"Since anything you have to say concerns Mrs. Bulfinch as much as it concerns me I think it much better that she should be present."

"As you wish."

Mrs. Bulfinch drew up a chair and sat down. Mrs. Albert Forrester had never seen her before but with a large apron over a print dress. She was wearing now an open-work blouse of white silk, a black skirt, and high-heeled, patent-leather shoes with silver buckles. She was a woman of about five-and-forty, with reddish hair and a reddish face, not pretty, but with a good-natured look, and buxom. She reminded Mrs. Albert Forrester of a serving-wench, somewhat overblown, in a jolly picture by an old Dutch master.

"Well, my dear, what have you to say to me?" asked Albert.

Mrs. Albert Forrester gave him her brightest and most affable smile. Her great black eyes shone with tolerant good-humour.

"Of course you know that this is perfectly absurd, Albert. I think you must be out of your mind."

"Do you, my dear? Fancy that."

"I'm not angry with you, I'm only amused, but a joke's a joke and should not be carried too far. I've come to take you home."

"Was my letter not quite clear?"

"Perfectly. I ask no questions and I will make no reproaches. We will look upon this as a momentary aberration and say no more about it."

"Nothing will induce me ever to live with you again, my dear," said Albert in, however, a perfectly friendly fashion.

"You're not serious?"

"Quite."

"Do you love this woman?"

Mrs. Albert Forrester still smiled with an eager and somewhat metallic brightness. She was determined to take the matter lightly. With her intimate sense of values she realised that the scene was comic. Albert looked at Mrs. Bulfinch and a smile broke out on his withered face.

"We get on very well together, don't we, old girl?"

"Not so bad," said Mrs. Bulfinch.

Mrs. Albert Forrester raised her eyebrows; her husband had never in all their married life called *her* "old girl": nor indeed would she have wished it.

"If Bulfinch has any regard or respect for you she must know that the thing is impossible. After the life you've led and the society you've moved in she can hardly expect to make you permanently happy in miserable furnished lodgings."

"They're not furnished lodgin's, ma'am," said Mrs. Bulfinch. "It's all me own furniture. You see, I'm very independent like and I've always liked to have a home of me own. So I keep these rooms on whether I'm in a situation or whether I'm not, and so I always have some place to go back to."

"And a very nice cosy little place it is," said Albert.

Mrs. Albert Forrester looked about her. There was a kitchen range in the fireplace on which a kettle was simmering and on the mantelshelf was a black marble clock flanked by black marble candelabra. There was a large table covered with a red cloth, a dresser, and a sewing-machine. On the walls were photographs and framed pictures from Christmas supplements. A door at the back, covered with a red plush portière, led into what, considering the size of the house, Mrs. Albert Forrester (who in her leisure moments had made a somewhat extensive study of architecture) could not but conclude was the only bedroom. Mrs. Bulfinch and Albert lived in a contiguity that allowed no doubt about their relations.

"Have you not been happy with me, Albert?" asked Mrs. Forrester in a deeper tone.

"We've been married for thirty-five years, my dear. It's too long. It's a great deal too long. You're a good woman in your way, but you don't suit me. You're literary and I'm not. You're artistic and I'm not."

"I've always taken care to make you share in all my interests. I've taken great pains that you shouldn't be overshadowed by my success. You can't say that I've ever left you out of things."

"You're a wonderful writer, I don't deny it for a moment, but the truth is I don't like the books you write."

"That, if I may be permitted to say so, merely shows that you have very bad taste. All the best critics admit their power and their charm."

"And I don't like your friends. Let me tell you a secret, my dear. Often at your parties I've had an almost irresistible impulse to take off all my clothes just to see what would happen."

"Nothing would have happened," said Mrs. Albert Forrester with a slight frown. "I should merely have sent for the doctor."

"Besides you haven't the figure for that, Albert," said Mrs. Bulfinch.

Mr. Simmons had hinted to Mrs. Albert Forrester that if the need arose she must not hesitate to use the allurements of her sex in order to bring back her erring husband to the conjugal roof, but she did not in the least know how to do this. It would have been easier, she could not but reflect, had she been in evening dress.

"Does the fidelity of five-and-thirty years count for nothing? I have never looked at another man, Albert. I'm used to you. I shall be lost without you."

"I've left all my menus with the new cook, ma'am. You've only got to tell her how many to luncheon and she'll manage," said Mrs. Bulfinch. "She's very reliable and she has as light a hand with pastry as anyone I ever knew."

Mrs. Albert Forrester began to be discouraged. Mrs. Bulfinch's remark, well-meant no doubt, made it difficult to bring the conversation on to the plane on which emotion could be natural.

"I'm afraid you're only wasting your time, my dear," said Albert. "My decision is irrevocable. I'm not very young any more and I want someone to take care of me. I shall of course make you as good an allowance as I can. Corinne wants me to retire."

"Who is Corinne?" asked Mrs. Forrester with the utmost surprise.

"It's my name," said Mrs. Bulfinch. "My mother was half French."

"That explains a great deal," replied Mrs. Forrester, pursing her lips, for though she admired the literature of our neighbours she knew that their morals left much to be desired.

"What I say is, Albert's worked long enough, and it's about time he started enjoying himself. I've got a little bit of property at Clacton-on-Sea. It's a very healthy neighbourhood and the air is wonderful. We could live there very comfortable. And what with the beach and the pier there's always something to do. They're a very nice lot of people down there. If you don't interfere with nobody, nobody'll interfere with you."

"I discussed the matter with my partners to-day and they're willing to buy me out. It means a certain sacrifice. When everything is settled I shall have an income of nine hundred pounds a year. There are three of us, so it gives us just three hundred a year apiece."

"How am I to live on that?" cried Mrs. Albert Forrester. "I have my position to keep up."

"You have a fluent, a fertile and a distinguished pen, my dear."

Mrs. Albert Forrester impatiently shrugged her shoulders.

"You know very well that my books don't bring me in anything but reputation. The publishers always say that they lose by them and in fact they only publish them because it gives them prestige."

It was then that Mrs. Bulfinch had the idea that was to have consequences of such magnitude.

"Why don't you write a good thrilling detective story?" she asked.

"Me?" exclaimed Mrs. Albert Forrester, for the first time in her life regardless of grammar.

"It's not a bad idea," said Albert. "It's not a bad idea at all."

"I should have the critics down on me like a thousand of bricks."

"I'm not so sure of that. Give the highbrow the chance of being lowbrow without demeaning himself and he'll be so grateful to you, he won't know what to do."

"For this relief much thanks," murmured Mrs. Albert Forrester reflectively.

"My dear, the critics'll eat it. And written in your beautiful English they won't be afraid to call it a masterpiece."

"The idea is preposterous. It's absolutely foreign to my genius. I could never hope to please the masses."

"Why not? The masses want to read good stuff, but they dislike being bored. They all know your name, but they don't read you, because you bore them. The fact is, my dear, you're dull."

"I don't know how you can say that, Albert," replied Mrs. Albert Forrester, with as little resentment as the equator might feel if someone called it chilly. "Everyone knows and acknowledges that I have an exquisite sense of humour and there is nobody who can extract so much good wholesome fun from a semi-colon as I can."

"If you can give the masses a good thrilling story and let them think at the same time that they are improving their minds you'll make a fortune."

"I've never read a detective story in my life," said Mrs. Albert Forrester. "I once heard of a Mr. Barnes of New York and I was told that he had written a book called *The Mystery of a Hansom Cab*. But I never read it."

"Of course you have to have the knack," said Mrs. Bulfinch. "The first thing to remember is that you don't want any love-making, it's out of place in a detective story, what you want is murder, and sleuth-hounds, and you don't want to be able to guess who done it till the last page."

"But you must play fair with your reader, my dear," said Albert. "It always annoys me when suspicion has been thrown on the secretary or the lady of title and it turns out to be the second footman who's never done

M

more than say, 'The carriage is at the door.' Puzzle your reader as much as you can, but don't make a fool of him."

"I love a good detective story," said Mrs. Bulfinch. "Give me a lady in evening dress, just streaming with diamonds, lying on the library floor with a dagger in her heart and I know I'm going to have a treat."

"There's no accounting for tastes," said Albert. "Personally, I prefer a respectable family solicitor, with side-whiskers, gold watch-chain, and a benign appearance, lying dead in Hyde Park."

"With his throat cut?" asked Mrs. Bulfinch eagerly.

"No, stabbed in the back. There's something peculiarly attractive to the reader in the murder of a middle-aged gentleman of spotless reputation. It is pleasant to think that the most apparently blameless of us have a mystery in our lives."

"I see what you mean, Albert," said Mrs. Bulfinch. "He was the repository of a fatal secret."

"We can give you all the tips, my dear," said Albert, smiling mildly at Mrs. Albert Forrester. "I've read hundreds of detective stories."

"You!"

"That's what first brought Corinne and me together. I used to pass them on to her when I'd finished them."

"Many's the time I've heard him switch off the electric light as the dawn was creeping through the window and I couldn't help smiling to myself as I said: 'There, he's finished it at last, now he can have a good sleep.'"

Mrs. Albert Forrester rose to her feet. She drew herself up.

"Now I see what a gulf separates us," she said, and her fine contralto shook a little. "You have been surrounded for thirty years with all that was best in English literature and you read hundreds of detective novels."

"Hundreds and hundreds," interrupted Albert with a smile of satisfaction.

"I came here willing to make any reasonable concession so that you should come back to your home, but now I wish it no longer. You have shown me that we have nothing in common and never had. There is an abyss between us."

"Very well, my dear," said Albert gently, "I will submit to your decision. But you think over the detective story."

"I will arise and go now," she murmured, "and go to Innisfree."

"I'll just show you downstairs," said Mrs. Bulfinch. "One has to be careful of the carpet if one doesn't exactly know where the holes are."

With dignity, but not without circumspection, Mrs. Albert Forrester walked downstairs and when Mrs. Bulfinch opened the door and asked her if she would like a taxi she shook her head.

"I shall take the tram."

"You need not be afraid that I won't take good care of Mr. Forrester, ma'am," said Mrs. Bulfinch pleasantly.

"He shall have every comfort. I nursed Mr. Bulfinch for three years during his last illness and there's very little I don't know about invalids. Not that Mr. Forrester isn't very strong and active for his years. And of course he'll have a hobby. I always think a man should have a hobby. He's going to collect postage-stamps."

Mrs. Albert Forrester gave a little start of surprise. But just then a tram came in sight and as a woman (even the greatest of them) will, she hurried at the risk of her life into the middle of the road and waved frantically. It stopped and she climbed in. She did not know how she was going to face Mr. Simmons. He would be waiting for her when she got home. Clifford Boyleston would probably be there too. They would all be there and she would have to tell them that she had miserably failed. At that moment she had no warm feeling of friendship towards her little group of devoted admirers. Wondering what the time was, she looked up at the man sitting opposite her to see whether he was the kind of person she could modestly ask, and suddenly started; for sitting there was a middle-aged gentleman of the most respectable appearance, with side-whiskers, a benign expression and a gold watch-chain. It was the very man whom Albert had described lying dead in Hyde Park and she could not but jump to the conclusion that he was a family solicitor. The coincidence was extraordinary and really it looked as though the hand of fate were beckoning to her. He wore a silk hat, a black coat and pepper-and-salt trousers, he was somewhat corpulent, of a powerful build, and by his side was a despatch-case. When the tram was half-way down the Vauxhall Bridge Road he asked the conductor to stop and she saw him go down a small, mean street. Why? Ah, why? When it reached Victoria, so deeply immersed in thought was she, until the conductor somewhat roughly told her where she was, she did not move. Edgar Allan Poe had written detective stories. She took a bus. She sat inside, buried in reflection, but when it arrived at Hyde Park Corner she suddenly made up her mind to get out. She couldn't sit still any longer. She felt she must walk. She entered the gates, walking slowly, and looked about her with an air that was at once intent and abstracted. Yes, there was Edgar Allan Poe; no one could deny that. After all he had invented the genre, and everyone knew how great his influence had been on the Parnassians. Or was it the Symbolists? Never mind. Baudelaire and all that. As she passed the Achilles Statue she stopped for a minute and looked at it with raised eyebrows.

At length she reached her flat and opening the door saw several hats in the hall. They were all there. She went into the drawing-room.

"Here she is at last," cried Miss Waterford.

Mrs. Albert Forrester advanced, smiling with animation, and shook the proffered hands. Mr. Simmons and Clifford Boyleston were there, Harry Oakland and Oscar Charles.

"Oh, you poor things, have you had no tea?" she cried brightly. "I haven't an idea what the time is, but I know I'm fearfully late."

"Well?" they said. "Well?"

"My dears, I've got something quite wonderful to tell you. I've had an inspiration. Why should the devil have all the best tunes?"

"What *do* you mean?"

She paused in order to give full effect to the surprise she was going to spring upon them. Then she flung it at them without preamble.

"I'M GOING TO WRITE A DETECTIVE STORY."

They stared at her with open mouths. She held up her hand to prevent them from interrupting her, but indeed no one had the smallest intention of doing so.

"I am going to raise the detective story to the dignity of Art. It came to me suddenly in Hyde Park. It's a murder story and I shall give the solution on the very last page. I shall write it in an impeccable English, and since it's occurred to me lately that perhaps I've exhausted the possibilities of the semi-colon, I am going to take up the colon. No one yet has explored its potentialities. Humour and mystery are what I aim at. I shall call it *The Achilles Statue*."

"What a title!" cried Mr. Simmons, recovering himself before any of the others. "I can sell the serial rights on the title and your name alone."

"But what about Albert?" asked Clifford Boyleston.

"Albert?" echoed Mrs. Forrester. "Albert?"

She looked at him as though for the life of her she could not think what he was talking about. Then she gave a little cry as if she had suddenly remembered.

"Albert! I knew I'd gone out on some errand and it absolutely slipped my memory. I was walking through Hyde Park and I had this inspiration. What a fool you'll all think me!"

"Then you haven't seen Albert?"

"My dear, I forgot all about him." She gave an amused laugh. "Let Albert keep his cook. I can't bother about Albert now. Albert belongs to the semi-colon period. I am going to write a detective story."

"My dear, you're too, too wonderful," said Harry Oakland.

WHEN Ashenden went on deck and saw before him a low-lying coast and a white town he felt a pleasant flutter of excitement. It was early and the sun had not long risen, but the sea was glassy and the sky was blue; it was warm already and one knew that the day would be sweltering. Vladivostok. It really gave one the sensation of being at the end of the world. It was a long journey that Ashenden had made from New York to San Francisco, across the Pacific in a Japanese boat to Yokohama, then from Tsuruki in a Russian boat, he the only Englishman on board, up the Sea of Japan. From Vladivostok he was to take the Trans-Siberian to Petrograd. It was the most important mission that he had ever had and he was pleased with the sense of responsibility that it gave him. He had no one to give him orders, unlimited funds (he carried in a belt next to his skin bills of exchange for a sum so enormous that he was staggered when he thought of them), and though he had been set to do something that was beyond human possibility he did not know this and was prepared to set about his task with confidence. He believed in his own astuteness. Though he had both esteem and admiration for the sensibility of the human race, he had little respect for their intelligence: man has always found it easier to sacrifice his life than to learn the multiplication table.

Ashenden did not much look forward to ten days on a Russian train, and in Yokohama he had heard rumours that in one or two places bridges had been blown up and the line cut. He was told that the soldiers, completely out of hand, would rob him of everything he possessed and turn him out on the steppe to shift for himself. It was a cheerful prospect. But the train was certainly starting and whatever happened later (and Ashenden had always a feeling that things never turned out as badly as you expected) he was determined to get a place on it. His intention on landing was to go at once to the British Consulate and find out what arrangements had been made for him; but as they neared the shore and he was able to discern the untidy and bedraggled town he felt not a little forlorn. He knew but a few words of Russian. The only man on the ship who spoke English was the purser and though he promised Ashenden to do anything he could to help him, Ashenden had the impression that he must not too greatly count upon him. It was a relief then, when they docked, to have a young man, small and with a mop of untidy hair, obviously a Jew, come up to him and ask if his name was Ashenden.

"Mine is Benedict. I'm the interpreter at the British Consulate. I've been told to look after you. We've got you a place on the train to-night."

Ashenden's spirits went up. They landed. The little

Jew looked after his luggage and had his passport examined and then, getting into a car that waited for them, they drove off to the Consulate.

"I've had instructions to offer you every facility," said the Consul, "and you've only got to tell me what you want. I've fixed you up all right on the train, but God knows if you'll ever get to Petrograd. Oh, by the way, I've got a travelling companion for you. He's a man called Harrington, an American, and he's going to Petrograd for a firm in Philadelphia. He's trying to fix up some deal with the Provisional Government."

"What's he like?" asked Ashenden.

"Oh, he's all right. I wanted him to come with the American Consul to luncheon, but they've gone for an excursion in the country. You must get to the station a couple of hours before the train starts. There's always an awful scrimmage and if you're not there in good time someone will pinch your seat."

The train started at midnight and Ashenden dined with Benedict at the station restaurant which was, it appeared, the only place in that slatternly town where you could get a decent meal. It was crowded. The service was intolerably slow. Then they went on to the platform, where, though they had still two hours to spare, there was already a seething mob. Whole families, sitting on piles of luggage, seemed to be camped there. People rushed to and fro, or stood in little groups violently arguing. Women screamed. Others were silently weeping. Here two men were engaged in a fierce quarrel. It was a scene of indescribable confusion. The light in the station was wan and cold and the white faces of all those people were like the white faces of the dead waiting, patient or anxious, distraught or penitent, for the judgment of the last day. The train was made up and most of the carriages were already filled to overflowing. When at last Benedict found that in which Ashenden had his place a man sprang out of it excitedly.

"Come in and sit down," he said. "I've had the greatest difficulty in keeping your seat. A fellow wanted to come in here with a wife and two children. My Consul has just gone off with him to see the station-master."

"This is Mr. Harrington," said Benedict.

Ashenden stepped into the carriage. It had two berths in it. The porter stowed his luggage away. He shook hands with his travelling companion.

Mr. John Quincy Harrington was a very thin man of somewhat less than middle height, he had a yellow, bony face, with large, pale-blue eyes and when he took off his hat to wipe his brow wet from the perturbation he had endured he showed a large, bald skull; it was very bony and the ridges and protuberances stood out disconcertingly. He wore a bowler hat, a black coat and waistcoat, and a pair of striped trousers; a very high white collar and a neat, unobtrusive tie. Ashenden did not know precisely how you should dress in order to take a ten days' journey across Siberia, but he could not but think that Mr. Harrington's costume was eccentric. He spoke with precision in a high-pitched voice and in an accent that Ashenden recognised as that of New England.

In a minute the station-master came accompanied by a bearded Russian, suffering evidently from profound emotion, and followed by a lady holding two children by the hand. The Russian, tears running down his face, was talking with quivering lips to the station-master and his wife between her sobs was apparently telling him the story of her life. When they arrived at the carriage the altercation became more violent and Benedict joined in with his fluent Russian. Mr. Harrington did not know a word of the language, but being obviously of an excitable turn broke in and explained in voluble English that these seats had been booked by the Consuls of Great Britain and the United States respectively, and though he didn't know about the King of England, he could tell them straight and they could take it from him that the President of the United States would never permit an American citizen to be done out of a seat on the train that he had duly paid for. He would yield to force, but to nothing else, and if they touched him he would register a complaint with the Consul at once. He said all this and a great deal more to the station-master, who of course had no notion what he was talking about, but with much emphasis and a good deal of gesticulation made him in reply a passionate speech. This roused Mr. Harrington to the utmost pitch of indignation, for shaking his fist in the station-master's face, his own pale with fury, he cried out:

"Tell him I don't understand a word he says and I don't want to understand. If the Russians want us to look upon them as a civilised people, why don't they talk a civilised language? Tell him that I am Mr. John Quincy Harrington and I'm travelling on behalf of Messrs. Crewe and Adams of Philadelphia with a special letter of introduction to Mr. Kerensky and if I'm not left in peaceful possession of this carriage Mr. Crewe will take the matter up with the Administration in Washington."

Mr. Harrington's manner was so truculent and his gestures so menacing that the station-master, throwing up the sponge, turned on his heel without another word and walked moodily away. He was followed by the bearded Russian and his wife arguing heatedly with him and the two apathetic children. Mr. Harrington jumped back into the carriage.

"I'm terribly sorry to have to refuse to give up my seat to a lady with two children," he said. "No one knows better than I the respect due to a woman and a mother, but I've got to get to Petrograd by this train if I don't want to lose a very important order and I'm not going to spend ten days in a corridor for all the mothers in Russia."

"I don't blame you," said Ashenden.

"I am a married man and I have two children myself. I know that travelling with your family is a difficult matter, but there's nothing that I know to prevent you from staying at home."

When you are shut up with a man for ten days in a railway carriage you can hardly fail to learn most of what there is to know about him, and for ten days (for eleven to be exact) Ashenden spent twenty-four hours a day with Mr. Harrington. It is true that they went into the dining-room three times a day for their meals, but they sat opposite to one another; it is true that the train stopped for an hour morning and afternoon so that they were able to have a tramp up and down the platform, but they walked side by side. Ashenden made acquaintance with some of his fellow-travellers and sometimes they came into the compartment to have a chat, but if they only spoke French or German Mr. Harrington would watch them with acidulous disapproval and if they spoke English he would never let them get a word in. For Mr. Harrington was a talker. He talked as though it were a natural function of the human being, automatically, as men breathe or digest their food; he talked not because he had something to say, but because he could not help himself, in a high-pitched, nasal voice, without inflection, at one dead level of tone. He talked with precision, using a copious vocabulary and forming his sentences with deliberation; he never used a short word when a longer one would do; he never paused. He went on and on. It was not a torrent, for there was nothing impetuous about it, it was like a stream of lava pouring irresistibly down the side of a volcano. It flowed with a quiet and steady force that overwhelmed everything that was in its path.

Ashenden thought he had never known as much about anyone as he knew about Mr. Harrington, and not only about him, with all his opinions, habits and circumstances, but about his wife and his wife's family, his children and their schoolfellows, his employers and the alliances they had made for three or four generations with the best families of Philadelphia. His own family had come from Devonshire early in the eighteenth century and Mr. Harrington had been to the village where the graves of his forebears were still to be seen in the churchyard. He was proud of his English ancestry, but proud too of his American birth, though to him America was a little strip of land along the Atlantic coast and Americans were a small number of persons of English or Dutch origin whose blood had never been sullied by foreign admixture. He looked upon the Germans, Swedes, Irish and the inhabitants of Central and Eastern Europe who for the last hundred years have descended upon the United States as interlopers. He turned his attention away from them as a maiden lady who lived in a secluded manor might avert her eyes from the factory chimneys that had trespassed upon her retirement.

When Ashenden mentioned a man of vast wealth who owned some of the finest pictures in America Mr. Harrington said:

"I've never met him. My great-aunt Maria Penn

Warmington always said his grandmother was a very good cook. My great-aunt Maria was terribly sorry when she left her to get married. She said she never knew anyone who could make an apple pancake as she could."

Mr. Harrington was devoted to his wife and he told Ashenden at unbelievable length how cultivated and what a perfect mother she was. She had delicate health and had undergone a great number of operations all of which he described in detail. He had had two operations himself, one on his tonsils and one to remove his appendix and he took Ashenden day by day through his experiences. All his friends had had operations and his knowledge of surgery was encyclopædic. He had two sons, both at school, and he was seriously considering whether he would not be well-advised to have them operated on. It was curious that one of them should have enlarged tonsils, and he was not at all happy about the appendix of the other. They were more devoted to one another than he had ever seen two brothers be and a very good friend of his, the brightest surgeon in Philadelphia, had offered to operate on them both together so that they should not be separated. He showed Ashenden photographs of the boys and their mother. This journey of his to Russia was the first time in their lives that he had been separated from them and every morning he wrote a long letter to his wife telling her everything that had happened and a good deal of what he had said during the day. Ashenden watched him cover sheet after sheet of paper with his neat legible and precise handwriting.

Mr. Harrington had read all the books on conversation and knew its technique to the last detail. He had a little book in which he noted down the stories he heard and he told Ashenden that when he was going out to dinner he always looked up half a dozen so that he should not be at a loss. They were marked with a G if they could be told in general society and with an M (for men) if they were more fit for rough masculine ears. He was a specialist in that peculiar form of anecdote that consists in narrating a long serious incident, piling detail upon detail, till a comic end is reached. He spared you nothing and Ashenden foreseeing the point long before it arrived would clench his hands and knit his brows in the strenuous effort not to betray his impatience and at last force from his unwilling mouth a grim and hollow laugh. If someone came into the compartment in the middle Mr. Harrington would greet him with cordiality.

"Come right in and sit down. I was just telling my friend a story. You must listen to it, it's one of the funniest things you ever heard."

Then he would begin again from the very beginning and repeat it word for word, without altering a single apt epithet, till he reached the humorous end. Ashenden suggested once that they should see whether they could find two people on the train who played cards so that they might while away the time with a game of bridge, but Mr. Harrington said he never touched cards and when Ashenden in desperation began to play patience he pulled a wry face.

"It beats me how an intelligent man can waste his time card-playing, and of all the unintellectual pursuits I have ever seen it seems to me that solitaire is the worst. It kills conversation. Man is a social animal and he exercises the highest part of his nature when he takes part in social intercourse."

"There is a certain elegance in wasting time," said Ashenden. "Any fool can waste money, but when you waste time you waste what is priceless. Besides," he added with bitterness, "you can still talk."

"How can I talk when your attention is taken up by whether you are going to get a black seven to put on a red eight? Conversation calls forth the highest powers of the intellect and if you have made a study of it you have the right to expect that the person you're talking to will give you the fullest attention he is capable of."

He did not say this acrimoniously, but with the good-humoured patience of a man who has been much tried. He was just stating a plain fact and Ashenden could take it or leave it. It was the claim of the artist to have his work taken seriously.

Mr. Harrington was a diligent reader. He read pencil in hand, underlining passages that attracted his attention and on the margin making in his neat writing comments on what he read. This he was fond of discussing and when Ashenden himself was reading and felt on a sudden that Mr. Harrington, book in one hand and pencil in the other, was looking at him with his large pale eyes he began to have violent palpitations of the heart. He dared not look up, he dared not even turn the page, for he knew that Mr. Harrington would regard this as ample excuse to break into a discourse, but remained with his eyes fixed desperately on a single word, like a chicken with its beak to a chalk line, and only ventured to breathe when he realised that Mr. Harrington, having given up the attempt, had resumed his reading. He was then engaged on a History of the American Constitution in two volumes and for recreation was perusing a stout volume that purported to contain all the great speeches of the world. For Mr. Harrington was an after-dinner speaker and had read all the best books on speaking in public. He knew exactly how to get on good terms with his audience, just where to put in the serious words that touched their hearts, how to catch their attention by a few apt stories and finally with what degree of eloquence, suiting the occasion, to deliver his peroration.

Mr. Harrington was very fond of reading aloud. Ashenden had had frequent occasion to observe the distressing propensity of Americans for this pastime. In hotel drawing-rooms at night after dinner he had often seen the father of a family seated in a retired corner and surrounded by his wife, his two sons and his daughter, reading to them. On ships crossing the Atlantic he had sometimes watched with awe the tall, spare gentleman of commanding aspect who sat in the centre of fifteen ladies no longer in their first youth and in a resonant voice read to them the history of Art. Walking up and down the promenade deck he had passed honeymooning couples lying on deck-chairs and caught the unhurried tones of the bride as she read to her young husband the pages of a popular novel. It had always seemed to him a curious way of showing affection. He had had friends who had offered to read to him and he had known women who had said they loved being read to, but he had always politely refused the invitation and firmly ignored the hint. He liked neither reading aloud nor being read aloud to. In his heart he thought the national predilection for this form of entertainment the only flaw in the perfection of the American character. But the immortal gods love a good laugh at the expense of human beings and now delivered him, bound and helpless, to the knife of the high priest. Mr. Harrington flattered himself that he was a very good reader and he explained to Ashenden the theory and practice of the art. Ashenden learned that there were two schools, the dramatic and the natural: in the first you imitated the voices of those who spoke (if you were reading a novel), and when the heroine wailed you wailed and when emotion choked her you choked too; but in the other you read as impassively as though you were reading the price-list of a mail-order house in Chicago. This was the school Mr. Harrington belonged to. In the seventeen years of his married life he had read aloud to his wife, and to his sons as soon as they were old enough to appreciate them, the novels of Sir Walter Scott, Jane Austen, Dickens, the Brontë Sisters, Thackeray, George Eliot, Nathaniel Hawthorne and W. D. Howells. Ashenden came to the conclusion that it was second nature with Mr. Harrington to read aloud and to prevent him from doing so made him as uneasy as cutting off his tobacco made the confirmed smoker. He would take you unawares.

"Listen to this," he would say, "you must listen to this," as though he were suddenly struck by the excellence of a maxim or the neatness of a phrase. "Now just tell me if you don't think this is remarkably well put. It's only three lines."

He read them and Ashenden was willing to give him a moment's attention, but having finished them, without pausing for a moment to take breath, he went on. He went right on. On and on. In his measured high-pitched voice, without emphasis or expression, he read page after page. Ashenden fidgeted, crossed and uncrossed his legs, lit cigarettes and smoked them, sat first in one position, then in another. Mr. Harrington went on and on. The train went leisurely through the interminable steppes of Siberia. They passed villages and crossed rivers. Mr. Harrington went on and on. When he finished a great speech by Edmund Burke he put down the book in triumph.

"Now that in my opinion is one of the finest orations in the English language. It is certainly a part of our common heritage that we can look upon with genuine pride."

"Doesn't it seem to you a little ominous that the people to whom Edmund Burke made that speech are all dead?" asked Ashenden gloomily.

Mr. Harrington was about to reply that this was hardly to be wondered at since the speech was made in the eighteenth century, when it dawned upon him that Ashenden (bearing up wonderfully under affliction as any unprejudiced person could not fail to admit) was making a joke. He slapped his knee and laughed heartily.

"Gee, that's a good one," he said. "I'll write that down in my little book. I see exactly how I can bring it in one time when I have to speak at our luncheon club."

Mr. Harrington was a highbrow; but that appellation, invented by the vulgar as a term of abuse, he had accepted like the instrument of a saint's martyrdom, the gridiron of Saint Laurence for instance or the wheel of Saint Catherine, as an honorific title. He gloried in it.

"Emerson was a highbrow," he said. "Longfellow was a highbrow. Oliver Wendell Holmes was a highbrow. James Russell Lowell was a highbrow."

Mr. Harrington's study of American literature had taken him no further down the years than the period during which those eminent, but not precisely thrilling authors, flourished.

Mr. Harrington was a bore. He exasperated Ashenden, and enraged him; he got on his nerves, and drove him to frenzy. But Ashenden did not dislike him. His self-satisfaction was enormous but so ingenuous that you could not resent it, his conceit was so childlike that you could only smile at it. He was so well-meaning, so thoughtful, so deferential, so polite that though Ashenden would willingly have killed him he could not but own that in that short while he had conceived for Mr. Harrington something very like affection. His manners were exquisite, formal, a trifle elaborate perhaps (there is no harm in that, for good manners are the product of an artificial state of society and so can bear a touch of the powdered wig and the lace ruffle), but though natural to his good breeding they gained a pleasant significance from his good heart. He was ready to do anyone a kindness and seemed to find nothing too much trouble if he could thereby oblige his fellow man. He was eminently *serviable*. And it may be that this is a word for which there is no exact translation because the charming quality it denotes is not very common among our practical people. When Ashenden was ill for a couple of days Mr. Harrington nursed him with devotion. Ashenden was embarrassed by the care he took of him and though racked with pain could not help laughing at the fussy attention with which Mr. Harrington took his temperature, from his neatly packed valise extracted a whole regiment of tabloids and firmly doctored him; and he was touched by the trouble he gave himself to get from the dining-car the things that he thought Ashenden could eat. He did everything in the world for him but stop talking.

It was only when he was dressing that Mr. Harrington

was silent, for then his maidenly mind was singly occupied with the problem of changing his clothes before Ashenden without indelicacy. He was extremely modest. He changed his linen every day, neatly taking it out of his suit-case and neatly putting back what was soiled; but he performed miracles of dexterity in order during the process not to show an inch of bare skin. After a day or two Ashenden gave up the struggle to keep neat and clean in that dirty train, with one lavatory for the whole carriage, and soon was as grubby as the rest of the passengers; but Mr. Harrington refused to yield to the difficulties. He performed his toilet with deliberation, notwithstanding the impatient persons who rattled the door-handle, and returned from the lavatory every morning washed, shining and smelling of soap. Once dressed, in his black coat, striped trousers and well-polished shoes, he looked as spruce as though he had just stepped out of his tidy little red-brick house in Philadelphia and was about to board the street-car that would take him down town to his office. At one point of the journey it was announced that an attempt had been made to blow up a bridge and that there were disturbances at the next station over the river; it might be that the train would be stopped and the passengers turned adrift or taken prisoners. Ashenden, thinking he might be separated from his luggage, took the precaution to change into his thickest clothes so that if he had to pass the winter in Siberia he need suffer as little as necessary from the cold; but Mr. Harrington would not listen to reason; he made no preparations for the possible experience and Ashenden had the conviction that if he spent three months in a Russian prison he would still preserve that smart and natty appearance. A troop of Cossacks boarded the train and stood on the platform of each carriage with their guns loaded, and the train rattled gingerly over the damaged bridge; then they came to the station at which they had been warned of danger, put on steam and dashed straight through it. Mr. Harrington was mildly satirical when Ashenden changed back into a light summer suit.

Mr. Harrington was a keen business man. It was obvious that it would need someone very astute to over-reach him and Ashenden was sure that his employers had been well-advised to send him on this errand. He would safeguard their interests with all his might and if he succeeded in driving a bargain with the Russians it would be a hard one. His loyalty to his firm demanded that. He spoke of the partners with affectionate reverence. He loved them and was proud of them; but he did not envy them because their wealth was great. He was quite content to work on a salary and thought himself adequately paid; so long as he could educate his boys and leave his widow enough to live on, what was money to him? He thought it a trifle vulgar to be rich. He looked upon culture as more important than money. He was careful of it and after every meal put down in his note-book exactly what it had cost him. His firm might be certain that he would not charge a penny more for his expenses than he had spent. But having discovered that poor people came to the station at the stopping places of the train to beg and seeing that the war had really brought them to destitution he took care before each halt to supply himself with ample small change and in a shame-faced way, mocking himself for being taken in by such imposters, distributed everything in his pocket.

"Of course I know they don't deserve it," he said, "and I don't do it for them. I do it entirely for my own peace of mind. I should feel so terribly badly if I thought some man really was hungry and I'd refused to give him the price of a meal."

Mr. Harrington was absurd, but lovable. It was inconceivable that anyone should be rude to him, it would have seemed as dreadful as hitting a child; and Ashenden, chafing inwardly but with a pretence of amiability, suffered meekly and with a truly Christian spirit the affliction of the gentle, ruthless creature's society. It took eleven days at that time to get from Vladivostok to Petrograd and Ashenden felt that he could not have borne another day. If it had been twelve he would have killed Mr. Harrington.

When at last (Ashenden tired and dirty, Mr. Harrington neat, sprightly and sententious) they reached the outskirts of Petrograd and stood at the window looking at the crowded houses of the city, Mr. Harrington turned to Ashenden and said:

"Well, I never would have thought that eleven days in the train would pass so quickly. We've had a wonderful time. I've enjoyed your company and I know you've enjoyed mine. I'm not going to pretend I don't know that I'm a pretty good conversationalist. But now we've come together like this we must take care to stay together. We must see as much of one another as we can while I'm in Petrograd."

"I shall have a great deal to do," said Ashenden. "I'm afraid my time won't be altogether my own."

"I know," answered Mr. Harrington cordially. "I expect to be pretty busy myself, but we can have breakfast together anyway and we'll meet in the evening and compare notes. It would be too bad if we drifted apart now."

"Too bad," sighed Ashenden.

When Ashenden found himself alone in his bedroom for the first time, he sat down and looked about him. It had seemed an age. He had not the energy to start immediately to unpack. How many of these hotel bedrooms had he known since the beginning of the war, grand or shabby, in one place and one land after another! It seemed to him that he had been living in his luggage for as long as he could remember. He was weary. He asked himself how he was going to set about the work that he had been sent to do. He felt lost in the immensity of Russia and very solitary. He had protested when he was chosen for this mission, it looked too large an order, but his protests were ignored. He was chosen not because those in authority thought him particularly suited for the job, but because there was no one to be found who was more suited. There was a knock at the door and Ashenden, pleased to make use of the few words of the language he knew, called out in Russian. The door was opened. He sprang to his feet.

"Come in, come in," he cried. "I'm awfully glad to see you."

Three men entered. He knew them by sight, since they had travelled on the same boat with him from San Francisco to Yokohama, but following their instructions no communications had passed between them and Ashenden. They were Czechs, exiled from their country for their revolutionary activity and long settled in America, who had been sent over to Russia to help Ashenden in his mission and put him in touch with Professor Z. whose authority over the Czechs in Russia was absolute. Their chief was a certain Dr. Egon Orth, a tall thin man, with a little grey head; he was minister to some church in the Middle West and a doctor of divinity; but had abandoned his cure to work for the liberation of his country, and Ashenden had the impression that he was an intelligent fellow who would not put too fine a point on matters of conscience. A parson with a fixed idea has this advantage over common men, that he can persuade himself of the Almighty's approval for almost any goings on. Dr. Orth had a merry twinkle in his eye and a dry humour.

Ashenden had had two secret interviews with him in Yokohama and had learnt that Professor Z., though eager to free his country from the Austrian rule and since he knew that this could only come about by the downfall of the Central Powers with the allies body and soul, yet had scruples; he would not do things that outraged his conscience, all must be straightforward and above board, and so some things that it was necessary to do had to be done without his knowledge. His influence was so great that his wishes could not be disregarded, but on occasion it was felt better not to let him know too much of what was going on.

Dr. Orth had arrived in Petrograd a week before Ashenden and now put before him what he had learned of the situation. It seemed to Ashenden that it was critical and if anything was to be done it must be done quickly. The army was dissatisfied and mutinous, the Government under the weak Kerensky was tottering and held power only because no one else had the courage to seize it, famine was staring the country in the face and already the possibility had to be considered that the Germans would march on Petrograd. The ambassadors of Great Britain and the United States had been apprised of Ashenden's coming, but his mission was secret even from them, and there were particular reasons why he could demand no assistance from them. He arranged with Dr. Orth to make an appointment with Professor Z. so that he could learn his views and explain to him that he had the financial means to support any scheme that seemed likely to prevent the catastrophe that the Allied governments foresaw of Russia's making a separate peace. But he had to get in touch with influential persons in all classes. Mr. Harrington with his business proposition and his letters to Ministers of State would be thrown in contact with members of the Government and Mr. Harrington wanted an interpreter. Dr. Orth spoke Russian almost as well as his own language and it struck Ashenden that he would be admirably suited to the post. He explained the circumstances to him and it was arranged that while Ashenden and Mr. Harrington were at luncheon Dr. Orth should come in, greeting Ashenden as though he had not seen him before, and be introduced to Mr. Harrington; then Ashenden, guiding the conversation, would suggest to Mr. Harrington that the heavens had sent in Dr. Orth the ideal man for his purpose.

But there was another person on whom Ashenden had fixed as possibly useful to him and now he said:

"Have you ever heard of a woman called Anastasia Alexandrovna Leonidov? She's the daughter of Alexander Denisiev."

"I know all about him of course."

"I have reason to believe she's in Petrograd. Will you find out where she lives and what she's doing?"

"Certainly."

Dr. Orth spoke in Czech to one of the two men who accompanied him. They were sharp-looking fellows, both of them, one was tall and fair and the other was short and dark, but they were younger than Dr. Orth and Ashenden understood that they were there to do as he bade them. The man nodded, got up, shook hands with Ashenden and went out.

"You shall have all the information possible this afternoon."

"Well, I think there's nothing more we can do for the present," said Ashenden. "To tell you the truth I haven't had a bath for eleven days and I badly want one."

Ashenden had never quite made up his mind whether the pleasure of reflection was better pursued in a railway carriage or in a bath. So far as the act of invention was concerned he was inclined to prefer a train that went smoothly and not too fast, and many of his best ideas had come to him when he was thus traversing the plains of France; but for the delight of reminiscence or the entertainment of embroidery upon a theme already in his head he had no doubt that nothing could compare with a hot bath. He considered now, wallowing in soapy water like a water-buffalo in a muddy pond, the grim pleasantry of his relations with Anastasia Alexandrovna Leonidov.

In these stories no more than the barest suggestion has been made that Ashenden was capable on occasions of the passion ironically called tender. The specialists in this matter, those charming creatures who make a business of what philosophers know is but a diversion, assert that writers, painters and musicians, all in short who are connected with the arts, in the relation of love, cut no very conspicuous figure. There is much cry but little wool. They rave or sigh, make phrases and strike many a romantic attitude, but in the end, loving art or themselves (which with them is one and the same thing) better than the object of their emotion, offer a shadow when the said object, with the practical common sense of the sex, demands a substance. It may be so and this may be the reason (never before suggested) why women in their souls look upon art with such a virulent hatred. Be this as it may Ashenden in the last twenty years had felt his heart go pit-a-pat because of one charming person after another. He had had a good deal of fun and had paid for it with a great deal of misery, but even when suffering most acutely from the pangs of un-requited love he had been able to say to himself, albeit with a wry face, after all, it's grist to the mill.

Anastasia Alexandrovna Leonidov was the daughter of a revolutionary who had escaped from Siberia after being sentenced to penal servitude for life and had settled in England. He was an able man and had supported himself for thirty years by the activity of a restless pen and had even made himself a distinguished position in English letters. When Anastasia Alexan-drovna reached a suitable age she married Vladimir Semenovich Leonidov, also an exile from his native country, and it was after she had been married to him for some years that Ashenden made her acquaintance. It was at the time when Europe discovered Russia. Every-one was reading the Russian novelists, the Russian dancers captivated the civilised world, and the Russian

composers set shivering the sensibility of persons who
were beginning to want a change from Wagner. Russian
art seized upon Europe with the virulence of an epidemic
of influenza. New phrases became the fashion, new
colours, new emotions, and the highbrows described
themselves without a moment's hesitation as members of
the intelligentsia. It was a difficult word to spell but an
easy one to say. Ashenden fell like the rest, changed the
cushions of his sitting-room, hung an eikon on the wall,
read Chekoff and went to the ballet.

Anastasia Alexandrovna was by birth, circumstances
and education very much a member of the intelligentsia.
She lived with her husband in a tiny house near Regent's
Park and here all the literary folk in London might gaze
with humble reverence at pale-faced bearded giants who
leaned against the wall like caryatids taking a day off;
they were revolutionaries to a man and it was a miracle
that they were not in the mines of Siberia. Women of
letters tremulously put their lips to a glass of vodka. If
you were lucky and greatly favoured you might shake
hands there with Diaghileff and now and again, like a
peach-blossom wafted by the breeze, Pavlova herself
hovered in and out. At this time Ashenden's success
had not been so great as to affront the highbrows, he
had very distinctly been one of them in his youth, and
though some already looked askance, others (optimistic
creatures with a faith in human nature) still had hopes of
him. Anastasia Alexandrovna told him to his face that
he was a member of the intelligentsia. Ashenden was

N

quite ready to believe it. He was in a state when he was ready to believe anything. He was thrilled and excited. It seemed to him that at last he was about to capture that illusive spirit of romance that he had so long been chasing. Anastasia Alexandrovna had fine eyes and a good, though for these days, too voluptuous figure, high cheek-bones and a snub nose (this was very Tartar), a wide mouth full of large square teeth and a pale skin. She dressed somewhat flamboyantly. In her dark melancholy eyes Ashenden saw the boundless steppes of Russia, and the Kremlin with its pealing bells, and the solemn ceremonies of Easter at St. Isaac's, and forests of silver beeches and the Nevsky Prospekt; it was astonishing how much he saw in her eyes. They were round and shining and slightly protuberant like those of a Pekinese. They talked together of Alyosha in the *Brothers Karamazov*, of Natasha in *War and Peace*, of Anna Karenina and of *Fathers and Sons*.

Ashenden soon discovered that her husband was quite unworthy of her and presently learned that she shared his opinion. Vladimir Semenovich was a little man with a large, long head that looked as though it had been pulled like a piece of liquorice, and he had a great shock of unruly Russian hair. He was a gentle, unobtrusive creature and it was hard to believe that the Czarist government had really feared his revolutionary activities. He taught Russian and wrote for papers in Moscow. He was amiable and obliging. He needed these qualities, for Anastasia Alexandrovna was a woman of character: when she had a toothache Vladimir Semenovich suffered the agonies of the damned and when her heart was wrung by the suffering of her unhappy country Vladimir Semenovich might well have wished he had never been born. Ashenden could not help admitting that he was a poor thing, but he was so harmless that he conceived quite a liking for him, and when in due course he had disclosed his passion to Anastasia Alexandrovna and to his joy found it was returned he was puzzled to know what to do about Vladimir Semenovich. Neither Anastasia Alexandrovna nor he felt that they could live another minute out of one another's pockets, and Ashenden feared that with her revolutionary views and all that she would never consent to marry him; but somewhat to his surprise, and very much to his relief, she accepted the suggestion with alacrity.

"Would Vladimir Semenovich let himself be divorced, do you think?" he asked, as he sat on the sofa, leaning against cushions the colour of which reminded him of raw meat just gone bad, and held her hand.

"Vladimir adores me," she answered. "It'll break his heart."

"He's a nice fellow, I shouldn't like him to be very unhappy. I hope he'll get over it."

"He'll never get over it. That is the Russian spirit. I know that when I leave him he'll feel that he has lost everything that made life worth living for him. I've never known anyone so wrapped up in a woman as he is in me. But of course he wouldn't want to stand in the way of my happiness. He's far too great for that. He'll see that when it's a question of my own self-development I haven't the right to hesitate. Vladimir will give me my freedom without question."

At that time the divorce law in England was even more complicated and absurd than it is now and in case she was not acquainted with its peculiarities Ashenden explained to Anastasia Alexandrovna the difficulties of the case. She put her hand gently on his.

"Vladimir would never expose me to the vulgar notoriety of the divorce court. When I tell him that I have decided to marry you he will commit suicide."

"That would be terrible," said Ashenden.

He was startled, but thrilled. It was really very much like a Russian novel and he saw the moving and terrible pages, pages and pages, in which Dostoievsky would have described the situation. He knew the lacerations his characters would have suffered, the broken bottles of champagne, the visits to the gipsies, the vodka, the swoonings, the catalepsy and the long, long speeches everyone would have made. It was all very dreadful and wonderful and shattering.

"It would make us horribly unhappy," said Anastasia Alexandrovna, "but I don't know what else he could do. I couldn't ask him to live without me. He would be like a ship without a rudder or a car without a carburettor. I know Vladimir so well. He will commit suicide."

"How?" asked Ashenden, who had the realist's passion for the exact detail.

"He will blow his brains out."

Ashenden remembered *Rosmerholm*. In his day he had been an ardent Ibsenite and had even flirted with the notion of learning Norwegian so that he might, by reading the master in the original, get at the secret essence of his thought. He had once seen Ibsen in the flesh drink a glass of Munich beer.

"But do you think we could ever pass another easy hour if we had the death of that man on our conscience?" he asked. "I have a feeling that he would always be between us."

"I know we shall suffer, we shall suffer dreadfully," said Anastasia Alexandrovna, "but how can we help it? Life is like that. We must think of Vladimir. There is his happiness to be considered too. He will prefer to commit suicide."

She turned her face away and Ashenden saw that the heavy tears were coursing down her cheeks. He was much moved. For he had a soft heart and it was dreadful to think of poor Vladimir lying there with a bullet in his brain.

These Russians, what fun they have!

But when Anastasia Alexandrovna had mastered her emotion she turned to him gravely. She looked at him with her humid, round and slightly protuberant eyes.

"We must be quite sure that we're doing the right

thing," she said. "I should never forgive myself if I'd allowed Vladimir to commit suicide and then found I'd made a mistake. I think we ought to make sure that we really love one another."

"But don't you know?" exclaimed Ashenden in a low, tense voice. "I know."

"Let's go over to Paris for a week and see how we get on. Then we shall know."

Ashenden was a trifle conventional and the suggestion took him by surprise. But only for a moment. Anastasia was wonderful. She was very quick and she saw the hesitation that for an instant troubled him.

"Surely you have no bourgeois prejudices?" she said.

"Of course not," he assured her hurriedly, for he would much sooner have been thought knavish than bourgeois, "I think it's a splendid idea."

"Why should a woman hazard her whole life on a throw? It's impossible to know what a man is really like till you've lived with him. It's only fair to give her the opportunity to change her mind before it's too late."

"Quite so," said Ashenden.

Anastasia Alexandrovna was not a woman to let the grass grow under her feet and so having made their arrangements forthwith on the following Saturday they started for Paris.

"I shall not tell Vladimir that I am going with you," she said. "It would only distress him."

"It would be a pity to do that," said Asbenden.

"And if at the end of the week I come to the conclusion that we've made a mistake he need never know anything about it."

"Quite so," said Ashenden.

They met at Victoria Station.

"What class have you got?" she asked him.

"First."

"I'm glad of that. Father and Vladimir travel third on account of their principles, but I always feel sick on a train and I like to be able to lean my head on somebody's shoulder. It's easier in a first-class carriage."

When the train started Anastasia Alexandrovna said she felt dizzy, so she took off her hat and leaned her head on Ashenden's shoulder. He put his arm round her waist.

"Keep quite still, won't you?" she said.

When they got on to the boat she went down to the ladies' cabin and at Calais was able to eat a very hearty meal, but when they got into the train she took off her hat again and rested her head on Ashenden's shoulder. He thought he would like to read and took up a book.

"Do you mind not reading?" she said. "I have to be held and when you turn the pages it makes me feel all funny."

Finally they reached Paris and went to a little hotel on the Left Bank that Anastasia Alexandrovna knew of. She said it had atmosphere. She could not bear those great big grand hotels on the other side; they were hopelessly vulgar and bourgeois.

"I'll go anywhere you like," said Ashenden, "as long as there's a bathroom."

She smiled and pinched his cheek.

"How adorably English you are. Can't you do without a bathroom for a week? My dear, my dear, you have so much to learn."

They talked far into the night about Maxim Gorki and Karl Marx, human destiny, love and the brotherhood of man; and drank innumerable cups of Russian tea, so that in the morning Ashenden would willingly have breakfasted in bed and got up for luncheon; but Anastasia Alexandrovna was an early riser. When life was so short and there was so much to do it was a sinful thing to have breakfast a minute after half-past eight. They sat down in a dingy little dining-room the windows of which showed no signs of having been opened for a month. It was full of atmosphere. Ashenden asked Anastasia Alexandrovna what she would have for breakfast.

"Scrambled eggs," she said.

She ate heartily. Ashenden had already noticed that she had a healthy appetite. He supposed it was a Russian trait: you could not picture Anna Karenina making her midday meal off a bath-bun and a cup of coffee, could you?

After breakfast they went to the Louvre and in the afternoon they went to the Luxembourg. They

dined early in order to go to the Comédie Française;
then they went to a Russian cabaret where they danced.
When next morning at eight-thirty they took their
places in the dining-room and Ashenden asked
Anastasia Alexandrovna what she fancied, her reply
was:

"Scrambled eggs."

"But we had scrambled eggs yesterday," he expostulated.

"Let's have them again to-day," she smiled.

"All right."

They spent the day in the same manner except that
they went to the Carnavalet instead of the Louvre and
the Musée Guimet instead of the Luxembourg. But
when the morning after in answer to Ashenden's
enquiry Anastasia Alexandrovna again asked for
scrambled eggs, his heart sank.

"But we had scrambled eggs yesterday and the day
before," he said.

"Don't you think that's a very good reason to have
them again to-day?"

"No, I don't."

"Is it possible that your sense of humour is a little
deficient this morning?" she asked. "I eat scrambled
eggs every day. It's the only way I like them."

"Oh, very well. In that case of course we'll have
scrambled eggs."

But the following morning he could not face them.

"Will you have scrambled eggs as usual?" he asked her.

"Of course," she smiled affectionately, showing him two rows of large square teeth.

"All right, I'll order them for you; I shall have mine fried."

The smile vanished from her lips.

"Oh?" She paused a moment. "Don't you think that's rather inconsiderate? Do you think it's fair to give the cook unnecessary work? You English, you're all the same, you look upon servants as machines. Does it occur to you that they have hearts like yours, the same feelings and the same emotions? How can you be surprised that the proletariat are seething with discontent when the bourgeoisie like you are so monstrously selfish?"

"Do you really think that there'll be a revolution in England if I have my eggs in Paris fried rather than scrambled?"

She tossed her pretty head in indignation.

"You don't understand. It's the principle of the thing. You think it's a jest, of course I know you're being funny, I can laugh at a joke as well as anyone, Chekoff was well-known in Russia as a humorist; but don't you see what is involved? Your whole attitude is wrong. It's a lack of feeling. You wouldn't talk like that if you had been through the events of 1905 in Petersburg. When I think of the crowds in front of the Winter Palace kneeling in the snow while the Cossacks charged them, women and children! No, no, no."

Her eyes filled with tears and her face was all twisted with pain. She took Ashenden's hand.

"I know you have a good heart. It was just thoughtless on your part and we won't say anything more about it. You have imagination. You're very sensitive. I know. You'll have your eggs done in the same way as mine, won't you?"

"Of course," said Ashenden.

He ate scrambled eggs for breakfast every morning after that. The waiter said: "*Monsieur aime les œufs brouillés.*" At the end of the week they returned to London. He held Anastasia Alexandrovna in his arms, her head resting on his shoulder, from Paris to Calais and again from Dover to London. He reflected that the journey from New York to San Francisco took five days. When they arrived at Victoria and stood on the platform waiting for a cab she looked at him with her round, shining and slightly protuberant eyes.

"We've had a wonderful time, haven't we?" she said.

"Wonderful."

"I've quite made up my mind. The experiment has justified itself. I'm willing to marry you whenever you like."

But Ashenden saw himself eating scrambled eggs every morning for the rest of his life. When he had put her in a cab, he called another for himself, went to the Cunard office and took a berth on the first ship that was going to America. No immigrant, eager for freedom and a new life, ever looked upon the statue of Liberty with more heartfelt thankfulness than did Ashenden, when on that bright and sunny morning his ship steamed into the harbour of New York.

Some years had passed since then and Ashenden had not seen Anastasia Alexandrovna again. He knew that on the outbreak of the revolution in March she and Vladimir Semenovich had gone to Russia. It might be that they would be able to help him, in a way Vladimir Semenovich owed him his life, and he made up his mind to write to Anastasia Alexandrovna to ask if he might come to see her.

When Ashenden went down to lunch he felt somewhat rested. Mr. Harrington was waiting for him and they sat down. They ate what was put before them.

"Ask the waiter to bring us some bread," said Mr. Harrington.

"Bread?" replied Ashenden. "There's no bread."

"I can't eat without bread," said Mr. Harrington.

"I'm afraid you'll have to. There's no bread, no butter, no sugar, no eggs, no potatoes. There's fish and meat and green vegetables, and that's all."

Mr. Harrington's jaw dropped.

"But this is war," he said.

"It looks very much like it."

Mr. Harrington was for a moment speechless, then he said: "I'll tell you what I'm going to do, I'm going to get through with my business as quick as I can and then I'm going to get out of this country. I'm sure Mrs.

Harrington wouldn't like me to go without sugar or butter. I've got a very delicate stomach. The firm would never have sent me here if they'd thought I wasn't going to have the best of everything."

In a little while Dr. Egan Orth came in and gave Ashenden an envelope. On it was written Anastasia Alexandrovna's address. He introduced him to Mr. Harrington. It was soon clear that he was pleased with Dr. Egan Orth and so without further to-do he suggested that here was the perfect interpreter for him.

"He talks Russian like a Russian. But he's an American citizen, so that he won't do you down. I've known him a considerable time and I can assure you that he's absolutely trustworthy."

Mr. Harrington was pleased with the notion and after luncheon Ashenden left them to settle the matter by themselves. He wrote a note to Anastasia Alexandrovna and presently received an answer to say that she was going to a meeting, but would look in at his hotel about seven. He awaited her with apprehension. Of course he knew now that he had not loved her, but Tolstoi and Dostoievsky, Rimsky-Korsakoff, Stravinsky and Bakst; but he was not quite sure if the point had occurred to her. When between eight and half-past she arrived he suggested that she should join Mr. Harrington and him at dinner. The presence of a third party, he thought, would prevent any awkwardness their meeting might have; but he need not have had any anxiety, for five minutes after they had sat down to a plate of soup it was borne in upon him that the feelings of Anastasia Alexandrovna towards him were as cool as were his towards her. It gave him a momentary shock. It is very hard for a man, however modest, to grasp the possibility that a woman who has once loved him may love him no longer, and though of course he did not imagine that Anastasia Alexandrovna had languished for five years with a hopeless passion for him, he did think that by a heightening of colour, a flutter of the eyelashes, or a quiver of the lips she would betray the fact that she had still a soft place in her heart for him. Not at all. She talked to him as though he were a friend she was very glad to see again after an absence of a few days, but whose intimacy with her was purely social. He asked after Vladimir Semenovich.

"He has been a disappointment to me," she said. "I never thought he was a clever man, but I thought he was an honest one. He's going to have a baby."

Mr. Harrington, who was about to put a piece of fish into his mouth, stopped, his fork in the air, and stared at Anastasia Alexandrovna with astonishment. In extenuation it must be explained that he had never read a Russian novel in his life. Ashenden, slightly perplexed too, gave her a questioning look.

"I'm not the mother," she said with a laugh. "I am not interested in that sort of thing. The mother is a friend of mine and a well-known writer on Political Economy. I do not think her views are sound, but I should be the last to deny that they deserve consideration. She has a good brain, quite a good brain." She turned to Mr. Harrington. "Are you interested in Political Economy?"

For once in his life Mr. Harrington was speechless. Anastasia Alexandrovna gave them her views on the subject and they began to speak on the situation in Russia. She seemed to be on intimate terms with the leaders of the various political parties and Ashenden made up his mind to sound her on the possibility of her working with him. His infatuation had not blinded him to the fact that she was an extremely intelligent woman. After dinner he told Mr. Harrington that he wished to talk business with Anastasia Alexandrovna and took her to a retired corner of the lounge. He told her all he thought necessary and found her interested and anxious to help. She had a passion for intrigue and a desire for power. When he hinted that he had command of large sums of money she saw at once that through him she might acquire an influence in the affairs of Russia. It tickled her vanity. She was immensely patriotic, but like many patriots she had an impression that her own aggrandisement tended to the good of her country. When they parted they had come to a working agreement.

"That was a very remarkable woman," said Mr. Harrington next morning when they met at breakfast.

"Don't fall in love with her," smiled Ashenden.

This, however, was not a matter on which Mr. Harrington was prepared to jest.

"I have never looked at a woman since I married Mrs. Harrington," he said. "That husband of hers must be a bad man."

"I could do with a plate of scrambled eggs," said Ashenden, irrelevantly, for their breakfast consisted of a cup of tea without milk and a little jam instead of sugar.

With Anastasia Alexandrovna to help him and Dr. Orth in the background, Ashenden set to work. Things in Russia were going from bad to worse. Kerensky, the head of the Provisional Government, was devoured by vanity and dismissed any minister who gave evidence of a capacity that might endanger his own position. He made speeches. He made endless speeches. At one moment there was a possibility that the Germans would make a dash for Petrograd. Kerensky made speeches. The food shortage grew more serious, the winter was approaching and there was no fuel. Kerensky made speeches. In the background the Bolsheviks were active, Lenin was hiding in Petrograd, it was said that Kerensky knew where he was, but dared not arrest him. He made speeches.

It amused Ashenden to see the unconcern with which Mr. Harrington wandered through this turmoil. History was in the making and Mr. Harrington minded his own business. It was uphill work. He was made to pay bribes to secretaries and underlings under the pretence that the ear of great men would be granted to him. He was kept waiting for hours in antechambers and then sent away without ceremony. When at last he saw the great men he found they had nothing to give him but idle words. They made him promises and in a day or two he discovered that the promises meant nothing. Ashenden advised him to throw in his hand and return to America; but Mr. Harrington would not hear of it; his firm had sent him to do a particular job, and, by gum, he was going to do it or perish in the attempt. Then Anastasia Alexandrovna took him in hand. A singular friendship had arisen between the pair. Mr. Harrington thought her a very remarkable and deeply wronged woman; he told her all about his wife and his two sons, he told her all about the Constitution of the United States; she on her side told him all about Vladimir Semenovich, and she told him about Tolstoi, Turgenev and Dostoievsky. They had great times together. He said he couldn't manage to call her Anastasia Alexandrovna, it was too much of a mouthful; so he called her Delilah. And now she placed her inexhaustible energy at his service and they went together to the persons who might be useful to him. But things were coming to a head. Riots broke out and the streets were growing dangerous. Now and then armoured cars filled with discontented reservists careered wildly along the Nevsky Prospekt and in order to show that they were not happy took pot-shots at the passers-by. On one occasion when Mr. Harrington and Anastasia Alexandrovna were in a tram together shots peppered the windows and they had to lie down on the floor for safety. Mr. Harrington was highly indignant.

"An old fat woman was lying right on top of me and

when I wriggled to get out Delilah caught me a clip on the side of the head and said, 'Stop still, you fool.' I don't like your Russian ways, Delilah."

"Anyhow you stopped still," she giggled.

"What you want in this country is a little less art and a little more civilisation."

"You are bourgeoisie, Mr. Harrington, you are not a member of the intelligentsia."

"You are the first person who's ever said that, Delilah. If I'm not a member of the intelligentsia I don't know who is," retorted Mr. Harrington with dignity.

Then one day when Ashenden was working in his room there was a knock at the door and Anastasia Alexandrovna stalked in followed somewhat sheepishly by Mr. Harrington. Ashenden saw that she was excited.

"What's the matter?" he asked.

"Unless this man goes back to America he'll get killed. You really must talk to him. If I hadn't been there something very unpleasant might have happened to him."

"Not at all, Delilah," said Mr. Harrington, with asperity. "I'm perfectly capable of taking care of myself and I wasn't in the smallest danger."

"What is it all about?" asked Ashenden.

"I'd taken Mr. Harrington to the Lavra of Alexander Nevsky to see Dostoievsky's grave," said Anastasia Alexandrovna, "and on our way back we saw a soldier being rather rough with an old woman."

"Rather rough!" cried Mr. Harrington. "There was

an old woman walking along the side-walk with a basket of provisions on her arm. Two soldiers came up behind her and one of them snatched the basket from her and walked off with it. She burst out screaming and crying, I don't know what she was saying, but I can guess, and the other soldier took his gun and with the butt-end of it hit her over the head. Isn't that right, Delilah?"

"Yes," she answered, unable to help smiling. "And before I could prevent it Mr. Harrington jumped out of the cab and ran up to the soldier who had the basket, wrenched it from him and began to abuse the pair of them like pickpockets. At first they were so taken aback they didn't know what to do and then they got in a rage.   ran after Mr. Harrington and explained to them that he was a foreigner and drunk."

"Drunk?" cried Mr. Harrington.

"Yes, drunk. Of course a crowd collected. It looked as though it wasn't going to be very nice."

Mr. Harrington smiled with those large, pale-blue eyes of his.

"It sounded to me as though you were giving them a piece of your mind, Delilah. It was as good as a play to watch you."

"Don't be stupid, Mr. Harrington," cried Anastasia, in a sudden fury, stamping her foot. "Don't you know that those soldiers might very easily have killed you and me too, and not one of the bystanders would have raised a finger to help us?"

"Me? I'm an American citizen, Delilah. They wouldn't dare touch a hair of my head."

"They'd have difficulty in finding one," said Anastasia Alexandrovna, who when she was in a temper had no manners. "But if you think Russian soldiers are going to hesitate to kill you because you're an American citizen you'll get a big surprise one of these days."

"Well, what happened to the old woman?" asked Ashenden.

"The soldiers went off after a little and we went back to her."

"Still with the basket?"

"Yes. Mr. Harrington clung on to that like grim death. She was lying on the ground with the blood pouring from her head. We got her into the cab and when she could speak enough to tell us where she lived we drove her home. She was bleeding dreadfully and we had some difficulty in staunching the blood."

Anastasia Alexandrovna gave Mr. Harrington an odd look and to his surprise Ashenden saw him turn scarlet.

"What's the matter now?"

"You see, we had nothing to bind her up with. Mr. Harrington's handkerchief was soaked. There was only one thing about me that I could get off quickly and so I took off my . . ."

But before she could finish Mr. Harrington interrupted her.

"You need not tell Mr. Ashenden what you took off. I'm a married man and I know ladies wear them, but I see no need to refer to them in general society."

Anastasia Alexandrovna giggled.

"Then you must kiss me, Mr. Harrington. If you don't I shall say."

Mr. Harrington hesitated a moment, considering evidently the pros and cons of the matter, but he saw that Anastasia Alexandrovna was determined.

"Go on then, you may kiss me, Delilah, though I'm bound to say I don't see what pleasure it can be to you."

She put her arms round his neck and kissed him on both cheeks, then without a word of warning burst into a flood of tears.

"You're a brave little man, Mr. Harrington. You're absurd but magnificent," she sobbed.

Mr. Harrington was less surprised than Ashenden would have expected him to be. He looked at Anastasia with a thin, quizzical smile and gently patted her.

"Come, come, Delilah, pull yourself together. It gave you a nasty turn, didn't it? You're quite upset. I shall have terrible rheumatism in my shoulder if you go on weeping all over it."

The scene was ridiculous and touching. Ashenden laughed, but he had the beginnings of a lump in his throat.

When Anastasia Alexandrovna had left them Mr. Harrington sat in a brown study.

"They're very queer, these Russians. Do you know what Delilah did?" he said, suddenly. "She stood up in the cab, in the middle of the street, with people passing on both sides, and took her pants off. She tore them in two and gave me one to hold while she made a bandage of the other. I was never so embarrassed in my life."

"Tell me what gave you the idea of calling her Delilah?" smiled Ashenden.

Mr. Harrington reddened a little.

"She's a very fascinating woman, Mr. Ashenden. She's been deeply wronged by her husband and I naturally felt a great deal of sympathy for her. These Russians are very emotional people and I did not want her to mistake my sympathy for anything else. I told her I was very much attached to Mrs. Harrington."

"You're not under the impression that Delilah was Potiphar's wife?" asked Ashenden.

"I don't know what you mean by that, Mr. Ashenden," replied Mr. Harrington. "Mrs. Harrington has always given me to understand that I'm very fascinating to women, and I thought if I called our little friend Delilah it would make my position quite clear."

"I don't think Russia's any place for you, Mr. Harrington," said Ashenden smiling. "If I were you I'd get out of it as quick as I could."

"I can't go now. I've got them to agree to my terms at last and we're going to sign next week. Then I shall pack my grip and go."

"I wonder if your signatures will be worth the paper they're written on," said Ashenden.

He had at length devised a plan of campaign. It took him twenty-four hours' hard work to code a telegram in which he put his scheme before the persons who had sent him to Petrograd. It was accepted and he was promised all the money he needed. Ashenden knew he could do nothing unless the Provisional Government remained in power for another three months; but winter was at hand and food was getting scarcer every day. The army was mutinous. The people clamoured for peace. Every evening at the Europe Ashenden drank a cup of chocolate with Professor Z. and discussed with him how best to make use of his devoted Czechs. Anastasia Alexandrovna had a flat in a retired spot and here he had meetings with all manner of persons. Plans were drawn up. Measures were taken. Ashenden argued, persuaded, promised. He had to overcome the vacillation of one and wrestle with the fatalism of another. He had to judge who was resolute and who was self-sufficient, who was honest and who was infirm of purpose. He had to curb his impatience with the Russian verbosity; he had to be good-tempered with people who were willing to talk of everything but the matter in hand; he had to listen sympathetically to ranting and rhodomontade. He had to beware of treachery. He had to humour the vanity of fools and elude the greed of the ambitious. Time was pressing. The rumours grew hot and many of the activities of the Bolsheviks. Kerensky ran hither and thither like a frightened hen.

Then the blow fell. On the night of November 7th, 1917, the Bolsheviks rose, Kerensky's ministers were arrested and the Winter Palace was sacked by the mob; the reins of power were seized by Lenin and Trotsky.

Anastasia Alexandrovna came to Ashenden's room at the hotel early in the morning. Ashenden was coding a telegram. He had been up all night, first at the Smolny, and then at the Winter Palace. He was tired out. Her face was white and her shining brown eyes were tragic.

"Have you heard?" she asked Ashenden.

He nodded.

"It's all over then. They say Kerensky has fled. They never even showed fight." Rage seized her. "The buffoon!" she screamed.

At that moment there was a knock at the door and Anastasia Alexandrovna looked at it with sudden apprehension.

"You know the Bolsheviks have got a list of people they've decided to execute. My name is on it, and it may be that yours is too."

"If it's they and they want to come in they only have to turn the handle," said Ashenden, smiling, but with ever so slightly odd a feeling at the pit of his stomach. "Come in."

The door was opened and Mr. Harrington stepped into the room. He was as dapper as ever, in his short black coat and striped trousers, his shoes neatly polished and a derby on his bald head. He took it off when he saw Anastasia Alexandrovna.

"Oh, fancy finding you here so early. I looked in on my way out, I wanted to tell you my news. I tried to find you yesterday evening, but couldn't. You didn't come in to dinner."

"No, I was at a meeting," said Ashenden.

"You must both congratulate me, I got my signatures yesterday, and my business is done."

Mr. Harrington beamed on them, the picture of self-satisfaction, and he arched himself like a bantam-cock who has chased away all rivals. Anastasia Alexandrovna burst into a sudden shriek of hysterical laughter. He stared at her in perplexity.

"Why, Delilah, what is the matter?" he said.

Anastasia laughed till the tears ran from her eyes and then began to sob in earnest. Ashenden explained.

"The Bolsheviks have overthrown the Government. Kerensky's ministers are in prison. The Bolsheviks are out to kill. Delilah says her name is on the list. Your minister signed your documents yesterday because he knew it did not matter what he did then. Your contracts are worth nothing. The Bolsheviks are going to make peace with Germany as soon as they can."

Anastasia Alexandrovna had recovered her self-control as quickly as she had lost it.

"You had better get out of Russia as soon as you can, Mr. Harrington. It's no place for a foreigner now and it may be that in a few days you won't be able to."

Mr. Harrington looked from one to the other.

"O my!" he said. "O my!" It seemed inadequate. "Are you going to tell me that that Russian minister was just making a fool of me?"

Ashenden shrugged his shoulders.

"How can one tell what he was thinking of? He may have a keen sense of humour and perhaps he thought it funny to sign a fifty-million-dollar contract yesterday when there was every chance of his being stood against the wall and shot to-day. Anastasia Alexandrovna's right, Mr. Harrington, you'd better take the first train that'll get you to Sweden."

"And what about you?"

"There's nothing for me to do here any more. I'm cabling for instructions and I shall go as soon as I get leave. The Bolsheviks have got in ahead of us and the people I was working with will have their work cut out to save their lives."

"Boris Petrovich was shot this morning," said Anastasia Alexandrovna with a frown.

They both looked at Mr. Harrington and he stared at the floor. His pride in this achievement of his was shattered and he sagged like a pricked balloon. But in a minute he looked up. He gave Anastasia Alexandrovna a little smile and for the first time Ashenden noticed how attractive and kindly his smile was. There was something peculiarly disarming about it.

"If the Bolsheviks are after you, Delilah, don't you think you'd better come with me? I'll take care of you and if you like to come to America I'm sure Mrs. Harrington would be glad to do anything she could for you."

"I can see Mrs. Harrington's face if you arrived in

Philadelphia with a Russian refugee," laughed Anastasia Alexandrovna. "I'm afraid it would need more explaining than you could ever manage. No, I shall stay here."

"But if you're in danger?"

"I'm a Russian. My place is here. I will not leave my country when most my country needs me."

"That is the bunk, Delilah," said Mr. Harrington very quietly.

Anastasia Alexandrovna had spoken with deep emotion, but now with a little start she shot a sudden quizzical look at him.

"I know it is, Samson," she answered. "To tell you the truth I think we're all going to have a hell of a time, God knows what's going to happen, but I want to see; I wouldn't miss a minute of it for the world."

Mr. Harrington shook his head.

"Curiosity is the bane of your sex, Delilah," he said.

"Go along and do your packing, Mr. Harrington," said Ashenden, smiling, "and then we'll take you to the station. The train will be besieged."

"Very well, I'll go. And I shan't be sorry either. I haven't had a decent meal since I came here and I've done a thing I never thought I should have to do in my life, I've drunk my coffee without sugar and when I've been lucky enough to get a little piece of black bread I've had to eat it without butter. Mrs. Harrington will never believe me when I tell her what I've gone through. What this country wants is organisation."

When he left them Ashenden and Anastasia Alexandrovna talked over the situation. Ashenden was depressed because all his careful schemes had come to nothing, but Anastasia Alexandrovna was excited and she hazarded every sort of guess about the outcome of this new revolution. She pretended to be very serious, but in her heart she looked upon it all very much as a thrilling play. She wanted more and more things to happen. Then there was another knock at the door and before Ashenden could answer Mr. Harrington burst in.

"Really the service at this hotel is a scandal," he cried heatedly. "I've been ringing my bell for fifteen minutes and I can't get anyone to pay the smallest attention to me."

"Service?" exclaimed Anastasia Alexandrovna. "There is not a servant left in the hotel."

"But I want my washing. They promised to let me have it back last night."

"I'm afraid you haven't got much chance of getting it now," said Ashenden.

"I'm not going to leave without my washing. Four shirts, two union suits, a pair of pyjamas, and four collars. I wash my handkerchiefs and socks in my room. I want my washing and I'm not going to leave this hotel without it."

"Don't be a fool," cried Ashenden. "What you've got to do is to get out of here while the going's good. If there are no servants to get it you'll just have to leave your washing behind you."

"Pardon me, sir, I shall do nothing of the kind. I'll go

and fetch it myself. I've suffered enough at the hands of this country and I'm not going to leave four perfectly good shirts to be worn by a lot of dirty Bolsheviks. No, sir. I do not leave Russia till I have my washing."

Anastasia Alexandrovna stared at the floor for a moment; then with a little smile looked up. It seemed to Ashenden that there was something in her that responded to Mr. Harrington's futile obstinacy. In her Russian way she understood that Mr. Harrington could not leave Petrograd without his washing. His insistence had given it the value of a symbol.

"I'll go downstairs and see if I can find anybody about who knows where the laundry is and if I can, I'll go with you and you can bring your washing away with you."

Mr. Harrington unbent. He answered with that sweet and disarming smile of his.

"That's terribly kind of you, Delilah. I don't mind if it's ready or not, I'll take it just as it is."

Anastasia Alexandrovna left them.

"Well, what do you think of Russia and the Russians now?" Mr. Harrington asked Ashenden.

"I'm fed up with them. I'm fed up with Tolstoi, I'm fed up with Turgenev and Dostoievsky, I'm fed up with Chekoff. I'm fed up with the Intelligentsia. I hanker after people who know their mind from one minute to another, who mean what they say an hour after they've said it, whose word you can rely on; I'm sick of fine phrases, and oratory and attitudinising."

Ashenden, bitten by the prevailing ill, was about to make a speech when he was interrupted by a rattle as of peas on a drum. In the city, so strangely silent, it sounded abrupt and odd.

"What's that?" asked Mr. Harrington.

"Rifle firing. On the other side of the river, I should think."

Mr. Harrington gave a funny little look. He laughed, but his face was a trifle pale; he did not like it, and Ashenden did not blame him.

"I think it's high time I got out. I shouldn't so much mind for myself, but I've got a wife and children to think of. I haven't had a letter from Mrs. Harrington for so long I'm a bit worried." He paused an instant. "I'd like you to know Mrs. Harrington, she's a very wonderful woman. She's the best wife a man ever had. Until I came here I'd not been separated from her for more than three days since we were married."

Anastasia Alexandrovna came back and told them that she had found the address.

"It's about forty minutes' walk from here and if you'll come now I'll go with you," she said.

"I'm ready."

"You'd better look out," said Ashenden. "I don't believe the streets are very healthy to-day."

Anastasia Alexandrovna looked at Mr. Harrington.

"I must have my washing, Delilah," he said. "I should never rest in peace if I left it behind me and Mrs. Harrington would never let me hear the last of it."

"Come on then."

They set out and Ashenden went on with the dreary business of translating into a very complicated code the shattering news he had to give. It was a long message, and then he had to ask for instructions upon his own movements. It was a mechanical job and yet it was one in which you could not allow your attention to wander. The mistake of a single figure might make a whole sentence incomprehensible.

Suddenly his door was burst open and Anastasia Alexandrovna flung into the room. She had lost her hat and was dishevelled. She was panting. Her eyes were starting out of her head and she was obviously in a state of great excitement.

"Where's Mr. Harrington?" she cried. "Isn't he here?"

"No."

"Is he in his bedroom?"

"I don't know. Why, what's the matter? We'll go and look if you like. Why didn't you bring him along with you?"

They walked down the passage and knocked at Mr. Harrington's door; there was no answer; they tried the handle; the door was locked.

"He's not there."

They went back to Ashenden's room. Anastasia Alexandrovna sank into a chair.

"Give me a glass of water, will you? I'm out of breath. I've been running."

She drank the water Ashenden poured out for her. She gave a sudden sob.

"I hope he's all right. I should never forgive myself if he was hurt. I was hoping he would have got here before me. He got his washing all right. We found the place. There was only an old woman there and they didn't want to let us take it, but we insisted. Mr. Harrington was furious because it hadn't been touched. It was exactly as he had sent it. They'd promised it last night and it was still in the bundle that Mr. Harrington had made himself. I said that was Russia and Mr. Harrington said he preferred coloured people. I'd led him by side streets because I thought it was better, and we started to come back again. We passed at the top of a street and at the bottom of it I saw a little crowd. There was a man addressing them.

" 'Let's go and hear what he's saying,' I said.

"I could see they were arguing. It looked exciting. I wanted to know what was happening.

" 'Come along, Delilah,' he said. 'Let us mind our own business.'

" 'You go back to the hotel and do your packing. I'm going to see the fun,' I said.

"I ran down the street and he followed me. There were about two or three hundred people there and a student was addressing them. There were some working men and they were shouting at him. I love a row and I edged my way into the crowd. Suddenly we heard the sound of shots and before you could realise what was happening two armoured cars came dashing down the street. There were soldiers in them and they were firing as they went. I don't know why. For fun, I suppose, or because they were drunk. We all scattered like a lot of rabbits. We just ran for our lives. I lost Mr. Harrington. I can't make out why he isn't here. Do you think something has happened to him?"

Ashenden was silent for a while.

"We'd better go out and look for him," he said. "I don't know why the devil he couldn't leave his washing."

"I understand, I understand so well."

"That's a comfort," said Ashenden irritably. "Let's go."

He put on his hat and coat, and they walked downstairs. The hotel seemed strangely empty. They went out into the street. There was hardly anyone to be seen. They walked along. The trams were not running and the silence in the great city was uncanny. The shops were closed. It was quite startling when a motor-car dashed by at breakneck speed. The people they passed looked frightened and downcast. When they had to go through a main thoroughfare they hastened their steps. A lot of people were there and they stood about irresolutely as though they did not know what to do next. Reservists in their shabby grey were walking down the middle of the roadway in little bunches. They did not speak. They looked like sheep looking for their shepherd. Then they came to the street down which

o

Anastasia Alexandrovna had run, but they entered it from the opposite end. A number of windows had been broken by the wild shooting. It was quite empty. You could see where the people had scattered, for strewn about were articles they had dropped in their haste, books, a man's hat, a lady's bag and a basket. Anastasia Alexandrovna touched Ashenden's arm to draw his attention: sitting on the pavement, her head bent right down to her lap, was a woman and she was dead. A little way on two men had fallen together. They were dead too. The wounded, one supposed, had managed to drag themselves away or their friends had carried them. Then they found Mr. Harrington. His derby had rolled in the gutter. He lay on his face, in a pool of blood, his bald head, with its prominent bones, very white; his neat black coat smeared and muddy. But his hand was clenched tight on the parcel that contained four shirts, two union suits, a pair of pyjamas and four collars. Mr. Harrington had not let his washing go.

THE DOOR OF OPPORTUNITY

THEY got a first-class carriage to themselves. It was lucky, because they were taking a good deal in with them, Alban's suit-case and a hold-all, Anne's dressing-case and her hat-box. They had two trunks in the van, containing what they wanted immediately, but all the rest of their luggage Alban had put in the care of an agent who was to take it up to London and store it till they had made up their minds what to do. They had a lot, pictures and books, curios that Alban had collected in the East, his guns and saddles. They had left Sondurah for ever. Alban, as was his way, tipped the porter generously and then went to the bookstall and bought papers. He bought "The New Statesman" and "The Nation," and "The Tatler" and "The Sketch," and the last number of "The London Mercury." He came back to the carriage and threw them on the seat.

"It's only an hour's journey," said Anne.

"I know, but I wanted to buy them. I've been starved so long. Isn't it grand to think that to-morrow morning we shall have to-morrow's 'Times,' and 'The Express' and 'The Mail'?"

She did not answer and he turned away, for he saw coming towards them two persons, a man and his wife, who had been fellow-passengers from Singapore.

"Get through the customs all right?" he cried to them cheerily.

The man seemed not to hear, for he walked straight on, but the woman answered.

"Yes, they never found the cigarettes."

She saw Anne, gave her a friendly little smile, and passed on. Anne flushed.

"I was afraid they'd want to come in here," said Alban. "Let's have the carriage to ourselves if we can."

She looked at him curiously.

"I don't think you need worry," she answered. "I don't think anyone will come in."

He lit a cigarette and lingered at the carriage door. On his face was a happy smile. When they had passed through the Red Sea and found a sharp wind in the Canal, Anne had been surprised to see how much the men who had looked presentable enough in the white ducks in which she had been accustomed to see them, were changed when they left them off for warmer clothes. They looked like nothing on earth then. Their ties were awful and their shirts all wrong. They wore grubby flannel trousers and shabby old golf-coats that had too obviously been bought off the nail, or blue serge suits that betrayed the provincial tailor. Most of the passengers had got off at Marseilles, but a dozen or so, either because after a long period in the East they thought the trip through the Bay would do them good,

or, like themselves, for economy's sake, had gone all
the way to Tilbury, and now several of them walked
along the platform. They wore solar topis or double-
brimmed terais, and heavy greatcoats, or else shapeless
soft hats or bowlers, not too well brushed, that looked
too small for them. It was a shock to see them. They
looked suburban and a trifle second-rate. But Alban
had already a London look. There was not a speck of
dust on his smart greatcoat, and his black Homburg
hat looked brand-new. You would never have guessed
that he had not been home for three years. His collar
fitted closely round his neck and his foulard tie was
neatly tied. As Anne looked at him she could not but
think how good-looking he was. He was just under
six feet tall, and slim, and he wore his clothes well,
and his clothes were well cut. He had fair hair, still
thick, and blue eyes and the faintly yellow skin common
to men of that complexion after they have lost the pink-
and-white freshness of early youth. There was no colour
in his cheeks. It was a fine head, well-set on rather a
long neck, with a somewhat prominent Adam's apple;
but you were more impressed with the distinction than
with the beauty of his face. It was because his features
were so regular, his nose so straight, his brow so
broad that he photographed so well. Indeed, from
his photographs you would have thought him extremely handsome. He was not that, perhaps because
his eyebrows and his eyelashes were pale, and his
lips thin, but he looked very intellectual. There was

refinement in his face and a spirituality that was oddly moving. That was how you thought a poet should look; and when Anne became engaged to him she told her girl friends who asked her about him that he looked like Shelley. He turned to her now with a little smile in his blue eyes. His smile was very attractive.

"What a perfect day to land in England!"

It was October. They had steamed up the Channel on a grey sea under a grey sky. There was not a breath of wind. The fishing boats seemed to rest on the placid water as though the elements had for ever forgotten their old hostility. The coast was incredibly green, but with a bright cosy greenness quite unlike the luxuriant, vehement verdure of Eastern jungles. The red towns they passed here and there were comfortable and homelike. They seemed to welcome the exiles with a smiling friendliness. And when they drew into the estuary of the Thames they saw the rich levels of Essex and in a little while Chalk Church on the Kentish shore, lonely in the midst of weather-beaten trees, and beyond it the woods of Cobham. The sun, red in a faint mist, set on the marshes, and night fell. In the station the arc-lamps shed a light that spotted the darkness with cold hard patches. It was good to see the porters lumbering about in their grubby uniforms and the stationmaster fat and important in his bowler hat. The station-master blew a whistle and waved his arm. Alban stepped into the carriage and seated himself in the corner opposite to Anne. The train started.

"We're due in London at six-ten," said Alban. "We ought to get to Jermyn Street by seven. That'll give us an hour to bath and change and we can get to the Savoy for dinner by eight-thirty. A bottle of pop to-night, my pet, and a slap-up dinner." He gave a chuckle. "I heard the Strouds and the Maundys arranging to meet at the Trocadero Grill-Room."

He took up the papers and asked if she wanted any of them. Anne shook her head.

"Tired?" he smiled.

"No."

"Excited?"

In order not to answer she gave a little laugh. He began to look at the papers, starting with the publishers' advertisements, and she was conscious of the intense satisfaction it was to him to feel himself through them once more in the middle of things. They had taken in those same papers in Sondurah, but they arrived six weeks old, and though they kept them abreast of what was going on in the world that interested them both, they emphasised their exile. But these were fresh from the Press. They smelt different. They had a crispness that was almost voluptuous. He wanted to read them all at once. Anne looked out of the window. The country was dark, and she could see little but the lights of their carriage reflected on the glass, but very soon the town encroached upon it, and then she saw little sordid houses, mile upon mile of them, with a light in a window here and there, and the chimneys made a dreary pattern against the sky. They passed through Barking and East Ham and Bromley—it was silly that the name on the platform as they went through the station should give her such a tremor—and then Stepney. Alban put down his papers.

"We shall be there in five minutes now."

He put on his hat and took down from the racks the things the porter had put in them. He looked at her with shining eyes and his lips twitched. She saw that he was only just able to control his emotion. He looked out of the window, too, and they passed over brightly lighted thoroughfares, close packed with tram-cars, buses and motor-vans, and they saw the streets thick with people. What a mob! The shops were all lit up. They saw the hawkers with their barrows at the curb.

"London," he said.

He took her hand and gently pressed it. His smile was so sweet that she had to say something. She tried to be facetious.

"Does it make you fell all funny inside?"

"I don't know if I want to cry or if I want to be sick."

Fenchurch Street. He lowered the window and waved his arm for a porter. With a grinding of brakes the train came to a standstill. A porter opened the door and Alban handed him out one package after another. Then in his polite way, having jumped out, he gave his hand to Anne to help her down to the platform. The porter went to fetch a barrow and they stood by the pile of their luggage. Alban waved to two passengers from the ship who passed them. The man nodded stiffly.

"What a comfort it is that we shall never have to be civil to those awful people any more," said Alban lightly.

Anne gave him a quick glance. He was really incomprehensible. The porter came back with his barrow, the luggage was put on and they followed him to collect their trunks. Alban took his wife's arm and pressed it.

"The smell of London. By God, it's grand."

He rejoiced in the noise and the bustle, and the crowd of people who jostled them; the radiance of the arc-lamps and the black shadows they cast, sharp but full-toned, gave him a sense of elation. They got out into the street and the porter went off to get them a taxi. Alban's eyes glittered as he looked at the buses and the policemen trying to direct the confusion. His distinguished face bore a look of something like inspiration. The taxi came. Their luggage was stowed away and piled up beside the driver, Alban gave the porter half-a-crown, and they drove off. They turned down Gracechurch Street and in Cannon Street were held up by a block in the traffic. Alban laughed out loud.

"What's the matter?" said Anne.

"I'm so excited."

They went along the Embankment. It was relatively quiet there. Taxis and cars passed them. The bells of

o*

the trams were music in his ears. At Westminster Bridge they cut across Parliament Square and drove through the green silence of St. James's Park. They had engaged a room at a hotel just off Jermyn Street. The reception clerk took them upstairs and a porter brought up their luggage. It was a room with twin beds and a bathroom.

"This looks all right," said Alban. "It'll do us till we can find a flat or something."

He looked at his watch.

"Look here, darling, we shall only fall over one another if we try to unpack together. We've got oodles of time and it'll take you longer to get straight and dress than me. I'll clear out. I want to go to the club and see if there's any mail for me. I've got my dinner-jacket in my suit-case and it'll only take me twenty minutes to have a bath and dress. Does that suit you?"

"Yes. That's all right."

"I'll be back in an hour."

"Very well."

He took out of his pocket the little comb he always carried and passed it through his long fair hair. Then he put on his hat. He gave himself a glance in the mirror.

"Shall I turn on the bath for you?"

"No, don't bother."

"All right. So long."

He went out.

When he was gone Anne took her dressing-case and

her hat-box and put them on the top of her trunk. Then she rang the bell. She did not take off her hat. She sat down and lit a cigarette. When a servant answered the bell she asked for the porter. He came. She pointed to the luggage.

"Will you take those things and leave them in the hall for the present. I'll tell you what to do with them presently."

"Very good, ma'am."

She gave him a florin. He took the trunk out and the other packages and closed the door behind him. A few tears slid down Anne's cheeks, but she shook herself; she dried her eyes and powdered her face. She needed all her calm. She was glad that Alban had conceived the idea of going to his club. It made things easier and gave her a little time to think them out.

Now that the moment had come to do what she had for weeks determined, now that she must say the terrible things she had to say, she quailed. Her heart sank. She knew exactly what she meant to say to Alban, she had made up her mind about that long ago, and had said the very words to herself a hundred times, three or four times a day every day of the long journey from Singapore, but she was afraid that she would grow confused. She dreaded an argument. The thought of a scene made her feel slightly sick. It was something at all events to have an hour in which to collect herself. He would say she was heartless and cruel and unreasonable. She could not help it.

"No, no, no," she cried aloud.

She shuddered with horror. And all at once she saw herself again in the bungalow, sitting as she had been sitting when the whole thing started. It was getting on towards tiffin time and in a few minutes Alban would be back from the office. It gave her pleasure to reflect that it was an attractive room for him to come back to, the large verandah which was their parlour, and she knew that though they had been there eighteen months he was still alive to the success she had made of it. The jalousies were drawn now against the midday sun and the mellowed light filtering through them gave an impression of cool silence. Anne was house-proud, and though they were moved from district to district according to the exigencies of the Service and seldom stayed anywhere very long, at each new post she started with new enthusiasm to make their house cosy and charming. She was very modern. Visitors were surprised because there were no knick-knacks. They were taken aback by the bold colour of her curtains and could not at all make out the tinted reproductions of pictures by Marie Laurencin and Gauguin in silvered frames which were placed on the walls with such cunning skill. She was conscious that few of them quite approved and the good ladies of Port Wallace and Pemberton thought such arrangements odd, affected and out of place; but this left her calm. They would learn. It did them good to get a bit of a jolt. And now she looked round the long, spacious verandah with the complacent sigh of the artist satisfied with his work. It was gay. It was bare. It was restful. It refreshed the spirit and gently excited the fancy. Three immense bowls of yellow cannas completed the colour scheme. Her eyes lingered for a moment on the book-shelves filled with books; that was another thing that disconcerted the colony, all the books they had, and strange books too, heavy they thought them for the most part; and she gave them a little affectionate look as though they were living things. Then she gave the piano a glance. A piece of music was still open on the rack, it was something of Debussy, and Alban had been playing it before he went to the office.

Her friends in the colony had condoled with her when Alban was appointed D.O. at Daktar, for it was the most isolated district in Sondurah. It was connected with the town which was the headquarters of the government neither by telegraph nor telephone. But she liked it. They had been there for some time and she hoped they would remain till Alban went home on leave in another twelve months. It was as large as an English county, with a long coast-line, and the sea was dotted with little islands. A broad, winding river ran through it and on each side of this stretched hills densely covered with virgin forest. The station, a good way up the river, consisted of a row of Chinese shops and a native village nestling amid coconut trees, the District Office, the D.O.'s bungalow, the Clerk's quarters and the barracks. Their only neighbours were the manager of a rubber estate a few miles up the river and the manager and his assistant, Dutchmen both, of a timber camp on one of the river's tributaries. The rubber estate's launch went up and down twice a month and was their only means of regular communication with the outside world. But though they were lonely they were not dull. Their days were full. Their ponies waited for them at dawn and they rode while the day was still fresh and in the bridle-paths through the jungle lingered the mystery of the tropical night. They came back, bathed, changed and had breakfast, and Alban went to the office. Anne spent the morning writing letters and working. She had fallen in love with the country from the first day she arrived in it and had taken pains to master the common language spoken. Her imagination was inflamed by the stories she heard of love and jealousy and death. She was told romantic tales of a time that was only just past. She sought to steep herself in the lore of those strange people. Both she and Alban read a great deal. They had for the country a considerable library and new books came from London by nearly every mail. Little that was noteworthy escaped them. Alban was fond of playing the piano. For an amateur he played very well. He had studied rather seriously, and he had an agreeable touch and a good ear; he could read music with ease, and it was always a pleasure to Anne to sit by him and follow the score when he tried something new. But their great delight was to tour the district. Sometimes they would be away for a fortnight at a time. They would go down the river in a prahu and then sail from one little island to another, bathe in the sea, and fish, or else row upstream till it grew shallow and the trees on either bank were so close to one another that you only saw a slim strip of sky between. Here the boatmen had to pole and they would spend the night in a native house. They bathed in a river pool so clear that you could see the sand shining silver at the bottom; and the spot was so lovely, so peaceful and remote, that you felt you could stay there for ever. Sometimes, on the other hand, they would tramp for days along the jungle paths, sleeping under canvas, and notwithstanding the mosquitoes that tormented them and the leeches that sucked their blood, enjoy every moment. Whoever slept so well as on a camp bed? And then there was the gladness of getting back, the delight in the comfort of the well-ordered establishment, the mail that had arrived with letters from home and all the papers, and the piano.

Alban would sit down to it then, his fingers itching to feel the keys, and in what he played, Stravinsky, Ravel, Darius Miehaud, she seemed to feel that he put in something of his own, the sounds of the jungle at night, dawn over the estuary, the starry nights and the crystal clearness of the forest pools.

Sometimes the rain fell in sheets for days at a time.

Then Alban worked at Chinese. He was learning it so that he could communicate with the Chinese of the country in their own language, and Anne did the thousand-and-one things for which she had not had time before. Those days brought them even more closely together; they always had plenty to talk about, and when they were occupied with their separate affairs they were pleased to feel in their bones that they were near to one another. They were wonderfully united. The rainy days that shut them up within the walls of the bungalow made them feel as if they were one body in face of the world.

On occasion they went to Port Wallace. It was a change, but Anne was always glad to get home. She was never quite at her ease there. She was conscious that none of the people they met liked Alban. They were very ordinary people, middle-class and suburban and dull, without any of the intellectual interests that made life so full and varied to Alban and her, and many of them were narrow-minded and ill-natured; but since they had to pass the better part of their lives in contact with them, it was tiresome that they should feel so unkindly towards Alban. They said he was conceited. He was always very pleasant with them, but she was aware that they resented his cordiality. When he tried to be jovial they said he was putting on airs, and when he chaffed them they thought he was being funny at their expense.

Once they stayed at Government House, and Mrs.

Hannay, the Governor's wife, who liked her, talked to her about it. Perhaps the Governor had suggested that she should give Anne a hint.

"You know, my dear, it's a pity your husband doesn't try to be more come-hither with people. He's very intelligent; don't you think it would be better if he didn't let others see he knows it quite so clearly? My husband said to me only yesterday: of course I know Alban Torel is the cleverest young man in the Service, but he does manage to put my back up more than anyone I know. I am the Governor, but when he talks to me he always gives me the impression that he looks upon me as a damned fool."

The worst of it was that Anne knew how low an opinion Alban had of the Governor's parts.

"He doesn't mean to be superior," Anne answered, smiling. "And he really isn't in the least conceited. I think it's only because he has a straight nose and high cheek-bones."

"You know, they don't like him at the club. They call him Powder-Puff Percy."

Anne flushed. She had heard that before and it made her very angry. Her eyes filled with tears.

"I think it's frightfully unfair."

Mrs. Hannay took her hand and gave it an affectionate little squeeze.

"My dear, you know I don't want to hurt your feelings. Your husband can't help rising very high in the Service. He'd make things so much easier for himself if he were a little more human. Why doesn't he play football?"

"It's not his game. He's always only too glad to play tennis."

"He doesn't give that impression. He gives the impression that there's no one here who's worth his while to play with."

"Well, there isn't," said Anne, stung.

Alban happened to be an extremely good tennis-player. He had played a lot of tournaments in England and Anne knew that it gave him a grim satisfaction to knock those beefy, hearty men all over the court. He could make the best of them look foolish. He could be maddening on the tennis court and Anne was aware that sometimes he could not resist the temptation.

"He does play to the gallery, doesn't he?" said Mrs. Hannay.

"I don't think so. Believe me, Alban has no idea he isn't popular. As far as I can see he's always pleasant and friendly with everybody."

"It's then he's most offensive," said Mrs. Hannay dryly.

"I know people don't like us very much," said Anne, smiling a little. "I'm very sorry, but really I don't know what we can do about it."

"Not you, my dear," cried Mrs. Hannay. "Everybody adores you. That's why they put up with your husband. My dear, who could help liking you?"

"I don't know why they should adore me," said Anne.

But she did not say it quite sincerely. She was deliberately playing the part of the dear little woman and within her she bubbled with amusement. They disliked Alban because he had such an air of distinction, and because he was interested in art and literature; they did not understand these things and so thought them unmanly; and they disliked him because his capacity was greater than theirs. They disliked him because he was better bred than they. They thought him superior; well, he was superior, but not in the sense they meant. They forgave her because she was an ugly little thing. That was what she called herself, but she wasn't that, or if she was it was with an ugliness that was most attractive. She was like a little monkey, but a very sweet little monkey and very human. She had a neat figure. That was her best point. That and her eyes. They were very large, of a deep brown, liquid and shining; they were full of fun, but they could be tender on occasion with a charming sympathy. She was dark, her frizzy hair was almost black, and her skin was swarthy; she had a small fleshy nose, with large nostrils, and much too big a mouth. But she was alert and vivacious. She could talk with a show of real interest to the ladies of the colony about their husbands and their servants and their children in England, and she could listen appreciatively to the men who told her stories that she had often heard before. They thought her a jolly good sort. They did not know what clever fun she made of them in private. It never occurred to them that she thought them narrow, gross and pretentious. They found no glamour in the East because they looked at it vulgarly with material eyes. Romance lingered at their threshold and they drove it away like an importunate beggar. She was aloof. She repeated to herself Landor's line:

"Nature I loved, and next to nature, art."

She reflected on her conversation with Mrs. Hannay, but on the whole it left her unconcerned. She wondered whether she should say anything about it to Alban; it had always seemed a little odd to her that he should be so little aware of his unpopularity; but she was afraid that if she told him of it he would become self-conscious. He never noticed the coldness of the men at the club. He made them feel shy and therefore uncomfortable. His appearance then caused a sort of awkwardness, but he, happily insensible, was breezily cordial to all and sundry. The fact was that he was strangely unconscious of other people. She was in a class by herself, she and a little group of friends they had in London, but he could never quite realise that the people of the colony, the government officials and the planters and their wives, were human beings. They were to him like pawns in a game. He laughed with them, chaffed them, and was amiably tolerant of them; with a chuckle Anne told herself that he was rather like the master of a preparatory school taking little boys out on a picnic and anxious to give them a good time.

She was afraid it wasn't much good telling Alban.

He was incapable of the dissimulation which, she happily realised, came so easily to her. What was one to do with these people? The men had come out to the colony as lads from second-rate schools, and life had taught them nothing. At fifty they had the outlook of hobbledehoys. Most of them drank a great deal too much. They read nothing worth reading. Their ambition was to be like everybody else. Their highest praise was to say that a man was a damned good sort. If you were interested in the things of the spirit you were a prig. They were eaten up with envy of one another and devoured by petty jealousies. And the women, poor things, were obsessed by petty rivalries. They made a circle that was more provincial than any in the smallest town in England. They were prudish and spiteful. What did it matter if they did not like Alban? They would have to put up with him because his ability was so great. He was clever and energetic. They could not say that he did not do his work well. He had been successful in every post he had occupied. With his sensitiveness and his imagination he understood the native mind and he was able to get the natives to do things that no one in his position could. He had a gift for languages, and he spoke all the local dialects. He not only knew the common tongue that most of the government officials spoke, but was acquainted with the niceties of the language and on occasion could make use of a ceremonial speech that flattered and impressed the chiefs. He had a gift for organisation. He was not afraid of responsibility. In due course he was bound to be made a Resident. Alban had some interest in England; his father was a brigadier-general killed in the war, and though he had no private means he had influential friends. He spoke of them with pleasant irony.

"The great advantage of democratic government," he said, "is that merit, with influence to back it, can be pretty sure of receiving its due reward."

Alban was so obviously the ablest man in the service that there seemed no reason why he should not eventually be made Governor. Then, thought Anne, his air of superiority, of which they complained, would be in place. They would accept him as their master and he would know how to make himself respected and obeyed. The position she foresaw did not dazzle her. She accepted it as a right. It would be fun for Alban to be Governor and for her to be the Governor's wife. And what an opportunity! They were sheep, the government servants and the planters; when Government House was the seat of culture they would soon fall into line. When the best way to the Governor's favour was to be intelligent, intelligence would become the fashion. She and Alban would cherish the native arts and collect carefully the memorials of a vanished past. The country would make an advance it had never dreamed of. They would develop it, but along lines of order and beauty. They would instil into their subordinates a passion for that beautiful land and a loving interest in these romantic races. They would make them realise what music meant. They would cultivate literature. They would create beauty. It would be the golden age.

Suddenly she heard Alban's footstep. Anne awoke from her day-dream. All that was far away in the future. Alban was only a District Officer yet and what was important was the life they were living now. She heard Alban go into the bath-house and splash water over himself. In a minute he came in. He had changed into a shirt and shorts. His fair hair was still wet.

"Tiffin ready?" he asked.

"Yes."

He sat down at the piano and played the piece that he had played in the morning. The silvery notes cascaded coolly down the sultry air. You had an impression of a formal garden with great trees and elegant pieces of artificial water and of leisurely walks bordered with pseudo-classical statues. Alban played with an exquisite delicacy. Lunch was announced by the head boy. He rose from the piano. They walked into the dining-room hand in hand. A punkah lazily fanned the air. Anne gave the table a glance. With its bright-coloured table-cloth and the amusing plates it looked very gay.

"Anything exciting at the office this morning?" she asked.

"No, nothing much. A buffalo case. Oh, and Prynne has sent along to ask me to go up to the estate. Some coolies have been damaging the trees and he wants me to come along and look into it."

Prynne was manager of the rubber estate up the river and now and then they spent a night with him. Sometimes when he wanted a change he came down to dinner and slept at the D.O.'s bungalow. They both liked him. He was a man of five-and-thirty, with a red face, with deep furrows in it, and very black hair. He was quite uneducated, but cheerful and easy, and being the only Englishman within two days' journey they could not but be friendly with him. He had been a little shy of them at first. News spreads quickly in the East and long before they arrived in the district he heard that they were highbrows. He did not know what he would make of them. He probably did not know that he had charm, which makes up for many more commendable qualities, and Alban with his almost feminine sensibilities was peculiarly susceptible to this. He found Alban much more human than he expected, and of course Anne was stunning. Alban played ragtime for him, which he would not have done for the Governor, and played dominoes with him. When Alban was making his first tour of the district with Anne, and suggested that they would like to spend a couple of nights on the estate, he had thought it as well to warn him that he lived with a native woman and had two children by her. He would do his best to keep them out of Anne's sight, but he could not send them away, there was nowhere to send them. Alban laughed.

"Anne isn't that sort of woman at all. Don't dream of hiding them. She loves children."

Anne quickly made friends with the shy, pretty little native woman and soon was playing happily with the children. She and the girl had long confidential chats. The children took a fancy to her. She brought them lovely toys from Port Wallace. Prynne, comparing her smiling tolerance with the disapproving acidity of the other white women of the colony, described himself as knocked all of a heap. He could not do enough to show his delight and gratitude.

"If all highbrows are like you," he said, "give me highbrows every time."

He hated to think that in another year they would leave the district for good and the chances were that, if the next D.O. was married, his wife would think it dreadful that, rather than live alone, he had a native woman to live with him and, what was more, was much attached to her.

But there had been a good deal of discontent on the estate of late. The coolies were Chinese and infected with communist ideas. They were disorderly. Alban had been obliged to sentence several of them for various crimes to terms of imprisonment.

"Prynne tells me that as soon as their term is up he's going to send them all back to China and get Javanese instead," said Alban. "I'm sure he's right. They're much more amenable."

"You don't think there's going to be any serious trouble?"

"Oh, no. Prynne knows his job and he's a pretty

determined fellow. He wouldn't put up with any nonsense and with me and our policemen to back him up I don't imagine they'll try any monkey tricks." He smiled. "The iron hand in the velvet glove."

The words were barely out of his mouth when a sudden shouting arose. There was a commotion and the sound of steps. Loud voices and cries.

"Tuan, Tuan."

"What the devil's the matter?"

Alban sprang from his chair and went swiftly on to the verandah. Anne followed him. At the bottom of the steps was a group of natives. There was the sergeant, and three or four policemen, boatmen and several men from the kampong.

"What is it?" called Alban.

Two or three shouted back in answer. The sergeant pushed others aside and Alban saw lying on the ground a man in a shirt and khaki shorts. He ran down the steps. He recognised the man as the assistant manager of Prynne's estate. He was a half-caste. His shorts were covered with blood and there was clotted blood all over one side of his face and head. He was unconscious.

"Bring him up here," called Anne.

Alban gave an order. The man was lifted up and carried on to the verandah. They laid him on the floor and Anne put a pillow under his head. She sent for water and for the medicine-chest in which they kept things for emergency.

"Is he dead?" asked Alban.

"No."

"Better try to give him some brandy."

The boatmen brought ghastly news. The Chinese coolies had risen suddenly and attacked the manager's office. Prynne was killed and the assistant manager, Oakley by name, had escaped only by the skin of his teeth. He had come upon the rioters when they were looting the office, he had seen Prynne's body thrown out of the window, and had taken to his heels. Some of the Chinese saw him and gave chase. He ran for the river and was wounded as he jumped into the launch. The launch managed to put off before the Chinese could get on board and they had come down-stream for help as fast as they could go. As they went they saw flames rising from the office buildings. There was no doubt that the coolies had burned down everything that would burn.

Oakley gave a groan and opened his eyes. He was a little, dark-skinned man, with flattened features and thick coarse hair. His great native eyes were filled with terror.

"You're all right," said Anne. "You're quite safe."

He gave a sigh and smiled. Anne washed his face and swabbed it with antiseptics. The wound on his head was not serious.

"Can you speak yet?" said Alban.

"Wait a bit," she said. "We must look at his leg."

Alban ordered the sergeant to get the crowd out of

the verandah. Anne ripped up one leg of the shorts. The material was clinging to the coagulated wound.

"I've been bleeding like a pig," said Oakley.

It was only a flesh wound. Alban was clever with his fingers, and though the blood began to flow again they stanched it. Alban put on a dressing and a bandage. The sergeant and a policeman lifted Oakley on to a long chair. Alban gave him a brandy and soda, and soon he felt strong enough to speak. He knew no more than the boatmen had already told. Prynne was dead and the estate was in flames.

"And the girl and the children?" asked Anne.

"I don't know."

"Oh, Alban."

"I must turn out the police. Are you sure Prynne is dead?"

"Yes, sir. I saw him."

"Have the rioters got fire-arms?"

"I don't know, sir."

"How d'you mean, you don't know?" Alban cried irritably. "Prynne had a gun, hadn't he?"

"Yes, sir."

"There must have been more on the estate. You had one, didn't you? The head overseer had one."

The half-caste was silent. Alban looked at him sternly.

"How many of those damned Chinese are there?"

"A hundred and fifty."

Anne wondered that he asked so many questions. It

seemed waste of time. The important thing was to collect coolies for the transport up-river, prepare the boats and issue ammunition to the police.

"How many policemen have you got, sir?" asked Oakley.

"Eight and the sergeant."

"Could I come too? That would make ten of us. I'm sure I shall be all right now I'm bandaged."

"I'm not going," said Alban.

"Alban, you must," cried Anne. She could not believe her ears.

"Nonsense. It would be madness. Oakley's obviously useless. He's sure to have a temperature in a few hours. He'd only be in the way. That leaves nine guns. There are a hundred and fifty Chinese and they've got fire-arms and all the ammunition in the world."

"How d'you know?"

"It stands to reason they wouldn't have started a show like this unless they had. It would be idiotic to go."

Anne stared at him with open mouth. Oakley's eyes were puzzled.

"What are you going to do?"

"Well, fortunately we've got the launch. I'll send it to Port Wallace with a request for reinforcements."

"But they won't be here for two days at least."

"Well, what of it? Prynne's dead and the estate burned to the ground. We couldn't do any good by going up now. I shall send a native to reconnoitre so

that we can find out exactly what the rioters are doing."
He gave Anne his charming smile. "Believe me, my
pet, the rascals won't lose anything by waiting a day or
two for what's coming to them."

Oakley opened his mouth to speak, but perhaps he
hadn't the nerve. He was a half-caste assistant manager
and Alban, the D.O., represented the power of the
Government. But the man's eyes sought Anne's and she
thought she read in them an earnest and personal
appeal.

"But in two days they're capable of committing the
most frightful atrocities," she cried. "It's quite un-
speakable what they may do."

"Whatever damage they do they'll pay for. I promise
you that."

"Oh, Alban, you can't sit still and do nothing. I
beseech you to go yourself at once."

"Don't be so silly. I can't quell a riot with eight
policemen and a sergeant. I haven't got the right to
take a risk of that sort. We'd have to go in boats.
You don't think we could get up unobserved. The
lalang along the banks is perfect cover and they could
just take pot shots at us as we came along. We shouldn't
have a chance."

"I'm afraid they'll only think it weakness if nothing is
done for two days, sir," said Oakley.

"When I want your opinion I'll ask for it," said
Alban acidly. "So far as I can see when there was
danger the only thing you did was to cut and run. I

can't persuade myself that your assistance in a crisis would be very valuable."

The half-caste reddened. He said nothing more. He looked straight in front of him with troubled eyes.

"I'm going down to the office," said Alban. "I'll just write a short report and send it down the river by launch at once."

He gave an order to the sergeant who had been standing all this time stiffly at the top of the steps. He saluted and ran off. Alban went into a little hall they had to get his topi. Anne swiftly followed him.

"Alban, for God's sake listen to me a minute," she whispered.

"I don't want to be rude to you, darling, but I am pressed for time. I think you'd much better mind your own business."

"You can't do nothing, Alban. You must go. Whatever the risk."

"Don't be such a fool," he said angrily.

He had never been angry with her before. She seized his hand to hold him back.

"I tell you I can do no good by going.'"

"You don't know. There's the woman and Prynne's children. We must do something to save them. Let me come with you. They'll kill them."

"They've probably killed them already."

"Oh, how can you be so callous! If there's a chance of saving them it's your duty to try."

"It's my duty to act like a reasonable human being.

I'm not going to risk my life and my policemen's for the sake of a native woman and her half-caste brats. What sort of a damned fool do you take me for?"

"They'll say you were afraid."

"Who?"

"Everyone in the colony."

He smiled disdainfully.

"If you only knew what a complete contempt I have for the opinion of everyone in the colony."

She gave him a long searching look. She had been married to him for eight years and she knew every expression of his face and every thought in his mind. She stared into his blue eyes as if they were open windows. She suddenly went quite pale. She dropped his hand and turned away. Without another word she went back on to the verandah. Her ugly little monkey face was a mask of horror.

Alban went to his office, wrote a brief account of the facts, and in a few minutes the motor launch was pounding down the river.

The next two days were endless. Escaped natives brought them news of happenings on the estate. But from their excited and terrified stories it was impossible to get an exact impression of the truth. There had been a good deal of bloodshed. The head overseer had been killed. They brought wild tales of cruelty and outrage. Anne could hear nothing of Prynne's woman and the two children. She shuddered when she thought of what might have been their fate. Alban collected as

many natives as he could. They were armed with
spears and swords. He commandeered boats. The
situation was serious, but he kept his head. He felt that
he had done all that was possible and nothing remained
but for him to carry on normally. He did his official
work. He played the piano a great deal. He rode with
Anne in the early morning. He appeared to have
forgotten that they had had the first serious difference of
opinion in the whole of their married life. He took it
that Anne had accepted the wisdom of his decision.
He was as amusing, cordial and gay with her as he had
always been. When he spoke of the rioters it was with
grim irony: when the time came to settle matters
a good many of them would wish they had never been
born.

"What'll happen to them?" asked Anne.

"Oh, they'll hang." He gave a shrug of distaste. "I
hate having to be present at executions. It always
makes me feel rather sick."

He was very sympathetic to Oakley, whom they had
put to bed and whom Anne was nursing. Perhaps he
was sorry that in the exasperation of the moment he
had spoken to him offensively, and he went out of his
way to be nice to him.

Then on the afternoon of the third day, when they
were drinking their coffee after luncheon, Alban's
quick ears caught the sound of a motor boat approaching. At the same moment a policeman ran up to say
that the government launch was sighted.

P

"At last," cried Alban.

He bolted out of the house. Anne raised one of the jalousies and looked out at the river. Now the sound was quite loud and in a moment she saw the boat come round the bend. She saw Alban on the landing-stage. He got into a prahu and as the launch dropped her anchor he went on board. She told Oakley that the reinforcements had come.

"Will the D.O. go up with them when they attack?" he asked her.

"Naturally," said Anne coldly.

"I wondered."

Anne felt a strange feeling in her heart. For the last two days she had had to exercise all her self-control not to cry. She did not answer. She went out of the room.

A quarter of an hour later Alban returned to the bungalow with the captain of constabulary who had been sent with twenty Sikhs to deal with the rioters. Captain Stratton was a little red-faced man with a red moustache and bow legs, very hearty and dashing, whom she had met often at Port Wallace.

"Well, Mrs. Torel, this is a pretty kettle of fish," he cried, as he shook hands with her, in a loud jolly voice. "Here I am, with my army all full of pep and ready for a scrap. Up, boys, and at 'em. Have you got anything to drink in this benighted place?"

"Boy," she cried, smiling.

"Something long and cool and faintly alcoholic, and then I'm ready to discuss the plan of campaign."

His breeziness was very comforting. It blew away the sullen apprehension that had seemed ever since the disaster to brood over the lost peace of the bungalow. The boy came in with a tray and Stratton mixed himself a stengah. Alban put him in possession of the facts. He told them clearly, briefly and with precision.

"I must say I admire you," said Stratton. "In your place I should never have been able to resist the temptation to take my eight cops and have a whack at the blighters myself."

"I thought it was a perfectly unjustifiable risk to take."

"Safety first, old boy, eh, what?" said Stratton jovially. "I'm jolly glad you didn't. It's not often we get the chance of a scrap. It would have been a dirty trick to keep the whole show to yourself."

Captain Stratton was all for steaming straight up the river and attacking at once, but Alban pointed out to him the inadvisability of such a course. The sound of the approaching launch would warn the rioters. The long grass at the river's edge offered them cover and they had enough guns to make a landing difficult. It seemed useless to expose the attacking force to their fire. It was silly to forget that they had to face a hundred and fifty desperate men and it would be easy to fall into an ambush. Alban expounded his own plan. Stratton listened to it. He nodded now and then. The plan was evidently a good one. It would enable them to take the rioters on the rear, surprise them, and in all probability finish the job without a single casualty.

He would have been a fool not to accept it.

"But why didn't you do that yourself?" asked Stratton.

"With eight men and a sergeant?"

Stratton did not answer.

"Anyhow it's not a bad idea and we'll settle on it. It gives us plenty of time, so with your permission, Mrs. Torel, I'll have a bath."

They set out at sunset, Captain Stratton and his twenty Sikhs, Alban with his policemen and the natives he had collected. The night was dark and moonless. Trailing behind them were the dug-outs that Alban had gathered together and into which after a certain distance they proposed to transfer their force. It was important that no sound should give warning of their approach. After they had gone for about three hours by launch they took to the dug-outs and in them silently paddled up stream. They reached the border of the vast estate and landed. Guides led them along a path so narrow that they had to march in single file. It had been long unused and the going was heavy. They had twice to ford a stream. The path led them circuitously to the rear of the coolie lines, but they did not wish to reach them till nearly dawn and presently Stratton gave the order to halt. It was a long cold wait. At last the night seemed to be less dark; you did not see the trunks of the trees, but were vaguely sensible of them against its darkness. Stratton had been sitting with his back to a tree. He gave a whispered order to a sergeant and in a few minutes the column was once more on the march. Suddenly they found themselves on a road. They formed fours. The dawn broke and in the ghostly light the surrounding objects were wanly visible. The column stopped on a whispered order. They had come in sight of the coolie lines. Silence reigned in them. The column crept on again and again halted. Stratton, his eyes shining, gave Alban a smile.

"We've caught the blighters asleep."

He lined up his men. They inserted cartridges in their guns. He stepped forward and raised his hand. The carbines were pointed at the coolie lines.

"Fire."

There was a rattle as the volley of shots rang out. Then suddenly there was a tremendous din and the Chinese poured out, shouting and waving their arms, but in front of them, to Alban's utter bewilderment, bellowing at the top of his voice and shaking his fist at them, was a white man.

"Who the hell's that?" cried Stratton.

A very big, very fat man, in khaki trousers and a singlet, was running towards them as fast as his fat legs would carry him and as he ran shaking both fists at them and yelling:

"*Smerige flikkers! Verlockte ploerten!*

"My God, it's Van Hasseldt," said Alban.

This was the Dutch manager of the timber camp which was situated on a considerable tributary of the river about twenty miles away.

"What the hell do you think you're doing?" he puffed as he came up to them.

"How the hell did you get here?" asked Stratton in turn.

He saw that the Chinese were scattering in all directions and gave his men instructions to round them up. Then he turned again to Van Hasseldt.

"What's it mean?"

"Mean? Mean?" shouted the Dutchman furiously. "That's what I want to know. You and your damned policemen. What do you mean by coming here at this hour in the morning and firing a damned volley. Target practice? You might have killed me. Idiots!"

"Have a cigarette," said Stratton.

"How did you get here, Van Hasseldt?" asked Alban again, very much at sea. "This is the force they've sent from Port Wallace to quell the riot."

"How did I get here? I walked. How did you think I got here? Riot be damned. I quelled the riot. If that's what you came for you can take your damned policemen home again. A bullet came within a foot of my head."

"I don't understand," said Alban.

"There's nothing to understand," spluttered Van Hasseldt, still fuming. "Some coolies came to my estate and said the chinks had killed Prynne and burned the bally place down, so I took my assistant and my head overseer and a Dutch friend I had staying with me and came over to see what the trouble was."

Captain Stratton opened his eyes wide.

"Did you just stroll in as if it was a picnic?" he asked.

"Well, you don't think after all the years I've been in this country I'm going to let a couple of hundred chinks put the fear of God into me? I found them all scared out of their lives. One of them had the nerve to pull a gun on me and I blew his bloody brains out. And the rest surrendered. I've got the leaders tied up. I was going to send a boat down to you this morning to come up and get them."

Stratton stared at him for a minute and then burst into a shout of laughter. He laughed till the tears ran down his face. The Dutchman looked at him angrily, then began to laugh too; he laughed with the big belly laugh of a very fat man and his coils of fat heaved and shook. Alban watched them sullenly. He was very angry.

"What about Prynne's girl and the kids?" he asked.

"Oh, they got away all right."

It just showed how wise he had been not to let himself be influenced by Anne's hysteria. Of course the children had come to no harm. He never thought they would.

Van Hasseldt and his little party started back for the timber camp, and as soon after as possible Stratton embarked his twenty Sikhs and leaving Alban with his sergeant and his policemen to deal with the situation departed for Port Wallace. Alban gave him a brief report for the Governor. There was much for him to do. It looked as though he would have to stay for a considerable time; but since every house on the estate had been burned to the ground and he was obliged to install himself in the coolie lines he thought it better that Anne should not join him. He sent her a note to that effect. He was glad to be able to reassure her of the safety of poor Prynne's girl. He set to work at once to make his preliminary enquiry. He examined a host of witnesses. But a week later he received an order to go to Port Wallace at once. The launch that brought it was to take him and he was able to see Anne on the way down for no more than an hour. Alban was a trifle vexed.

"I don't know why the Governor can't leave me to get things straight without dragging me off like this. It's extremely inconvenient."

"Oh, well, the Government never bothers very much about the convenience of its subordinates, does it?" smiled Anne.

"It's just red-tape. I would offer to take you along, darling, only I shan't stay a minute longer than I need. I want to get my evidence together for the Sessions Court as soon as possible. I think in a country like this it's very important that justice should be prompt."

When the launch came in to Port Wallace one of the harbour police told him that the harbour-master had a chit for him. It was from the Governor's secretary and informed him that His Excellency desired to see him as soon as convenient after his arrival. It was ten in the morning. Alban went to the club, had a bath and shaved, and then in clean ducks, his hair neatly brushed, he called a rickshaw and told the boy to take him to the Governor's office. He was at once shown in to the secretary's room. The secretary shook hands with him.

"I'll tell H.E. you're here," he said. "Won't you sit down?"

The secretary left the room and in a little while came back.

"H.E. will see you in a minute. Do you mind if I get on with my letters?"

Alban smiled. The secretary was not exactly come-hither. He waited, smoking a cigarette, and amused himself with his own thoughts. He was making a good job of the preliminary enquiry. It interested him. Then an orderly came in and told Alban that the Governor was ready for him. He rose from his seat and followed him into the Governor's room.

"Good morning, Torel."

"Good morning, sir."

The Governor was sitting at a large desk. He nodded to Alban and motioned to him to take a seat. The Governor was all grey. His hair was grey, his face, his eyes; he looked as though the tropical suns had washed the colour out of him; he had been in the country for thirty years and had risen one by one through all the ranks of the Service; he looked tired and depressed.

P*

Even his voice was grey. Alban liked him because he was quiet; he did not think him clever, but he had an unrivalled knowledge of the country, and his great experience was a very good substitute for intelligence. He looked at Alban for a full moment without speaking and the odd idea came to Alban that he was embarrassed. He very nearly gave him a lead.

"I saw Van Hasseldt yesterday," said the Governor suddenly.

"Yes, sir?"

"Will you give me your account of the occurrences at the Alud Estate and of the steps you took to deal with them."

Alban had an orderly mind. He was self-possessed. He marshalled his facts well and was able to state them with precision. He chose his words with care and spoke them fluently.

"You had a sergeant and eight policemen. Why did you not immediately go to the scene of the disturbance?"

"I thought the risk was unjustifiable."

A thin smile was outlined on the Governor's grey face.

"If the officers of this Government had hesitated to take unjustifiable risks it would never have become a province of the British Empire."

Alban was silent. It was difficult to talk to a man who spoke obvious nonsense.

"I am anxious to hear your reasons for the decision you took."

Alban gave them coolly. He was quite convinced of the rightness of his action. He repeated, but more fully, what he had said in the first place to Anne. The Governor listened attentively.

"Van Hasseldt, with his manager, a Dutch friend of his, and a native overseer, seems to have coped with the situation very efficiently," said the Governor.

"He had a lucky break. That doesn't prevent him from being a damned fool. It was madness to do what he did."

"Do you realise that by leaving a Dutch planter to do what you should have done yourself, you have covered the Government with ridicule?"

"No, sir."

"You've made yourself a laughing-stock in the whole colony."

Alban smiled.

"My back is broad enough to bear the ridicule of persons to whose opinion I am entirely indifferent."

"The utility of a Government official depends very largely on his prestige, and I'm afraid his prestige is likely to be inconsiderable when he lies under the stigma of cowardice."

Alban flushed a little.

"I don't quite know what you mean by that, sir."

"I've gone into the matter very carefully. I've seen Captain Stratton, and Oakley, poor Prynne's assistant, and I've seen Van Hasseldt. I've listened to your defence."

"I didn't know that I was defending myself, sir."

"Be so good as not to interrupt me. I think you committed a grave error of judgment. As it turns out the risk was very small, but whatever it was, I think you should have taken it. In such matters promptness and firmness are essential. It is not for me to conjecture what motive led you to send for a force of constabulary and do nothing till they came. I am afraid, however, that I consider that your usefulness in the Service is no longer very great."

Alban looked at him with astonishment.

"But would you have gone under the circumstances?" he asked him.

"I should."

Alban shrugged his shoulders.

"Don't you believe me?" rapped out the Governor.

"Of course I believe you, sir. But perhaps you will allow me to say that if you had been killed the colony would have suffered an irreparable loss."

The Governor drummed on the table with his fingers. He looked out of the window and then looked again at Alban. When he spoke it was not unkindly.

"I think you are unfitted by temperament for this rather rough-and-tumble life, Torel. If you'll take my advice you'll go home. With your abilities I feel sure that you'll soon find an occupation much better suited to you."

"I'm afraid I don't understand what you mean, sir."

"Oh, come, Torel, you're not stupid. I'm trying to

make things easy for you. For your wife's sake as well as for your own I do not wish you to leave the colony with the stigma of being dismissed from the Service for cowardice. I'm giving you the opportunity of resigning."

"Thank you very much, sir. I'm not prepared to avail myself of the opportunity. If I resign I admit that I committed an error and that the charge you make against me is justified. I don't admit it."

"You can please yourself. I have considered the matter very carefully and I have no doubt about it in my mind. I am forced to discharge you from the Service. The necessary papers will reach you in due course. Meanwhile you will return to your post and hand over to the officer appointed to succeed you on his arrival."

"Very good, sir," replied Alban, a twinkle of amusement in his eyes. "When do you desire me to return to my post?"

"At once."

"Have you any objection to my going to the club and having tiffin before I go?"

The Governor looked at him with surprise. His exasperation was mingled with an unwilling admiration.

"Not at all. I'm sorry, Torel, that this unhappy incident should have deprived the Government of a servant whose zeal has always been so apparent and whose tact, intelligence and industry seemed to point him out in the future for very high office."

"Your Excellency does not read Schiller, I suppose. You are probably not acquainted with his celebrated line: *mit der Dummheit kämpfen die Götter selbst vergebens*."

"What does it mean?"

"Roughly: against stupidity the gods themselves battle in vain."

"Good-morning."

With his head in the air, a smile on his lips, Alban left the Governor's office. The Governor was human, and he had the curiosity to ask his secretary later in the day if Alban Torel had really gone to the club.

"Yes, sir. He had tiffin there."

"It must have wanted some nerve."

Alban entered the club jauntily and joined the group of men standing at the bar. He talked to them in the breezy, cordial tone he always used with them. It was designed to put them at their ease. They had been discussing him ever since Stratton had come back to Port Wallace with his story, sneering at him and laughing at him, and all that had resented his superciliousness, and they were the majority, were triumphant because his pride had had a fall. But they were so taken aback at seeing him now, so confused to find him as confident as ever, that it was they who were embarrassed.

One man, though he knew perfectly, asked him what he was doing in Port Wallace.

"Oh, I came about the riot on the Alud Estate. H.E. wanted to see me. He does not see eye to eye with me about it. The silly old ass has fired me. I'm going home as soon as he appoints a D.O. to take over."

There was a moment of awkwardness. One, more kindly disposed than the others, said:

"I'm awfully sorry."

Alban shrugged his shoulders.

"My dear fellow, what can you do with a perfect damned fool? The only thing is to let him stew in his own juice."

When the Governor's secretary had told his chief as much of this as he thought discreet, the Governor smiled.

"Courage is a queer thing. I would rather have shot myself than go to the club just then and face all those fellows."

A fortnight later, having sold to the incoming D.O. all the decorations that Anne had taken so much trouble about, with the rest of their things in packing-cases and trunks, they arrived at Port Wallace to await the local steamer that was to take them to Singapore. The padre's wife invited them to stay with her, but Anne refused; she insisted that they should go to the hotel. An hour after their arrival she received a very kind little letter from the Governor's wife asking her to go and have tea with her. She went. She found Mrs. Hannay alone, but in a minute the Governor joined them. He expressed his regret that she was leaving and told her how sorry he was for the cause.

"It's very kind of you to say that," said Anne, smiling gaily, "but you mustn't think I take it to heart.

I'm entirely on Alban's side. I think what he did was absolutely right and if you don't mind my saying so I think you've treated him most unjustly."

"Believe me, I hated having to take the step I took."

"Don't let's talk about it," said Anne.

"What are your plans when you get home?" asked Mrs. Hannay.

Anne began to chat brightly. You would have thought she had not a care in the world. She seemed in great spirits at going home. She was jolly and amusing and made little jokes. When she took leave of the Governor and his wife she thanked them for all their kindness. The Governor escorted her to the door.

The next day but one, after dinner, they went on board the clean and comfortable little ship. The padre and his wife saw them off. When they went into their cabin they found a large parcel on Anne's bunk. It was addressed to Alban. He opened it and saw that it was an immense powder-puff.

"Hullo, I wonder who sent us this," he said, with a laugh. "It must be for you, darling."

Anne gave him a quick look. She went pale. The brutes! How could they be so cruel? She forced herself to smile.

"It's enormous, isn't it? I've never seen such a large powder-puff in my life."

But when he had left the cabin and they were out at sea, she threw it passionately overboard.

And now, now that they were back in London and

Sondurah was nine thousand miles away, she clenched her hands as she thought of it. Somehow, it seemed the worst thing of all. It was so wantonly unkind to send that absurd object to Alban, Powder-puff Percy; it showed such a petty spite. Was that their idea of humour? Nothing had hurt her more and even now she felt that it was only by holding on to herself that she could prevent herself from crying. Suddenly she started, for the door opened and Alban came in. She was still sitting in the chair in which he had left her.

"Hullo, why haven't you dressed?" He looked about the room. "You haven't unpacked."

"No."

"Why on earth not?"

"I'm not going to unpack. I'm not going to stay here. I'm leaving you."

"What are you talking about?"

"I've stuck it out till now. I made up my mind I would till we got home. I set my teeth, I've borne more than I thought it possible to bear, but now it's finished. I've done all that could be expected of me. We're back in London now and I can go."

He looked at her in utter bewilderment.

"Are you mad, Anne?"

"Oh, my God, what I've endured! The journey to Singapore, with all the officers knowing, and even the Chinese stewards. And at Singapore, the way people looked at us at the hotel, and the sympathy I had to put up with, the bricks they dropped and their embarrassment when they realised what they'd done. My God, I could have killed them. That interminable journey home. There wasn't a single passenger on the ship who didn't know. The contempt they had for you and the kindness they went out of their way to show me. And you so self-complacent and so pleased with yourself, seeing nothing, feeling nothing. You must have the hide of a rhinoceros. The misery of seeing you so chatty and agreeable. Pariahs, that's what we were. You seemed to ask them to snub you. How can anyone be so shameless?"

She was flaming with passion. Now that at last she need not wear the mask of indifference and pride that she had forced herself to assume she cast aside all reserve and all self-control. The words poured from her trembling lips in a virulent stream.

"My dear, how can you be so absurd?" he said good-naturedly, smiling. "You must be very nervous and high-strung to have got such ideas in your head. Why didn't you tell me? You're like a country bumpkin who comes to London and thinks everyone is staring at him. Nobody bothered about us and if they did what on earth did it matter? You ought to have more sense than to bother about what a lot of fools say. And what do you imagine they were saying?"

"They were saying you'd been fired."

"Well, that was true," he laughed.

"They said you were a coward."

"What of it?"

"Well, you see, that was true too."

He looked at her for a moment reflectively. His lips tightened a little.

"And what makes you think so?" he asked acidly.

"I saw it in your eyes, that day the news came, when you refused to go to the estate and I followed you into the hall when you went to fetch your topi. I begged you to go, I felt that whatever the danger you must take it, and suddenly I saw the fear in your eyes. I nearly fainted with the horror."

"I should have been a fool to risk my life to no purpose. Why should I? Nothing that concerned me was at stake. Courage is the obvious virtue of the stupid. I don't attach any particular importance to it."

"How do you mean that nothing that concerned you was at stake? If that's true then your whole life is a sham. You've given away everything you stood for, everything we both stand for. You've let all of us down. We did set ourselves up on a pinnacle, we did think ourselves better than the rest of them because we loved literature and art and music, we weren't content to live a life of ignoble jealousies and vulgar tittle-tattle, we did cherish the things of the spirit, and we loved beauty. It was our food and drink. They laughed at us and sneered at us. That was inevitable. The ignorant and the common naturally hate and fear those who are interested in things they don't understand. We didn't care. We called them Philistines. We despised them and we had a right to despise them. Our justification was that we were better and nobler and wiser and braver than they were. And you weren't better, you weren't nobler, you weren't braver. When the crisis came you slunk away like a whipped cur with his tail between his legs. You of all people hadn't the right to be a coward. They despise *us* now and they have the right to despise us. Us and all we stood for. Now they can say that art and beauty are all rot; when it comes to a pinch people like us always let you down. They never stopped looking for a chance to turn and rend us and you gave it to them. They can say that they always expected it. It's a triumph for them. I used to be furious because they called you Powder-Puff Percy. Did you know they did?"

"Of course. I thought it very vulgar, but it left me entirely indifferent."

"It's funny that their instinct should have been so right."

"Do you mean to say you've been harbouring this against me all these weeks? I should never have thought you capable of it."

"I couldn't let you down when everyone was against you. I was too proud for that. Whatever happened I swore to myself that I'd stick to you till we got home. It's been torture."

"Don't you love me any more?"

"Love you? I loathe the very sight of you."

"Anne."

"God knows I loved you. For eight years I worshipped the ground you trod on. You were everything to me. I believed in you as some people believe in God. When I saw the fear in your eyes that day, when you told me that you weren't going to risk your life for a kept woman and her half-caste brats, I was shattered. It was as though someone had wrenched my heart out of my body and trampled on it. You killed my love there and then, Alban. You killed it stone-dead. Since then when you've kissed me I've had to clench my hands so as not to turn my face away. The mere thought of anything else makes me feel physically sick. I loathe your complacence and your frightful insensitiveness. Perhaps I could have forgiven it if it had been just a moment's weakness and if afterwards you'd been ashamed. I should have been miserable, but I think my love was so great that I should only have felt pity for you. But you're incapable of shame. And now I believe in nothing. You're only a silly, pretentious vulgar poseur. I would rather be the wife of a second-rate planter so long as he had the common human virtues of a man than the wife of a fake like you."

He did not answer. Gradually his face began to discompose. Those handsome, regular features of his horribly distorted and suddenly he broke out into loud sobs. She gave a little cry.

"Don't, Alban, don't."

"Oh, darling, how can you be so cruel to me? I

adore you. I'd give my whole life to please you. I can't live without you."

She put out her arms as though to ward off a blow. "No, no, Alban, don't try to move me. I can't. I must go. I can't live with you any more. It would be frightful. I can never forget. I must tell you the truth, I have only contempt for you and repulsion."

He sank down at her feet and tried to cling to her knees. With a gasp she sprang up and he buried his head in the empty chair. He cried painfully with sobs that tore his chest. The sound was horrible. The tears streamed from Anne's eyes and, putting her hands to her ears to shut out that dreadful, hysterical sobbing, blindly stumbling she rushed to the door and ran out.

NEIL MACADAM

CAPTAIN BREDON was good-natured. When Angus Munro, the Curator of the museum at Kuala Solor, told him that he had advised Neil MacAdam, his new assistant, on his arrival at Singapore to put up at the Van Dyke Hotel, and asked him to see that the lad got into no mischief during the few days he must spend there, he said he would do his best. Captain Bredon commanded the "Sultan Ahmed," and when he was at Singapore always stayed at the Van Dyke. He had a Japanese wife and kept a room there. It was his home. When he got back after his fortnight's trip along the coast of Borneo the Dutch manager told him that Neil had been there for two days. The boy was sitting in the little dusty garden of the hotel reading old numbers of "The Straits Times." Captain Bredon took a look at him first and then went up.

"You're MacAdam, aren't you?"

Neil rose to his feet, flushed to the roots of his hair and answered shyly: "I am."

"My name's Bredon. I'm skipper of the 'Sultan Ahmed.' You're sailing with me next Tuesday. Munro asked me to look after you. What about a stengah? I suppose you've learned what that means by now."

"Thank you very much, but I don't drink."

465

He spoke with a broad Scots accent.

"I don't blame you. Drink's been the ruin of many a good man in this country."

He called the Chinese boy and ordered himself a double whisky and a small soda.

"What have you been doing with yourself since you got in?"

"Walking about."

"There's nothing much to see in Singapore."

"I've found plenty."

Of course the first thing he had done was to go to the museum. There was little that he had not seen at home, but the fact that those beasts and birds, those reptiles, moths, butterflies and insects, were native to the country excited him. There was one section devoted to that part of Borneo of which Kuala Solor was the capital, and since these were the creatures that for the next three years would chiefly concern him, he examined them with attention. But it was outside, in the streets, that it was most thrilling, and except that he was a grave and sober young man he would have laughed aloud with joy. Everything was new to him. He walked till he was footsore. He stood at the corner of a busy street and wondered at the long line of rickshaws and the little men between the shafts running with dogged steps. He stood on a bridge over a canal and looked at the sampans wedged up against one another like sardines in a tin. He peered into the Chinese shops in Victoria Road where so many strange things were sold.

Bombay merchants, fat and exuberant, stood at their shop doors and sought to sell him silks and tinsel jewellery. He watched the Tamils, pensive and forlorn, who walked with a sinister grace, and the bearded Arabs, in white skull-caps, who bore themselves with scornful dignity. The sun shone upon the varied scene with a hard, acrid brilliance. He was confused. He thought it would take him years to find his bearings in this multi-coloured and excessive world.

After dinner that night Captain Bredon asked him if he would like to go round the town.

"You ought to see a bit of life while you're here," he said.

They stepped into rickshaws and drove to the Chinese quarter. The Captain, who never drank at sea, had been making up for his abstinence during the day. He was feeling good. The rickshaws stopped at a house in a side street and they knocked at the door. It was opened and they passed through a narrow passage into a large room with benches all round it covered with red plush. A number of women were sitting about—French, Italian and American. A mechanical piano was grinding out harsh music and a few couples were dancing. Captain Bredon ordered drinks. Two or three women, waiting for an invitation, gave them inciting glances.

"Well, young feller, is there anyone you fancy here?" the Captain asked facetiously.

"To sleep with, d'you mean? No."

"No white girls where you're going, you know."

"Oh, well."

"Like to go an' see some natives?"

"I don't mind."

The Captain paid for the drinks and they strolled on. They went to another house. Here the girls were Chinese, small and dainty, with tiny feet and hands like flowers, and they wore suits of flowered silk. But their painted faces were like masks. They looked at the strangers with black derisive eyes. They were strangely inhuman.

"I brought you here because I thought you ought to see the place," said Captain Bredon, with the air of a man doing his bounden duty, "but just look see is all. They don't like us for some reason. In some of these Chinese joints they won't even let a white man in. Fact is, they say we stink. Funny, ain't it? They say we smell of corpses."

"We?"

"Give me Japs," said the Captain. "They're fine. My wife's a Jap, you know. You come along with me and I'll take you to a place where they have Japanese girls, and if you don't see something you like there I'm a Dutchman."

Their rickshaws were waiting and they stepped into them. Captain Bredon gave a direction and the boys started off. They were let into the house by a stout middle-aged Japanese woman, who bowed low as they entered. She took them into a neat, clean room furnished only with mats on the floor; they sat down and

presently a little girl came in with a tray on which were
two bowls of pale tea. With a shy bow she handed one
to each of them. The Captain spoke to the middle-aged
woman and she looked at Neil and giggled. She said
something to the child, who went out, and presently
four girls tripped in. They were sweet in their kimonos,
with their shining black hair artfully dressed; they were
small and plump, with round faces and laughing eyes.
They bowed low as they came in and with good manners
murmured polite greetings. Their speech sounded like
the twittering of birds. Then they knelt, one on each
side of the two men, and charmingly flirted with them.
Captain Bredon soon had his arms round two slim
waists. They all talked nineteen to the dozen. They
were very gay. It seemed to Neil that the Captain's girls
were mocking him, for their gleaming eyes were mis-
chievously turned towards him, and he blushed. But
the other two cuddled up to him, smiling, and spoke in
Japanese as though he understood every word they said.
They seemed so happy and guileless that he laughed.
They were very attentive. They handed him the
bowl so that he should drink his tea, and then took
it from him so that he should not have the trouble
of holding it. They lit his cigarette for him and
one put out a small, delicate hand to take the ash
so that it should not fall on his clothes. They
stroked his smooth face and looked with curiosity
at his large young hands. They were as playful as
kittens.

"Well, which is it to be?" said the Captain after a while. "Made your choice yet?"

"What d'you mean?"

"I'll just wait and see you settled and then I'll fix myself up."

"Oh, I don't want either of them. I'm going home to bed."

"Why, what's the matter? You're not scared, are you?"

"No, I just don't fancy it. But don't let me stand in your way. I'll get back to the hotel all right."

"Oh, if you're not going to do anything I won't either. I only wanted to be matey."

He spoke to the middle-aged woman and what he said caused the girls to look at Neil with sudden surprise. She answered and the Captain shrugged his shoulders. Then one of the girls made a remark that set them all laughing.

"What does she say?" asked Neil.

"She's pulling your leg," replied the Captain, smiling.

But he gave Neil a curious look. The girl, having made them laugh once, now said something directly to Neil. He could not understand, but the mockery of her eyes made him blush and frown. He did not like to be made fun of. Then she laughed outright and throwing her arm round his neck lightly kissed him.

"Come on, let's be going," said the Captain.

When they dismissed their rickshaws and walked into the hotel Neil asked him:

"What was it that girl said that made them all laugh?"

"She said you were a virgin."

"I don't see anything to laugh at in that," said Neil, with his slow Scots accent.

"Is it true?"

"I suppose it is."

"How old are you?"

"Twenty-two."

"What are you waiting for?"

"Till I marry."

The Captain was silent. At the top of the stairs he held out his hand. There was a twinkle in his eyes when he bade the lad good-night, but Neil met it with a level, candid and untroubled gaze.

Three days later they sailed. Neil was the only white passenger. When the Captain was busy he read. He was reading again Wallace's "Malay Archipelago." He had read it as a boy, but now it had a new and absorbing interest for him. When the Captain was at leisure they played cribbage or sat in long chairs on the deck, smoking, and talked. Neil was the son of a country doctor, and he could not remember when he had not been interested in natural history. When he had done with school he went to the University of Edinburgh and there took a B.Sc. with Honours. He was looking out for a job as demonstrator in biology when he chanced to see in "Nature" an advertisement for an assistant curator of the museum at Kuala Solor. The

Curator, Angus Munro, had been at Edinburgh with his uncle, a Glasgow merchant, and his uncle wrote to ask him if he would give the boy a trial. Though Neil was especially interested in entomology he was a trained taxidermist, which the advertisement said was essential; he enclosed certificates from Neil's old teachers; he added that Neil had played football for his university. In a few weeks a cable arrived engaging him and a fortnight later he sailed.

"What's Mr. Munro like?" asked Neil.

"Good fellow. Everybody likes him."

"I looked out his papers in the scientific journals. He had one in the last number of 'The Ibis' on the Gymnathidæ."

"I don't know anything about that. I know he's got a Russian wife. They don't like her much."

"I got a letter from him at Singapore saying they'd put me up for a bit till I could look round and see what I wanted to do."

Now they were steaming up the river. At the mouth was a straggling fishermen's village standing on piles in the water; on the bank grew thickly nipah palm and the tortured mangrove; beyond stretched the dense green of the virgin forest. In the distance, darkly silhouetted against the blue sky, was the rugged outline of a mountain. Neil, his heart beating with the excitement that possessed him, devoured the scene with eager eyes. He was surprised. He knew his Conrad almost by heart and he was expecting a land of brooding

mystery. He was not prepared for the blue milky sky.
Little white clouds on the horizon, like sailing boats
becalmed, shone in the sun. The green trees of the
forest glittered in the brilliant light. Here and there, on
the banks, were Malay houses with thatched roofs, and
they nestled cosily among fruit trees. Natives in dug-
outs rowed, standing, up the river. Neil had no feeling
of being shut in, nor in that radiant morning, of gloom,
but of space and freedom. The country offered him a
gracious welcome. He knew he was going to be happy
in it. Captain Bredon from the bridge threw a friendly
glance at the lad standing below him. He had taken
quite a fancy to him during the four days the journey
had lasted. It was true he did not drink, and when you
made a joke he was as likely as not to take you seriously,
but there was something very taking in his seriousness;
everything was interesting and important to him—that,
of course, was why he did not find your jokes amusing;
but even though he didn't see them he laughed, because
he felt you expected it. He laughed because life was
grand. He was grateful for every little thing you told
him. He was very polite. He never asked you to pass
him anything without saying "please" and always said
"thank you" when you gave it. And he was a good-
looking fellow, no one could deny that. Neil was
standing with his hands on the rail, bare-headed, looking
at the passing bank. He was tall, six foot two, with
long, loose limbs, broad shoulders and narrow hips;
there was something charmingly coltish about him, so

that you expected him at any moment to break into a caper. He had brown curly hair with a peculiar shine in it; sometimes when the light caught it, it glittered like gold. His eyes, large and very blue, shone with good humour. They reflected his happy disposition. His nose was short and blunt and his mouth big, his chin determined; his face was rather broad. But his most striking feature was his skin; it was very white and smooth, with a lovely patch of red on either cheek. It would have been a beautiful skin even for a woman. Captain Bredon made the same joke to him every morning.

"Well, my lad, have you shaved to-day?"

Neil passed his hand over his chin.

"No, d'you think I need it?"

The Captain always laughed at this.

"Need it? Why, you've got a face like a baby's bottom."

And invariably Neil reddened to the roots of his hair.

"I shave once a week," he retorted.

But it wasn't only his looks that made you like him. It was his ingenuousness, his candour and the freshness with which he confronted the world. For all his intentness and the solemn way in which he took everything, and his inclination to argue upon every point that came up, there was something strangely simple in him that gave you quite an odd feeling. The Captain couldn't make it out.

"I wonder if it's because he's never had a woman," he said to himself. "Funny. I should have thought the girls never left him alone. With a complexion like that."

But the "Sultan Ahmed" was nearing the bend after rounding which Kuala Solor would be in sight and the Captain's reflections were interrupted by the necessities of his work. He rang down to the engine room. The ship slackened to half speed. Kuala Solor straggled along the left bank of the river, a white neat and trim little town, and on the right on a hill were the fort and the Sultan's Palace. There was a breeze and the Sultan's flag, at the top of a tall staff, waved bravely against the sky. They anchored in midstream. The doctor and a police officer came on board in the government launch. They were accompanied by a tall thin man in white ducks. The Captain stood at the head of the gangway and shook hands with them. Then he turned to the last comer.

"Well, I've brought you your young hopeful safe and sound." And with a glance at Neil: "This is Munro."

The tall thin man held out his hand and gave Neil an appraising look. Neil flushed a little and smiled. He had beautiful teeth.

"How do you do, sir?"

Munro did not smile with his lips, but faintly with his grey eyes. His cheeks were hollow and he had a thin aquiline nose and pale lips. He was deeply sunburned.

Q

His face looked tired, but his expression was very gentle, and Neil immediately felt confidence in him. The Captain introduced him to the doctor and the policeman and suggested that they should have a drink. When they sat down and the boy brought bottles of beer Munro took off his topi. Neil saw that he had close-cropped brown hair turning grey. He was a man of forty, quiet, self-possessed in manner, with an intellectual air that distinguished him from the brisk little doctor and the heavy swaggering police officer.

"MacAdam doesn't drink," said the Captain when the boy poured out four glasses of beer.

"All the better," said Munro. "I hope you haven't been trying to lure him into evil ways."

"I tried to in Singapore," returned the Captain, with a twinkle in his eyes, "but there was nothing doing."

When he had finished his beer Munro turned to Neil.

"Well, we'll be getting ashore, shall we?"

Neil's baggage was put in charge of Munro's boy and the two men got into a sampan. They landed.

"Do you want to go straight up to the bungalow or would you like to have a look round first? We've got a couple of hours before tiffin."

"Couldn't we go to the museum?" said Neil.

Munro's eyes smiled gently. He was pleased. Neil was shy and Munro not by nature talkative, so they walked in silence. By the river were the native huts and here, living their immemorial lives, dwelt the

Malays. They were busy, but without haste, and you were conscious of a happy, normal activity. There was a sense of the rhythm of life of which the pattern was birth and death, love and the affairs common to mankind. They came to the bazaars, narrow streets with arcades, where the teeming Chinese, working and eating, noisily talking, as is their way, indefatigably strove with eternity.

"It's not much after Singapore," said Munro, "but I always think it's rather picturesque."

He spoke with an accent less broad than Neil's, but the Scots burr was there and it put Neil at his ease. He could never quite get it out of his head that the English of English people was affected.

The museum was a handsome stone building and as they entered its portals Munro instinctively straightened himself. The attendant at the door saluted and Munro spoke to him in Malay, evidently explaining who Neil was, for the attendant gave him a smile and saluted again. It was cool in there in comparison with the heat without and the light was pleasant after the glare of the street.

"I'm afraid you'll be disappointed," said Munro. "We haven't got half the things we ought to have, but up to now we've been handicapped by lack of money. We've had to do the best we could. So you must make allowances."

Neil stepped in like a swimmer diving confidently into a summer sea. The specimens were admirably arranged. Munro had sought to please as well as to instruct, and birds and beasts and reptiles were presented, as far as possible in their natural surroundings, in such a way as to give a vivid impression of life. Neil lost his shyness and began with boyish enthusiasm to talk of this and that. He asked an infinity of questions. He was excited. Neither of them was conscious of the passage of time, and when Munro glanced at his watch he was surprised to see what the hour was. They got into rickshaws and drove to the bungalow.

Munro led the young man into a drawing-room. A woman was lying on a sofa reading a book and as they came in she slowly rose.

"This is my wife. I'm afraid we're dreadfully late, Darya."

"What does it matter?" she smiled. "What is more unimportant than time?"

She held out her hand, a rather large hand, to Neil and gave him a long, reflective, but friendly look.

"I suppose you've been showing him the museum."

She was a woman of five-and-thirty, of medium height, with a pale brown face of a uniform colour and pale blue eyes. Her hair, parted in the middle and wound into a knot on the nape of her neck, was untidy; it had a moth-like quality and was of a curious pale brown. Her face was broad, with high cheek-bones, and she had a rather fleshy nose. She was not a pretty woman, but there was in her slow movements a sensual grace and in her manner as it were a physical casualness that only very dull people could have failed to find interesting. She wore a frock of green cotton. She spoke English perfectly, but with a slight accent.

They sat down to tiffin. Neil was overcome once more with shyness, but Darya did not seem to notice it. She talked freely and easily. She asked him about his journey and what he had thought of Singapore. She told him about the people he would have to meet. That afternoon Munro was to take him to call on the Resident, the Sultan being away, and later they would go to the club. There he would see everybody.

"You will be popular," she said, her pale blue eyes resting on him with attention. A man less ingenuous than Neil might have noticed that she took stock of his size and youthful virility, his shiny, curling hair and his lovely skin. "They don't think much of us."

"Oh, nonsense, Darya. You're too sensitive. They're English, that's all."

"They think it's rather funny of Angus to be a scientist and they think it's rather vulgar of me to be a Russian. I don't care. They're fools. They're the most commonplace, the most narrow-minded, the most conventional people it has ever been my misfortune to live amongst."

"Don't put MacAdam off the moment he arrives. He'll find them kind and hospitable."

"What is your first name?" she asked the boy.

"Neil."

"I shall call you by it. And you must call me Darya. I hate being called Mrs. Munro. It makes me feel like a minister's wife."

Neil blushed. He was embarrassed that she should ask him so soon to be so familiar. She went on.

"Some of the men are not bad."

"They do their jobs competently and that's what they're here for," said Munro.

"They shoot. They play football and tennis and cricket. I get on with them quite well. The women are intolerable. They are jealous and spiteful and lazy. They can talk of nothing. If you introduce an intellectual subject they look down their noses as though you were indecent. What can they talk about? They're interested in nothing. If you speak of the body they think you improper, and if you speak of the soul they think you priggish."

"You mustn't take what my wife says too literally," smiled Munro, in his gentle, tolerant way. "The community here is just like any other in the East, neither very clever, nor very stupid, but amiable and kindly. And that's a good deal."

"I don't want people to be amiable and kindly. I want them to be vital and passionate. I want them to be interested in mankind. I want them to attach more importance to the things of the spirit than to a gin pahit or a curry tiffin. I want art to matter to them and literature." She addressed herself abruptly to Neil: "Have you got a soul?"

"Oh, I don't know. I don't know exactly what you mean."

"Why do you blush when I ask you? Why should you be ashamed of your soul? It is what is important in you. Tell me about it. I am interested in you and I want to know."

It seemed very awkward to Neil to be tackled in this way by a perfect stranger. He had never met anyone like this. But he was a serious young man and when he was asked a question straight out he did his best to answer it. It was Munro's presence that embarrassed him.

"I don't know what you mean by the soul. If you mean an immaterial or spiritual entity, separately produced by the creator, in temporary conjunction with the material body, then my answer is in the negative. It seems to me that such a radically dualistic view of human personality cannot be defended by anyone who is able to take a calm view of the evidence. If, on the other hand, you mean by soul the aggregate of psychic elements which form what we know as the personality of the individual, then, of course, I have."

"You're very sweet and you're wonderfully handsome," she said, smiling. "No, I mean the heart with its longings and the body with its desires and the infinite in us. Tell me, what did you read on the journey, or did you only play deck tennis?"

Neil was taken aback at the inconsequence of her reply. He would have been a little affronted except for the good humour in her eyes and the naturalness in her manner. Munro smiled quietly at the young man's bewilderment. When he smiled the lines that ran from the wings of his nostrils to the corners of his mouth became deep furrows.

"I read a lot of Conrad."

"For pleasure or to improve your mind?"

"Both. I admire him awfully."

Darya threw up her arms in an extravagant gesture of protest.

"That Pole," she cried. "How can you English ever have let yourselves be taken in by that wordy mountebank? He has all the superficiality of his countrymen. That stream of words, those involved sentences, the showy rhetoric, that affectation of profundity: when you get through all that to the thought at the bottom, what do you find but a trivial commonplace? He was like a second-rate actor who puts on a romantic dress and declaims a play by Victor Hugo. For five minutes you say this is heroic, and then your whole soul revolts and you cry, no, this is false, false, false."

She spoke with a passion that Neil had never known anyone show when speaking of art or literature. Her cheeks, usually colourless, flushed and her pale eyes glowed.

"There's no one who got atmosphere like Conrad," said Neil. "I can smell and see and feel the East when I read him."

"Nonsense. What do you know about the East?

Everyone will tell you that he made the grossest blunders. Ask Angus."

"Of course he was not always accurate," said Munro, in his measured, reflective way. "The Borneo he described is not the Borneo we know. He saw it from the deck of a merchant vessel and he was not an acute observer even of what he saw. But does it matter? I don't know why fiction should be hampered by fact. I don't think it's a mean achievement to have created a country, a dark, sinister, romantic and heroic country of the soul."

"You're a sentimentalist, my poor Angus." And then again to Neil: "You must read Turgeniev, you must read Tolstoi, you must read Dostoevsky."

Neil did not in the least know what to make of Darya Munro. She skipped over the first stages of acquaintance and treated him at once like someone she had known intimately all her life. It puzzled him. It seemed so reckless. When he met anyone his own instinct was to go cautiously. He was amiable, but he did not like to step too far before he saw his way before him. He did not want to give anyone his confidence before he thought himself justified. But with Darya you could not help yourself; she forced your confidence. She poured out the feelings and thoughts that most people keep to themselves like a prodigal flinging gold pieces to a scrambling crowd. She did not talk, she did not act like anyone he had ever known. She did not mind what she said. She would speak of the natural functions

Q*

of the human animal in a way that brought the blushes coursing to his cheeks. They excited her ridicule.

"Oh, what a prig you are! What is there indecent in it? When I'm going to take a purge, why shouldn't I say so and when I think you want one, why shouldn't I tell you?"

"Theoretically I daresay you're right," said Neil, always judicious and reasonable.

She made him tell her of his father and mother, his brothers, his life at school and at the university. She told him about herself. Her father was a general killed in the war and her mother a Princess Lutchkov. They were in Eastern Russia when the Bolsheviks seized power, and fled to Yokohama. Here they had subsisted miserably on the sale of their jewels and such objects of art as they had been able to save, and here she married a fellow exile. She was unhappy with him and in two years divorced him. Her mother died and, penniless, she was driven to earn her living as best she could. She was employed by an American relief organisation. She taught in a mission school. She worked in a hospital. She made Neil's blood boil, and at the same time embarrassed him very much, when she spoke of the men who tried to take advantage of her defencelessness and her poverty. She spared him no details.

"Brutes," he said.

"Oh, all men are like that," she replied, with a shrug of her shoulders.

She told him how once she protected her virtue at the point of her revolver.

"I swore I'd kill him if he took another step, and if he had I'd have shot him like a dog."

"Gosh!" said Neil.

It was at Yokohama that she met Angus. He was spending his leave in Japan. She was captivated by his straightforwardness, the decency which was so obvious in him, his tenderness and his consideration. He was not a business man; he was a scientist, and science is milk-brother to art. He offered her peace. He offered her security. And she was tired of Japan. Borneo was a land of mystery. They had been married for five years.

She gave Neil the Russian novelists to read. She gave him "Fathers and Sons," "Anna Karenina" and "The Brothers Karamazoff."

"Those are the three peaks of our literature. Read them. They are the greatest novels the world has ever seen."

Like many of her countrymen she talked as though no other literature counted, and as though a few novels and stories, some indifferent poetry and half a dozen good plays had made whatever else the world has produced negligible. Neil was fascinated and overwhelmed.

"You're rather like Alyosha yourself, Neil," she said, looking at him with eyes that were now so soft and tender, "an Alyosha with a Scotch dourness, suspicious and prudent, that will not let the soul in you, the spiritual beauty, come out."

"I'm not a bit like Alyosha," he answered self-consciously.

"You don't know what you're like. You don't know anything about yourself. Why are you a naturalist? Is it for money? You could have made much more money by going into your uncle's office in Glasgow. I feel in you something strange and unearthly. I could bow down at your feet as Father Zossima did to Dimitri."

"Please don't," he said, smiling, but flushing a little too.

But the novels he read made her seem a little less strange to him. They gave her an environment and he recognised in her traits which, however unusual in the women he knew in Scotland, his mother and the daughters of his uncle in Glasgow, were common to many of the characters in Russian fiction. He no longer wondered that she should like to sit up so late, drinking innumerable cups of tea, and lie on the sofa nearly all day long reading and incessantly smoking cigarettes. She could do nothing at all for days on end without being bored. She had a curious mixture of languor and zest. She often said, with a shrug of her shoulders, that she was an Oriental and a European only by chance. She had a feline grace that indeed suggested the Oriental. She was immensely untidy and it did not seem to affect her that cigarette ends, old papers and empty

tins should lie about their living-room. But he thought
she had something of Anna Karenina in her, and he
transferred to her the sympathy he felt for that pathetic
creature. He understood her arrogance. It was not
unnatural that she despised the women of the community, whose acquaintance little by little he made; they
were commonplace; her mind was quicker than theirs,
she had a wider culture, and she had above all a sort of
tremulous sensitiveness that made *them* extraordinarily
colourless. She certainly took no pains to conciliate
them. Though at home she slopped about in a sarong
and baju, when she and Angus went out to dinner she
dressed with a splendour that was somewhat out of
place. She liked to display her ample bosom and her
shapely back. She painted her cheeks and made up her
eyes like an actress for the footlights. Though it made
Neil angry to see the amused or outraged glances that her
appearance provoked, he could not in his heart but think
it a pity that she should make such an object of herself.
She looked grand, of course, but if you hadn't known
who she was you would have thought she wasn't
respectable. There were things about her that he could
never get over. She had an enormous appetite and it
fashed him that she ate more than he and Angus
together. He could never quite get used to the bluntness
with which she discussed sexual matters. She took it
for granted that at home and in Edinburgh he had had
affairs with a host of women. She pressed him for
details of his adventures. His Scotch pawkiness

helped him to parry her thrusts and he evaded her questions with native caution. She laughed at his reticence.

Sometimes she shocked him. He grew accustomed to the frankness with which she admired his looks, and when she told him that he was as beautiful as a young Norse god he did not turn a hair. Flattery fell off him like water from a duck's back. But he did not like it when she ran her hand, though large, very soft, with caressing fingers, through his curly hair or, a smile on her lips, stroked his smooth face. He couldn't bear being mussed about. One day she wanted a drink of tonic water and began pouring some out in a glass that stood on the table.

"That's my glass," he said quickly. "I've just been drinking out of it."

"Well, what of it? You haven't got syphilis, have you?"

"I hate drinking out of other people's glasses myself."

She was funny about cigarettes too. Once, when he hadn't been there very long, he had just lit one, when she passed and said:

"I want that."

She took it out of his mouth and began to smoke it. After two or three puffs, she said she did not want any more and handed it back to him. The end she had had in her mouth was red from the rouge on her lips, and he didn't want to go on smoking it at all. But he was afraid she would think it rude if he threw it away. It somewhat disgusted him. Often she would ask him for a cigarette and when he handed it to her, say:

"Oh, light it for me, will you?"

When he did so, and held it out to her, she opened her mouth so that he should put it in. He hadn't been able to help wetting the end a little. He wondered she could bear to put it in her mouth after it had been in his. The whole thing seemed to him awfully familiar. He was sure Munro wouldn't like it. She had even done this once or twice at the club. Neil had felt himself go purple. He wished she hadn't got these rather unpleasant habits, but he supposed they were Russian, and one couldn't deny that she was wonderfully good company. Her conversation was very stimulating. It was like champagne (which Neil had tasted once and thought wretched stuff), "metaphorically speaking." There was nothing she couldn't talk about. She didn't talk like a man; with a man you generally knew what he would say next, but with her you never did; her intuition was quite remarkable. She gave you ideas. She enlarged your mind and excited your imagination. Neil felt alive as he had never felt alive before. He seemed to walk on mountain peaks and the horizons of the spirit were unbounded. Neil felt a certain complacency when he stopped to reflect on what an exalted plane his mind communed with hers. Such conversations made very small beer of the vaunted pleasure of sense. She was in many ways (he was of a cautious nature and seldom made a statement even to himself that he did not qualify) the most intelligent woman he had ever met. And besides, she was Angus Munro's wife.

For, whatever Neil's reservations were about Darya, ne had none about Munro, and she would have had to be a much less remarkable woman not to profit by the enormous admiration he conceived for her husband. With him Neil let himself go. He felt for him what he had never felt for anyone before. He was so sane, so balanced, so tolerant. This was the sort of man he would himself like to be when he was older. He talked little, but when he did, with good sense. He was wise. He had a dry humour that Neil understood. It made the hearty English fun of the men at the club seem inane. He was kind and patient. He had a dignity that made it impossible to conceive of anyone taking a liberty with him, but he was neither pompous nor solemn. He was honest and absolutely truthful. But Neil admired him no less as a scientist than as a man. He had imagination. He was careful and painstaking. Though his interest was in research he did the routine work of the museum conscientiously. He was just then much interested in stick-insects and intended to write a paper on their powers of parthenogenetic reproduction. An incident occurred in connection with the experiments he was making that made a great impression on Neil. One day, a little captive gibbon escaped from its chain and ate up all the larvæ and so destroyed the whole of Munro's evidence. Neil nearly cried. Angus

Munro took the gibbon in his arms and, smiling, stroked it.

"Diamond, Diamond," he said, quoting Sir Isaac Newton, "you little know the damage you have done."

He was also studying mimicry and instilled into Neil his absorbed interest in this controversial subject. They had interminable talks about it. Neil was astonished at the Curator's wonderful knowledge. It was encyclopædic, and he was abashed at his own ignorance. But it was when Munro spoke of the trips into the country to collect specimens that his enthusiasm was most contagious. That was the perfect life, a life of hardship, difficulty, often of privation and sometimes of danger, but rewarded by the thrill of finding a rare, or even a new species, by the beauty of the scenery and the intimate observation of nature, and above all by the sense of freedom from every tie. It was for this part of the work that Neil had been chiefly engaged. Munro was occupied in research work that made it difficult for him to be away from home for several weeks at a time, and Darya had always refused to accompany him. She had an unreasoning fear of the jungle. She was terrified of wild beasts, snakes and venomous insects. Though Munro had told her over and over again that no animal hurt you unless you molested or frightened it, she could not get over her instinctive horror. He did not like leaving her. She cared little for the local society and with him away he realised that life for her must be intolerably dull. But the Sultan was keenly interested in natural history and was anxious that the museum should be completely representative of the country's fauna. One expedition Munro and Neil were to make together, so that Neil should learn how to go to work, and the plans for this were discussed by them for months. Neil looked forward to it as he had never looked forward to anything in his life.

Meanwhile he learned Malay and acquired a smattering of the dialects that would be useful to him on future journeys. He played tennis and football. He soon knew everyone in the community. On the football field he threw off his absorption in science and his interest in Russian fiction and gave himself up to the pleasure of the game. He was strong, quick and active. After it was all over it was grand to have a sluice down and a long tonic with a slice of lemon and go over it all with the other fellows. It had never been intended that Neil should live permanently with the Munros. There was a roomy Rest House at Kuala Solor, but the rule was that no one should stay in it for more than a fortnight and such of the bachelors as had no official quarters clubbed together and took a house between them. When Neil arrived it so happened that there was no vacancy in any of these messes. One evening, however, when he had been about four months in the colony, two men, Waring and Jonson, when they were sitting together after a game of tennis, told him that one member of their mess was going home and if he would like to join them they would be glad to have him. They were young fellows of his own age, in the football team, and Neil liked them both. Waring was in the customs and Jonson in the police. He jumped at the suggestion. They told him how much it would cost and fixed a day, a fortnight later, when it would be convenient for him to move in.

At dinner he told the Munros.

"It's been awfully good of you to let me stay so long. It's made me very uncomfortable planting myself on you like this, I've been quite ashamed, but now there's no excuse for me."

"But we like having you here," said Darya. "You don't need an excuse."

"I can hardly go on staying here indefinitely?"

"Why not? Your salary's miserable, what's the use of wasting it on board and lodging? You'd be bored stiff with Jonson and Waring. Stupids. They haven't an idea in their heads outside playing the gramophone and knocking balls about."

It was true that it had been very convenient to live free of cost. He had saved the greater part of his salary. He had a thrifty soul and had never been used to spending money when it wasn't necessary, but he was proud. He could not go on living at other people's expense. Darya looked at him with her quiet, observant eyes.

"Angus and I have got used to you now. I think we'd miss you. If you like, you can pay us for your board. You don't cost anything, but if it'll make you easier I'll find out exactly what difference you make in cookie's book and you can pay that."

"It must be an awful nuisance having a stranger in the house," he answered uncertainly.

"It'll be miserable for you there. Good heavens, the filth they eat."

It was true also that at the Munros' you ate better than anywhere else at Kuala Solor. He had dined out now and then, and even at the Resident's you didn't get a very good dinner. Darya liked her food and kept the cook up to the mark. He made Russian dishes which were a fair treat. That cabbage soup of Darya's was worth walking five miles for. But Munro hadn't said anything.

"I'd be glad if you'd stay here," he said now. "It's very convenient to have you on the spot. If anything comes up we can talk it over there and then. Waring and Jonson are very good fellows, but I daresay you'd find them rather limited after a bit."

"Oh, well, then I'll be very pleased. Heaven knows, I couldn't want anything better than this. I was only afraid I was in the way."

Next day it was raining cats and dogs and it was impossible to play tennis or football, but towards six Neil put on a mackintosh and went to the club. It was empty but for the Resident, who was sitting in an armchair reading "The Fortnightly." His name was Trevelyan, and he claimed to be related to the friend of Byron. He was a tall fat man, with close-cropped white hair and the large red face of a comic actor. He was fond of amateur theatricals and specialised in cynical dukes and facetious butlers. He was a bachelor, but generally supposed to be fond of the girls, and he liked his gin pahit before dinner. He owed his position to the Sultan's friendship. He was a slack, complacent man, a great talker, not very fond of work, who wanted everything to go smoothly and no one to give trouble. Though not considered especially competent he was popular in the community because he was easy-going and hospitable, and he certainly made life more comfortable than if he had been energetic and efficient. He nodded to Neil.

"Well, young fellow, how are bugs to-day?"

"Feeling the weather, sir," said Neil gravely.

"Hi-hi."

In a few minutes Waring, Jonson and another man, called Bishop, came in. He was in the Civil Service. Neil did not play bridge, so Bishop went up to the Resident.

"Would you care to make a fourth, sir?" he asked him. "There's nobody much in the club to-day."

The Resident gave the others a glance.

"All right. I'll just finish this article and join you. Cut for me and deal. I shall only be five minutes."

Neil went up to the three men.

"Oh, I say, Waring, thanks awfully, but I can't move over to you after all. The Munros have asked me to stay on with them for good."

A broad smile broke on Waring's face.

"Fancy that."

"It's awfully nice of them, isn't it? They made rather a point of it. I couldn't very well refuse."

"What did I tell you?" said Bishop.

"I don't blame the boy," said Waring.

There was something in their manner that Neil did not like. They seemed to be amused. He flushed.

"What the hell are you talking about?" he cried.

"Oh, come off it," said Bishop. "We know our Darya. You're not the first good-looking young fellow she's had a romp with, and you won't be the last."

The words were hardly out of his mouth before Neil's clenched fist shot out like a flash. He hit Bishop on the face and he fell heavily to the floor. Jonson sprang at Neil and seized him round the middle, for he was beside himself.

"Let me go," he shouted. "If he doesn't withdraw that I'll kill him."

The Resident, startled by the commotion, looked up and rose to his feet. He walked heavily towards them.

"What's this? What's this? What the hell are you boys playing at?"

They were taken aback. They had forgotten him. He was their master. Jonson let go of Neil and Bishop picked himself up. The Resident, a frown on his face, spoke to Neil sharply.

"What's the meaning of this? Did you hit Bishop?"

"Yes, sir."

"Why?"

"He made a foul suggestion reflecting on a woman's honour," said Neil, very haughtily, and still white with rage.

The Resident's eyes twinkled, but he kept a grave face.

"What woman?"

"I refuse to answer," said Neil, throwing back his head and drawing himself up to his full imposing height.

It would have been more effective if the Resident hadn't been a good two inches taller, and very much stouter.

"Don't be a damned young fool."

"Darya Munro," said Jonson.

"What did you say, Bishop?"

"I forget the exact words I used. I said she'd hopped into bed with a good many young chaps here, and I supposed she hadn't missed the chance of doing the same with MacAdam."

"It was a most offensive suggestion. Will you be so good as to apologise and shake hands. Both of you."

"I've had a hell of a biff, sir. My eye's going to look like the devil. I'm damned if I apologise for telling the truth."

"You're old enough to know that the fact that your statement is true only makes it more offensive, and as far as your eye is concerned I'm told that a raw beefsteak is very efficacious in these circumstances. Though I put my desire that you should apologise in the form of a request out of politeness, it is in point of fact an order."

There was a moment's silence. The Resident looked bland.

"I apologise for what I said, sir," Bishop said sulkily.

"Now then, MacAdam."

"I'm sorry I hit him, sir. I apologise, too."

"Shake hands."

The two young men solemnly did so.

"I shouldn't like this to go any further. It wouldn't be very nice for Munro, whom I think we all like. Can I count on you all holding your tongues?"

They nodded.

"Now be off with you. You stay, MacAdam, I want to have a few words with you."

When the two of them were left alone, the Resident sat down and lit himself a cheroot. He offered one to Neil, but he only smoked cigarettes.

"You're a very violent young man," said the Resident, with a smile. "I don't like my officers to make scenes in a public place like this."

"Mrs. Munro is a great friend of mine. She's been kindness itself to me. I won't hear a word said against her."

"Then I'm afraid you'll have your job cut out for you if you stay here much longer."

Neil was silent for a moment. He stood, tall and slim, before the Resident, and his grave young face was guileless. He flung back his head defiantly. His emotion made him speak in broader Scots even than usual.

"I've lived with the Munros for four months, and I give you my word of honour that so far as I am concerned there is not an iota of truth in what that beast said. Mrs. Munro has never treated me with anything that you could call undue familiarity. She's never by word or deed given me the smallest hint that she had an improper idea in her head. She's been like a mother to me or an elder sister."

The Resident watched him with ironical eyes.

"I'm very glad to hear it. That's the best thing I've heard about her for a long time."

"You believe me, sir, don't you?"

"Of course. Perhaps you've reformed her." He called out. "Boy. Bring me a gin pahit." And then to Neil. "That'll do. You can go now if you want to. But no more fighting, mind you, or you'll get the order of the boot."

When Neil walked back to the Munros' bungalow the rain had stopped and the velvet sky was bright with stars. In the garden the fire-flies were flitting here and there. From the earth rose a scented warmth and you felt that if you stopped you would hear the growth of that luxuriant vegetation. A white flower of the night gave forth an overwhelming perfume. In the verandah Munro was typing some notes and Darya, lying at full length on a long chair, was reading. The lamp behind her lit her smoky hair so that it shone like an aureole. She looked up at Neil and putting down her book, smiled. Her smile was very friendly.

"Where have you been, Neil?"

"At the club."

"Anybody there?"

The scene was so cosy and domestic, Darya's manner so peaceful and quietly assured, that it was impossible not to be touched. The two of them there, each occupied with his own concerns, seemed so united, their intimacy so natural, that no one could have conceived that they were not perfectly happy in one another. Neil did not believe a single word of what Bishop had said and the Resident had hinted. It was incredible. After all, he knew that what they had suspected of *him* was untrue, so what reason was there to think that the rest was any truer? They had dirty minds, all those people; because they were a lot of swine they thought everyone else as bad as they were. His knuckle hurt him a little. He was glad he had hit Bishop. He wished he knew who had started that filthy story. He'd wring his neck.

But now Munro fixed a date for the expedition that they had so much discussed, and in his careful way began to make preparations so that at the last moment nothing should be forgotten. The plan was to go as far up the river as possible and then make their way through the jungle and hunt for specimens on the little-known Mount Hitam. They expected to be away two months. As the day on which they were to start grew nearer Munro's spirits rose, and though he did not say very much, though he remained quiet and self-controlled, you could tell by the light in his eyes and the jauntiness of his step how much he looked forward to it. One morning, at the museum, he was almost sprightly.

"I've got some good news for you," he said suddenly to Neil, after they had been looking at some experiments they were making, "Darya's coming with us."

"Is she? That's grand."

Neil was delighted. That made it perfect.

"It's the first time I've ever been able to induce her to accompany me. I told her she'd enjoy it, but she would never listen to me. Queer cattle, women. I'd given it up and never thought of asking her to come this time, and suddenly, last night, out of a blue sky she said she'd like to."

"I'm awfully glad," said Neil.

"I didn't much like the idea of leaving her by herself so long; now we can stay just as long as we want to."

They started early one morning in four prahus, manned by Malays, and besides themselves the party consisted of their servants and four Dyak hunters. The three of them lay on cushions side by side, under an awning; in the other boats were the Chinese servants and the Dyaks. They carried bags of rice for the whole party, provisions for themselves, clothes, books and all that was necessary for their work. It was heavenly to leave civilisation behind them and they were all excited.

They talked. They smoked. They read. The motion of the river was exquisitely soothing. They lunched on a grassy bank. Dusk fell and they moored for the night. They slept at a long house and their Dyak hosts celebrated their visit with arak, eloquence and a fantastic dance. Next day the river, narrowing, gave them more definitely the feeling that they were adventuring into the unknown, and the exotic vegetation that crowded the banks to the water's edge, like an excited mob pushed from behind by a multitude, caused Neil a breathless ravishment. O wonder and delight! On the third day, because the water was shallower and the stream more rapid, they changed into lighter boats, and soon it grew so strong that the boatmen could paddle no longer, and they poled against the current with powerful and magnificent gestures. Now and then they came to rapids and had to disembark, unload and haul the boats through a rock-strewn passage. After five days they reached a point beyond which they could go no further. There was a government bungalow there, and they settled in for a couple of nights while Munro made arrangements for their excursion into the interior. He wanted bearers for their baggage, and men to build a house for them when they reached Mount Hitam. It was necessary for Munro to see the headman of a village in the vicinity and thinking it would save time if he went himself rather than let the headman come to him, the day after they arrived he set out at dawn with a guide and a couple of Dyaks. He expected to be back in a few hours. When he had seen him off Neil thought he would have a bathe. There was a pool a little way from the bungalow, and the water was so clear that you saw every grain of the sandy bottom. The river was so narrow there that the trees over-arched it. It was a lovely spot. It reminded Neil of the pools in Scotch streams he had bathed in as a boy, and yet it was strangely different. It had an air of romance, a feeling of virgin nature, that filled him with sensations that he found hard to analyse. He tried, of course, but older heads than his have found it difficult to anatomize happiness. A kingfisher was sitting on an overhanging branch and its vivid blue was reflected as bluely in the crystal stream. It flew away with a flashing glitter of jewelled wings when Neil, stripping off his sarong and baju, scrambled down into the water. It was fresh without being cold. He splashed and tumbled about. He enjoyed the movement of his strong limbs. He floated and looked at the blue sky peeping through the leaves and the sun that here and there gilded the water. Suddenly he heard a voice.

"How white your body is, Neil."

With a gasp he let himself sink and turning round saw Darya standing on the bank.

"I say, I haven't got any clothes on."

"So I saw. It's much nicer bathing without. Wait a minute, I'll come in, it looks lovely."

She also was wearing a sarong and a baju. He turned away his head quickly, for he saw that she was taking them off. He heard her splash into the water. He gave two or three strokes in order that she should have room to swim about at a good distance from him, but she swam up to him.

"Isn't the feel of the water on one's body lovely?" she said.

She laughed and opening her hand splashed water in his face. He was so embarrassed he did not know which way to look. In that limpid water it was impossible not to see that she was stark naked. It was not so bad now, but he could not help thinking how difficult it would be to get out. She seemed to be having a grand time.

"I don't care if I do get my hair wet," she said.

She turned over on her back and with strong strokes swam round the pool. When she wanted to get out, he thought, the best thing would be if he turned his back, and when she was dressed she could go and he would get out later. She seemed quite unconscious of the awkwardness of the situation. He was vexed with her. It really was rather tactless to behave like that. She kept on talking to him just as if they were on dry land and properly dressed. She even called his attention to herself.

"Does my hair look awful? It's so fine it gets like rat tails when it's wet. Hold me under the shoulders a moment while I try to screw it up."

"Oh, it's all right," he said. "You'd better leave it now."

"I'm getting frightfully hungry," she said presently.

"What about breakfast?"

"If you'll get out first and put on your things, I'll follow you in a minute."

"All right."

She swam the two strokes needed to bring her to the side, and he modestly looked away so that he should not see her get out nude from the water.

"I can't get up," she cried. "You'll have to help me."

It had been easy enough to get in, but the bank overhung the water and one had to lift oneself up by the branch of a tree.

"I can't. I haven't got a stitch of clothing on."

"I know that. Don't be so Scotch. Get up on the bank and give me a hand."

There was no help for it. Neil swung himself up and pulled her after him. She had left her sarong beside his. She took it up unconcernedly and began to dry herself with it. There was nothing for him but to do the same, but for decency's sake he turned his back on her.

"You really have a most lovely skin," she said. "It's as smooth and white as a woman's. It's funny on such a manly virile figure. And you haven't got a hair on your chest."

Neil wrapped the sarong round him and slipped his arms into the baju.

"Are you ready?"

She had porridge for breakfast, and eggs and bacon, cold meat and marmalade. Neil was a trifle sulky.

She was really almost too Russian. It was stupid of her to behave like that; of course there was no harm in it, but it was just that sort of thing that made people think the things they did about her. The worst of it was that you couldn't give her a hint. She'd only laugh at you. But the fact was that if any of those men at Kuala Solor had seen them bathing like that together, stark naked, nothing would have persuaded them that something improper hadn't happened. In his judicious way Neil admitted to himself that you could hardly blame them. It was too bad of her. She had no right to put a fellow in such a position. He had felt such a fool. And say what you liked it was indecent.

Next morning, having seen their carriers on the way, a long procession in single file, each man carrying his load in a creel on his back, with their servants, guides and hunters, they started to walk. The path ran over the foothills of the mountain, through scrub and tall grass, and now and then they came to narrow streams which they crossed by rickety bridges of bamboo. The sun beat on them fiercely. In the afternoon they reached the shade of a bamboo forest, grateful after the glare, and the bamboos in their slender elegance rose to incredible heights, and the green light was like the light under the sea. At last they reached the primeval forest, huge trees swathed in luxuriant creepers, an inextricable tangle, and awe descended upon them. They cut their way through the undergrowth. They walked in twilight and only now and then caught through the dense foliage above them a glimpse of sunshine. They saw neither man nor beast, for the denizens of the jungle are shy and at the first sound of footsteps vanish from sight. They heard birds up high in the tall trees, but saw none save the twittering sunbirds that flew in the underwoods and delicately coquetted with the wild flowers. They halted for the night. The carriers made a floor of branches and on this spread water-proof sheets. The Chinese cook made them their dinner and then they turned in.

It was the first night Neil had ever spent in the jungle and he could not sleep. The darkness was profound. The noise was deafening of innumerable insects, but like the roar of traffic in a great city it was so constant that in a little while it was like an impenetrable silence, and when on a sudden he heard the shriek of a monkey seized by a snake or the scream of a night-bird he nearly jumped out of his skin. He had a mysterious sensation that all around creatures were watching them. Over there, beyond the camp fires, savage warfare was waged and they three on their bed of branches were defenceless and alone in face of the horror of nature. By his side Munro was breathing quietly in his deep sleep.

"Are you awake, Neil?" Darya whispered.

"Yes. Is anything the matter?"

"I'm terrified."

"It's all right. There's nothing to be afraid of."

"The silence is so awful. I wish I hadn't come."

She lit a cigarette.

Neil, having at last dozed off, was awakened by the hammering of a woodpecker, and its complacent laugh as it flew from one tree to another seemed to mock the sluggards. A hurried breakfast and the caravan started. The gibbons swung from branch to branch, gathering in the dawn dew from the leaves, and their strange cry was like the call of a bird. The light had driven away Darya's fears, and notwithstanding a sleepless night she was alert and gay. They continued to climb. In the afternoon they reached the spot that the guides had told them would be a good camping place, and here Munro decided to build a house. The men set to work. With their long knives they cut palm leaves and saplings and soon had erected a two-roomed hut raised on piles from the ground. It was neat and fresh and green. It smelt good.

The Munros, he from old habit, she because she had for years wandered about the world and had a catlike knack of making herself comfortable wherever she went, were at home anywhere. In a day they had arranged everything and settled down. Their routine was invariable. Every morning early Neil and Munro started out separately, collecting. The afternoon was devoted to pinning insects in boxes, placing butterflies between sheets of paper and skinning birds. When dusk came they caught moths. Darya busied herself with the hut and the servants, sewed and read and smoked innumerable cigarettes. The days passed very pleasantly.

monotonous but eventful. Neil was enraptured. He explored the mountain in all directions. One day, to his pride, he found a new species of stick-insect. Munro named it Cuniculina MacAdami. This was fame. Neil (at twenty-two) realised that he had not lived in vain. But another day he only just escaped being bitten by a viper. Owing to its green colour he had not seen it and was only saved from lurching against it by the Dyak hunter who was with him. They killed it and brought it back to camp. Darya shuddered at the sight of it. She had a terror of the wild creatures of the jungle that was almost hysterical. She would never go more than a few yards from the camp for fear of being lost.

"Has Angus ever told you how he was lost?" she asked Neil one evening when they were sitting quietly together after dinner.

"It wasn't a very pleasant experience," he smiled.

"Tell him, Angus."

He hesitated a little. It was not a thing he liked to recall.

"It was some years ago, I'd gone out with my butterfly net and I'd been very lucky, I'd got several rare specimens that I'd been looking for a long time. After a while I thought I was getting hungry so I turned back. I walked for some time and it struck me I'd come a good deal farther than I knew. Suddenly I caught sight of an empty match-box. I swore. I knew at once what had happened. I'd thrown it away when I started to come back, I'd been walking in a circle and was exactly where I was an hour before. I was not pleased. But I had a look round and set off again. It was fearfully hot and I was simply dripping with sweat. I knew more or less the direction the camp was in and I looked about for traces of my passage to see if I had come that way. I thought I found one or two and went on hopefully. I was frightfully thirsty. I walked on and on, picking my way over snags and trailing plants, and suddenly I knew I was lost. I couldn't have gone so far in the right direction without hitting the camp. I can tell you I was startled. I knew I must keep my head, so I sat down and thought the situation over. I was tortured by thirst. It was long past midday and in three or four hours it would be dark. I didn't like the idea of spending a night in the jungle at all. The only thing I could think of was to try and find a stream; if I followed its course, it would eventually bring me to a larger stream and sooner or later to the river. But of course it might take a couple of days. I cursed myself for being such a fool, but there was nothing better to do and I began walking. At all events if I found a stream I should be able to get a drink. I couldn't find a trickle of water anywhere, not the smallest brook that might lead to something like a stream. I began to be alarmed. I saw myself wandering on till at last I fell exhausted. I knew there was a lot of game in the forest and if I came upon a rhino I was done for. The maddening thing was I knew I couldn't be more than ten miles from my camp. I forced myself to keep my head. The day was waning and in the depths of the jungle it was growing dark already. If I'd brought a gun I could have fired it. In the camp they must have realised I was lost and would be looking for me. The undergrowth was so thick that I couldn't see six feet into it and presently, I don't know if it was nerves or not, I had the sensation that some animal was walking stealthily beside me. I stopped and it stopped too. I went on and it went on. I couldn't see it. I could see no movement in the undergrowth. I didn't even hear the breaking of a twig or the brushing of a body through leaves, but I knew how silently those beasts could move, and I was positive something was stalking me. My heart beat so violently against my ribs that I thought it would break. I was scared out of my wits. It was only by the exercise of all the self-control I had that I prevented myself from breaking into a run. I knew if I did that I was lost. I should be tripped up before I had gone twenty yards by a tangled root and when I was down it would spring on me. And if I started to run God knew where I should get to. And I had to husband my strength. I felt very like crying. And that intolerable thirst. I've never been so frightened in my life. Believe me, if I'd had a revolver I think I'd have blown my brains out. It was so awful I just wanted to finish with it. I was so exhausted I could hardly stagger. If I had an enemy who'd done me a deadly injury I wouldn't wish him the agony I endured then. Suddenly I heard two shots. My heart stood still. They were looking for me. Then I did lose my head. I ran in the direction of the sound, screaming at the top of my voice, I fell, I picked myself up again, I ran on, I shouted till I thought my lungs would burst, there was another shot, nearer, I shouted again, I heard answering shouts; there was a scramble of men in the undergrowth. In a minute I was surrounded by Dyak hunters. They wrung and kissed my hands. They laughed and cried. I very nearly cried too. I was down and out, but they gave me a drink. We were only three miles from the camp. It was pitch dark when we got back. By God, it was a near thing."

A convulsive shudder passed through Darya.

"Believe me, I don't want to be lost in the jungle again."

"What would have happened if you hadn't been found?"

"I can tell you. I should have gone mad. If I hadn't been stung by a snake or attacked by a rhino I should have gone on blindly till I fell exhausted. I should have starved to death. I should have died of thirst. Wild beasts would have eaten my body and ants cleaned my bones."

Silence fell upon them.

Then it happened, when they had spent nearly a month on Mount Hitam, that Neil, notwithstanding the quinine Munro had made him take regularly, was stricken with fever. It was not a bad attack, but he felt very sorry for himself and was obliged to stay in bed. Darya nursed him. He was ashamed to give her so much trouble, but she would not listen to his protests. She was certainly very capable. He resigned himself to letting her do things for him that one of the Chinese boys could have done just as well. He was touched. She waited on him hand and foot. But when the fever was at its height and she sponged him all over with cold water, though the comfort was indescribable, he was excessively embarrassed. She insisted on washing him night and morning.

"I wasn't in the British hospital at Yokohama for six months without learning at least the routine of nursing," she said, smiling.

She kissed him on the lips each time after she had finished. It was friendly and sweet of her. He rather liked it, but attached no importance to it; he even went so far, a rare thing for him, as to be facetious on the subject.

"Did you always kiss your patients at the hospital?" he asked her.

"Don't you like me to kiss you?" she smiled.

"It doesn't do me any harm."

"It may even hasten your recovery," she mocked.

One night he dreamt of her. He awoke with a start. He was sweating profusely. The relief was wonderful, and he knew that his temperature had fallen; he was well. He did not care. For what he had dreamt filled him with shame. He was horrified. That he should have such thoughts, even in his sleep, made him feel awful. He must be a monster of depravity. Day was breaking, and he heard Munro getting up in the room next door that he occupied with Darya. She slept late, and he took care not to disturb her. When he passed through Neil's room, Neil in a low voice called him.

"Hullo, are you awake?"

"Yes, I've had the crisis. I'm all right now."

"Good. You'd better stay in bed to-day. To-morrow you'll be as fit as a fiddle."

"Send Ah Tan to me when you've had your breakfast, will you?"

"Right-ho."

He heard Munro start out. The Chinese boy came and asked him what he wanted. An hour later Darya awoke. She came in to bid him good morning. He could hardly look at her.

"I'll just have my breakfast and then I'll come in and wash you," she said.

"I'm washed. I got Ah Tan to do it."

"Why?"

"I wanted to spare you the trouble."

"It isn't a trouble. I like doing it."

She came over to the bed and bent down to kiss him, but he turned away his head.

"Oh, don't," he said.

"Why not?"

"It's silly."

She looked at him for a moment, surprised, and then with a slight shrug of the shoulders left him. A little later she came back to see if there was anything he wanted. He pretended to be asleep. She very gently stroked his cheek.

"For God's sake don't do that," he cried.

"I thought you were sleeping. What's the matter with you to-day?"

"Nothing."

"Why are you being horrid to me? Have I done anything to offend you?"

"No."

"Tell me what it is."

She sat down on the bed and took his hand. He turned his face to the wall. He was so ashamed he could hardly speak.

"You seem to forget I'm a man. You treat me as if I was a boy of twelve."

"Oh?"

He was blushing furiously. He was angry with himself and vexed with her. She really should be more tactful. He plucked nervously at the sheet.

"I know it means nothing to you and it ought not to mean anything to me. It doesn't when I'm well and up and about. One can't help one's dreams, but they are an indication of what is going on in the subconscious."

"Have you been dreaming about me? Well, I don't think there's any harm in that."

He turned his head and looked at her. Her eyes were gleaming, but his were sombre with remorse.

"You don't know men," he said.

She gave a little burble of laughter. She bent down

ℓ*

and threw her arms round his neck. She had nothing on but her sarong and baju.

"You darling," she cried. "Tell me, what did you dream?"

He was startled out of his wits. He pushed her violently aside.

"What are you doing? You're crazy."

He jumped half out of bed.

"Don't you know that I'm madly in love with you?" she said.

"What *are* you talking about?"

He sat down on the side of the bed. He was frankly bewildered. She chuckled.

"Why do you suppose I came up to this horrible place? To be with you, ducky. Don't you know I'm scared stiff of the jungle? Even in here I'm frightened there'll be snakes or scorpions or something. I adore you."

"You have no right to speak to me like that," he said sternly.

"Oh, don't be so prim," she smiled.

"Let's get out of here."

He walked out on to the verandah and she followed him. He threw himself into a chair. She knelt by his side and tried to take his hands, but he withdrew them.

"I think you must be mad. I hope to God you don't mean what you say."

"I do. Every word of it," she smiled.

It exasperated him that she seemed unconscious of the frightfulness of her confession.

"Have you forgotten your husband?"

"Oh, what does he matter?"

"Darya."

"I can't be bothered about Angus now."

"I'm afraid you're a very wicked woman," he said slowly, a frown darkening his smooth brow.

She giggled.

"Because I've fallen in love with you? Darling, you shouldn't be so absurdly good-looking."

"For God's sake don't laugh."

"I can't help it; you're comic—but still adorable. I love your white skin and your shining curly hair. I love you because you're so prim and Scotch and humourless. I love your strength. I love your youth."

Her eyes glowed and her breath came quickly. She stooped and kissed his naked feet. He drew them away quickly, with a cry of protest, and in the agitation of his gesture nearly overthrew the rickety chair.

"Woman, you're insane. Have you no shame?"

"No."

"What do you want of me?" he asked fiercely.

"Love."

"What sort of a man do you take me for?"

"A man like any other," she replied calmly.

"Do you think after all that Angus Munro has done for me I could be such a damned beast as to play about with his wife? I admire him more than any man I've ever known. He's grand. He's worth a dozen of me and you put together. I'd sooner kill myself than betray him. I don't know how you can think me capable of such a dastardly act."

"Oh, my dear, don't talk such bilge. What harm is it going to do him? You mustn't take that sort of thing so tragically. After all life is very short; we're fools if we don't take what pleasure we can out of it."

"You can't make wrong right by talking about it."

"I don't know about that. I think that's a very controvertible statement."

He looked at her with amazement. She was sitting at his feet, cool to all appearance and collected, and she seemed to be enjoying the situation. She seemed quite unconscious of its seriousness.

"Do you know that I knocked a fellow down at the club because he made an insulting remark about you?"

"Who?"

"Bishop."

"Dirty dog. What did he say?"

"He said you'd had affairs with men."

"I don't know why people won't mind their own business. Anyhow, who cares what they say? I love you. I've never loved anyone like you. I'm absolutely sick with love for you."

"Be quiet. Be quiet."

"Listen, to-night when Angus is asleep, I'll slip into your room. He sleeps like a rock. There's no risk."

"You mustn't do that."

"Why not?"

"No, no, no."

He was frightened out of his wits. Suddenly she sprang to her feet and went into the house.

Munro came back at noon, and in the afternoon they busied themselves as usual. Darya, as she sometimes did, worked with them. She was in high spirits. She was so gay that Munro suggested that she was beginning to enjoy the life.

"It's not so bad," she admitted. "I'm feeling happy to-day."

She teased Neil. She seemed not to notice that he was silent and kept his eyes averted from her.

"Neil's very quiet," said Munro. "I suppose you're feeling a bit weak still."

"No, I just don't feel very talkative."

He was harassed. He was convinced that Darya was capable of anything. He remembered the hysterical frenzy of Nastasya Filipovna in "The Idiot," and felt that she too could behave with that unfortunate lack of balance. He had seen her more than once fly into a temper with one of the Chinese servants and he knew how completely she could lose her self-control. Resistance only exasperated her. If she did not immediately get what she wanted she would go almost insane with rage. Fortunately she lost interest in a thing with the same suddenness with which she hankered for it, and if you could distract her attention for a minute she forgot all about it. It was in such situations that Neil had most admired Munro's tact. He had often been slyly amused to see with what a pawky and yet tender cunning he appeased her feminine tantrums. It was on Munro's account that Neil's indignation was so great. Munro was a saint, and from what a state of humiliation and penury and random shifts had he not taken her to make her his wife! She owed everything to him. His name protected her. She had respectability. The commonest gratitude should have made it impossible for her to harbour such thoughts as she had that morning expressed. It was all very well for men to make advances, that was what men did, but for women to do so was disgusting. His modesty was outraged. The passion he had seen in her face, and the indelicacy of her gestures, scandalised him.

He wondered whether she would really carry out her threat to come to his room. He didn't think she would dare. But when night came and they all went to bed, he was so terrified that he could not sleep. He lay there listening anxiously. The silence was broken only by the repeated and monotonous cry of an owl. Through the thin wall of woven palm leaves he heard Munro's steady breathing. Suddenly he was conscious that someone was stealthily creeping into his room. He had already made up his mind what to do.

"Is that you, Mr. Munro?" he called in a loud voice.

Darya stopped suddenly. Munro awoke.

"There's someone in my room. I thought it was you."

"It's all right," said Darya. "It's only me. I couldn't sleep, so I thought I'd go and smoke a cigarette on the verandah."

"Oh, is that all?" said Munro. "Don't catch cold."

She walked through Neil's room and out. He saw her light a cigarette. Presently she went back and he heard her get into bed.

He did not see her next morning, for he started out collecting before she was up, and he took care not to get in till he was pretty sure Munro also would be back. He avoided being alone with her till it was dark and Munro went down for a few minutes to arrange the moth-traps.

"Why did you wake Angus last night?" she said in a low angry whisper.

He shrugged his shoulders and going on with his work did not answer.

"Were you frightened?"

"I have a certain sense of decency."

"Oh, don't be such a prig."

"I'd rather be a prig than a dirty swine."

"I hate you."

"Then leave me alone."

She did not answer, but with her open hand smartly slapped his face. He flushed, but did not speak. Munro returned and they pretended to be intent on whatever they were doing.

For the next few days Darya, except at meal-times and in the evenings, never spoke to Neil. Without prearrangement they exerted themselves to conceal from Munro that their relations were strained. But the effort with which Darya roused herself from a brooding silence would have been obvious to anyone more suspicious than Angus, and sometimes she could not help herself from being a trifle sharp with Neil. She chaffed him, but in her chaff was a sting. She knew how to wound and caught him on the raw, but he took care not to let her see it. He had an inkling that the good humour he affected infuriated her.

Then, one day when Neil came back from collecting, though he had delayed till the last possible minute before tiffin, he was surprised to find that Munro had not yet returned. Darya was lying on a mattress on the verandah, sipping a gin pahit and smoking. She did not speak to him when he passed through to wash. In a minute the Chinese boy came into his room and told him that tiffin was ready. He walked out.

"Where's Mr. Munro?" he asked.

"He's not coming," said Darya. "He sent a message to say that the place he's at is so good he won't come down till night."

Munro had set out that morning for the summit of the mountain. The lower levels had yielded poor results in the way of mammals, and Munro's idea was, if he could find a good place higher up, with a supply of water, to transfer the camp. Neil and Darya ate their meal in silence. After they had finished he went into the house and came out again with his topi and his collecting gear. It was unusual for him to go out in the afternoon.

"Where are you going?" she asked abruptly.

"Out."

"Why?"

"I don't feel tired. I've got nothing much else to do this afternoon."

Suddenly she burst into tears.

"How can you be so unkind to me?" she sobbed. "Oh, it is cruel to treat me like this."

He looked down at her from his great height, his handsome, somewhat stolid face bearing a harassed look.

"What have *I* done?"

"You've been beastly to me. Bad as I am I haven't deserved to suffer like this. I've done everything in the world for you. Tell me one single little thing I could do that I haven't done gladly. I'm so terribly unhappy."

He moved on his feet uneasily. It was horrible to hear her say that. He loathed and feared her, but he had still the respect for her that he had always felt, not only because she was a woman, but because she was Angus Munro's wife. She wept uncontrollably. Fortunately the Dyak hunters had gone that morning with Munro. There was no one about the camp but the three Chinese servants and they, after tiffin, were asleep in their own quarters fifty yards away. They were alone.

"I don't want to make you unhappy. It's all so silly. It's absurd of a woman like you to fall in love with a fellow like me. It makes me look such a fool.

Haven't you got any self-control?"

"Oh, God. Self-control!"

"I mean, if you really cared for me you couldn't want me to be such a cad. Doesn't it mean anything to you that your husband trusts us implicitly? The mere fact of his leaving us alone like this puts us on our honour. He's a man who would never hurt a fly. I should never respect myself again if I betrayed his confidence."

She looked up suddenly.

"What makes you think he would never hurt a fly? Why, all those bottles and cases are full of the harmless animals he's killed."

"In the interests of science. That's quite another thing."

"Oh, you fool, you fool."

"Well, if I am a fool I can't help it. Why do you bother about me?"

"Do you think I wanted to fall in love with you?"

"You ought to be ashamed of yourself."

"Ashamed? How stupid! My God, what have I done that I should eat my heart out for such a pretentious ass?"

"You talk about what you've done for me. What has Munro done for you?"

"Munro bores me to death. I'm sick of him. Sick to death of him."

"Then I'm not the first?"

Ever since her amazing avowal he had been tortured by the suspicion that what those men at Kuala Solor had said of her was true. He had refused to believe a word of it, and even now he could not bring himself to think that she could be such a monster of depravity. It was frightful to think that Angus Munro, so trusting and tender, should have lived in a fool's paradise. She could not be as bad as that. But she misunderstood him. She smiled through her tears.

"Of course not. How can you be so silly? Oh, darling, don't be so desperately serious. I love you."

Then it was true. He had sought to persuade himself that what she felt for him was exceptional, a madness that together they could contend with and vanquish. But she was simply promiscuous.

"Aren't you afraid Munro will find out?"

She was not crying any more. She adored talking about herself, and she had a feeling that she was inveigling Neil into a new interest in her.

"I sometimes wonder if he doesn't know, if not with his mind, then with his heart. He's got the intuition of a woman and a woman's sensitiveness. Sometimes I've been certain he suspected and in his anguish I've sensed a strange, spiritual exaltation. I've wondered if in his pain he didn't find an infinitely subtle pleasure. There are souls, you know, that feel a voluptuous joy in laceration."

"How horrible!" Neil had no patience with these conceits. "The only excuse for you is that you're insane."

She was now much more sure of herself. She gave him a bold look.

"Don't you think I'm attractive? A good many men have. You must have had dozens of women in Scotland who weren't so well made as I am."

She looked down at her shapely, sensual figure with calm pride.

"I've never had a woman," he said gravely.

"Why not?"

She was so surprised that she sprang to her feet. He shrugged his shoulders. He could not bring himself to tell her how disgusting the idea of such a thing was to him, and how vile he had thought the haphazard amours of his fellow-students at Edinburgh. He took a mystical joy in his purity. Love was sacred. The sexual act horrified him. Its excuse was the procreation of children and its sanctification marriage. But Darya, her whole body rigid, stared at him, panting; and suddenly, with a sobbing cry in which there was exultation and at the same time wild desire, she flung herself on her knees and seizing his hand passionately kissed it.

"Alyosha," she gasped. "Alyosha."

And then, crying and laughing, she crumpled up in a heap at his feet. Strange, hardly human sounds issued from her throat and convulsive tremors passed through her body so that you would have thought she was receiving one electric shock after another. Neil did not know if it was an attack of hysteria or an epileptic fit.

"Stop it," he cried. "Stop it."

He took her up in his strong arms and laid her in the chair. But when he tried to leave her she would not let him. She flung her arms round his neck and held him. She covered his face with kisses. He struggled. He turned his face away. He put his hand between her face and his to protect himself. Suddenly she dug her teeth into it. The pain was so great that, without thinking, he gave her a great swinging blow.

"You devil," he cried.

His violent gesture had forced her to release him. He held his hand and looked at it. She had caught him by the fleshy part on the side and it was bleeding. Her eyes blazed. She was feeling alert and active.

"I've had enough of this. I'm going out," he said.

She sprang to her feet.

"I'll come with you."

He put on his topi and, snatching up his collecting gear, without a word turned on his heel. With one stride he leaped down the three steps that led from the floor of the house to the ground. She followed him.

"I'm going into the jungle," he said.

"I don't care."

In the ravening desire that possessed her she forgot her morbid fear of the jungle. She recked nothing of snakes and wild beasts. She did not mind the branches that hit her face or the creepers that entangled her feet. For a month Neil had explored all that part of the forest and he knew every yard of it. He told himself grimly that he'd teach her to come with him. He forced his way through the undergrowth with rapid strides; she followed him, stumbling but determined; he crashed on.

blind with rage, and she crashed after him. She talked; he did not listen to what she said. She besought him to have pity on her. She bemoaned her fate. She made herself humble. She wept and wrung her hands. She tried to cajole him. The words poured from her lips in an unceasing stream. She was like a mad woman. At last in a little clearing he stopped suddenly and turning round faced her.

"This is impossible," he cried. "I'm fed up. When Angus comes back I must tell him I've got to go. I shall go back to Kuala Solor to-morrow morning and go home."

"He won't let you go, he wants you. He finds you invaluable."

"I don't care. I'll fake up something."

"What?"

He mistook her.

"Oh, you needn't be frightened, I shan't tell him the truth. You can break his heart if you want to; I'm not going to."

"You worship him, don't you? That dull, phlegmatic man."

"He's worth a hundred of you."

"It would be rather funny if I told him you'd gone because I wouldn't yield to your advances."

He gave a slight start and looked at her to see if she was serious.

"Don't be such a fool. You don't think he'd believe that, do you? He knows it would never occur to me."

"Don't be too sure."

She had spoken carelessly, with no particular intention other than to continue the argument, but she saw that he was frightened and some instinct of cruelty made her press the advantage.

"Do you expect mercy from me? You've humiliated me beyond endurance. You've treated me like dirt. I swear that if you make any suggestion of going I shall go straight to Angus and say that you took advantage of his absence to try and assault me."

"I can deny it. After all it's only your word against mine."

"Yes, but my word'll count. I can prove what I say."

"What do you mean?"

"I bruise easily. I can show him the bruise where you struck me. And look at your hand." He turned and gave it a sudden glance. "How did those teeth marks get there?"

He stared at her stupidly. He had gone quite pale. How could he explain that bruise and that scar? If he was forced to in self-defence he could tell the truth, but was it likely that Angus would believe it? He worshipped Darya. He would take her word against anyone's. What monstrous ingratitude it would seem for all Munro's kindness and what treachery in return for so much confidence! He would think him a filthy skunk and from his standpoint with justice. That was what shattered him, the thought that Munro, for whom he would willingly have laid down his life, should think

ill of him. He was so unhappy that tears, unmanly tears
that he hated, came to his eyes. Darya saw that he was
broken. She exulted. She was paying him back for the
misery he had made her suffer. She held him now. He
was in her power. She savoured her triumph and in the
midst of her anguish laughed in her heart because he
was such a fool. At that moment she did not know
whether she loved or despised him.

"Now will you be good?" she said.

He gave a sob and blindly, with a sudden instinct of
escape from that abominable woman, took to his heels
and ran as hard as he could. He plunged through the
jungle, like a wounded animal, not looking where he
was going, till he was out of breath. Then, panting, he
stopped. He took out his handkerchief and wiped away
the sweat that was pouring into his eyes and blinding
him. He was exhausted and he sat down to rest.

"I must take care I don't get lost," he said to himself.

That was the least of his troubles, but all the same he
was glad that he had a pocket compass, and he knew
in which direction he must go. He heaved a deep
sigh and rose wearily to his feet. He started walking.
He watched his way and with another part of his
mind miserably asked himself what he should do. He
was convinced that Darya would do what she had
threatened. They were to be another three weeks in that
accursed place. He dared not go; he dared not stay. His
mind was in a whirl. The only thing was to get back to
camp and think it out quietly. In about a quarter of an

hour he came to a spot that he recognised. In an hour
he was back. He flung himself miserably into a chair.
And it was Angus who filled his thoughts. His heart
bled for him. Neil saw now all sorts of things that
before had been dark to him. They were revealed to
him in a flash of bitter insight. He knew why the
women at Kuala Solor were so hostile to Darya and why
they looked at Angus so strangely. They treated him
with a sort of affectionate levity. Neil thought it was
because Angus was a man of science and so in their
foolish eyes somewhat absurd. He knew now it was
because they were sorry for him and at the same time
found him ridiculous. Darya had made him the laughing-stock of the community. If ever there was a man
who hadn't deserved ill usage at a woman's hands it was
he. Suddenly Neil gasped and began to tremble all
over. It had suddenly occurred to him that Darya did
not know her way through the jungle; in his anguish he
had hardly been conscious of where they went. Supposing she could not find her way home? She would be
terrified. He remembered the ghastly story Angus had
told them of being lost in the forest. His first instinct
was to go back and find her, and he sprang to his feet.
Then a fierce anger seized him. No, let her shift for
herself. She had gone of her own free will. Let her find
her own way back. She was an abominable woman and
deserved all that might come to her. Neil threw back his
head defiantly, a frown of indignation on his smooth
young brow, and clenched his hands. Courage. He

made up his mind. It would be better for Angus if she
never returned. He sat down and began trying to make
a skin of a Mountain Trogon. But the Trogon has a
skin like wet tissue-paper and his hands trembled. He
tried to apply his mind to the work he was doing, but
his thoughts fluttered desperately, like moths in a trap,
and he could not control them. What was happening
over there in the jungle? What had she done when he
suddenly bolted? Every now and then, against his will,
he looked up. At any moment she might appear in the
clearing and walk calmly up to the house. He was not to
blame. It was the hand of God. He shuddered. Storm
clouds were gathering in the sky and night fell quickly.

Just after dusk Munro arrived.

"Just in time," he said. "There's going to be a hell of
a storm."

He was in great spirits. He had come upon a fine
plateau, with lots of water, from which there was a
magnificent view to the sea. He had found two or three
rare butterflies and a flying squirrel. He was full of plans
to move the camp to this new place. All about it he had
seen abundant evidence of animal life. Presently he
went into the house to take off his heavy walking boots.
He came out at once.

"Where's Darya?"

Neil stiffened himself to behave with naturalness.

"Isn't she in her room?"

"No. Perhaps she's gone down to the servants'
quarters for something."

He walked down the steps and strolled a few yards.

"Darya," he called. "Darya." There was no answer "Boy."

A Chinese servant came running up and Angus asked him where his mistress was. He did not know. He had not seen her since tiffin.

"Where can she be?" asked Munro, coming back, puzzled.

He went to the back of the house and shouted.

"She can't have gone out. There's nowhere to go. When did you see her last, Neil?"

"I went out collecting after tiffin. I'd had a rather unsatisfactory morning and I thought I'd try my luck again."

"Strange."

They hunted everywhere round the camp. Munro thought she might have made herself comfortable somewhere and gone to sleep.

"It's too bad of her to frighten one like this."

The whole party joined in the search. Munro began to grow alarmed.

"It's not possible that she should have gone for a stroll in the jungle and lost her way. She's never moved more than a hundred yards from the house to the best of my knowledge since we've been here."

Neil saw the fear in Munro's eyes and looked down.

"We'd better get everyone along and start hunting. There's one thing, she can't be far. She knows that if you get lost the best thing is to stay where you are and

wait for people to come and find you. She'll be scared
out of her wits, poor thing."

He called out the Dyak hunters and told the Chinese
servants to bring lanterns. He fired his gun as a signal.
They separated into two parties, one under Munro, the
other under Neil, and went down the two rough paths
that in the course of the month they had made in their
comings and goings. It was arranged that whoever
found Darya should fire three shots in quick succession.
Neil walked with his face stern and set. His conscience
was clear. He seemed to bear in his hands the decree of
imminent justice. He knew that Darya would never be
found. The two parties met. It was not necessary to
look at Munro's face. He was distracted. Neil felt like a
surgeon who is forced to perform a dangerous operation
without assistance or appliances to save the life of
someone he loves. It behoved him to be firm.

"She could never have got so far as this," said Munro.
"We must go back and beat the jungle within the radius
of a mile from the house inch by inch. The only
explanation is that she was frightened by something or
fainted or was stung by a snake."

Neil did not answer. They started out again and,
making lines, combed the undergrowth. They shouted.
Every now and then they fired a gun and listened for a
faint call in answer. Birds of the night flew with a
whirring of wings, frightened, as they advanced with
their lanterns; and now and then they half saw, half
guessed at an animal, deer, boar or rhino, that fled at

their approach. The storm broke suddenly. A great wind blew and then the lightning rent the darkness, like the scream of a woman in pain, and the tortured flashes, quick, quick, one on the heels of the other, like demon dancers in a frantic reel, wriggled down the night. The horror of the forest was revealed in an unearthly day. The thunder crashed down the sky in huge rollers, peal upon peal, like vast, primeval waves dashing against the shores of eternity. That fearful din hurtled through space as though sound had size and weight. The rain pelted in fierce torrents. Rocks and gigantic trees came tumbling down the mountain. The tumult was awful. The Dyak hunters cowered, gibbering in terror of the angry spirits who spoke in the storm, but Munro urged them on. The rain fell all night, with lightning and thunder, and did not cease till dawn. Wet through and shivering they returned to the camp. They were exhausted. When they had eaten Munro meant to resume the desperate search. But he knew that it was hopeless. They would never see her alive again. He flung himself down wearily. His face was tired and white and anguished.

"Poor child. Poor child."

THE VESSEL OF WRATH

THERE are few books in the world that contain
more meat than the "Sailing Directions" published
by the Hydrographic Department by order of the Lords
Commissioners of the Admiralty. They are handsome
volumes, bound (very flimsily) in cloth of different
colours, and the most expensive of them is cheap. For
four shillings you can buy the "Yangste Kiang Pilot,"
'containing a description of, and sailing directions for,
the Yangste Kiang from the Wusung river to the
highest navigable point, including the Han Kiang, the
Kialing Kiang, and the Min Kiang'; and for three shillings you can get Part III of the "Eastern Archipelago
Pilot," 'comprising the N.E. end of Celebes, Molucca
and Gilolo passages, Banda and Arafura Seas, and
North, West, and South-West coasts of New Guinea.'
But it is not very safe to do so if you are a creature of
settled habits that you have no wish to disturb or if
you have an occupation that holds you fast to one
place. These business-like books take you upon
enchanted journeys of the spirit; and their matter-of-
fact style, the admirable order, the concision with
which the material is set before you, the stern sense of
the practical that informs every line, cannot dim the
poetry that, like the spice-laden breeze that assails your

senses with a more than material languor when you approach some of those magic islands of the Eastern seas, blows with so sweet a fragrance through the printed pages. They tell you the anchorages and the landing places, what supplies you can get at each spot, and where you can get water; they tell you the lights and buoys, tides, winds and weather that you will find there. They give you brief information about the population and the trade. And it is strange when you think how sedately it is all set down, with no words wasted, that so much else is given you besides. What? Well, mystery and beauty, romance and the glamour of the unknown. It is no common book that offers you casually turning its pages such a paragraph as this: 'Supplies. A few jungle fowl are preserved, the island is also the resort of vast numbers of sea birds. Turtle are found in the lagoon, as well as quantities of various fish, including grey mullet, shark, and dog-fish; the seine cannot be used with any effect; but there is a fish which may be taken on a rod. A small store of tinned provisions and spirits is kept in a hut for the relief of shipwrecked persons. Good water may be obtained from a well near the landing-place.' Can the imagination want more material than this to go on a journey through time and space?

In the volume from which I have copied this passage, the compilers with the same restraint have described the Alas Islands. They are composed of a group or chain of islands, 'for the most part low and wooded, extending about 75 miles east and west, and 40 miles north and south.' The information about them, you are told, is very slight; there are channels between the different groups, and several vessels have passed through them, but the passages have not been thoroughly explored, and the positions of many of the dangers not yet determined; it is therefore advisable to avoid them. The population of the group is estimated at about 8,000, of whom 200 are Chinese and 400 Mohammedans. The rest are heathen. The principal island is called Baru, it is surrounded by a reef, and here lives a Dutch Contrôleur. His white house with its red roof on the top of a little hill is the most prominent object that the vessels of the Royal Netherlands Steam Packet Company see when every other month on their way up to Macassar and every four weeks on their way down to Merauke in Dutch New Guinea they touch at the island.

At a certain moment of the world's history the Contrôleur was Mynheer Evert Gruyter and he ruled the people who inhabited the Alas Islands with firmness tempered by a keen sense of the ridiculous. He had thought it a very good joke to be placed at the age of twenty-seven in a position of such consequence and at thirty he was still amused by it. There was no cable communication between his islands and Batavia, and the mail arrived after so long a delay that even if he asked advice, by the time he received it, it was useless, and so he equably did what he thought best and trusted to his

good fortune to keep out of trouble with the authorities
He was very short, not more than five feet four in
height, and extremely fat; he was of a florid complexion.
For coolness' sake he kept his head shaved and his face
was hairless. It was round and red. His eyebrows were
so fair that you hardly saw them; and he had little
twinkling blue eyes. He knew that he had no dignity,
but for the sake of his position made up for it by
dressing very dapperly. He never went to his office, nor
sat in court, nor walked abroad but in spotless white.
His stengah-shifter, with its bright brass buttons,
fitted him very tightly and displayed the shocking fact
that, young though he was, he had a round and pro-
truding belly. His good-humoured face shone with
sweat and he constantly fanned himself with a palm-
leaf fan.

But in his house Mr. Gruyter preferred to wear
nothing but a sarong and then with his white podgy
little body he looked like a fat funny boy of sixteen. He
was an early riser and his breakfast was always ready for
him at six. It never varied. It consisted of a slice of
papaia, three cold fried eggs, Edam cheese, sliced thin,
and a cup of black coffee. When he had eaten it, he
smoked a large Dutch cigar, read the papers if he had
not read them through and through already, and then
dressed to go down to his office.

One morning while he was thus occupied his head
boy came into his bedroom and told him that Tuan
Jones wanted to know if he could see him. Mr. Gruyter

s

was standing in front of a looking-glass. He had his trousers on and was admiring his smooth chest. He arched his back in order to throw it out and throw in his belly and with a good deal of satisfaction gave his breast three or four resounding slaps. It was a manly chest. When the boy brought the message he looked at his own eyes in the mirror and exchanged a slightly ironic smile with them. He asked himself what the devil his visitor could want. Evert Gruyter spoke English, Dutch and Malay with equal facility, but he thought in Dutch. He liked to do this. It seemed to him a pleasantly ribald language.

"Ask the Tuan to wait and say I shall come directly." He put on his tunic, over his naked body, buttoned it up, and strutted into the sitting-room. The Rev. Owen Jones got up.

"Good morning, Mr. Jones," said the Contrôleur. "Have you come in to have a peg with me before I start my day's work?"

Mr. Jones did not smile.

"I've come to see you upon a very distressing matter, Mr. Gruyter," he answered.

The Contrôleur was not disconcerted by his visitor's gravity nor depressed by his words. His little blue eyes beamed amiably.

"Sit down, my dear fellow, and have a cigar."

Mr. Gruyter knew quite well that the Rev. Owen Jones neither drank nor smoked, but it tickled something prankish in his nature to offer him a drink and a smoke whenever they met. Mr. Jones shook his head.

Mr. Jones was in charge of the Baptist Mission on the Alas Islands. His headquarters were at Baru, the largest of them, with the greatest population, but he had meeting-houses under the care of native helpers in several other islands of the group. He was a tall, thin melancholy man, with a long face, sallow and drawn, of about forty. His brown hair was already white on the temples and it receded from the forehead. This gave him a look of somewhat vacuous intellectuality. Mr. Gruyter both disliked and respected him. He disliked him because he was narrow-minded and dogmatic. Himself a cheerful pagan who liked the good things of the flesh and was determined to get as many of them as his circumstances permitted, he had no patience with a man who disapproved of them all. He thought the customs of the country suited its inhabitants and had no patience with the missionary's energetic efforts to destroy a way of life that for centuries had worked very well. He respected him because he was honest, zealous and good. Mr. Jones, an Australian of Welsh descent, was the only qualified doctor in the group and it was a comfort to know that if you fell ill you need not rely only on a Chinese practitioner, and none knew better than the Contrôleur how useful to all Mr. Jones's skill had been and with what charity he had given it. On the occasion of an epidemic of influenza the missionary had done the work of ten men and no storm short of a typhoon could

prevent him from crossing to one island or another
if his help was needed.

He lived with his sister in a little white house about
half a mile from the village and when the Contrôleur
had arrived, came on board to meet him and begged
him to stay till he could get his own house in order.
The Contrôleur had accepted and soon saw for himself
with what simplicity the couple lived. It was more than
he could stand. Tea at three sparse meals a day and
when he lit his cigar Mr. Jones politely but firmly
asked him to be good enough not to smoke, since both
his sister and he strongly disapproved of it. In twenty-
four hours Mr. Gruyter moved into his own house.
He fled, with panic in his heart, as though from a
plague-stricken city. The Contrôleur was fond of a
joke and he liked to laugh; to be with a man who took
your nonsense in deadly earnest and never even smiled
at your best story was more than flesh and blood could
stand. The Rev. Owen Jones was a worthy man, but as
a companion he was impossible. His sister was worse.
Neither had a sense of humour, but whereas the
missionary was of a melancholy turn, doing his duty
so conscientiously, with the obvious conviction that
everything in the world was hopeless, Miss Jones was
resolutely cheerful. She grimly looked on the bright
side of things. With the ferocity of an avenging angel
she sought out the good in her fellow-men. Miss Jones
taught in the mission school and helped her brother in
his medical work. When he did operations she gave

the anæsthetic and was matron, dresser and nurse of the
tiny hospital which on his own initiative Mr. Jones had
added to the mission. But the Contrôleur was an
obstinate little fellow and he never lost his capacity of
extracting amusement from the Rev. Owen's dour
struggle with the infirmities of human nature, and Miss
Jones's ruthless optimism. He had to get his fun where
he could. The Dutch boats came in three times in
two months for a few hours and then he could have a
good old crack with the captain and chief engineer,
and once in a blue moon a pearling lugger came in from
Thursday Island or Port Darwin and for two or three
days he had a grand time. They were rough fellows,
the pearlers, for the most part, but they were full of
guts, and they had plenty of liquor on board, and good
stories to tell, and the Contrôleur had them up to his
house and gave them a fine dinner and the party was
only counted a success if they were all too drunk to get
back on the lugger again that night. But beside the
missionary the only white man who lived on Baru was
Ginger Ted, and he, of course, was a disgrace to civilisation. There was not a single thing to be said in his
favour. He cast discredit on the white race. All the
same, but for Ginger Ted the Contrôleur sometimes
thought he would find life on the island of Baru almost
more than he could bear.

Oddly enough it was on account of this scamp
that Mr. Jones, when he should have been instructing
the pagan young in the mysteries of the Baptist

faith, was paying Mr. Gruyter this early visit.

"Sit down, Mr. Jones," said the Contrôleur. "What can I do for you?"

"Well, I've come to see you about the man they call Ginger Ted. What are you going to do now?"

"Why, what's happened?"

"Haven't you heard? I thought the sergeant would have told you."

"I don't encourage the members of my staff to come to my private house unless the matter is urgent," said the Contrôleur rather grandly. "I am unlike you, Mr. Jones, I only work in order to have leisure and I like to enjoy my leisure without disturbance."

But Mr. Jones did not care much for small talk and he was not interested in general reflections.

"There was a disgraceful row in one of the Chinese shops last night. Ginger Ted wrecked the place and half killed a Chinaman."

"Drunk again, I suppose," said the Contrôleur placidly.

"Naturally. When is he anything else? They sent for the police and he assaulted the sergeant. They had to have six men to get him to the gaol."

"He's a hefty fellow," said the Contrôleur.

"I suppose you'll send him to Macassar."

Evert Gruyter returned the missionary's outraged look with a merry twinkle. He was no fool and he knew already what Mr. Jones was up to. It gave him considerable amusement to tease him a little.

"Fortunately my powers are wide enough to enable me to deal with the situation myself," he answered.

"You have power to deport anyone you like, Mr. Gruyter, and I'm sure it would save a lot of trouble if you got rid of the man altogether."

"I have the power of course, but I am sure you would be the last person to wish me to use it arbitrarily."

"Mr. Gruyter, the man's presence here is a public scandal. He's never sober from morning till night; it's notorious that he has relations with one native woman after another."

"That is an interesting point, Mr. Jones. I had always heard that alcoholic excess, though it stimulated sexual desire, prevented its gratification. What you tell me about Ginger Ted does not seem to bear out this theory."

The missionary flushed a dull red.

"These are physiological matters which at the moment I have no wish to go into," he said, frigidly. "The behaviour of this man does incalculable damage to the prestige of the white race, and his example seriously hampers the efforts that are made in other quarters to induce the people of these islands to lead a less vicious life. He's an out-and-out bad lot."

"Pardon my asking, but have you made any attempts to reform him?"

"When he first drifted here I did my best to get in touch with him. He repelled all my advances. When there was that first trouble I went to him and talked to him straight from the shoulder. He swore at me."

"No one has a greater appreciation than I of the excellent work that you and other missionaries do on these islands, but are you sure that you always exercise your calling with all the tact possible?"

The Contrôleur was rather pleased with this phrase. It was extremely courteous and yet contained a reproof that he thought worth administering. The missionary looked at him gravely. His sad brown eyes were full of sincerity.

"Did Jesus exercise tact when he took a whip and drove the money-changers from the Temple? No, Mr. Gruyter. Tact is the subterfuge the lax avail themselves of to avoid doing their duty."

Mr. Jones's remark made the Contrôleur feel suddenly that he wanted a bottle of beer. The missionary leaned forward earnestly.

"Mr. Gruyter, you know this man's transgressions just as well as I do. It's unnecessary for me to remind you of them. There are no excuses for him. Now he really has overstepped the limit. You'll never have a better chance than this. I beg you to use the power you have and turn him out once for all."

The Contrôleur's eyes twinkled more brightly than ever. He was having a lot of fun. He reflected that human beings were much more amusing when you did not feel called upon in dealing with them to allot praise or blame.

"But, Mr. Jones, do I understand you right? Are you asking me to give you an assurance to deport this man before I've heard the evidence against him and listened to his defence?"

"I don't know what his defence can be."

The Contrôleur rose from his chair and really he managed to get quite a little dignity into his five feet four inches.

"I am here to administer justice according to the laws of the Dutch Government. Permit me to tell you that I am exceedingly surprised that you should attempt to influence me in my judicial functions."

The missionary was a trifle flustered. It had never occurred to him that this little whipper-snapper of a boy, ten years younger than himself, would dream of adopting such an attitude. He opened his mouth to explain and apologise, but the Contrôleur raised a podgy little hand.

"It is time for me to go to my office, Mr. Jones. I wish you good morning."

The missionary, taken aback, bowed and without another word walked out of the room. He would have been surprised to see what the Contrôleur did when his back was turned. A broad grin broke on his lips and he put his thumb to his nose and cocked a snook at the Rev. Owen Jones.

A few minutes later he went down to his office. His head clerk, who was a Dutch half-caste, gave him his version of the previous night's row. It agreed pretty

s*

well with Mr. Jones's. The Court was sitting that day.

"Will you take Ginger Ted first, sir?" asked the clerk.

"I see no reason to do that. There are two or three cases held over from the last sitting. I will take him in his proper order."

"I thought perhaps as he was a white man you would like to see him privately, sir."

"The majesty of the law knows no difference between white and coloured, my friend," said Mr. Gruyter, somewhat pompously.

The Court was a big square room with wooden benches on which, crowded together, sat natives of all kinds, Polynesians, Bugis, Chinese, Malays, and they all rose when a door was opened and a sergeant announced the arrival of the Contrôleur. He entered with his clerk and took his place on a little dais at a table of varnished pitch pine. Behind him was a large engraving of Queen Wilhelmina. He despatched half a dozen cases and then Ginger Ted was brought in. He stood in the dock, handcuffed, with a warder on either side of him. The Contrôleur looked at him with a grave face, but he could not keep the amusement out of his eyes.

Ginger Ted was suffering from a hang-over. He swayed a little as he stood and his eyes were vacant. He was a man still young, thirty perhaps, of somewhat over the middle height, rather fat, with a bloated red face and a shock of curly red hair. He had not come out of the tussle unscathed. He had a black eye and his mouth was cut and swollen. He wore khaki shorts, very dirty and ragged, and his singlet had been almost torn off his back. A great rent showed the thick mat of red hair with which his chest was covered, but showed also the astonishing whiteness of his skin. The Contrôleur looked at the charge sheet. He called the evidence. When he had heard it, when he had seen the Chinaman whose head Ginger Ted had broken with a bottle, when he had heard the agitated story of the sergeant who had been knocked flat when he tried to arrest him, when he had listened to the tale of the havoc wrought by Ginger Ted who in his drunken fury had smashed everything he could lay hands on, he turned and addressed the accused in English.

"Well, Ginger, what have you got to say for yourself?"

"I was blind. I don't remember a thing about it. If they say I half killed 'im I suppose I did. I'll pay the damage if they'll give me time."

"You will, Ginger," said the Contrôleur, "but it's me who'll give you time."

He looked at Ginger Ted for a minute in silence. He was an unappetising object. A man who had gone completely to pieces. He was horrible. It made you shudder to look at him and if Mr. Jones had not been so officious, at that moment the Contrôleur would certainly have ordered him to be deported.

"You've been a trouble ever since you came to the islands, Ginger. You're a disgrace. You're incorrigibly idle. You've been picked up in the street dead drunk time and time again. You've kicked up row after row. You're hopeless. I told you the last time you were brought here that if you were arrested again I should deal with you severely. You've gone the limit this time and you're for it. I sentence you to six months' hard labour."

"Me?"

"You."

"By God, I'll kill you when I come out."

He burst into a string of oaths both filthy and blasphemous. Mr. Gruyter listened scornfully. You can swear much better in Dutch than in English and there was nothing that Ginger Ted said that he could not have effectively capped.

"Be quiet," he ordered. "You make me tired."

The Contrôleur repeated his sentence in Malay and the prisoner was led struggling away.

Mr. Gruyter sat down to tiffin in high good humour. It was astonishing how amusing life could be if you exercised a little ingenuity. There were people in Amsterdam, and even in Batavia and Surabaya, who looked upon his island home as a place of exile. They little knew how agreeable it was and what fun he could extract from unpromising material. They asked him whether he did not miss the club and the races and the cinema, the dances that were held once a week at the Casino and the society of Dutch ladies. Not at all. He liked comfort. The substantial furniture of the room

in which he sat had a satisfying solidity. He liked
reading French novels of a frivolous nature and he
appreciated the sensation of reading one after the other
without the uneasiness occasioned by the thought that
he was wasting his time. It seemed to him a great luxury
to waste time. When his young man's fancy turned to
thoughts of love his head boy brought to the house a
little dark-skinned bright-eyed creature in a sarong. He
took care to form no connection of a permanent nature.
He thought that change kept the heart young. He
enjoyed freedom and was not weighed down by a sense
of responsibility. He did not mind the heat. It made a
sluice over with cold water half a dozen times a day a
pleasure that had almost an æsthetic quality. He played
the piano. He wrote letters to his friends in Holland.
He felt no need for the conversation of intellectual
persons. He liked a good laugh, but he could get that
out of a fool just as well as out of a professor of
philosophy. He had a notion that he was a very wise
little man.

Like all good Dutchmen in the Far East he began his
lunch with a small glass of Hollands gin. It has a musty
acrid flavour, and the taste for it must be acquired, but
Mr. Gruyter preferred it to any cocktail. When he
drank it he felt besides that he was upholding the
traditions of his race. Then he had *rysttafel*. He had it
every day. He heaped a soup-plate high with rice, and
then, his three boys waiting on him, helped himself to
the curry that one handed him, to the fried egg that

another brought, and to the condiment presented by the third. Then each one brought another dish, of bacon, or bananas, or pickled fish, and presently his plate was piled high in a huge pyramid. He stirred it all together and began to eat. He ate slowly and with relish. He drank a bottle of beer.

He did not think while he was eating. His attention was applied to the mass in front of him and he consumed it with a happy concentration. It never palled on him. And when he had emptied the great plate it was a compensation to think that next day he would have *rysttafel* again. He grew tired of it as little as the rest of us grow tired of bread. He finished his beer and lit his cigar. The boy brought him a cup of coffee. He leaned back in his chair then and allowed himself the luxury of reflection.

It tickled him to have sentenced Ginger Ted to the richly deserved punishment of six months' hard labour, and he smiled when he thought of him working on the roads with the other prisoners. It would have been silly to deport from the island the one man with whom he could occasionally have a heart-to-heart talk, and besides, the satisfaction it would have given the missionary would have been bad for that gentleman's character. Ginger Ted was a scamp and a scallywag, but the Contrôleur had a kindly feeling for him. They had drunk many a bottle of beer in one another's company and when the pearl fishers from Port Darwin came in and they all made a night of it, they had got

gloriously tight together. The Contrôleur liked the
reckless way in which Ginger Ted squandered the
priceless treasure of life.

Ginger Ted had wandered in one day on the ship
that was going up from Merauke to Macassar. The
captain did not know how he had found his way there,
but he had travelled steerage with the natives, and he
stopped off at the Alas Islands because he liked the
look of them. Mr. Gruyter had a suspicion that their
attraction consisted perhaps in their being under the
Dutch flag and so out of British jurisdiction. But his
papers were in order, so there was no reason why he
should not stay. He said that he was buying pearl-shell
for an Australian firm, but it soon appeared that his
commercial undertakings were not serious. Drink,
indeed, took up so much of his time that he had little
left over for other pursuits. He was in receipt of two
pounds a week, paid monthly, which came regularly to
him from England. The Contrôleur guessed that this
sum was paid only so long as he kept well away from
the persons who sent it. It was anyway too small to
permit him any liberty of movement. Ginger Ted was
reticent. The Contrôleur discovered that he was an
Englishman, this he learnt from his passport, which
described him as Edward Wilson, and that he had been
in Australia. But why he had left England and what
he had done in Australia he had no notion. Nor could
he ever quite tell to what class Ginger Ted belonged.
When you saw him in a filthy singlet and a pair of ragged

trousers, a battered topi on his head, with the pearl-fishers and heard his conversation, coarse, obscene and illiterate, you thought he must be a sailor before the mast who had deserted his ship, or a labourer, but when you saw his handwriting you were surprised to find that it was that of a man not without at least some education, and on occasion when you got him alone, if he had had a few drinks but was not yet drunk, he would talk of matters that neither a sailor nor a labourer would have been likely to know anything about. The Contrôleur had a certain sensitiveness and he realised that Ginger Ted did not speak to him as an inferior to a superior but as an equal. Most of his remittance was mortgaged before he received it, and the Chinamen to whom he owed money were standing at his elbow when the monthly letter was delivered to him, but with what was left he proceeded to get drunk. It was then that he made trouble, for when drunk he grew violent and was then likely to commit acts that brought him into the hands of the police. Hitherto Mr. Gruyter had contented himself with keeping him in gaol till he was sober and giving him a talking to. When he was out of money he cadged what drink he could from anyone who would give it him. Rum, brandy, arak, it was all the same to him. Two or three times Mr. Gruyter had got him work on plantations run by Chinese in one or other of the islands, but he could not stick to it, and in a few weeks was back again at Baru on the beach. It was a miracle how he kept body and

soul together. He had, of course, a way with him. He
picked up the various dialects spoken on the islands,
and knew how to make the natives laugh. They
despised him, but they respected his physical strength,
and they liked his company. He was as a result never at
a loss for a meal or a mat to sleep on. The strange thing
was, and it was this that chiefly outraged the Rev. Owen
Jones, that he could do anything he liked with a woman.
The Contrôleur could not imagine what it was they saw
in him. He was casual with them and rather brutal.
He took what they gave him, but seemed incapable of
gratitude. He used them for his pleasure and then flung
them indifferently away. Once or twice this had got
him into trouble, and Mr. Gruyter had had to sentence
an angry father for sticking a knife in Ginger Ted's back
one night, and a Chinese woman had sought to poison
herself by swallowing opium because he had deserted
her. Once Mr. Jones came to the Contrôleur in a great
state because the beachcomber had seduced one of his
converts. The Contrôleur agreed that it was very
deplorable, but could only advise Mr. Jones to keep
a sharp eye on these young persons. The Contrôleur
liked it less when he discovered that a girl whom
he fancied a good deal himself and had been seeing
for several weeks had all the time been according
her favours also to Ginger Ted. When he thought of
this particular incident he smiled again at the thought
of Ginger Ted doing six months' hard labour. It is
seldom in this life that in the process of doing your

bounden duty you can get back on a fellow who has played you a dirty trick.

A few days later Mr. Gruyter was taking a walk, partly for exercise and partly to see that some job he wanted done was being duly proceeded with, when he passed a gang of prisoners working under the charge of a warder. Among them he saw Ginger Ted. He wore the prison sarong, a dingy tunic called in Malay a baju, and his own battered topi. They were repairing the road, and Ginger Ted was wielding a heavy pick. The way was narrow and the Contrôleur saw that he must pass within a foot of him. He remembered his threats. He knew that Ginger Ted was a man of violent passion and the language he had used in the dock made it plain that he had not seen what a good joke it was of the Contrôleur's to sentence him to six months' hard labour. If Ginger Ted suddenly attacked him with the pick, nothing on God's earth could save him. It was true that the warder would immediately shoot him down, but meanwhile the Contrôleur's head would be bashed in. It was with a funny little feeling in the pit of his stomach that Mr. Gruyter walked through the gang of prisoners. They were working in pairs a few feet from one another. He set his mind on neither hastening his pace nor slackening it. As he passed Ginger Ted, the man swung his pick into the ground and looked up at the Contrôleur and as he caught his eye winked. The Contrôleur checked the smile that rose to his lips and with official dignity strode on. But

that wink, so lusciously full of sardonic humour, filled
him with satisfaction. If he had been the Caliph of
Bagdad instead of a junior official in the Dutch Civil
Service, he would forthwith have released Ginger Ted,
sent slaves to bath and perfume him, and having
clothed him in a golden robe entertained him to a
sumptuous repast.

Ginger Ted was an exemplary prisoner and in a
month or two the Contrôleur, having occasion to send
a gang to do some work on one of the outlying islands,
included him in it. There was no gaol there, so the
ten fellows he sent, under the charge of a warder, were
billeted on the natives and after their day's work lived
like free men. The job was sufficient to take up the
rest of Ginger Ted's sentence. The Contrôleur saw him
before he left.

"Look here, Ginger," he said to him, "here's ten
guilder for you so that you can buy yourself tobacco
when you're gone."

"Couldn't you make it a bit more? There's eight
pounds a month coming in regularly."

"I think that's enough. I'll keep the letters that
come for you, and when you get back you'll have a
tidy sum. You'll have enough to take you anywhere
you want to go."

"I'm very comfortable here," said Ginger Ted.

"Well, the day you come back, clean yourself up
and come over to my house. We'll have a bottle of beer
together."

"That'll be fine. I guess I'll be ready for a good crack then."

Now chance steps in. The island to which Ginger Ted had been sent was called Maputiti, and like all the rest of them it was rocky, heavily wooded and surrounded by a reef. There was a village among coconuts on the sea-shore opposite the opening of the reef and another village on a brackish lake in the middle of the island. Of this some of the inhabitants had been converted to Christianity. Communication with Baru was effected by a launch that touched at the various islands at irregular intervals. It carried passengers and produce. But the villagers were seafaring folk, and if they had to communicate urgently with Baru, manned a prahu and sailed the fifty miles or so that separated them from it. It happened that when Ginger Ted's sentence had but another fortnight to run the Christian headman of the village on the lake was taken suddenly ill. The native remedies availed him nothing and he writhed in agony. Messengers were sent to Baru imploring the missionary's help; but as ill luck would have it Mr. Jones was suffering at the moment from an attack of malaria. He was in bed and unable to move. He talked the matter over with his sister.

"It sounds like acute appendicitis," he told her.

"You can't go, Owen," she said.

"I can't let the man die."

Mr. Jones had a temperature of a hundred and four. His head was aching like mad. He had been delirious all night. His eyes were shining strangely and his sister felt that he was holding on to his wits by a sheer effort of will.

"You couldn't operate in the state you're in."

"No, I couldn't. Then Hassan must go."

Hassan was the dispenser.

"You couldn't trust Hassan. He'd never dare to do an operation on his own responsibility. And they'd never let him. I'll go. Hassan can stay here and look after you."

"You can't remove an appendix?"

"Why not? I've seen you do it. I've done lots of minor operations."

Mr. Jones felt he didn't quite understand what she was saying.

"Is the launch in?"

"No, it's gone to one of the islands. But I can go in the prahu the men came in."

"You? I wasn't thinking of you. You can't go."

"I'm going, Owen."

"Going where?" he said.

She saw that his mind was wandering already. She put her hand soothingly on his dry forehead. She gave him a dose of medicine. He muttered something and she realised that he did not know where he was. Of course she was anxious about him, but she knew that his illness was not dangerous, and she could leave him safely to the mission boy who was helping her nurse him and to the native dispenser. She slipped out of the room. She put her toilet things, a night-dress, and a change of clothes into a bag. A little chest with surgical instruments, bandages and antiseptic dressings was kept always ready. She gave them to the two natives who had come over from Maputiti, and telling the dispenser what she was going to do gave him instructions to inform her brother when he was able to listen. Above all he was not to be anxious about her. She put on her topi and sallied forth. The mission was about half a mile from the village. She walked quickly. At the end of the jetty the prahu was waiting. Six men manned it. She took her place in the stern and they set off with a rapid stroke. Within the reef the sea was calm, but when they crossed the bar they came upon a long swell. But this was not the first journey of the sort Miss Jones had taken and she was confident in the seaworthiness of the boat she was in. It was noon and the sun beat down from a sultry sky. The only thing that harassed her was that they could not arrive before dark, and if she found it necessary to operate at once she could count only on the light of hurricane lamps.

Miss Jones was a woman of hard on forty. Nothing in her appearance would have prepared you for such determination as she had just shown. She had an odd drooping gracefulness, which suggested that she might be swayed by every breeze; it was almost an affectation; and it made the strength of character which you soon discovered in her seem positively monstrous. She was flat-chested, tall and extremely thin. She had a long sallow face and she was much afflicted with prickly heat. Her lank brown hair was drawn back straight from her forehead. She had rather small eyes, grey in colour, and because they were somewhat too close they gave her face a shrewish look. Her nose was long and thin and a trifle red. She suffered a good deal from indigestion. But this infirmity availed nothing against her ruthless determination to look upon the bright side of things. Firmly persuaded that the world was evil and men unspeakably vicious, she extracted any little piece of decency she could find in them with the modest pride with which a conjurer extracts a rabbit from a hat. She was quick, resourceful and competent. When she arrived on the island she saw that there was not a moment to lose if she was to save the headman's life. Under the greatest difficulties, showing a native how to give the anæsthetic, she operated, and for the next three days nursed the patient with anxious assiduity. Everything went very well and she realised that her brother could not have made a better job of it. She waited long enough to take out the stitches and then prepared to go home. She could flatter herself that she had not wasted her time. She had given medical attention to such as needed it, she had strengthened the small Christian community in its faith, admonished such as were lax and cast the good seed in places where it might be hoped under divine providence to take root.

The launch, coming from one of the other islands, put in somewhat late in the afternoon, but it was full

moon and they expected to reach Baru before midnight. They brought her things down to the wharf
and the people who were seeing her off stood about
repeating their thanks. Quite a little crowd collected.
The launch was loaded with sacks of copra, but Miss
Jones was used to its strong smell and it did not
incommode her. She made herself as comfortable a
place to sit in as she could, and waiting for the launch
to start, chatted with her grateful flock. She was the
only passenger. Suddenly a group of natives emerged
from the trees that embowered the little village on
the lagoon and she saw that among them was a white
man. He wore a prison sarong and a baju. He had
long red hair. She at once recognised Ginger Ted.
A policeman was with him. They shook hands and
Ginger Ted shook hands with the villagers who
accompanied him. They bore bundles of fruit and a jar
which Miss Jones guessed contained native spirit, and
these they put in the launch. She discovered to her
surprise that Ginger Ted was coming with her. His
term was up and instructions had arrived that he was
to be returned to Baru in the launch. He gave her a
glance, but did not nod—indeed Miss Jones turned
away her head—and stepped in. The mechanic started
his engine and in a moment they were jug-jugging
through the channel in the lagoon. Ginger Ted
clambered on to a pile of sacks and lit a cigarette.

Miss Jones ignored him. Of course she knew him
very well. Her heart sank when she thought that he

was going to be once more in Baru, creating a scandal and drinking, a peril to the women and a thorn in the flesh of all decent people. She knew the steps her brother had taken to have him deported and she had no patience with the Contrôleur, who would not see a duty that stared him so plainly in the face. When they had crossed the bar and were in the open sea Ginger Ted took the stopper out of the jar of arak and putting his mouth to it took a long pull. Then he handed the jar to the two mechanics who formed the crew. One was a middle-aged man and the other a youth.

"I do not wish you to drink anything while we are on the journey," said Miss Jones sternly to the elder one.

He smiled at her and drank.

"A little arak can do no one any harm," he answered. He passed the jar to his companion, who drank also.

"If you drink again I shall complain to the Contrôleur," said Miss Jones.

The elder man said something she could not understand, but which she suspected was very rude, and passed the jar back to Ginger Ted. They went along for an hour or more. The sea was like glass and the sun set radiantly. It set behind one of the islands and for a few minutes changed it into a mystic city of the skies. Miss Jones turned round to watch it and her heart was filled with gratitude for the beauty of the world.

"And only man is vile," she quoted to herself.

They went due east. In the distance was a little

island which she knew they passed close by. It was uninhabited. A rocky islet thickly grown with virgin forest. The boatman lit his lamps. The night fell and immediately the sky was thick with stars. The moon had not yet risen. Suddenly there was a slight jar and the launch began to vibrate strangely. The engine rattled. The head mechanic, calling to his mate to take the helm, crept under the housing. They seemed to be going more slowly. The engine stopped. She asked the youth what was the matter, but he did not know. Ginger Ted got down from the top of the copra sacks and slipped under the housing. When he reappeared she would have liked to ask him what had happened, but her dignity prevented her. She sat still and occupied herself with her thoughts. There was a long swell and the launch rolled slightly. The mechanic emerged once more into view and started the engine. Though it rattled like mad they began to move. The launch vibrated from stem to stern. They went very slowly. Evidently something was amiss, but Miss Jones was exasperated rather than alarmed. The launch was supposed to do six knots, but now it was just crawling along; at that rate they would not get into Baru till long, long after midnight. The mechanic, still busy under the housing, shouted out something to the man at the helm. They spoke in Bugi, of which Miss Jones knew very little. But after a while she noticed that they had changed their course and seemed to be heading for the little uninhabited island a good deal to the lee of which they should have passed.

"Where are we going?" she asked the helmsman with sudden misgiving.

He pointed to the islet. She got up and went to the housing and called to the man to come out.

"You're not going there? Why? What's the matter?"

"I can't get to Baru," he said.

"But you must. I insist. I order you to go to Baru."

The man shrugged his shoulders. He turned his back on her and slipped once more under the housing. Then Ginger Ted addressed her.

"One of the blades of the propeller has broken off. He thinks he can get as far as that island. We shall have to stay the night there and he'll put on a new propeller in the morning when the tide's out."

"I can't spend the night on an uninhabited island with three men," she cried.

"A lot of women would jump at it."

"I insist on going to Baru. Whatever happens we must get there to-night."

"Don't get excited, old girl. We've got to beach the boat to put a new propeller on, and we shall be all right on the island."

"How dare you speak to me like that. I think you're very insolent."

"You'll be O.K. We've got plenty of grub and we'll have a snack when we land. You have a drop of arak and you'll feel like a house on fire."

"You're an impertinent man. If you don't go to Baru I'll have you all put in prison."

"We're not going to Baru. We can't. We're going to that island and if you don't like it you can get out and swim."

"Oh, you'll pay for this."

"Shut up, you old cow," said Ginger Ted.

Miss Jones gave a gasp of anger. But she controlled herself. Even out there, in the middle of the ocean, she had too much dignity to bandy words with that vile wretch. The launch, the engine rattling horribly, crawled on. It was pitch dark now, and she could no longer see the island they were making for. Miss Jones, deeply incensed, sat with lips tight shut and a frown on her brow; she was not used to being crossed. Then the moon rose and she could see the bulk of Ginger Ted sprawling on the top of the piled sacks of copra. The glimmer of his cigarette was strangely sinister. Now the island was vaguely outlined against the sky. They reached it and the boatman ran the launch on to the beach. Suddenly Miss Jones gave a gasp. The truth had dawned on her and her anger changed to fear. Her heart beat violently. She shook in every limb. She felt dreadfully faint. She saw it all. Was the broken propeller a put-up job or was it an accident? She could not be certain; anyhow, she knew that Ginger Ted would seize the opportunity. Ginger Ted would rape her. She knew his character. He was mad about women. That was what he had done, practically, to the

girl at the mission, such a good little thing she was
and an excellent sempstress; they would have prosecuted
him for that and he would have been sentenced to years
of imprisonment only very unfortunately the innocent
child had gone back to him several times and indeed
had only complained of his ill usage when he left her
for somebody else. They had gone to the Contrôleur
about it, but he had refused to take any steps, saying
in that coarse way of his that even if what the girl said
was true, it didn't look very much as though it had been
an altogether unpleasant experience. Ginger Ted was
a scoundrel. And she was a white woman. What
chance was there that he would spare her? None. She
knew men. But she must pull herself together. She
must keep her wits about her. She must have courage.
She was determined to sell her virtue dearly, and if he
killed her——well, she would rather die than yield. And
if she died she would rest in the arms of Jesus. For a
moment a great light blinded her eyes and she saw the
mansions of her Heavenly Father. They were a grand
and sumptuous mixture of a picture palace and a railway
station. The mechanics and Ginger Ted jumped out
of the launch and, waist-deep in water, gathered round
the broken propeller. She took advantage of their pre-
occupation to get her case of surgical instruments out
of the box. She took out the four scalpels it contained
and secreted them in her clothing. If Ginger Ted
touched her she would not hesitate to plunge a scalpel
in his heart.

"Now then, miss, you'd better get out," said Ginger Ted. "You'll be better off on the beach than in the boat."

She thought so too. At least there she would have freedom of action. Without a word she clambered over the copra sacks. He offered her his hand.

"I don't want your help," she said coldly.

"You can go to hell," he answered.

It was a little difficult to get out of the boat without showing her legs, but by the exercise of considerable ingenuity she managed it.

"Damned lucky we've got something to eat. We'll make a fire and then you'd better have a snack and a nip of arak."

"I want nothing. I only want to be left alone."

"It won't hurt me if you go hungry."

She did not answer. She walked, with head erect, along the beach. She held the largest scalpel in her closed fist. The moon allowed her to see where she was going. She looked for a place to hide. The thick forest came down to the very edge of the beach; but, afraid of its darkness (after all, she was but a woman), she dared not plunge into its depth. She did not know what animals lurked there or what dangerous snakes. Besides, her instinct told her that it was better to keep those three bad men in sight; then if they came towards her she would be prepared. Presently she found a little hollow. She looked round. They seemed to be occupied with their own affairs and they could not see her.

She slipped in. There was a rock between them and
her so that she was hidden from them and yet could
watch them. She saw them go to and from the boat
carrying things. She saw them build a fire. It lit them
luridly and she saw them sit around it and eat, and she
saw the jar of arak passed from one to the other. They
were all going to get drunk. What would happen to
her then? It might be that she could cope with Ginger
Ted, though his strength terrified her, but against three
she would be powerless. A mad idea came to her to
go to Ginger Ted and fall on her knees before him and
beg him to spare her. He must have some spark of
decent feeling in him and she had always been so convinced that there was good even in the worst of men.
He must have had a mother. Perhaps he had a sister.
Ah, but how could you appeal to a man blinded with
lust and drunk with arak? She began to feel terribly
weak. She was afraid she was going to cry. That would
never do. She needed all her self-control. She bit her
lip. She watched them, like a tiger watching his prey;
no, not like that, like a lamb watching three hungry
wolves. She saw them put more wood on the fire and
Ginger Ted, in his sarong, silhouetted by the flames.
Perhaps after he had had his will of her he would pass
her on to the others. How could she go back to her
brother when such a thing had happened to her? Of
course he would be sympathetic, but would he ever feel
quite the same to her again? It would break his heart.
And perhaps he would think that she ought to have

resisted more. For his sake perhaps it would be better
if she said nothing about it. Naturally the men would
say nothing. It would mean twenty years in prison
for them. But then supposing she had a baby. Miss
Jones instinctively clenched her hands with horror and
nearly cut herself with the scalpel. Of course it would
only infuriate them if she resisted.

"What shall I do?" she cried. "What have I done to
deserve this?"

She flung herself down on her knees and prayed to
God to save her. She prayed long and earnestly. She
reminded God that she was a virgin and just mentioned,
in case it had slipped the divine memory, how much
St. Paul had valued that excellent state. And then she
peeped round the rock again. The three men appeared
to be smoking and the fire was dying down. Now was
the time that Ginger Ted's lewd thoughts might be
expected to turn to the woman who was at his mercy.
She smothered a cry, for suddenly he got up and walked
in her direction. She felt all her muscles grow taut,
and though her heart was beating furiously she clenched
the scalpel firmly in her hand. But it was for another
purpose that Ginger Ted had got up. Miss Jones
blushed and looked away. He strolled slowly back to
the others and sitting down again raised the jar of arak
to his lips. Miss Jones, crouching behind the rock,
watched with straining eyes. The conversation round
the fire grew less and presently she divined, rather than
saw, that the two natives wrapped themselves in

blankets and composed themselves to slumber. She
understood. This was the moment Ginger Ted had
been waiting for. When they were fast asleep he
would get up cautiously and without a sound, in
order not to wake the others, creep stealthily towards
her. Was it that he was unwilling to share her with
them or did he know that his deed was so dastardly
that he did not wish them to know of it? After all, he
was a white man and she was a white woman. He could
not have sunk so low as to allow her to suffer the
violence of natives. But his plan, which was so obvious
to her, had given her an idea; when she saw him coming
she would scream, she would scream so loudly that it
would wake the two mechanics. She remembered now
that the elder, though he had only one eye, had a kind
face. But Ginger Ted did not move. She was feeling
terribly tired. She began to fear that she would not
have the strength now to resist him. She had gone
through too much. She closed her eyes for a minute.

When she opened them it was broad daylight. She
must have fallen asleep and, so shattered was she by
emotion, have slept till long after dawn. It gave her
quite a turn. She sought to rise, but something caught
in her legs. She looked and found that she was covered
with two empty copra sacks. Someone had come in
the night and put them over her. Ginger Ted! She
gave a little scream. The horrible thought flashed
through her mind that he had outraged her in her sleep.
No. It was impossible. And yet he had had her at his

T

mercy. Defenceless. And he had spared her. She blushed furiously. She raised herself to her feet, feeling a little stiff, and arranged her disordered dress. The scalpel had fallen from her hand and she picked it up. She took the two copra sacks and emerged from her hiding-place. She walked towards the boat. It was floating in the shallow water of the lagoon.

"Come on, Miss Jones," said Ginger Ted. "We've finished. I was just going to wake you up."

She could not look at him, but she felt herself as red as a turkey cock.

"Have a banana?" he said.

Without a word she took it. She was very hungry, and ate it with relish.

"Step on this rock and you'll be able to get in without wetting your feet."

Miss Jones felt as though she could sink into the ground with shame, but she did as he told her. He took hold of her arm—good heavens! his hand was like an iron vice, never, never could she have struggled with him—and helped her into the launch. The mechanic started the engine and they slid out of the lagoon. In three hours they were at Baru.

That evening, having been officially released, Ginger Ted went to the Contrôleur's house. He wore no longer the prison uniform, but the ragged singlet and the khaki shorts in which he had been arrested. He had had his hair cut and it fitted his head now like a little curly red cap. He was thinner. He had lost his bloated flabbiness and looked younger and better. Mr. Gruyter, a friendly grin on his round face, shook hands with him and asked him to sit down. The boy brought two bottles of beer.

"I'm glad to see you hadn't forgotten my invitation, Ginger," said the Contrôleur.

"Not likely. I've been looking forward to this for six months."

"Here's luck, Ginger Ted."

"Same to you, Contrôleur."

They emptied their glasses and the Contrôleur clapped his hands. The boy brought two more bottles.

"Well, you don't bear me any malice for the sentence I gave you, I hope."

"No bloody fear. I was mad for a minute, but I got over it. I didn't have half a bad time, you know. Nice lot of girls on that island, Contrôleur. You ought to give 'em a look over one of these days."

"You're a bad lot, Ginger."

"Terrible."

"Good beer, isn't it?"

"Fine."

"Let's have some more."

Ginger Ted's remittance had been arriving every month and the Contrôleur now had fifty pounds for him. When the damage he had done to the Chinaman's shop was paid for there would still be over thirty.

"That's quite a lot of money, Ginger. You ought to do something useful with it."

"I mean to," answered Ginger. "Spend it."

The Contrôleur sighed.

"Well, that's what money's for, I guess."

The Contrôleur gave his guest the news. Not much had happened during the last six months. Time on the Alas Islands did not matter very much and the rest of the world did not matter at all.

"Any wars anywhere?" asked Ginger Ted.

"No. Not that I've noticed. Harry Jervis found a pretty big pearl. He says he's going to ask a thousand quid for it."

"I hope he gets it."

"And Charlie McCormack's married."

"He always was a bit soft."

Suddenly the boy appeared and said Mr. Jones wished to know if he might come in. Before the Contrôleur could give an answer Mr. Jones walked in.

"I won't detain you long," he said. "I've been trying to get hold of this good man all day and when I heard he was here I thought you wouldn't mind my coming."

"How is Miss Jones?" asked the Contrôleur politely. "None the worse for her night in the open, I trust."

"She's naturally a bit shaken. She had a temperature and I've insisted on her going to bed, but I don't think it's serious."

The two men had got up on the missionary's entrance, and now the missionary went up to Ginger Ted and held out his hand.

"I want to thank you. You did a great and noble

thing. My sister is right, one should always look for the good in their fellow-men; I am afraid I misjudged you in the past: I beg your pardon."

He spoke very solemnly. Ginger Ted looked at him with amazement. He had not been able to prevent the missionary taking his hand. He still held it.

"What the hell are you talking about?"

"You had my sister at your mercy and you spared her. I thought you were all evil and I am ashamed. She was defenceless. She was in your power. You had pity on her. I thank you from the bottom of my heart. Neither my sister nor I will ever forget. God bless and guard you always."

Mr. Jones's voice shook a little and he turned his head away. He released Ginger Ted's hand and strode quickly to the door. Ginger Ted watched him with a blank face.

"What the blazes does he mean?" he asked.

The Contrôleur laughed. He tried to control himself but the more he did the more he laughed. He shook and you saw the folds of his fat belly ripple under the sarong. He leaned back in his long chair and rolled from side to side. He did not laugh only with his face, he laughed with his whole body, and even the muscles of his podgy legs shook with mirth. He held his aching ribs. Ginger Ted looked at him frowning, and because he did not understand what the joke was he grew angry. He seized one of the empty beer bottles by the neck.

"If you don't stop laughing, I'll break your bloody head open," he said.

The Contrôleur mopped his face. He swallowed a mouthful of beer. He sighed and groaned because his sides were hurting him.

"He's thanking you for having respected the virtue of Miss Jones," he spluttered at last.

"Me?" cried Ginger Ted.

The thought took quite a long time to travel through his head, but when at last he got it he flew into a violent rage. There flowed from his mouth such a stream of blasphemous obscenities as would have startled a marine.

"That old cow," he finished. "What does he take me for?"

"You have the reputation of being rather hot stuff with the girls, Ginger," giggled the little Contrôleur.

"I wouldn't touch her with the fag-end of a barge-pole. It never entered my head. The nerve. I'll wring his blasted neck. Look here, give me my money, I'm going to get drunk."

"I don't blame you," said the Contrôleur.

"That old cow," repeated Ginger Ted. "That old cow."

He was shocked and outraged. The suggestion really shattered his sense of decency.

The Contrôleur had the money at hand and having got Ginger Ted to sign the necessary papers gave it to him.

"Go and get drunk, Ginger Ted," he said, "but I warn you, if you get into mischief it'll be twelve months next time."

"I shan't get into mischief," said Ginger Ted sombrely. He was suffering from a sense of injury. "It's an insult," he shouted at the Contrôleur. "That's what it is, it's a bloody insult."

He lurched out of the house, and as he went he muttered to himself: "dirty swine, dirty swine." Ginger Ted remained drunk for a week. Mr. Jones went to see the Contrôleur again.

"I'm very sorry to hear that poor fellow has taken up his evil course again," he said. "My sister and I are dreadfully disappointed. I'm afraid it wasn't very wise to give him so much money at once."

"It was his own money. I had no right to keep it back."

"Not a legal right, perhaps, but surely a moral right."

He told the Contrôleur the story of that fearful night on the island. With her feminine instinct, Miss Jones had realised that the man, inflamed with lust, was determined to take advantage of her, and, resolved to defend herself to the last, had armed herself with a scalpel. He told the Contrôleur how she had prayed and wept and how she had hidden herself. Her agony was indescribable, and she knew that she could never have survived the shame. She rocked to and fro and every moment she thought he was coming. And there was no help anywhere and at last she had fallen asleep; she was tired out, poor thing, she had undergone more than any human being could stand, and then when she awoke she found that he had covered her with copra sacks. He had found her asleep, and surely it was her innocence, her very helplessness that had moved him, he hadn't the heart to touch her; he covered her gently with two copra sacks and crept silently away.

"It shows you that deep down in him there is something sterling. My sister feels it's our duty to save him. We must do something for him."

"Well, in your place I wouldn't try till he's got through all his money," said the Contrôleur, "and then if he's not in gaol you can do what you like."

But Ginger Ted didn't want to be saved. About a fortnight after his release from prison he was sitting on a stool outside a Chinaman's shop looking vacantly down the street when he saw Miss Jones coming along. He stared at her for a minute and once more amazement seized him. He muttered to himself and there can be little doubt that his mutterings were disrespectful. But then he noticed that Miss Jones had seen him and he quickly turned his head away; he was conscious, notwithstanding, that she was looking at him. She was walking briskly, but she sensibly diminished her pace as she approached him. He thought she was going to stop and speak to him. He got up quickly and went into the shop. He did not venture to come out for at least five minutes. Half an hour later Mr. Jones himself came along and he went straight up to Ginger Ted with outstretched hand.

"How do you do, Mr. Edward? My sister told me I should find you here."

Ginger Ted gave him a surly look and did not take the proffered hand. He made no answer.

"We'd be so very glad if you'd come to dinner with us next Sunday. My sister's a capital cook and she'll make you a real Australian dinner."

"Go to hell," said Ginger Ted.

"That's not very gracious," said the missionary, but with a little laugh to show that he was not affronted. "You go and see the Contrôleur from time to time, why shouldn't you come and see us? It's pleasant to talk to white people now and then. Won't you let bygones be bygones? I can assure you of a very cordial welcome."

"I haven't got clothes fit to go out in," said Ginger Ted sulkily.

"Oh, never mind about that. Come as you are."

"I won't."

"Why not? You must have a reason."

Ginger Ted was a blunt man. He had no hesitation in saying what we should all like to when we receive unwelcome invitations.

"I don't want to."

"I'm sorry. My sister will be very disappointed."

Mr. Jones, determined to show that he was not in the least offended, gave him a breezy nod and walked

T*

on. Forty-eight hours later there mysteriously arrived at the house in which Ginger Ted lodged a parcel containing a suit of ducks, a tennis shirt, a pair of socks and some shoes. He was unaccustomed to receiving presents and next time he saw the Contrôleur asked him if it was he who had sent the things.

"Not on your life," replied the Contrôleur. "I'm perfectly indifferent to the state of your wardrobe."

"Well, then, who the hell can have?"

"Search me."

It was necessary from time to time for Miss Jones to see Mr. Gruyter on business and shortly after this she came to see him one morning in his office. She was a capable woman and though she generally wanted him to do something he had no mind to, she did not waste his time. He was a little surprised then to discover that she had come on a very trivial errand. When he told her that he could not take cognizance of the matter in question, she did not as was her habit try to convince him, but accepted his refusal as definite. She got up to go and then as though it were an afterthought said:

"Oh, Mr. Gruyter, my brother is very anxious that we should have the man they call Ginger Ted to supper with us and I've written him a little note inviting him for the day after to-morrow. I think he's rather shy, and I wonder if you'd come with him."

"That's very kind of you."

"My brother feels that we ought to do something for the poor fellow."

"A woman's influence and all that sort of thing," said the Contrôleur demurely.

"Will you persuade him to come? I'm sure he will if you make a point of it, and when he knows the way he'll come again. It seems such a pity to let a young man like that go to pieces altogether."

The Contrôleur looked up at her. She was several inches taller than he. He thought her very unattractive. She reminded him strangely of wet linen hung on a clothes-line to dry. His eyes twinkled, but he kept a straight face.

"I'll do my best," he said.

"How old is he?" she asked.

"According to his passport he's thirty-one."

"And what is his real name?"

"Wilson."

"Edward Wilson," she said softly.

"It's astonishing that after the life he's led he should be so strong," murmured the Contrôleur. "He has the strength of an ox."

"Those red-headed men sometimes are very powerful," said Miss Jones, but spoke as though she were choking.

"Quite so," said the Contrôleur.

Then for no obvious reason Miss Jones blushed. She hurriedly said good-bye to the Controleur and left his office.

"*Godverdomme!*" said the Contrôleur.

He knew now who had sent Ginger Ted the new clothes.

He met him during the course of the day and asked him whether he had heard from Miss Jones. Ginger Ted took a crumpled ball of paper out of his pocket and gave it to him. It was the invitation. It ran as follows:

Dear Mr. Wilson,—

My brother and I would be so very glad if you would come and have supper with us next Thursday at 7.30. The Contrôleur has kindly promised to come. We have some new records from Australia which I am sure you will like. I am afraid I was not very nice to you last time we met, but I did not know you so well then, and I am big enough to admit it when I have committed an error. I hope you will forgive me and let me be your friend.

Yours sincerely,

Martha Jones.

The Contrôleur noticed that she addressed him as Mr. Wilson and referred to his own promise to go, so that when she told him she had already invited Ginger Ted she had a little anticipated the truth.

"What are you going to do?"

"I'm not going, if that's what you mean. Damned nerve."

"You must answer the letter."

"Well, I won't."

"Now look here, Ginger, you put on those new clothes and you come as a favour to me. I've got to go, and damn it all, you can't leave me in the lurch. It won't hurt you just once."

Ginger Ted looked at the Contrôleur suspiciously, but his face was serious and his manner sincere: he could not guess that within him the Dutchman bubbled with laughter.

"What the devil do they want me for?"

"I don't know. The pleasure of your society, I suppose."

"Will there be any booze?"

"No, but come up to my house at seven, and we'll have a tiddly before we go."

"Oh, all right," said Ginger Ted sulkily.

The Contrôleur rubbed his little fat hands with joy. He was expecting a great deal of amusement from the party. But when Thursday came and seven o'clock Ginger Ted was dead drunk and Mr. Gruyter had to go alone. He told the missionary and his sister the plain truth. Mr. Jones shook his head.

"I'm afraid it's no good, Martha, the man's hopeless."

For a moment Miss Jones was silent and the Contrôleur saw two tears trickle down her long thin nose. She bit her lip.

"No one is hopeless. Everyone has some good in him. I shall pray for him every night. It would be wicked to doubt the power of God."

Perhaps Miss Jones was right in this, but the divine providence took a very funny way of effecting its ends. Ginger Ted began to drink more heavily than ever. He was so troublesome that even Mr. Gruyter lost patience with him. He made up his mind that he could not have the fellow on the islands any more and resolved to deport him on the next boat that touched at Baru. Then a man died under mysterious circumstances after having been for a trip to one of the islands and the Contrôleur learnt that there had been several deaths on the same island. He sent the Chinese who was the official doctor of the group to look into the matter, and very soon received intelligence that the deaths were due to cholera. Two more took place at Baru and the certainty was forced upon him that there was an epidemic.

The Contrôleur cursed freely. He cursed in Dutch, he cursed in English and he cursed in Malay. Then he drank a bottle of beer and smoked a cigar. After that he took thought. He knew the Chinese doctor would be useless. He was a nervous little man from Java and the natives would refuse to obey his orders. The Contrôleur was efficient and knew pretty well what must be done, but he could not do everything single-handed. He did not like Mr. Jones, but just then he was thankful that he was at hand, and he sent for him at once. In ten minutes Mr. Jones was in the office. He was accompanied by his sister.

"You know what I want to see you about, Mr. Jones," he said abruptly.

"Yes. I've been expecting a message from you.

That is why my sister has come with me. We are ready to put all our resources at your disposal. I need not tell you that my sister is as competent as a man."

"I know. I shall be very glad of her assistance."

They set to without further delay to discuss the steps that must be taken. Hospital huts would have to be erected and quarantine stations. The inhabitants of the various villages on the islands must be forced to take proper precautions. In a good many cases the infected villages drew their water from the same well as the uninfected, and in each case this difficulty would have to be dealt with according to circumstances. It was necessary to send round people to give orders and make sure that they were carried out. Negligence must be ruthlessly punished. The worst of it was that the natives would not obey other natives, and orders given by native policemen, themselves unconvinced of their efficacy, would certainly be disregarded. It was advisable for Mr. Jones to stay at Baru where the population was largest and his medical attention most wanted; and what with the official duties that forced him to keep in touch with his headquarters, it was impossible for Mr. Gruyter to visit all the other islands himself. Miss Jones must go; but the natives of some of the outlying islands were wild and treacherous; the Contrôleur had had a good deal of trouble with them. He did not like the idea of exposing her to danger.

"I'm not afraid," she said.

"I daresay. But if you have your throat cut I shall get into trouble, and besides, we're so short-handed I don't want to risk losing your help."

"Then let Mr. Wilson come with me. He knows the natives better than anyone and can speak all their dialects."

"Ginger Ted?" The Contrôleur stared at her. "He's just getting over an attack of D.Ts."

"I know," she answered.

"You know a great deal, Miss Jones."

Even though the moment was so serious Mr. Gruyter could not but smile. He gave her a sharp look, but she met it coolly.

"There's nothing like responsibility for bringing out what there is in a man, and I think something like this may be the making of him."

"Do you think it would be wise to trust yourself for days at a time to a man of such infamous character?" said the missionary.

"I put my trust in God," she answered gravely.

"Do you think he'd be any use?" asked the Contrôleur. "You know what he is."

"I'm convinced of it." Then she blushed. "After all, no one knows better than I that he's capable of self-control."

The Contrôleur bit his lip.

"Let's send for him."

He gave a message to the sergeant and in a few minutes Ginger Ted stood before them. He looked ill. He had evidently been much shaken by his recent attack and his nerves were all to pieces. He was in rags and he had not shaved for a week. No one could have looked more disreputable.

"Look here, Ginger," said the Contrôleur, "it's about this cholera business. We've got to force the natives to take precautions and we want you to help us."

"Why the hell should I?"

"No reason at all. Except philanthropy."

"Nothing doing, Contrôleur. I'm not a philanthropist."

"That settles that. That was all. You can go."

But as Ginger Ted turned to the door Miss Jones stopped him.

"It was my suggestion, Mr. Wilson. You see, they want me to go to Labobo and Sakunchi, and the natives there are so funny I was afraid to go alone. I thought if you came I should be safer."

He gave her a look of extreme distaste.

"What do you suppose I care if they cut your throat?"

Miss Jones looked at him and her eyes filled with tears. She began to cry. He stood and watched her stupidly.

"There's no reason why you should." She pulled herself together and dried her eyes. "I'm being silly. I shall be all right. I'll go alone."

"It's damned foolishness for a woman to go to Labobo."

She gave him a little smile.

"I daresay it is, but you see, it's my job and I can't help myself. I'm sorry if I offended you by asking you. You must forget about it. I daresay it wasn't quite fair to ask you to take such a risk."

For quite a minute Ginger Ted stood and looked at her. He shifted from one foot to the other. His surly face seemed to grow black.

"Oh, hell, have it your own way," he said at last. "I'll come with you. When d'you want to start?"

They set out next day, with drugs and disinfectants, in the Government launch. Mr. Gruyter as soon as he had put the necessary work in order was to start off in a prahu in the other direction. For four months the epidemic raged. Though everything possible was done to localise it one island after another was attacked. The Contrôleur was busy from morning to night. He had no sooner got back to Baru from one or other of the islands to do what was necessary there than he had to set off again. He distributed food and medicine. He cheered the terrified people. He supervised everything. He worked like a dog. He saw nothing of Ginger Ted, but he heard from Mr. Jones that the experiment was working out beyond all hopes. The scamp was behaving himself. He had a way with the natives; and by cajolery, firmness and on occasion the use of his fist, managed to make them take the steps necessary for their own safety. Miss Jones could congratulate herself on the success of the scheme. But the Contrôleur was too tired to be amused. When the epidemic had run its course he rejoiced because out of a population of eight thousand only six hundred had died.

Finally he was able to give the district a clean bill of health.

One evening he was sitting in his sarong on the verandah of his house and he read a French novel with the happy consciousness that once more he could take things easy. His head boy came in and told him that Ginger Ted wished to see him. He got up from his chair and shouted to him to come in. Company was just what he wanted. It had crossed the Contrôleur's mind that it would be pleasant to get drunk that night, but it is dull to get drunk alone, and he had regretfully put the thought aside. And heaven had sent Ginger Ted in the nick of time. By God, they would make a night of it. After four months they deserved a bit of fun. Ginger Ted entered. He was wearing a clean suit of white ducks. He was shaved. He looked another man.

"Why, Ginger, you look as if you'd been spending a month at a health resort instead of nursing a pack of natives dying of cholera. And look at your clothes. Have you just stepped out of a band-box?"

Ginger Ted smiled rather sheepishly. The head boy brought two bottles of beer and poured them out.

"Help yourself, Ginger," said the Contrôleur as he took his glass.

"I don't think I'll have any, thank you."

The Contrôleur put down his glass and looked at Ginger Ted with amazement.

"Why, what's the matter? Aren't you thirsty?"

"I don't mind having a cup of tea."

"A cup of what?"

"I'm on the wagon. Martha and I are going to be married."

'Ginger!"

The Contrôleur's eyes popped out of his head. He scratched his shaven pate.

"You can't marry Miss Jones," he said. "No one could marry Miss Jones."

"Well, I'm going to. That's what I've come to see you about. Owen's going to marry us in chapel, but we want to be married by Dutch law as well."

"A joke's a joke, Ginger. What's the idea?"

"She wanted it. She fell for me that night we spent on the island when the propeller broke. She's not a bad old girl when you get to know her. It's her last chance, if you understand what I mean, and I'd like to do something to oblige her. And she wants someone to take care of her, there's no doubt about that."

"Ginger, Ginger, before you can say knife she'll make you into a damned missionary."

"I don't know that I'd mind that so much if we had a little mission of our own. She says I'm a bloody marvel with the natives. She says I can do more with a native in five minutes than Owen can do in a year. She says she's never known anyone with the magnetism I have. It seems a pity to waste a gift like that."

The Contrôleur looked at him without speaking and slowly nodded his head three or four times. She'd nobbled him all right.

"I've converted seventeen already," said Ginger Ted.

"You? I didn't know you believed in Christianity."

"Well, I don't know that I did exactly, but when I talked to 'em and they just came into the fold like a lot of blasted sheep, well, it gave me quite a turn. Blimey, I said, I daresay there's something in it after all."

"You should have raped her, Ginger. I wouldn't have been hard on you. I wouldn't have given you more than three years' and three years' is soon over."

"Look here, Contrôleur, don't you ever let on that the thought never entered my head. Women are touchy, you know, and she'd be as sore as hell if she knew that."

"I guessed she'd got her eye on you, but I never thought it would come to this." The Contrôleur in an agitated manner walked up and down the verandah. "Listen to me, old boy," he said after an interval of reflection, "we've had some grand times together and a friend's a friend. I'll tell you what I'll do, I'll lend you the launch and you can go and hide on one of the islands till the next ship comes along and then I'll get 'em to slow down and take you on board. You've only got one chance now and that's to cut and run."

Ginger Ted shook his head.

"It's no good, Contrôleur, I know you mean well, but I'm going to marry the blasted woman, and that's that. You don't know the joy of bringing all them bleeding sinners to repentance, and Christ! that girl can make a treacle pudding. I haven't eaten a better one since I was a kid."

The Contrôleur was very much disturbed. The drunken scamp was his only companion on the islands and he did not want to lose him. He discovered that he had even a certain affection for him. Next day he went to see the missionary.

"What's this I hear about your sister marrying Ginger Ted?" he asked him. "It's the most extraordinary thing I've ever heard in my life."

"It's true nevertheless."

"You must do something about it. It's madness."

"My sister is of full age and entitled to do as she pleases."

"But you don't mean to tell me you approve of it. You know Ginger Ted. He's a bum and there are no two ways about it. Have you told her the risk she's running? I mean, bringing sinners to repentance and all that sort of thing's all right, but there are limits. And does the leopard ever change his spots?"

Then for the first time in his life the Contrôleur saw a twinkle in the missionary's eye.

"My sister is a very determined woman, Mr. Gruyter," he replied. "From that night they spent on the island he never had a chance."

The Contrôleur gasped. He was as surprised as the prophet when the Lord opened the mouth of the ass, and she said unto Balaam, What have I done unto thee, that thou hast smitten me these three times? Perhaps Mr. Jones was human after all.

"*Allejesus!*" muttered the Contrôleur.

Before anything more could be said Miss Jones swept into the room. She was radiant. She looked ten years younger. Her cheeks were flushed and her nose was hardly red at all.

"Have you come to congratulate me, Mr. Gruyter?" she cried, and her manner was sprightly and girlish. "You see, I was right after all. Everyone has some good in them. You don't know how splendid Edward has been all through this terrible time. He's a hero. He's a saint. Even I was surprised."

"I hope you'll be very happy, Miss Jones."

"I know I shall. Oh, it would be wicked of me to doubt it. For it is the Lord who has brought us together."

"Do you think so?"

"I know it. Don't you see? Except for the cholera Edward would never have found himself. Except for the cholera we should never have learnt to know one another. I have never seen the hand of God more plainly manifest."

The Contrôleur could not but think that it was rather a clumsy device to bring those two together that necessitated the death of six hundred innocent persons, but not being well versed in the ways of omnipotence he made no remark.

"You'll never guess where we're going for our honeymoon," said Miss Jones, perhaps a trifle archly.

"Java?"

"No, if you'll lend us the launch, we're going to that island where we were marooned. It has very tender recollections for both of us. It was there that I first guessed how fine and good Edward was. It's there I want him to have his reward."

The Contrôleur caught his breath. He left quickly, for he thought that unless he had a bottle of beer at once he would have a fit. He was never so shocked in his life.

THE FORCE OF CIRCUMSTANCE

SHE was sitting on the verandah waiting for her husband to come in for luncheon. The Malay boy had drawn the blinds when the morning lost its freshness, but she had partly raised one of them so that she could look at the river. Under the breathless sun of midday it had the white pallor of death. A native was paddling along in a dug-out so small that it hardly showed above the surface of the water. The colours of the day were ashy and wan. They were but the various tones of the heat. (It was like an Eastern melody, in the minor key, which exacerbates the nerves by its ambiguous monotony; and the ear awaits impatiently a resolution, but waits in vain.) The cicadas sang their grating song with a frenzied energy; it was as continual and monotonous as the rustling of a brook over the stones; but on a sudden it was drowned by the loud singing of a bird mellifluous and rich; and for an instant, with a catch at her heart, she thought of the English blackbird.

Then she heard her husband's step on the gravel path behind the bungalow, the path that led to the courthouse in which he had been working, and she rose from her chair to greet him. He ran up the short flight of steps, for the bungalow was built on piles, and at the door the boy was waiting to take his topee. He came into the room which served them as a dining-room and parlour, and his eyes lit up with pleasure as he saw her.

"Hulloa, Doris. Hungry?"

"Ravenous."

"It'll only take me a minute to have a bath and then I'm ready."

"Be quick," she smiled.

He disappeared into his dressing-room and she heard him whistling cheerily while, with the carelessness with which she was always remonstrating, he tore off his clothes and flung them on the floor. He was twenty-nine, but he was still a schoolboy; he would never grow up. That was why she had fallen in love with him, perhaps, for no amount of affection could persuade her that he was good-looking. He was a little round man, with a red face like the full moon, and blue eyes. He was rather pimply. She had examined him carefully and had been forced to confess to him that he had not a single feature which she could praise. She had told him often that he wasn't her type at all.

"I never said I was a beauty," he laughed.

"I can't think what it is I see in you."

But of course she knew perfectly well. He was a gay, jolly little man, who took nothing very solemnly, and he was constantly laughing. He made her laugh too. He found life an amusing rather than a serious business and he had a charming smile. When she was with him she felt happy and good-tempered. And the deep affection which she saw in those merry blue eyes of his touched her. It was very satisfactory to be loved like that. Once, sitting on his knees, during their honeymoon, she had taken his face in her hands and said to him:

"You're an ugly, little fat man, Guy, but you've got charm. I can't help loving you."

A wave of emotion swept over her and her eyes filled with tears. She saw his face contorted for a moment with the extremity of his feeling and his voice was a little shaky when he answered:

"It's a terrible thing for me to have married a woman who's mentally deficient," he said.

She chuckled. It was the characteristic answer which she would have liked him to make.

It was hard to realise that nine months ago she had never even heard of him. She had met him at a small place by the seaside where she was spending a month's holiday with her mother. Doris was secretary to a member of parliament. Guy was home on leave. They were staying at the same hotel, and he quickly told her all about himself. He was born in Sembulu, where his father had served for thirty years under the second Sultan, and on leaving school he had entered the same service. He was devoted to the country.

"After all England's a foreign land to me," he told her. "My home's Sembulu."

And now it was her home too. He asked her to

marry him at the end of the month's holiday. She had known he was going to, and had decided to refuse him. She was her widowed mother's only child and she could not go so far away from her, but when the moment came she did not quite know what happened to her, she was carried off her feet by an unexpected emotion, and she accepted him. They had been settled now for four months in the little outstation of which he was in charge. She was very happy.

She told him once that she had quite made up her mind to refuse him.

"Are you sorry you didn't?" he asked, with a merry smile in his twinkling blue eyes.

"I should have been a perfect fool if I had. What a bit of luck that fate or chance or whatever it was stepped in and took the matter entirely out of my hands!"

Now she heard Guy clatter down the steps to the bath-house. He was a noisy fellow and even with bare feet he could not be quiet. But he uttered an exclamation. He said two or three words in the local dialect and she could not understand. Then she heard someone speaking to him, not aloud, but in a sibilant whisper. Really it was too bad of people to waylay him when he was going to have his bath. He spoke again, and though his voice was low she could hear that he was vexed. The other voice was raised now; it was a woman's. Doris supposed it was someone who had a complaint to make. It was like a Malay woman to come in that surreptitious way. But she was evidently getting

very little from Guy, for she heard him say: "Get out!"
That at all events she understood, and then she heard
him bolt the door. There was a sound of the water he
was throwing over himself (the bathing arrangements
still amused her, the bath-houses were under the bedrooms, on the ground; you had a large tub of water
and you sluiced yourself with a little tin pail) and in a
couple of minutes he was back again in the dining-
room. His hair was still wet. They sat down to
luncheon.

"It's lucky I'm not a suspicious or a jealous person,"
she laughed. "I don't know that I should altogether
approve of your having animated conversations with
ladies while you're having your bath."

His face, usually so cheerful, had borne a sullen look
when he came in, but now it brightened.

"I wasn't exactly pleased to see her."

"So I judged by the tone of your voice. In fact, I
thought you were rather short with the young person."

"Damned cheek, waylaying me like that!"

"What did she want?"

"Oh, I don't know. It's a woman from the kampong.
She's had a row with her husband or something."

"I wonder if it's the same one who was hanging about
this morning."

He frowned a little.

"Was there someone hanging about?"

"Yes, I went into your dressing-room to see that
everything was nice and tidy, and then I went down to

the bath-house. I saw someone slink out of the door as I went down the steps and when I looked out I saw a woman standing there."

"Did you speak to her?"

"I asked her what she wanted and she said something, but I couldn't understand."

"I'm not going to have all sorts of stray people prowling about here," he said. "They've got no right to come."

He smiled, but Doris, with the quick perception of a woman in love, noticed that he smiled only with his lips, not as usual with his eyes also, and wondered what it was that troubled him.

"What have you been doing this morning?" he asked.

"Oh, nothing much. I went for a little walk."

"Through the kampong?"

"Yes. I saw a man send a chained monkey up a tree to pick coconuts, which rather thrilled me."

"It's rather a lark, isn't it?"

"Oh, Guy, there were two little boys watching him who were much whiter than the others. I wondered if they were half-castes. I spoke to them, but they didn't know a word of English."

"There are two or three half-caste children in the kampong," he answered.

"Whom do they belong to?"

"Their mother is one of the village girls."

"Who is their father?"

"Oh, my dear, that's the sort of question we think it a little dangerous to ask out here." He paused. "A lot of fellows have native wives, and then when they go home or marry they pension them off and send them back to their village."

Doris was silent. The indifference with which he spoke seemed a little callous to her. There was almost a frown on her frank, open, pretty English face when she replied:

"But what about the children?"

"I have no doubt they're properly provided for. Within his means, a man generally sees that there's enough money to have them decently educated. They get jobs as clerks in a Government office, you know; they're all right."

She gave him a slightly rueful smile.

"You can't expect me to think it's a very good system."

"You mustn't be too hard," he smiled back.

"I'm not hard. But I'm thankful you never had a Malay wife. I should have hated it. Just think if those two little brats were yours."

The boy changed their plates. There was never much variety in their menu. They started luncheon with river fish, dull and insipid, so that a good deal of tomato ketchup was needed to make it palatable, and then went on to some kind of stew. Guy poured Worcester Sauce over it.

"The old Sultan didn't think it was a white woman's

country," he said presently. "He rather encouraged people to—keep house with native girls. Of course things have changed now. The country's perfectly quiet and I suppose we know better how to cope with the climate."

"But, Guy, the eldest of those boys wasn't more than seven or eight and the other was about five."

"It's awfully lonely on an outstation. Why, often one doesn't see another white man for six months on end. A fellow comes out here when he's only a boy." He gave her that charming smile of his which transfigured his round, plain face. "There are excuses, you know."

She always found that smile irresistible. It was his best argument. Her eyes grew once more soft and tender.

"I'm sure there are." She stretched her hand across the little table and put it on his. "I'm very lucky to have caught you so young. Honestly, it would upset me dreadfully if I were told that you had lived like that."

He took her hand and pressed it.

"Are you happy here, darling?"

"Desperately."

She looked very cool and fresh in her linen frock. The heat did not distress her. She had no more than the prettiness of youth, though her brown eyes were fine; but she had a pleasing frankness of expression, and her dark, short hair was neat and glossy. She gave you the impression of a girl of spirit and you felt sure that the member of parliament for whom she worked had in her a very competent secretary.

"I loved the country at once," she said. "Although I'm alone so much I don't think I've ever once felt lonely."

Of course she had read novels about the Malay Archipelago and she had formed an impression of a sombre land with great ominous rivers and a silent, impenetrable jungle. When the little coasting steamer set them down at the mouth of the river, where a large boat, manned by a dozen Dyaks, was waiting to take them to the station, her breath was taken away by the beauty, friendly rather than awe-inspiring, of the scene. It had a gaiety, like the joyful singing of birds in the trees, which she had never expected. On each bank of the river were mangroves and nipah palms, and behind them the dense green of the forest. In the distance stretched blue mountains, range upon range, as far as the eye could see. She had no sense of confinement nor of gloom, but rather of openness and wide spaces where the exultant fancy could wander with delight. The green glittered in the sunshine and the sky was blithe and cheerful. The gracious land seemed to offer her a smiling welcome.

They rowed on, hugging a bank, and high overhead flew a pair of doves. A flash of colour, like a living jewel, dashed across their path. It was a kingfisher. Two monkeys, with their dangling tails, sat side by side on a branch. On the horizon, over there on the other

U

side of the broad and turbid river, beyond the jungle, was a row of little white clouds, the only clouds in the sky, and they looked like a row of ballet-girls, dressed in white, waiting at the back of the stage, alert and merry, for the curtain to go up. Her heart was filled with joy; and now, remembering it all, her eyes rested on her husband with a grateful, assured affection.

And what fun it had been to arrange their living-room! It was very big. On the floor, when she arrived, was a torn and dirty matting; on the walls of unpainted wood hung (much too high up) photogravures of Academy pictures, Dyak shields and parangs. The tables were covered with Dyak cloth in sombre colours, and on them stood pieces of Brunei brass-ware, much in need of cleaning, empty cigarette tins and bits of Malay silver. There was a rough wooden shelf with cheap editions of novels and a number of old travel books in battered leather; and another shelf was crowded with empty bottles. It was a bachelor's room, untidy but stiff; and though it amused her she found it intolerably pathetic. It was a dreary, comfortless life that Guy had led there, and she threw her arms round his neck and kissed him.

"You poor darling," she laughed.

She had deft hands and she soon made the room habitable. She arranged this and that, and what she could not do with she turned out. Her wedding presents helped. Now the room was friendly and comfortable. In glass vases were lovely orchids and in great bowls huge masses of flowering shrubs. She felt an inordinate pride because it was her house (she had never in her life lived in anything but a poky flat) and she had made it charming for him.

"Are you pleased with me?" she asked when she had finished.

"Quite," he smiled.

The deliberate understatement was much to her mind. How jolly it was that they should understand each other so well! They were both of them shy of displaying emotion, and it was only at rare moments that they used with one another anything but ironic banter.

They finished luncheon and he threw himself into a long chair to have a sleep. She went towards her room. She was a little surprised that he drew her to him as she passed and, making her bend down, kissed her lips. They were not in the habit of exchanging embraces at odd hours of the day.

"A full tummy is making you sentimental, my poor lamb," she chaffed him.

"Get out and don't let me see you again for at least two hours."

"Don't snore."

She left him. They had risen at dawn and in five minutes were fast asleep.

Doris was awakened by the sound of her husband's splashing in the bath-house. The walls of the bungalow were like a sounding-board and not a thing that one of them did escaped the other. She felt too lazy to move, but she heard the boy bring the tea-things in, so she jumped up and ran down into her own bath-house. The water, not cold but cool, was deliciously refreshing. When she came into the sitting-room Guy was taking the rackets out of the press, for they played tennis in the short cool of the evening. The night fell at six.

The tennis-court was two or three hundred yards from the bungalow and after tea, anxious not to lose time, they strolled down to it.

"Oh, look," said Doris, "there's that girl that I saw this morning."

Guy turned quickly. His eyes rested for a moment on a native woman, but he did not speak.

"What a pretty sarong she's got," said Doris. "I wonder where it comes from."

They passed her. She was slight and small, with the large, dark, starry eyes of her race and a mass of raven hair. She did not stir as they went by, but stared at them strangely. Doris saw then that she was not quite so young as she had at first thought. Her features were a trifle heavy and her skin was dark, but she was very pretty. She held a small child in her arms. Doris smiled a little as she saw it, but no answering smile moved the woman's lips. Her face remained impassive. She did not look at Guy, she looked only at Doris, and he walked on as though he did not see her. Doris turned to him.

"Isn't that baby a duck?"

"I didn't notice."

She was puzzled by the look of his face. It was deathly white, and the pimples which not a little distressed her were more than commonly red.

"Did you notice her hands and feet? She might be a duchess."

"All natives have good hands and feet," he answered, but not jovially as was his wont; it was as though he forced himself to speak.

But Doris was not intrigued.

"Who is she, d'you know?"

"She's one of the girls in the kampong."

They had reached the court now. When Guy went up to the net to see that it was taut he looked back. The girl was still standing where they had passed her. Their eyes met.

"Shall I serve?" said Doris.

"Yes, you've got the balls on your side."

He played very badly. Generally he gave her fifteen and beat her, but to-day she won easily. And he played silently. Generally he was a noisy player, shouting all the time, cursing his foolishness when he missed a ball and chaffing her when he placed one out of her reach.

"You're off your game, young man," she cried.

"Not a bit," he said.

He began to slam the balls, trying to beat her, and sent one after the other into the net. She had never seen him with that set face. Was it possible that he was a little out of temper because he was not playing well? The light fell, and they ceased to play. The woman whom they had passed stood in exactly the same position as when they came and once more, with expressionless face, she watched them go.

The blinds on the verandah were raised now and on the table between their two long chairs were bottles and soda-water. This was the hour at which they had the first drink of the day and Guy mixed a couple of gin slings. The river stretched widely before them and on the further bank the jungle was wrapped in the mystery of the approaching night. A native was silently rowing up-stream, standing at the bow of the boat, with two oars.

"I played like a fool," said Guy, breaking a silence. "I'm feeling a bit under the weather."

"I'm sorry. You're not going to have fever, are you?"

"Oh, no. I shall be all right to-morrow."

Darkness closed in upon them. The frogs croaked loudly and now and then they heard a few short notes from some singing bird of the night. Fireflies flitted across the verandah and they made the trees that surrounded it look like Christmas trees lit with tiny candles. They sparkled softly. Doris thought she heard a little sigh. It vaguely disturbed her. Guy was always so full of gaiety.

"What is it, old man?" she said gently. "Tell mother."

"Nothing. Time for another drink," he answered breezily.

Next day he was as cheerful as ever and the mail came. The coasting steamer passed the mouth of the river twice a month, once on its way to the coalfields and once on its way back. On the outward journey it brought mail, which Guy sent a boat down to fetch. Its arrival was the excitement of their uneventful lives. For the first day or two they skimmed rapidly all that had come, letters, English papers and papers from Singapore, magazines and books, leaving for the ensuing weeks a more exact perusal. They snatched the illustrated papers from one another. If Doris had not been so absorbed she might have noticed that there was a change in Guy. She would have found it hard to describe and harder still to explain. There was in his eyes a sort of watchfulness and in his mouth a slight droop of anxiety.

Then, perhaps a week later, one morning when she was sitting in the shaded room studying a Malay grammar (for she was industriously learning the language), she heard a commotion in the compound. She heard the house-boy's voice, he was speaking angrily, the voice of another man, perhaps it was the water-carrier's, and then a woman's, shrill and vituperative. There was a scuffle. She went to the window and opened the shutters. The water-carrier had hold of a woman's arm and was dragging her along, while the house-boy was pushing her from behind with both hands. Doris recognised her at once as the woman she had seen one morning loitering in the compound and later in the day outside the tennis-court. She was holding a baby against her breast. All three were shouting angrily.

"Stop," cried Doris. "What are you doing?"

At the sound of her voice the water-carrier let go suddenly and the woman, still pushed from behind, fell to the ground. There was a sudden silence and the house-boy looked sullenly into space. The water-carrier hesitated a moment and then slunk away. The woman raised herself slowly to her feet, arranged the baby on her arm, and stood impassive, staring at Doris. The boy said something to her which Doris could not have heard even if she had understood; the woman by no change of face showed that his words meant anything to her; but she slowly strolled away. The boy followed her to the gate of the compound. Doris called to him as he walked back, but he pretended not to hear. She was growing angry now and she called more sharply.

"Come here at once," she cried.

Suddenly, avoiding her wrathful glance, he came towards the bungalow. He came in and stood at the door. He looked at her sulkily.

"What were you doing with that woman?" she asked abruptly.

"Tuan say she no come here."

"You mustn't treat a woman like that. I won't have it. I shall tell the Tuan exactly what I saw."

The boy did not answer. He looked away, but she felt that he was watching her through his long eyelashes. She dismissed him.

"That'll do."

Without a word he turned and went back to the servants' quarters. She was exasperated and she found it impossible to give her attention once more to the Malay exercises. In a little while the boy came in to lay the cloth for luncheon. On a sudden he went to the door.

"What is it?" she asked.

"Tuan just coming."

He went out to take Guy's hat from him. His quick ears had caught the footsteps before they were audible to her. Guy did not as usual come up the steps immediately; he paused, and Doris at once surmised that the boy had gone down to meet him in order to tell him of the morning's incident. She shrugged her shoulders. The boy evidently wanted to get his story in first. But she was astonished when Guy came in. His face was ashy.

"Guy, what on earth's the matter?"

He flushed a sudden hot red.

"Nothing. Why?"

She was so taken aback that she let him pass into his room without a word of what she had meant to speak of at once. It took him longer than usual to have his bath and change his clothes and luncheon was served when he came in.

"Guy," she said, as they sat down, "that woman we saw the other day was here again this morning."

"So I've heard," he answered.

υ*

"The boys were treating her brutally. I had to stop them. You must really speak to them about it."

Though the Malay understood every word she said, he made no sign that he heard. He handed her the toast.

"She's been told not to come here. I gave instructions that if she showed herself again she was to be turned out."

"Were they obliged to be so rough?"

"She refused to go. I don't think they were any rougher than they could help."

"It was horrible to see a woman treated like that. She had a baby in her arms."

"Hardly a baby. It's three years old."

"How d'you know?"

"I know all about her. She hasn't the least right to come here pestering everybody."

"What does she want?"

"She wants to do exactly what she did. She wants to make a disturbance."

For a little while Doris did not speak. She was surprised at her husband's tone. He spoke tersely. He spoke as though all this were no concern of hers. She thought him a little unkind. He was nervous and irritable.

"I doubt if we shall be able to play tennis this afternoon," he said. "It looks to me as though we were going to have a storm."

The rain was falling when she awoke and it was

impossible to go out. During tea Guy was silent and abstracted. She got her sewing and began to work. Guy sat down to read such of the English papers as he had not yet gone through from cover to cover; but he was restless; he walked up and down the large room and then went out on the verandah. He looked at the steady rain. What was he thinking of? Doris was vaguely uneasy.

It was not till after dinner that he spoke. During the simple meal he had exerted himself to be his usual gay self, but the exertion was apparent. The rain had ceased and the night was starry. They sat on the verandah. In order not to attract insects they had put out the lamp in the sitting-room. At their feet, with a mighty, formidable sluggishness, silent, mysterious and fatal, flowed the river. It had the terrible deliberation and the relentlessness of destiny.

"Doris, I've got something to say to you," he said suddenly.

His voice was very strange. Was it her fancy that he had difficulty in keeping it quite steady? She felt a little pang in her heart because he was in distress, and she put her hand gently into his. He drew it away.

"It's rather a long story. I'm afraid it's not a very nice one and I find it rather difficult to tell. I'm going to ask you not to interrupt me, or to say anything, till I've finished."

In the darkness she could not see his face, but she felt that it was haggard. She did not answer. He spoke in a voice so low that it hardly broke the silence of the night.

"I was only eighteen when I came out here. I came straight from school. I spent three months in Kuala Solor, and then I was sent to a station up the Sembulu River. Of course there was a Resident there and his wife. I lived in the court-house, but I used to have my meals with them and spend the evening with them. I had an awfully good time. Then the fellow who was here fell ill and had to go home. We were short of men on account of the war and I was put in charge of this place. Of course I was very young, but I spoke the language like a native, and they remembered my father. I was as pleased as Punch to be on my own."

He was silent while he knocked the ashes out of his pipe and refilled it. When he lit a match Doris, without looking at him, noticed that his hand was unsteady.

"I'd never been alone before. Of course at home there'd been father and mother and generally an assistant. And then at school naturally there were always fellows about. On the way out, on the boat, there were people all the time, and at K.S., and the same at my first post. The people there were almost like my own people. I seemed always to live in a crowd. I like people. I'm a noisy blighter. I like to have a good time. All sorts of things make me laugh and you must have somebody to laugh with. But it was different here. Of course it was all right in the daytime; I had my work and I could talk to the Dyaks. Although they were head-hunters in those days and now and then I had a bit of trouble with them, they were an awfully decent lot of fellows. I got on very well with them. Of course I should have liked a white man to gas to, but they were better than nothing, and it was easier for me because they didn't look upon me quite as a stranger. I liked the work too. It was rather lonely in the evening to sit on the verandah and drink a gin and bitters by myself, but I could read. And the boys were about. My own boy was called Abdul. He'd known my father. When I got tired of reading I could give him a shout and have a bit of a jaw with him.

"It was the nights that did for me. After dinner the boys shut up and went away to sleep in the kampong. I was all alone. There wasn't a sound in the bungalow except now and then the croak of the chik-chak. It used to come out of the silence, suddenly, so that it made me jump. Over in the kampong I heard the sound of a gong or fire-crackers. They were having a good time, they weren't so far away, but I had to stay where I was. I was tired of reading. I couldn't have been more of a prisoner if I'd been in gaol. Night after night it was the same. I tried drinking three or four whiskies, but it's poor fun drinking alone, and it didn't cheer me up; it only made me feel rather rotten next day. I tried going to bed immediately after dinner, but I couldn't sleep. I used to lie in bed, getting hotter and hotter, and more wide awake, till I didn't know what to do with myself. By George, those nights were long. D'you know, I got so low, I was so sorry for myself that sometimes—it makes me laugh now when I think of it, but I was only nineteen and a half—sometimes I used to cry.

"Then, one evening, after dinner, Abdul had cleared away and was just going off, when he gave a little cough. He said, wasn't I lonely in the house all night by myself? 'Oh, no, that's all right,' I said. I didn't want him to know what a damned fool I was, but I expect he knew all right. He stood there without speaking, and I knew he wanted to say something to me. 'What is it?' I said. 'Spit it out.' Then he said that if I'd like to have a girl to come and live with me he knew one who was willing. She was a very good girl and he could recommend her. She'd be no trouble and it would be someone to have about the bungalow. She'd mend my things for me. . . . I felt awfully low. It had been raining all day and I hadn't been able to get any exercise. I knew I shouldn't sleep for hours. It wouldn't cost me very much money, he said, her people were poor and they'd be quite satisfied with a small present. Two hundred Straits dollars. 'You look,' he said. 'If you don't like her you send her away.' I asked him where she was. 'She's here,' he said. 'I call her.' He went to the door. She'd been waiting on the steps with her mother. They came in and sat down on the floor. I gave them some sweets. She was shy, of course, but cool enough, and when I said something to her she gave me a smile. She was very young, hardly more than a child, they said she was fifteen. She was awfully pretty, and she had her best clothes on. We began to talk. She didn't say much, but she laughed a lot when I chaffed her. Abdul said I'd find she had plenty to say for herself when she got to know me. He told her to come and sit by me. She giggled and refused, but her mother told her to come, and I made room for her on the chair. She blushed and laughed, but she came, and then she snuggled up to me. The boy laughed too. 'You see, she's taken to you already,' he said. 'Do you want her to stay?' he asked. 'Do you want to?' I said to her. She hid her face, laughing, on my shoulder. She was very soft and small. 'Very well,' I said, 'let her stay.' "

Guy leaned forward and helped himself to a whisky and soda.

"May I speak now?" asked Doris.

"Wait a minute, I haven't finished yet. I wasn't in love with her, not even at the beginning. I only took her so as to have somebody about the bungalow. I think I should have gone mad if I hadn't, or else taken to drink. I was at the end of my tether. I was too young to be quite alone. I was never in love with anyone but you." He hesitated a moment. "She lived here till I went home last year on leave. It's the woman you've seen hanging about."

"Yes, I guessed that. She had a baby in her arms. Is that your child?"

"Yes. It's a little girl."

"Is it the only one?"

"You saw the two small boys the other day in the kampong. You mentioned them."

"She has three children then?"

"Yes."

"It's quite a family you've got."

She felt the sudden gesture which her remark forced from him, but he did not speak.

"Didn't she know that you were married till you suddenly turned up here with a wife?" asked Doris.

"She knew I was going to be married."

"When ?"

"I sent her back to the village before I left here. I told her it was all over. I gave her what I'd promised. She always knew it was only a temporary arrangement. I was fed up with it. I told her I was going to marry a white woman."

"But you hadn't even seen me then."

"No, I know. But I'd made up my mind to marry when I was home." He chuckled in his old manner. "I don't mind telling you that I was getting rather despondent about it when I met you. I fell in love with you at first sight and then I knew it was either you or nobody."

"Why didn't you tell me? Don't you think it would have been only fair to give me a chance of judging for myself? It might have occurred to you that it would be rather a shock to a girl to find out that her husband had lived for ten years with another girl and had three children."

"I couldn't expect you to understand. The circumstances out here are peculiar. It's the regular thing. Five men out of six do it. I thought perhaps it would shock you and I didn't want to lose you. You see, I was most awfully in love with you. I am now, darling. There was no reason that you should ever know. I didn't expect to come back here. One seldom goes back to the same station after home leave. When we came here I offered her money if she'd go to some other village. First she said she would and then she changed her mind."

"Why have you told me now?"

"She's been making the most awful scenes. I don't know how she found out that you knew nothing about it. As soon as she did she began to blackmail me. I've had to give her an awful lot of money. I gave orders that she wasn't to be allowed in the compound. This morning she made that scene just to attract your attention. She wanted to frighten me. It couldn't go on like that. I thought the only thing was to make a clean breast of it."

There was a long silence as he finished. At last he put his hand on hers.

"You do understand, Doris, don't you? I know I've been to blame."

She did not move her hand. He felt it cold beneath his.

"Is she jealous?"

"I daresay there were all sorts of perks when she was

living here, and I don't suppose she much likes not getting them any longer. But she was never in love with me any more than I was in love with her. Native women never do really care for white men, you know."

"And the children?"

"Oh, the children are all right. I've provided for them. As soon as the boys are old enough I shall send them to school at Singapore."

"Do they mean nothing to you at all?"

He hesitated.

"I want to be quite frank with you. I should be sorry if anything happened to them. When the first one was expected I thought I'd be much fonder of it than I ever had been of its mother. I suppose I should have been if it had been white. Of course, when it was a baby it was rather funny and touching, but I had no particular feeling that it was mine. I think that's what it is; you see, I have no sense of their belonging to me. I've reproached myself sometimes, because it seemed rather unnatural, but the honest truth is that they're no more to me than if they were somebody else's children. Of course a lot of slush is talked about children by people who haven't got any."

Now she had heard everything. He waited for her to speak, but she said nothing. She sat motionless.

"Is there anything more you want to ask me, Doris?" he said at last.

"No, I've got rather a headache. I think I shall go to bed." Her voice was as steady as ever. "I don't quite know what to say. Of course it's been all very unexpected. You must give me a little time to think."

"Are you very angry with me?"

"No. Not at all. Only—only I must be left to myself for a while. Don't move. I'm going to bed."

She rose from her long chair and put her hand on his shoulder.

"It's so very hot to-night. I wish you'd sleep in your dressing-room. Good-night."

She was gone. He heard her lock the door of her bedroom.

She was pale next day and he could see that she had not slept. There was no bitterness in her manner, she talked as usual, but without ease; she spoke of this and that as though she were making conversation with a stranger. They had never had a quarrel, but it seemed to Guy that so would she talk if they had had a disagreement and the subsequent reconciliation had left her still wounded. The look in her eyes puzzled him; he seemed to read in them a strange fear. Immediately after dinner she said:

"I'm not feeling very well to-night. I think I shall go straight to bed."

"Oh, my poor darling, I'm so sorry," he cried.

"It's nothing. I shall be all right in a day or two."

"I shall come in and say good-night to you later."

"No, don't do that. I shall try and get straight off to sleep."

"Well, then, kiss me before you go."

He saw that she flushed. For an instant she seemed to hesitate; then, with averted eyes, she leaned towards him. He took her in his arms and sought her lips, but she turned her face away and he kissed her cheek. She left him quickly and again he heard the key turn softly in the lock of her door. He flung himself heavily on the chair. He tried to read, but his ear was attentive to the smallest sound in his wife's room. She had said she was going to bed, but he did not hear her move. The silence in there made him unaccountably nervous. Shading the lamp with his hand he saw that there was a glimmer under her door; she had not put out her light. What on earth was she doing? He put down his book. It would not have surprised him if she had been angry and had made him a scene, or if she had cried; he could have coped with that; but her calmness frightened him. And then what was that fear which he had seen so plainly in her eyes? He thought once more over all he had said to her on the previous night. He didn't know how else he could have put it. After all, the chief point was that he'd done the same as everybody else, and it was all over long before he met her. Of course as things turned out he had been a fool, but anyone could be wise after the event. He put his hand to his heart. Funny how it hurt him there.

"I suppose that's the sort of thing people mean when they say they're heart-broken," he said to himself. "I wonder how long it's going on like this?"

Should he knock at the door and tell her he must

speak to her? It was better to have it out. He *must* make her understand. But the silence scared him. Not a sound! Perhaps it was better to leave her alone. Of course it had been a shock. He must give her as long as she wanted. After all, she knew how devotedly he loved her. Patience, that was the only thing; perhaps she was fighting it out with herself; he must give her time; he must have patience.

Next morning he asked her if she had slept better.

"Yes, much," she said.

"Are you very angry with me?" he asked piteously.

She looked at him with candid, open eyes.

"Not a bit."

"Oh, my dear, I'm so glad. I've been a brute and a beast. I know it's been hateful for you. But do forgive me. I've been so miserable."

"I do forgive you. I don't even blame you."

He gave her a little rueful smile, and there was in his eyes the look of a whipped dog.

"I haven't much liked sleeping by myself the last two nights."

She glanced away. Her face grew a trifle paler.

"I've had the bed in my room taken away. It took up so much space. I've had a little camp bed put there instead."

"My dear, what are you talking about?"

Now she looked at him steadily.

"I'm not going to live with you as your wife again."

"Never?"

She shook her head. He looked at her in a puzzled way. He could hardly believe he had heard aright and his heart began to beat painfully.

"But that's awfully unfair to me, Doris."

"Don't you think it was a little unfair to me to bring me out here in the circumstances?"

"But you just said you didn't blame me."

"That's quite true. But the other's different. I can do it."

"But how are we going to live together like that?"

She stared at the floor. She seemed to ponder deeply.

"When you wanted to kiss me on the lips last night I —it almost made me sick."

"Doris."

She looked at him suddenly and her eyes were cold and hostile.

"That bed I slept on, is that the bed in which she had her children?" She saw him flush deeply. "Oh, it's horrible. How could you?" She wrung her hands, and her twisting, tortured fingers looked like little writhing snakes. But she made a great effort and controlled herself. "My mind is quite made up. I don't want to be unkind to you, but there are some things that you can't ask me to do. I've thought it all over. I've been thinking of nothing else since you told me, night and day, till I'm exhausted. My first instinct was to get up and go. At once. The steamer will be here in two or three days."

"Doesn't it mean anything to you that I love you?"

"Oh, I know you love me. I'm not going to do that. I want to give us both a chance. I have loved you so, Guy." Her voice broke, but she did not cry. "I don't want to be unreasonable. Heaven knows, I don't want to be unkind. Guy, will you give me time?"

"I don't know quite what you mean."

"I just want you to leave me alone. I'm frightened by the feelings that I have."

He had been right, then; she was afraid.

"What feelings?"

"Please don't ask me. I don't want to say anything to wound you. Perhaps I shall get over them. Heaven knows, I want to. I'll try, I promise you. I'll try. Give me six months. I'll do everything in the world for you but just that one thing." She made a little gesture of appeal. "There's no reason why we shouldn't be happy enough together. If you really love me you'll—you'll have patience."

He sighed deeply.

"Very well," he said. "Naturally I don't want to force you to do anything you don't like. It shall be as you say."

He sat heavily for a little, as though, on a sudden grown old, it was an effort to move; then he got up.

"I'll be getting along to the office."

He took his topee and went out.

A month passed. Women conceal their feelings better than men and a stranger visiting them would never have guessed that Doris was in any way troubled.

But in Guy the strain was obvious; his round, good-natured face was drawn, and in his eyes was a hungry, harassed look. He watched Doris. She was gay and she chaffed him as she had been used to do; they played tennis together; they chatted about one thing and another. But it was evident that she was merely playing a part, and at last, unable to contain himself, he tried to speak again of his connection with the Malay woman.

"Oh, Guy, there's no object in going back on all that," she answered breezily. "We've said all we had to say about it and I don't blame you for anything."

"Why do you punish me, then?"

"My poor boy, I don't want to punish you. It's not my fault if . . ." she shrugged her shoulders. "Human nature is very odd."

"I don't understand."

"Don't try."

The words might have been harsh, but she softened them with a pleasant, friendly smile. Every night when she went to bed she leaned over Guy and lightly kissed his cheek. Her lips only touched it. It was as though a moth had just brushed his face in its flight.

A second month passed, then a third, and suddenly the six months which had seemed so interminable were over. Guy asked himself whether she remembered. He gave a strained attention now to everything she said, to every look on her face and to every gesture of her hands. She remained impenetrable. She had asked him to give her six months; well, he had.

The coasting steamer passed the mouth of the river, dropped their mail, and went on its way. Guy busily wrote the letters which it would pick up on the return journey. Two or three days passed by. It was a Tuesday and the prahu was to start at dawn on Thursday to await the steamer. Except at meal-time when Doris exerted herself to make conversation they had not of late talked very much together; and after dinner as usual they took their books and began to read; but when the boy had finished clearing away and was gone for the night Doris put down hers.

"Guy, I have something I want to say to you," she murmured.

His heart gave a sudden thud against his ribs and he felt himself change colour.

"Oh, my dear, don't look like that, it's not so very terrible," she laughed.

But he thought her voice trembled a little.

"Well?"

"I want you to do something for me."

"My darling, I'll do anything in the world for you."

He put out his hand to take hers, but she drew it away.

"I want you to let me go home."

"You?" he cried, aghast. "When? Why?"

"I've borne it as long as I can. I'm at the end of my tether."

"How long do you want to go for? For always?"

"I don't know. I think so." She gathered

determination. "Yes, for always."

"Oh, my God!"

His voice broke and she thought he was going to cry.

"Oh, Guy, don't blame me. It really is not my fault. I can't help myself."

"You asked me for six months. I accepted your terms. You can't say I've made a nuisance of myself."

"No, no."

"I've tried not to let you see what a rotten time I was having."

"I know. I'm very grateful to you. You've been awfully kind to me. Listen, Guy, I want to tell you again that I don't blame you for a single thing you did. After all, you were only a boy, and you did no more than the others; I know what the loneliness is here. Oh, my dear, I'm so dreadfully sorry for you. I knew all that from the beginning. That's why I asked you for six months. My commonsense tells me that I'm making a mountain out of a molehill. I'm unreasonable; I'm being unfair to you. But, you see, commonsense has nothing to do with it; my whole soul is in revolt. When I see the woman and her children in the village I just feel my legs shaking. Everything in this house; when I think of that bed I slept in it gives me goose-flesh. . . . You don't know what I've endured."

"I think I've persuaded her to go away. And I've applied for a transfer."

"That wouldn't help. She'd be there always. You belong to them, you don't belong to me. I think perhaps I could have stood it if there'd only been one child, but three; and the boys are quite big boys. For ten years you lived with her." And now she came out with what she had been working up to. She was desperate. "It's a physical thing, I can't help it, it's stronger than I am. I think of those thin black arms of hers round you and it fills me with a physical nausea. I think of you holding those little black babies in your arms. Oh, it's loathsome. The touch of you is odious to me. Each night, when I've kissed you, I've had to brace myself up to it, I've had to clench my hands and force myself to touch your cheek." Now she was clasping and unclasping her fingers in a nervous agony, and her voice was out of control. "I know it's I who am to blame now. I'm a silly, hysterical woman. I thought I'd get over it. I can't, and now I never shall. I've brought it all on myself; I'm willing to take the consequences; if you say I must stay here, I'll stay, but if I stay I shall die. I beseech you to let me go."

And now the tears which she had restrained so long overflowed and she wept broken-heartedly. He had never seen her cry before.

"Of course I don't want to keep you here against your will," he said hoarsely.

Exhausted, she leaned back in her chair. Her features were all twisted and awry. It was horribly painful to see the abandonment of grief on that face which was habitually so placid.

"I'm so sorry, Guy. I've broken your life, but I've

broken mine too. And we might have been so happy."

"When do you want to go? On Thursday?"

"Yes."

She looked at him piteously. He buried his face in his hands. At last he looked up.

"I'm tired out," he muttered.

"May I go?"

"Yes."

For two minutes perhaps they sat there without a word. She started when the chik-chak gave its piercing, hoarse and strangely human cry. Guy rose and went out on to the verandah. He leaned against the rail and looked at the softly flowing water. He heard Doris go into her room.

Next morning, up earlier than usual, he went to her door and knocked.

"Yes?"

"I have to go up-river to-day. I shan't be back till late."

"All right."

She understood. He had arranged to be away all day in order not to be about while she was packing. It was heart-breaking work. When she had packed her clothes she looked round the sitting-room at the things that belonged to her. It seemed dreadful to take them. She left everything but the photograph of her mother. Guy did not come in till ten o'clock at night.

"I'm sorry I couldn't get back to dinner," he said. "The head-man at the village I had to go to had a lot of things for me to attend to."

She saw his eyes wander about the room and notice that her mother's photograph no longer stood in its place.

"Is everything quite ready?" he asked. "I've ordered the boatman to be at the steps at dawn."

"I told the boy to wake me at five."

"I'd better give you some money." He went to his desk and wrote out a cheque. He took some notes from a drawer. "Here's some cash to take you as far as Singapore and at Singapore you'll be able to change the cheque."

"Thank you."

"Would you like me to come to the mouth of the river with you?"

"Oh, I think it would be better if we said good-bye here."

"All right. I think I shall turn in. I've had a long day and I'm dead-beat."

He did not even touch her hand. He went into his room. In a few minutes she heard him throw himself on his bed. For a little while she sat looking for the last time round that room in which she had been so happy and so miserable. She sighed deeply. She got up and went into her own room. Everything was packed except the one or two things she needed for the night.

It was dark when the boy awakened them. They dressed hurriedly and when they were ready breakfast was waiting for them. Presently they heard the boat row up to the landing-stage below the bungalow, and then the servants carried down her luggage. It was a poor pretence they made of eating. The darkness thinned away and the river was ghostly. It was not yet day, but it was no longer night. In the silence the voices of the natives at the landing-stage were very clear. Guy glanced at his wife's untouched plate.

"If you're finished we might stroll down. I think you ought to be starting."

She did not answer. She rose from the table. She went into her room to see that nothing had been forgotten and then side by side with him walked down the steps. A little winding path led them to the river. At the landing-stage the native guards in their smart uniform were lined up and they presented arms as Guy and Doris passed. The head boatman gave her his hand as she stepped into the boat. She turned and looked at Guy. She wanted desperately to say one last word of comfort, once more to ask for his forgiveness, but she seemed to be struck dumb.

He stretched out his hand.

"Well, good-bye, I hope you'll have a jolly journey."

They shook hands.

Guy nodded to the head boatman and the boat pushed off. The dawn now was creeping along the river mistily, but the night lurked still in the dark trees of the jungle. He stood at the landing-stage till the boat was lost in the shadows of the morning. With a sigh he turned away. He nodded absent-mindedly when the guard once more presented arms. But when he reached the bungalow he called the boy. He went round the room, picking out everything that had belonged to Doris.

"Pack all these things up," he said. "It's no good leaving them about."

Then he sat down on the verandah and watched the day advance gradually like a bitter, an unmerited and an overwhelming sorrow. At last he looked at his watch. It was time for him to go to the office.

In the afternoon he could not sleep, his head ached miserably, so he took his gun and went for a tramp in the jungle. He shot nothing, but he walked in order to tire himself out. Towards sunset he came back and had two or three drinks, and then it was time to dress for dinner. There wasn't much use in dressing now; he might just as well be comfortable; he put on a loose native jacket and a sarong. That was what he had been accustomed to wear before Doris came. He was barefoot. He ate his dinner listlessly and the boy cleared away and went. He sat down to read *The Tatler*. The bungalow was very silent. He could not read and let the paper fall on his knees. He was exhausted. He could not think and his mind was strangely vacant. The chik-chak was noisy that night and its hoarse and sudden cry seemed to mock him. You could hardly believe that this reverberating sound came from so small a throat. Presently he heard a discreet cough.

"Who's there?" he cried.

There was a pause. He looked at the door. The chik-chak laughed harshly. A small boy sidled in and stood on the threshold. It was a little half-caste boy in a tattered singlet and a sarong. It was the elder of his two sons.

"What do you want?" said Guy.

The boy came forward into the room and sat down, tucking his legs away under him.

"Who told you to come here?"

"My mother sent me. She says, do you want anything?"

Guy looked at the boy intently. The boy said nothing more. He sat and waited, his eyes cast down shyly. Then Guy in deep and bitter reflection buried his face in his hands. What was the use? It was finished. Finished! He surrendered. He sat back in his chair and sighed deeply.

"Tell your mother to pack up her things and yours. She can come back."

"When?" asked the boy, impassively.

Hot tears trickled down Guy's funny, round spotty face.

"To-night."